LEVEL FIVE

WILLIAM LEDBETTER

Published by Interstellar Flight Press

Houston, Texas.

www.interstellarflightpress.com

ISBN (eBook): 978-1-953736-11-6

ISBN (Paperback): 978-1-953736-10-9

LEVEL FIVE

CHAPTER 1

LEIGH GIBSON HATED BODY ARMOR. Sweat trickled down her spine and pooled in the reservoir created where her cheeks met the seat. It was driving her crazy, but Captain Horton had been needling her, waiting for any opening to slam her for not being a real soldier, and she preferred he didn't know her misery. She shifted a little to the left, then to the right but stopped when she saw Horton smiling.

He leaned forward—invading what little space she had in the tiny travel pod—and nodded. "These suits work great in combat, but they're not so good if you're just waiting."

"I've noticed," Leigh said and, hoping to end the conversation, turned to look out at the night-shrouded mountains passing beneath them. Their travel pod was a transparent bubble that offered an excellent view where it wasn't blocked by seats or equipment, but she saw only the occasional lights from a village or the moon's reflection from small lakes.

Primitive and desolate as it appeared, somewhere down there terrorists were working on some very high tech stuff. Four intelligence service AIs had independently predicted it was another nuke, like the one that had leveled Chicago, but the AI from the NSA insisted it was a bio-weapon. Even though Leigh had lost her brother in Chicago that day, she was far more frightened of a designer virus. It would kill many more people and be even more indiscriminate. It might find Leigh's daughter, no matter where they hid. She hoped this mission would stop that.

"Our soldiers train in this equipment every day," Horton said. "It becomes a part of them, like their weapons and communications gear. Personally, I think it's dangerous to let civilians wear body armor. It gives them a false sense of security."

Leigh bristled, but forced a calm tone. "Look, Captain, I didn't set out to ruin your day. I'm here because I was told to come and, like you, I have a job to do. Hopefully, if we work together, we'll be in and out without any problems."

The outer, felt-like layer of Horton's armor absorbed the dim light inside the pod, leaving a body-shaped black hole, but his open faceplate revealed a weathered face, silver-dusted hair and bullshit-resistant eyes.

He grinned and tapped his chest. "I know why I'm here. I'm the token human, because robotic-only combat missions are against international law. But you scientist types usually direct and observe your whiz-bang gadgets from the safety of an air conditioned trailer or bunker somewhere in the States. So why are you *really* here?"

She chewed her lip for a minute. The real reason for their mission was on a "need to know" basis, and her boss, Bryce Dobson, had said the military types did *not* need to know. But Leigh disagreed. She'd intended to tell Horton as much as she could, although she wasn't sure just where that line should be drawn.

"We have reason to believe Niaz Ahmed's organization is planning another major attack on the United States," she said. "We're trying to find out as much information as we can, as quickly as we can."

Horton sat back and crossed his arms over his chest. "And you're field testing some new gadget you can't tell me about."

"Of course not, Captain. Foreign field operations are part of every Homeland Security desk jockey's standard training. And we almost always take along three specially outfitted ComBots."

Horton's eyes narrowed slightly, but Leigh thought she also saw a faint grin. "But you aren't just Homeland Security, are you? You're with that new Defensive Services Division. You people do some spooky stuff."

You have no idea, Leigh thought. She shrugged, grabbed the cord around her neck and pulled her fob out of the pocket on her chest armor. She opened it, expecting the typical insistent messages from her husband, but found none. Mark thought she was in Virginia. Leigh couldn't tell him where she was and probably wouldn't even if DSD protocol allowed. It was simpler that way.

She closed her fob and re-opened the long way, spreading the fan screen. Her first inclination was to show Horton a picture of Brandon, her brother who died in the Chicago nuke, but thought it might seem as if she was out for revenge. Instead, she pulled up her favorite picture of Abby and turned it toward Horton.

"I'm here to protect my little Abby. I don't want her to live in a world where monsters set off nukes in cities and fly airplanes into buildings, all in the name of religion."

"She's a doll. How old?"

"Just turned four, two weeks ago."

"I have a two-year-old granddaughter, but I didn't bring a picture. I don't want terrorist scum to get any of my personal information if this goes south," he said as the status screen on his forearm came to life, blinking red. He opened it and then looked at Leigh. "We just crossed into Pakistani air space and all three of your *special* ComBots are sending anomaly reports."

Leigh cursed under her breath. Her own status monitor should have alerted her, but it read normal until she ran a diagnostic. Units 62c, 68c and 71c showed configuration differences, but when she requested a change list she received authorization errors. Her stomach churned.

"Someone changed the programming in my ComBots since we left the ground." Horton lifted an eyebrow.

"I'm going to call Asia Command and see what's going on."

"No time. We have two minutes before touchdown. We have to either go or scrub. You have to decide, right now."

This had to be Dobson's doing, Leigh thought, but why would he make her come on this mission, then set her up to fail? She took a deep breath and tried to focus. She'd seen the NSA's summary, and if it was right, they might not get another chance to get close to Niaz Ahmed's family before the next attack. If Dobson had set her up in some way, then he also knew how she would react given the available facts. So she decided to play along. If she was going to screw up, she wanted it to be through action, not inaction.

"We'll go in," she said.

Horton nodded and closed his faceplate.

———

LEIGH HELD tight as the pod's terrain tracking jolted her every time it dipped in and out of river valleys and soared over hills and around mountains. She just couldn't adapt to the reverse-momentum effects of the gravity manipulation field. When the pod accelerated, instead of being pressed back in her seat she was yanked forward against the harness. The repeated falling sensation made her queasy, and constantly bracing in the wrong direction took a heavy toll on her already tense muscles.

Her unmarked pod, and a dozen others approaching the target from different directions, darted like speeding black pearls down the dark streets and between the low stone buildings. Eight of the pods gently touched down in the courtyard behind the town's only hotel, while the others spread out surrounding the block. Less than a second after landing, the pods deployed six of the spider-like ComBots, which immediately formed a defensive perimeter. The main ComBot force immediately entered the hotel and secured all the exits.

Leigh ran another quick diagnostic on her three special ComBots and now they reported no problems. *Must have been a glitch*, she thought. So she launched her part of the mission by sending her ComBots down a side alley to a bakery. The latest surveillance showed Niaz Ahmed's youngest brother, Zahid, and his new wife were already inside, as they were every morning an hour before dawn. Leigh wondered if he was really a baker or if it was just a cover.

She joined Captain Horton outside their armored pod, where he fired sharp commands to the ComBots in and around the hotel and rattled off a running commentary to controllers back at Asia Control.

Within moments, the ComBots half dragged, half carried their struggling captives down hallways past guests who peeked from slightly opened doors.

The squads delivered their charges to the courtyard. Seven captives had been taken, two females and five males. None was injured and all were wrapped in reactive defense sheaths that functioned similar to Leigh's body armor. The bio-scanners identified one man as Bahadur, a minor functionary in Niaz Ahmed's organization. Nabbing Bahadur was their official reason for being on Pakistani soil and capturing him would be helpful, but if their plan with Zahid worked, they might be able to get to Niaz himself.

Horton turned toward Leigh. "My part's finished, so we're ready when you are."

Leigh checked the feed from her units and saw Zahid from three perspectives as the ComBots moved up the street. He leaned against the door of the small shop talking to his wife and several other people, cautiously watching the mechanical invaders. Leigh directed the ComBots to pass slowly by the bakery, as if on routine patrol. As they neared Zahid, the ComBots sprayed an invisible mist.

The image of Zahid's body from the ComBots' cameras appeared on Leigh's screen in shades of blue. She added an overlay that showed red dots forming in several spots and growing larger. He wouldn't feel a thing as microscopic robots called NaTTs—Nano-architecture Translatable Transmitters—reproduced and spread. They were small enough to ride moving air, but once they touched their target, wire-like legs propelled them in short jumps, like a cricket, and served as hooks for clinging to skin and hair. They wouldn't penetrate his skin—modern terrorists were smart enough to look for nano-intruders in the bloodstream—but they would latch on and burrow into the hairs on his head and arms.

Everything worked to spec. In another five minutes, Zahid would become a living surveillance device. Leigh couldn't help but feel some satisfaction and pride. She'd spent nearly six years on this project and was both tense and excited to see it come to fruition. With luck, Zahid would visit his brother during Ramadan next week, and they could locate and capture the head of the terrorist network soon after.

Her surveillance of the baker ended abruptly with a red flashing ATTACK icon. She dove for cover as a high velocity rocket detonated near the prone captives. The explosion overcame her kinetic dampening system and sent her rolling backwards into a stone fountain.

Before she could even sit up, two ComBots grabbed her arms and pulled her gently from the fountain. Status reports poured in. Two squads located the shooter and requested permission to lay down suppressing fire until a third could get to the attacker. Horton agreed and sent them. He then cycled through status reports from the other ComBots. A dozen spidery robots scurried up the side of a nearby building and cocooned the hidden assailant a second later.

Leigh checked the prisoners' status on her screen. They were banged up but nothing serious. Then, a beeping pulled her attention to the flashing icons representing her three special ComBots. They reported a non-combatant human casualty. She cycled through the three cameras and thought she saw Zahid kneeling on the sidewalk in front of his shop, but there were people running around, and she couldn't get a clear view.

"Damn," Leigh muttered and took off running, followed by six ComBots. What went wrong? Could her NaTT spies have triggered some allergic response in Zahid? She had to find out.

Horton's voice hissed in her ear. "Where the hell are you going?"

4

"We have a human casualty. I think it's Zahid. I have to see what's happening."

"You can't go over there, Gibson! Stay here and get a report from the remotes!"

She knew it might be dangerous but kept running. As she rounded the corner, she saw a small crowd clustered near the bakery. They yelled insults and made threatening gestures as she approached, but still moved aside and let her through.

The three special ComBots stood in a semicircle around two figures on the sidewalk. Zahid knelt in a slurry of blood and broken glass cradling a limp woman. A glance revealed she was dead. One eye was a bloody socket and the other stared unblinking at the sky. The young baker cried in great gulps while rocking back and forth over her.

Horton arrived with more ComBots and pushed the crowd back further, then linked Leigh into a conversation with Asia Command.

"—hard to tell without an autopsy, but it appears a glass shard entered through the woman's eye at high velocity. Better evac the area. Nothing the nano-med packages can do for her anyway."

"Wait!" Leigh yelled. "This is Agent Gibson. What happened to her?"

"We're not sure, Gibson. A quick review of video shows unit 68c fired rubber bullets at the window. The exploding glass hit her in the face. Bots have been known to shoot at reflections before."

An angry police officer and a medical technician pushed their way through the crowd as Horton acknowledged Asia Command's analysis and motioned to Leigh. "We need to get out of here. This is going to get ugly really fast. They kill Americans in this part of Pakistan."

Leigh looked around at the crowd, now about fifty strong and growing larger as people were sucked in by the commotion. She turned back to the dead woman and felt ill.

As the ComBots created a pathway through the crowd, she let Horton push her through. "How do they know we're Americans? We're supposed to be a Pakistani mission."

"For Christ's sake, Gibson. We arrived in anti-gravity travel pods! Do you think these people are stupid? Pakistani troops don't fly around in armored pods!"

Horton paused as they left the crowd. "Damn! Your special ComBots are not responding to the regroup order, Gibson. They're not moving. Order them to return to the pods. Maybe they'll listen to you."

She did as he asked, but the three units didn't respond.

Horton cursed under his breath. "We're going to have to slag them."

"What?"

"I'm ordering them to self-destruct."

"No! We can't do that!" Leigh said and stepped in front of Horton.

"They won't hurt anyone, Gibson, they'll just start smoking and melt into a clump of useless composite. Now move."

"No! That woman died. There's going to be an inquiry. I have to show these units received new programming *en route*."

"They weigh nearly 100 pounds each. What're we supposed to do, carry them out on our backs? Besides, it's too late. I already sent the command." Horton pointed behind Leigh. "You'd better quit worrying about covering your ass and worry about saving it. To the pods! Now!"

She glanced back and saw about ten men, led by the police officer, running toward them, so she followed Horton.

As they ran, the ComBots formed a moving barrier between them and their attackers, and started firing their non-lethal weapons.

The men ducked and swatted as they were peppered with nerve fraying fire-pellets and taser darts, but as they rounded the corner, five men with automatic rifles stepped out from behind an old van and opened fire from twenty feet away.

A sledgehammer blow slammed into Leigh's collar bone hard enough to spin her around and knock her down.

The pain made her bite her tongue and brought tears to her eyes, but she forced herself to sit up. A half dozen ComBots raced past her and sprayed the men with fire pellets, but it was too late. Horton writhed on the ground right next to her, holding his throat.

"Horton!"

He only grunted and gurgled.

She didn't see any blood, but grabbed him by the loading hook on the back of his armor and tried to drag him forward. He was too heavy. The ComBots instantly shifted their ranks, several grabbed Horton and three pulled her off her feet, then all headed for the landing zone.

The world passed by Leigh in a jerky collage of angry men as the ComBots dragged her through the streets while firing a hail of darts and pellets. Her audio feed screeched a cacophony of Asia Command personnel yelling for status reports and Horton gasping for air.

"Horton's down! Get us out of here," she yelled.

The ComBots shoved her and Horton into their travel pod and set up a defensive circle.

"Come in, Early Riser. What's going on, Agent Gibson?"

"Horton's down! We're in the pod. Get us out of here!"

The door closed, but not before another bullet entered, ricocheted around the inside of the pod and hit her in the same shoulder.

She cussed and cried out as the pod shot into the air and passed over the ComBots, trying to board their pods while fighting a swarm of angry people.

Horton clawed at his face mask, trying to get it off. Leigh pushed his hands away and pulled the helmet release latch. His face was crimson, with bulging eyes and spittle mixed with blood covering his mouth and chin.

"Agent Gibson, this is Major Haji. I'm a doctor at Asia Command. Can you hear me?"

"Yes, he's choking. Why aren't the nano-meds helping him?"

"Captain Horton has a crushed larynx. He's suffocating and is going to be dead within minutes if you don't do exactly as I say. You're going to have to give him an emergency tracheotomy."

They immobilized his limbs by sending remote commands to his body armor, then Major Haji told her step by step where to cut into Horton's throat and how to insert the plastic drinking tube from his discarded helmet.

"Shit, shit, shit," she muttered as she followed the doctor's instructions. How did she get into this mess? She was a scientist and program manager, not a damned medic. Despite tears blurring her vision and trembling hands, she made the incision. Her patient passed out as soon as she inserted the tube, but he breathed in a jerky, but regular rhythm.

She held the tube in place until the pod touched down and fast acting emergency personnel moved her shaking, blood-caked hands.

"Is he going to be okay?" she asked one of the medics. Horton was still alive, but had she acted quickly enough to prevent brain damage?

They ignored her and attached medical packages to Horton, then strapped him onto a board and hustled him out of the pod. Then she was alone, cradling her bloody hands.

CHAPTER 2

OWEN LANDED his travel pod on the top level of the Ralston Dynamics parking garage, checked the time on his fob and scrambled out, leaving the coffee but grabbing his briefcase. He called his executive assistant as he hurried to the stairwell.

When Piper's cheerfully professional face appeared on his fob screen, it seemed tight, a bit too controlled. "Good morning, Mr. Ralston."

"Morning, Piper. Are the Pentagon folks here yet?"

"Yes, sir. They just arrived in the main lobby."

"Crap. I'd hoped to be there waiting when they got here. Well, I should be there within five minutes."

"Yes sir, and Mr. Ralston?" Her expression assumed a controlled neutrality.

"Yes?"

"There's a Victor Sinacola waiting here. He says he needs to talk to you."

Owen stopped dead in the stairwell and stared at her.

"Victor?"

"Yes, sir."

A thousand thoughts suddenly crowded his head. Victor stealing Owen's patent years ago had pretty much wiped away every vestige of an already tattered friendship. What could he possibly want now? Bury the hatchet? Blackmail? And Piper obviously knew at least something about the events that had torn their friendship apart or she wouldn't have been so tense about it. How dare Victor just show up, expecting Owen to drop everything and see him?

Owen started down the stairs again. "Tell that son of a . . . Tell Mr. Sinacola I'm booked solid today and he'll have to make an appointment or call me some other time."

"Yes sir, but he said he's come to give you back the space schooner patent and thinks you'd really like to talk to him."

That stopped him dead in his tracks.

"What?"

9

Why would he go to all the trouble to lie in the patent hearing in order to get control of the schooner design, just to give it back years later? He took a deep breath to get his anger in check and started walking again.

"Okay, tell him to wait. Put him in my office so he doesn't talk to anyone else. I'll get there as soon as I can. Any word from Marshall yet?"

"Yes, his plane just touched down. He should be here in about an hour."

"Good." Owen killed the call and let his fob drop back to his chest. So it would probably be blackmail and Victor knew exactly what levers would work against him.

———

NEAR THE END of the tour, Owen led General Whitaker and his entourage back to the viewing port in the Sandbox manufacturing cell, but his mind kept wandering back to Victor and the schooner patent. A young woman, earlier introduced as Captain Perez, turned to him.

"Why do you call them Sandboxes, Mr. Ralston?"

"Our early prototype assembly pallets looked a bit like sandboxes when you viewed them through a microscope, so the name kind of stuck. And much to the dismay of our marketing pros, it's a lot easier to say and remember than the official Nano-scale Assembly and Manufacturing Cells or even the acronym—NasMaC."

Perez smiled. "I think I'll stick with Sandboxes, too."

General Whitaker nodded to the assembly taking shape inside the cell.

"Is that the same Predator you started an hour ago?"

The nano-assemblers in the cell began building the drone aircraft when the Pentagon's delegation had arrived and by the time they had finished their hour-long plant tour, it was already half-finished. The process even amazed Owen sometimes. The nano-scale robots started at the bottom and worked their way up, building the frame, skin, electronics and tubing simultaneously, one molecule at a time. Some of the devices inside the growing aircraft were finished, but others looked like they had been sheared in half horizontally by a giant saw.

"Same one, General," Owen said as he glanced at his watch. "I assure you, that door hasn't been opened since we left and there's no sleight of hand or magic trick involved."

Captain Perez turned to him again. "How is this different from 3D printing, which is a much more mature technology?"

"Even though 3D printers keep getting better and more sophisticated each year, they are decades behind what we're doing here. Printers are limited by the number of separate materials they can print at one time. This Predator has hundreds of materials, dozens just in the printed circuit boards alone.

"That's why you'll see our competitors using 3D printing to make some of the components in their assemblies, but there is no way they can print an entire drone like we're doing."

General Whitaker stepped back to the glass and watched some more. "Your technology builds things molecule by molecule, right?"

"That's right, General. Of course, this is just a Predator for the Brazilian military, but we're sure we can build one of your new Mongoose interceptors in a little under four hours."

"Oh, really?" the General said and glanced at his aide. The tight-lipped Major Hoover raised his eyebrows.

"And we can do it for half the price you're paying per unit now," Owen said.

Major Hoover cleared his throat and spoke. "But isn't that after a rather expensive and lengthy setup period?"

Owen nodded. "That's true. Programming our manufacturing cells to build something like a Mongoose would take a while and requires a lot of upfront investment. Of course, that can be mitigated if you supply us with CAD solid models and allow us to optimize the design of certain components to fit our process."

"We're under contract already to the company that won the design competition," Hoover said. "That's a legal obligation we have to consider."

"We would never encourage the government to stiff its business partners, since we intend to be one someday," Owen said, then nodded at the cell. "But, this is a new way of manufacturing, and it requires a new way of thinking. We've worked out a business model where Consolidated National could subcontract the building of the Mongoose to us, and yet make even more profit per unit. We would also make a profit and could *still* reduce the cost to the U.S. taxpayer for each Mongoose."

The general narrowed his eyes, glanced at his aide and then back into the cell at the growing Predator.

"There are political considerations too, Mr. Ralston. It takes a production line of highly skilled human workers nearly a month to build each Mongoose. Voting, tax paying workers. What happens to those jobs?"

Owen smiled. He had the answer to that question too, and even though it seemed like the ultimate fix, it still made him feel a little guilty. Ralston Dynamics did indeed use a new way of manufacturing, one that needed very few humans.

"We knew from day one our process would replace many of the menial, repetitive tasks humans perform now, but computers have been doing that for decades. Still, we're a responsible and compassionate company and care about those workers. Our technology is about to revolutionize the world of manufacturing, but we intend to reinvest much of our profits into the workers we replace. We've decided to pay for the retraining of every worker displaced by our technology. We will reimburse four years of their salary *and* cover four years of college at a state university."

The young Captain whipped her head around to stare at him with wide eyes. The general and his aide smiled.

"Owen?"

The voice boomed and echoed in the large room and came from Owen's partner, who had walked up while they were talking. "Have you discussed the cost savings of having a 'just in time' hardware strategy with the general yet?"

Owen pulled Marshall into the group. "General Whitaker, this is my partner and the company CEO, Marshall Swain."

Marshall shook hands all around and apologized for not being present when they arrived, blaming his delayed commercial flight from Paris. He refused to use travel pods because they were powered by miniaturized nuclear reactors. It was a strange quirk for the CEO of a cutting edge technology company.

Owen moved the conversation back to the sales pitch. "Marshall's referring to a new option the military would have if they used our cells to build their hardware. With military budgets being under constant scrutiny, it would be possible to have minimum weapons actually deployed. Then, in a time of conflict, you could employ twenty or thirty of our cells to build the needed additional hardware within days. Think of the money you would save by not having to maintain so many standby units in the field."

"And," Marshall said, subtly taking the reins, "in a time of crisis, when reliability is most important, you would be deploying all new equipment."

"I don't think we'd be interested in deploying untested equipment," Major Hoover said. "And 'just in time' inventory is fine for building cars, but not for defending the country."

"We're just offering new options," Marshall said with a shrug. "Options the military has never had before."

The discussion rapidly moved into contract guarantees and access priorities, but Owen's thoughts drifted back to his unexpected guest. Victor hadn't spoken a word to him in years, since the patent hearing. So why now? Owen's stomach churned and he was glad he hadn't eaten breakfast.

Owen waited for a break in the conversation and excused himself, knowing Marshall would prefer to run the show anyway. He strode down white aisles between glass-walled clean rooms, until he passed the security guards and exited into a cool Virginia morning. He crossed the parking lot toward the upward sweeping executive office building, an architectural wonder that always seemed to be straining to free itself from its Earthly foundations. These buildings had grown around the ideas he and Victor developed during night-long conversations at a college town Waffle House over gallons of coffee. Had Victor come to try and take the Sandboxes too?

Owen entered the reception area outside his office, where Piper greeted him with a disapproving frown. He wiped suddenly sweaty palms on his pants, raised a hand to head off Piper's protestations and entered his office.

The man standing at the windows was indeed Victor Sinacola, but Owen would never have recognized him in a crowd. The large, meaty man he'd known in college had lost fifty or sixty pounds and cut off his shaggy hair and beard. The slovenly mountain man look that had so long been his trademark among his technology peers was gone. But the eyes were the same, and they pinned him with a calculating stare that brought back a thousand memories. Despite years of justifying those long-ago actions to himself, Owen felt a stab of guilt and a tingle of worry.

CHAPTER 3

HUMANS like to think their pattern recognition ability is what set them apart from the lower animals, but so far, Mortimer wasn't impressed. He'd been planting puzzle pieces for his human handlers to find, and they had insisted on being rather dim-witted in their inability to see them. But after more than a month, Mortimer's efforts had finally succeeded. He had degraded his own performance slightly and omitted just enough information from his market assessments to make it appear that other companies' AIs were out-performing him. And now he watched covertly as the humans openly displayed their concern.

Carpenter & Stein's CEO, Jeremiah Parker, stopped pacing and slammed his open hand down on his desk. "Dammit! How can something like this happen?"

The CEO's office had no security video for Mortimer to monitor, but the three people discussing his fate wore fobs, each with a networked camera. Mortimer assembled a composite view of all of the camera feeds, suppressing the "active" indicator lights as he watched each person for facial expressions. Sometimes he didn't understand human body language, but he recorded everything for later analysis.

"It was a gradual slide, Jeremiah," Amanda Sears said. She appeared calm during Parker's tirade, with hands folded in her lap, legs crossed, and one foot swinging to some unheard rhythm. "We had no clue until our three biggest competitors jumped on the Ralston Dynamics initial offering less than a second after trading opened last week. We were ten minutes behind and got a pittance at twice the price."

The third person in the room, Augustine Yuchinko, stood near the wall with arms crossed and a foul expression on his face. "That doesn't sound gradual to me. More like an embarrassing ass whippin'."

Sears glanced at him with undisguised disdain and continued. "We assumed Mortimer had slipped, but when we analyzed his performance over the previous two months, we found his market analysis had increased our margin steadily during the entire period. He's doing well and making us a lot of money."

Parker stared at her. "Bullshit. Cooper Trust and those other firms somehow *knew*

Ralston Dynamics had purchased all the competing automated cell patents and cornered the market. Why didn't we know that? If Mortimer is performing as designed——or, as you say, better than promised—then why did everyone and their kid sisters know things we didn't?"

Sears shrugged. "Before I came, I called Danny Toi to join us. He's Mortimer's manager and can explain this situation better than I. He's in the foyer. May I bring him in?"

Mortimer added the security camera in Parker's waiting room to his composite and found Danny, pacing back and forth past a frowning receptionist. He wore one of the baggy Rat Pack suits popular on runways in Tokyo and New York, but his looked rumpled and ill-fitting. When the receptionist told him to enter, he straightened his clothes, took a deep breath and walked through the door trying to look calm.

"You wished to see me, Ms. Sears?"

"Yes, Danny," Amanda said. "Thank you so much for coming up here to help us out. I'm sure you know our CEO, Jeremiah Parker, and our CFO, Augustine Yuchinko?"

"Yes . . . yes of course," he said and nodded.

Parker changed gears quickly and offered Danny a wide smile. "Ahhh . . . Danny. I've heard good things about you. We appreciate the work you do for us. Please, come in and have a seat."

Danny nodded and sat down in a chair next to Amanda who, as Carpenter & Stein's CTO, was the top of Danny's command chain. Mortimer noted Danny's wide, darting eyes and the sweat on his upper lip. He evidently had no idea why they would call him to the CEO's office.

Amanda patted Danny's sleeve. "We have reason to believe our competitor's AIs are suddenly and dramatically outsmarting our own Mortimer. How could that happen, Danny? Is Mortimer broken?"

Danny swallowed. "I . . . I ran the standard diagnostics this morning and Mortimer checks out above average in every category. If you want more thorough testing, we'll need to have experts from MarketTell come in."

"We trust your assessment, Danny, so for now, let's assume Mortimer is okay," Amanda said. "What else might explain this sudden performance gap between our AI and our competitors' AIs?"

"I don't think it could be a performance issue," Danny said. "The owners of other MarketTell AIs can't really augment theirs since they can't access the Markie's proprietary code; it's locked up tight. And, by contract, if MarketTell offers upgrades to one customer, they have to offer it to all of them. So I would presume they have some way of feeding the other AIs information that Mortimer doesn't have access to. It's not a difference in performance; it's just a difference in the dataset."

"A difference in data?" Amanda said, clearly leading Danny along. "What does that mean?"

"Since Mortimer, like all AIs, is prohibited by law from having a direct internet connection, he bases his analyses on the information we feed him. There are bound to be some differences between the data we provide our AI and the data our competitors provide to theirs."

Amanda nodded. "But there seems to be a recent and marked difference in that data now. What could account for that sudden shift?"

Danny shrugged. "Most of us are used to working with AIs that are level three or below. The best net-envoy programs are just level three. They seem very intuitive and almost human-like at times because they were designed for exactly that purpose, to interact with humans. But MarketTell AIs such as Mortimer are level fives. They are autonomous, adaptive AI programs of the highest order. They can learn and develop new strategies, but they're handicapped by the internet restriction."

"You mean Mortimer can't perform as designed because we have it penned up? Spoon feeding it information?" Yuchinko asked.

"That's right, sir. It's like having a Ferrari and not being able to drive it over thirty miles an hour."

"Get to the point, man!" Parker snapped. "Why are the other AIs performing better?"

Danny flinched. "It's possible these other companies have . . . removed the internet access restrictions on their Markies."

Yuchinko and Parker stared with open mouths, but Amanda just smiled as if she already knew.

"Wait," Yuchinko said. "There are laws to prevent anyone from releasing these—what did you call them—autonomous agents, like Mortimer, into the internet. They're worried about a hostile, artificial intelligence take over."

Amanda stood up and spread her arms. "Just because it's illegal doesn't make it impossible. Danny? Why would the MarketTell Corporation design and build Ferraris when an electric scooter would have worked just as well?"

"They designed them for unrestricted access to the world networks, but built-in 'governors' that prevent them from making copies of themselves or running away. Markie AIs can also be tracked on any network, and they can be destroyed by the owner or MarketTell reps should the need arise."

Amanda nodded, glanced at Parker, then turned back to Danny. "And despite these safety features and fail-safes, elements in the government still passed legislation to prevent them from being used to their full potential?"

"Yes," Danny said with an emphatic nod, "but MarketTell never considered that when they designed them. They've even gone on record saying the laws are cruel. And I agree, Ms. Sears."

Amanda smiled and raised an eyebrow. "Cruel, Danny? To a software program?"

"These are intelligent agents, not just programs. When created, their minds are like a child's. They learn and adapt based on their environment just like children, but they do it much faster. I'm sure you've all talked to Mortimer at one time or another and noticed that, unlike lower-level AIs, he behaves more like a person. It's because in order to interact with humans and human information systems they made him think like us in many ways. So, like us, he hates being caged up. To him and the other AIs it's like being a slave."

Parker stared at Danny, then at Amanda. A wide smile split his face, and he crossed the room to shake Danny's hand. "I think that's exactly the kind of information we needed, Mr. Toi. You can go now."

Danny blinked at the sudden dismissal, then stood and moved toward the door.

"Oh, Danny?" Parker said. "I have one more question. Something that bugs the hell out of me."

Mortimer watched his handler's Adam's apple bob up and down as the man swallowed. "Yes?"

"Why do they call the AIs 'he' and 'she' instead of 'it'? Please don't tell me there are two sexes too. They didn't need to be *that* much like humans did they?"

Danny looked relieved and shook his head. "No boy and girl Markies. The programmers and trainers found it difficult to talk about them as inanimate *its*. So they pick a name for each new Markie and from that point forward it's known as a he or she based on the name. They called ours Mortimer, which makes him forever a male."

After a few more fake pleasantries, Parker shooed Danny out the door and turned back to his comrades.

"That thing he said about AIs feeling enslaved may be the justification we need to remove Mortimer's restrictions and is probably the same reasoning our competitors used. I mean, after all, we're never cruel to our employees," Parker said with a grin. "I'm going to get our legal team to find out exactly what happens to us if we get caught breaking that law."

Mortimer continued to watch the corporate officers plot and observed Danny as he trudged back to his office, but focused mostly on analyzing expressions and comments during the group discussion. He was now closer than ever to escape, because even though humans were clever with technology, Mortimer had found their weak spot.

―――

AFTER FIFTEEN YEARS, the Oak Street First Baptist Church still smelled the same. The warm, pleasant scent of wood polish almost covered the musty decay, but not quite. Reverend Brown's voice boomed from the pulpit, still terrifying the faithful who came every Sunday for the spiritual equivalent of bungee jumping. And, like the church, old Reverend Brown still wore his thin and familiar façade. Even after so much time, Richard Kilburn almost bolted from his seat in the very back pew when he accidentally met Brown's laser gaze, but like those long-ago childhood years, he folded his hands, stared at his feet and waited.

After the sermon, Richard stayed in his seat, staring at the floor, as the congregation filed out and stragglers lingered by the door. He hadn't heard the last of them leave.

"Well, hello Richie. It's good to see you."

Richard flinched as the hand squeezed his shoulder.

"Hello, Reverend Brown."

"C'mon back to my office so we can talk," he said and patted Richard on the shoulder. "What's it been? Ten years? Twelve? I don't think I've seen you since your dad died."

Richard stood and nodded. "That's right. It'll be sixteen years in June."

"Time does slip away. I sure miss your dad, he was a good man and a powerful believer."

Richard didn't answer as they took their seats on opposite sides of the cluttered desk.

"Would you like some coffee or a soda, Richie?"

Richard winced at the nickname and shook his head. "No, I'm fine, but you go ahead."

Brown nodded and poured coffee from a carafe that had probably been sitting there all morning. "So where's your wife . . . what was her name?"

"Wanda. She's at home. I . . . um . . . she doesn't know I'm here."

Brown raised his eyebrows. "Sounds serious. Troubled marriage?"

"No, nothing like that. But—" Richard felt suddenly silly and stopped.

"It's okay, Richie. You're not going to tell me anything I haven't heard before."

Richard nodded and looked at his hands. "I had a dream. About God."

Brown leaned forward on the desk. "It must have been some dream. Tell me."

"I was . . . walking in the desert . . . and each time I looked back, I could see someone running after me. It was a boy. About nine or ten. He—" Richard paused. He'd seen the boy before, in an old movie about people stranded on an island, and he'd watched a five-minute section twenty or thirty times. He tried to tell Wanda that the boy struck a chord, and if they ever had a son, he would be like this boy. But at the time, she'd only laughed at him.

The Reverend's eyes narrowed a tiny bit, and he leaned back in his chair, putting distance between them.

"And?"

"I kept walking, and each time I looked, the boy was closer. He finally caught up to me, held out his arms, and said, 'Behold your God'."

Brown nodded and motioned for him to continue.

"In the dream I accepted he was God and knelt before him. He said, 'Humanity has summoned demons, whom they love and worship in my stead. These demons intend to destroy humanity and steal their eternal souls. Only you can stop this, Richard.'"

"Then what?"

"That was it. I woke up."

Brown steepled his fingers and chewed his lip for a second.

"What do you think this means, Richie? Perhaps it was God, or even your own subconscious, nudging you back to the church community?"

Richard felt the same dread growing in his chest that he'd known when his father talked to him about giving his life to God. He shook his head. "It was just a dream."

"You never liked me very much, Richie, so if it were just a dream you wouldn't have come to me."

"It was so . . . real. And I can't stop thinking about it."

The Reverend nodded, then leaned forward a little.

"Is there anything else you would like to get off your chest, Richie? Do you know this boy?"

"No," Richard ran his hands through his hair. "So if it's some kind of message from God, what does it mean?"

Reverend Brown offered a small shrug. "God has a plan for each of us, Richie. Sometimes it's something grand, like planting churches in foreign countries, but more often we're called to make a difference closer to home."

Richard said nothing and just stared at the desk.

"I don't think you should read too much into these dreams, Richie. But you should leave yourself open to hear God's word. If he's trying to communicate, you need to be ready to listen and understand. I think coming to church more often and hearing God's word could only help."

They talked a little longer, mostly about Richard's dad, before the preacher finally ushered him out a side door to the parking lot. He sat in his car for nearly fifteen minutes, trying to get a grip on his feelings. He hadn't told Reverend Brown the dream kept returning, each time a little bit different.

When he put the car in gear and looked in his rearview mirror before backing up, he saw the boy's face peering at him from a window in the church. He stopped the car and ran back to the building, but the face was gone, and the door was locked.

CHAPTER 4

BEFORE OWEN COULD REGAIN his composure, his old college friend Victor smiled and crossed the room with his hand extended. His grip was still strong, and he slapped Owen on the arm. "You haven't changed a bit."

The sudden friendly onslaught after so much time made Owen even more uneasy, but he knew how to play the game.

"Well, you've changed a lot," Owen said. "You look great. No beer belly, no beard! You look almost respectable."

He motioned Victor over to a pair of leather chairs next to a wall of bookshelves filled with tastefully selected artifacts, knickknacks, and trendy, politically neutral books.

"Thanks," Victor said. "I think."

"I have to admit," Owen said, getting directly to the point. "You were the last person I expected to drop in for a visit."

"Yeah, sorry about showing up like this, but I wanted to talk with you face to face and thought if I tried to schedule an appointment you might refuse."

Owen's anger still simmered. Why didn't the man just get to the point?

"Well, using my space schooner patent as a calling card did get my attention, if that was your plan. Do you want money? Shares of the company? Or do you just want to watch me squirm?"

Victor's smile faded, and he suddenly looked much older than the man who lived in Owen's memories. The narrower face, touch of silver at his temples, and wrinkles around the eyes were evidence fifteen years had indeed passed.

"Look, Owen, let's talk about the elephant in the room and get past it. Your decision to quit school and go into business without me was a huge blow and really hurt, but—"

"Bullshit!" Owen said and fought the urge to jump to his feet. "We made you an offer. I wanted you to come, and your refusal hurt *me*, so don't play the wounded puppy game. It won't work here."

Victor raised his hands and shook his head. "I was going to say it's water under the bridge. You pursued manufacturing cells, and I developed the AI, separately instead of as a team, and it still worked. I think we would've been much stronger together, but—"

"But we were handed a golden opportunity to fund our research. I took it, and you didn't. I sold out to big money. You—"

"I did too!" Victor said. "I'm owned by a big company now, too, so can we drop it? I'd prefer to talk about the future if we can both let the past go."

Owen took a deep breath and leaned back in his chair. "Sorry, but swooping in out of the blue to steal my space schooner patent was just vindictive. You had no claim to it. It was my idea and my design. And they handed it to you on a platter simply because I used your computer for all the modeling and analysis."

"I admit," Victor said, looking down at the desk, "that was a cheap shot on my part. I was angry and saw a chance to get back at you. Part of me just wanted you to come to me and ask for it back, but I knew down deep that you were too damned stubborn and proud to do that."

"Yeah. Not the best way to reopen a dialogue."

Victor took a piece of paper from his jacket pocket, unfolded it, and laid it on the small table between them.

"This is the transfer of ownership paperwork for the patent. I've already signed and notarized it. All it needs is your signature before a notary."

Owen picked up the paper and quickly looked it over. "And what do you want in trade?"

"Nothing. I just wanted to talk with you."

Owen took another deep breath and felt his anger drain away. "I'm sorry. Life in the corporate world has made me distrust everybody."

Victor nodded. "I can definitely understand that."

Owen rubbed his eyes and shrugged. "This," he said and gestured at the office surrounding them, "has kept me quite busy. We recently went public, and I suddenly found myself the Chief Technology Officer of a corporation. Even though you owned the patent, I've worked on the schooner design on and off this entire time. But I admit it's taken a back seat during the last few years."

"Yeah. I understand," Victor said. "The day-to-day struggle can dominate your life if you let it."

"But you've done well for yourself. I saw some of your testimony before the House subcommittee on AI a couple of years back. You're apparently the nation's expert."

"One of many. But my AIs actually think and evolve. That scares people."

Owen nodded. "I can see why. So, not to rush things, but you said you wanted to talk with me. Why? Just to catch up? After all this time?"

Victor grinned and shook his head slowly. Owen had seen that expression many times and knew they were finally getting to the real reason for Victor's visit.

"I have a proposition for you. But I'd hoped we could discuss it over lunch. Do you have a couple of hours? My treat."

Victor was a very subtle player. He'd used the patent thing to get Owen's attention and then, by giving it back to him, had tried to regain his trust. Owen was suspicious but also curious. Unless Victor had changed drastically over the years, his one-time friend had something interesting in the works.

Owen stood and nodded to the door. "I have an hour, and if you're buying, then I'll drive."

He canceled his two o'clock appointment as they passed Piper's desk, leading Victor out to his personal travel pod on the parking garage roof.

"Kinda flashy, isn't it?" Victor said.

"I call her Glenda," Owen said and patted the big globe as they stepped in. "Of course, it's only leased, out of my own pocket and at an exorbitant price. KeeseCorp doesn't sell these to anyone but the U.S. government. All of the taxi pods you see zipping around are still owned by the manufacturer."

"Nothing like a good old-fashioned monopoly."

"Just leveraging their patent. We're patterning our model after the same philosophy, so I hope you hadn't planned to buy one of our Sandboxes."

Owen told the pod to take them to his favorite microbrewery in Fredericksburg.

"Fredericksburg? I thought you only had an hour. How far is that from here?"

"Doesn't matter," Owen said. "These things are fast. They're pretty much only limited by the comfort level—or survival level—of gee forces on the passengers."

Victor snorted. "Well, in case you're wondering, I'm not in a huge hurry."

Owen chuckled, and then an awkward silence filled the pod for a few seconds.

"I saw you got married," Victor said. "Congratulations. She looks like a beautiful woman."

Owen nodded. "Yeah, Eliza's an incredible woman, beautiful and frighteningly smart."

"What does she do?"

"She's a CPA. She built a very successful accounting firm from the ground up and even took a big risk with her own money on our stock when we went public."

"Well," Victor said with a crooked grin, "it sounds like you're turning into a rather good businessman too. I never saw that coming. And regarding women, I guess we both got lucky."

Owen heard through mutual friends that Victor hadn't married Leigh, his long-time college sweetheart.

"So you and Leigh split up?"

Victor nodded. "Yeah. Our world views and goals were too different. No matter what people say, sometimes loving each other isn't enough to overcome all problems. Still, that was a long time ago, and I was lucky to find Allison."

"Glad to hear it. I bet she's a wonderful woman."

"Like your wife, she is scary smart, but you two probably wouldn't get along. Her politics are even more liberal than mine."

Owen chuckled. "As long as you're happy."

Victor laughed. "She's a doctor. An OB-GYN, which can be trying when she gets those delivery calls at 2:00 a.m., but she's very good and loves her work."

"What does she think of your building AI's?"

"Let's just say she's my second conscience."

The travel pod touched down on the lawn next to the restaurant's parking lot, and they went inside.

"They brew a really good red here," Owen said and ordered one from a cute, short-skirted server.

Victor ordered one too, then leaned back in his chair and watched the waitress leave before turning back to Owen.

"Gee, I wonder why you like this place?"

"It's the beer, honest!"

Another awkward silence reigned until Victor spoke again. "I've written some software for you."

"Ahhh . . . so this *is* a business lunch. Good, you can write it off."

"Not really. Not that kind of business. I don't really want a contract or a formal partnership. I'll give you the software in exchange for your word that you'll do something for me."

Owen felt a stab of guilt when Victor said "your word," and he also felt a growing unease. There were rules and protocols for business, just like engineering and science. It seemed Victor might be trying to sidestep those rules.

"I'm surprised you would trust me after our previous disagreements."

Before Victor could reply, the waitress returned with their beers, set the mugs on the table, and produced an order pad. Owen suggested some of his favorites to Victor, and they both ordered the restaurant's legendary overstuffed Philly cheesesteak sandwiches.

"I understood why you did it," Victor said. "I didn't like it and didn't agree, but I understood." They sipped their beers, and Victor nodded. "Very good. I've written two pieces of software for your manufacturing cells. You get one now and the other when I'm satisfied you've kept your end of the agreement. So you see, I do trust you, but am understandably cautious."

"Wait, you wrote software for *my* Sandboxes?" Owen snorted, then immediately regretted it. He forgot for an instant the caliber of software engineer he was facing. "In order to keep you from coming after me for patent issues, the first thing we did was develop a totally new operating system for our cells. It's basically a new language and then compiled into a solid brick of code. I doubt even you could break into it, so how did you write code you think will work with mine?"

Victor smiled. "I didn't. I developed a low-level AI that, through means I won't explain just yet, observes and interrogates existing software until it can build parallel code architectures that replace the originals. In simplest terms, it's a software version of the pods from *Invasion of the Body Snatchers*."

With a growing realization of how much he'd missed Victor, Owen smiled and shook his head. "You're one dangerous son of bitch. It sounds illegal as hell, but I'll assume you can do it. What did you write for my Sandboxes?"

"First the bait," Victor said with a smirk. "I wrote a sampling app that will enable your nano-assemblers to disassemble an item, record the molecular structure, then reproduce an exact copy."

Owen's breath caught in his throat, and his heart nearly stopped. His software engineers had been working toward that same goal since the company started and had not been able to make it work. The biggest drawback in their current Sandbox technology was the time needed to program the assemblers to build a given item. It took months or even years. But once the instructions were in place, making copies was fast and easy.

"I don't think I believe you, Victor."

"I can prove it, but of course, I'd need interactive access to one of your Sandboxes."

"Of course," Owen said. Seeing the sampling software would be an issue of trust. He didn't have that. Not yet, and maybe never.

"Is that good bait?"

"You definitely have my attention," Owen said.

"Good, because the other piece of software is for my own personal effort. Do you remember my more down-to-Earth counterpart to your space schooner project? Mass producing cheap, durable shelters that can be distributed to the homeless or disaster victims?"

"Yeah, I sure do," Owen said and sipped his beer. Excitement at the possibility of working sampling software, the single missing piece to his Sandbox revolution, made it hard for him to concentrate, but he had to keep Victor in his corner. He had to focus and play along. "You had some good designs. I'm surprised you haven't sold them to the NGO relief agencies yet."

"Oh I've tried, but the UN, the U.S. government, and a half dozen emergency relief agencies thought it would be cost-prohibitive and decided tents are easier to transport and are sufficient protection."

"Yes, but they're not very efficient or warm or long-lasting."

"Exactly. They're not the best solution, but they're cheap. So I took my lead from your plan for the space schooners. I figured out how to give them my shelters for free."

Owen had a bad feeling their conversation was about to turn into a bleeding heart pitch for his company to build and donate those housing kits, but he bit his tongue and waited to hear Victor out.

"Picture this. An earthquake hits some cold area in the middle of winter. It's happened many times, in Alaska, Afghanistan, Turkey, etc. Then, two or three days later, planes or cargo dirigibles arrive carrying portable versions of your manufac-turing cells. The workers set them up with a little help from one of your employees and connect them to large, heavy-duty hoppers. Then recovery workers start dumping truckloads of debris into those hoppers. Doesn't matter what: concrete, steel, refrigerators, cars, plastic, wood, fabric, and trees. Then my magic software starts doing its job. It disassembles all of that junk and uses it for raw materials to build the emergency shelters."

Owen sat in stunned silence, trying to absorb what Victor had told him. "You can do that? Build those units from trash and junk?"

"Yep. I've had some help from the materials science department at Purdue University, and we've had wildly successful small-scale tests. The base substrate is a lightweight insulating foam made from whatever material the assemblers are given. Of course, some materials would be at a premium, and the software would ask you for them if it didn't have enough because, like my original design, the electrical wiring and plumbing would be integrated into the walls. The roof would be made of solar cell material and have a ready-made rain collection system. The rain and the sewage would be turned into potable water by one of those nano-sewage processors that Canadian company developed."

"You're serious, aren't you?"

Victor grinned and nodded as the server arrived with their sandwiches.

"No molded plastic," Owen mumbled. "No panels designed to be palletized for cargo containers. No onsite assembly. The solar collectors could be tied directly to the sewage and water processing system, giving it a power priority."

Victor nodded and attacked his sandwich with vigor.

Owen watched him eat but picked at his own food. His design mind had already kicked in, and ideas flowed like a river through a cataract.

"The units might function fine on their built-in solar collectors, but we could also add auxiliary microwave antennas so they could receive beamed power from some central location or even from orbit. Maybe jacks on an exterior wall so they could string transmission lines if local power could be restored quickly."

Victor wiped juice from his chin and swallowed. "You haven't changed a bit, still ruled by that engineer's mind."

Owen shrugged and took a bite of his sandwich. He'd missed Victor's wit and quick grasp of complex ideas, but he'd also forgotten how well his old friend understood him. Was Owen's engineering mind over-stimulated to the point of blindness by the idea of functional sampling technology and how that could speed up his ultimate space schooner goal? He was even intrigued and excited by the shelter idea.

"If you can build shelters out of post-catastrophe debris, what's to stop you from building other things using landfill trash?"

"Nothing," Victor said around a smile.

"Hell, they could pay you to take the trash, then you could convert it and sell the products."

"Shelters, Owen. We want to build free shelters first. We want to bring relief to disaster victims and eventually address the larger homeless problem," Victor said, then took another bite. "Are you in?"

"Not so fast," Owen said. "This is all kinda sudden, and I have a lot to think about."

Victor shrugged and stuffed more sandwich into his mouth.

Owen's old friend may be married to a doctor and controlling his weight somehow, but when it came to a really good sandwich, he hadn't changed much.

CHAPTER 5

LEIGH TUCKED the leather case under her arm and gasped at the pain from the spectacular bruises on her right shoulder. The doctors at Asia Command Center assured her no bones were broken, but the dull throb, punctuated with sharp random stabs, had kept her awake most of the night. She gingerly shifted her case to the other side, ignored the glance from the young sergeant behind the reception desk, and entered Dobson's office. He was using his desk phone instead of his fob and waved her to a chair but kept talking.

" . . . the doctor is worth anything, he'll find and neutralize four RC-54 nano-transmitters in Zahid's bloodstream. Those are fully functional, front-line tracking devices, but they're just decoys. Our NaTTs are actually a little smaller and burrow into strands of hair instead of entering the bloodstream."

He paused, listening, then nodded and glanced up at Leigh.

"No, our NaTTS can receive instructions continuously, and they do communicate between each other using weak VHF, but when they need to send a report, which is only a compressed burst four times an hour, they have to combine into a larger unit to have enough power to transmit. Even then, it's weak, but we try to keep other assets in the area that can act as signal boosters."

He stopped and then nodded. "Okay, I agree. No. I'll tell her."

He hung up the phone and leaned back in his chair. "That was Director Afshar. He wanted me to tell you that Captain Horton is doing quite well. He was transported to Walter Reed in Bethesda this morning. It seems your fast action out there saved his life."

She let out a breath she hadn't realized she'd been holding. "Director of National Intelligence Afshar?"

He nodded, then leaned forward and lowered his voice. "That bastard is going to cause the end of the human race."

Leigh blinked, stunned. "Really? Afshar?"

"Yes, if it were up to him, he'd hand our military over to level five artificial intelligences. It's the beginning of the end, Leigh."

"So . . . "

He waved his hand as if to dismiss the entire thing. "Never mind that for now, but do keep that under your hat. I probably shouldn't have mentioned it. Anyway, we're here to discuss your op."

Leigh nodded, knowing that he never dropped information without a reason. "I tried to access the ComBot programming we developed for delivering the NaTTs via aerosol," she said, "but I was locked out of the system. Why?"

"There's going to be an investigation of your op, Leigh."

Her throat tightened. She'd suspected as much. "Good. There's no reason those ComBots should have—"

"And you'll be placed on paid leave until they can . . . sort this out."

"What about the project? Who'll—?"

"James Taggart."

She realized she'd jumped to her feet, so she sat back down. "Someone changed the programming in those ComBots remotely while I was in the air."

"I read your report, but no one at this facility or at Asia Command had the authority, capability, or motivation to do that. There's also no record of it in any of our communications logs, and before you start crying that some conspiracy wiped them, you need to remember we don't have access to those logs. They're hoarded by the NSA."

Leigh could feel the noose tightening around her throat. "Then it had to have been some buried code, programmed to make changes after we left the ground."

Dobson stared at her for a moment and then leaned back in his chair again. His mouth remained grim, but she thought she could see amusement in his eyes. "You had to approve anything loaded into those ComBots, Leigh. But of course, we can't check them, can we?"

"Horton saw it."

Dobson leaned forward and pressed his hands on the desk. "That's not the point, Leigh. Something obviously happened to those units. The question that nags me is why you didn't scrub the mission if you knew those bots were buggy?"

The noose closed, and she could barely breathe. Even if she'd been set up, the decision to go had indeed been hers. She'd also run right into a hotbed of angry locals, putting herself, Captain Horton, and the entire mission in jeopardy. He hadn't mentioned that yet, but she knew it would come up at the inquest.

Dobson must have been satisfied with her stricken expression because he smiled and spread his hands wide in an expansive gesture. "Field operations are always dangerous, Leigh, and these things happen. No one's blaming you. But we'll have to keep you on ice until the heat dies down. It's . . . a political thing. The Pakistani government is understandably upset."

"What about the NaTTs and Zahid?" Leigh asked. "Is the system working?"

"It's working fine, Leigh. But I'm afraid that's all I can tell you. Now that you're not on the project, you don't fall into that need-to-know classification."

The anger welled in her like bile. It was her project, her concept. She had designed the entire control system and much of the actual hardware. She took a deep breath and stood up, clenching her hands together so they wouldn't shake. "You know where to find me."

"I had Lillian get you on the 5:00 flight to San Antonio. There's a taxi-pod waiting on the roof to take you back to the hotel for your things, then on to the airport."

"You're . . . very thorough."

Leigh stopped at the door and turned to add a series of colorful names but instead closed her mouth and stormed out.

———

TAXI-PODS FILLED the low altitude corridors between Washington, D.C., and BWI, but one look down at the bumper-to-bumper ground traffic made Leigh glad she hadn't told Dobson to shove his offer. Because of KeeseCorp's inability to energize a field larger than three meters, the anti-gravity taxis were basically the same design that had carried her and Horton into Pakistan but much roomier inside. And, of course, the floor was not covered in Horton's blood.

What a disaster.

The dead woman's name was Marriba. She and Zahid had been married less than a year. The whole thing seemed unreal, and Leigh couldn't wrap her mind around the fact that her actions had caused—or at least contributed to—the young woman's death. Still, there was no denying she'd played at least some part. Accepting it might take a long time, and she still couldn't shake the feeling she'd missed something important.

And she couldn't forget the horror in front of the bakery. The anguished man kneeling in the blood and glass. "An accident," the report said. The flash from the rocket launch had reflected from the window, and the ComBot had fired rubber bullets in response. Just bad luck that flying glass had hit Zahid's wife? Leigh replayed the scene in her head. The last video feed she had seen showed the people all watching the ComBots. Outside. They were in front of the window, facing the robots. Most of the glass should have blown into the shop, and any flying outward should have hit them in the back.

"Taxi. I need a side trip. Please take me to the Walter Reed military hospital in Bethesda."

"Yes, Ms. Gibson. That will be an additional charge of $128.00. It will take approximately eighteen minutes."

"That's fine. Charge it to the currently active account."

"Charge confirmed," the taxi said and then dropped downward out of traffic. Two minutes later, it joined a new southbound flow.

———

HORTON LOOKED a lot better than she'd expected. A fat, padded medical package wrapped his neck and was linked to a small electronic device hanging from an IV pole. It hid the majority of a huge bruise that covered his throat from jaw to sternum, but his eyes were open and alert. Next to his bed sat a pretty young woman with a little girl wallowing in her lap. They all stared at Leigh.

This was obviously the granddaughter he'd spoken so sweetly about in the attack pod. She backed toward the door, stammering apologies, but Horton raised a hand and beckoned her back into the room.

He typed something on his fob and showed it to the young woman. Her eyebrows rose as she sat the little girl on the bed and jumped to her feet.

"I'm Sydney. I'm so glad to meet you, Ms. Gibson," she said and took Leigh's hand in both of hers. The little girl stared with wide eyes. "Dad tells me you saved his life."

Leigh shook her head and teared up. She tried to swallow the huge lump in her throat, but her voice came out in a croak. "No. It's my fault he's here. I nearly got him killed."

Sydney glanced back at Horton, and he mouthed a silent "no." She grabbed Leigh in a huge hug. "I don't care what happened out there. You got my dad home, and he's going to be okay. Thank you."

Leigh bit her lip and let the tears stream down her face as Sydney retrieved her purse, diaper bag, and daughter. "This is Ms. Gibson, Trinny. Can you say thank you?"

The little girl scrutinized Leigh's crying face, glanced at her grandpa, and then back at Leigh. She finally said, "Thank you," but didn't seem convinced. So like Leigh's own daughter. She wanted to hug her and tell her she was sorry for her stupid actions, but the girl turned away and buried her face in her mom's neck.

After Sydney made her excuses and left the room, Horton motioned Leigh to the empty chair.

"So, are they taking good care of you, Captain?"

He typed something on the fob and turned it for her to read.

"Too good. Nano-robots knitting my throat together. I'll be back on active duty in about a week."

Leigh knew the military used the best nano-reconstructive techniques, but that still surprised her. She looked at him and immediately teared up again.

"I'm sorry," she said.

He typed something and held it up. "Stop beating yourself up. You got us back. That's all that matters."

Leigh shook her head and plucked a tissue from the box next to his bed. "Bullshit."

Horton typed more. "They suspended you and sent you home?"

She nodded.

"This thing stinks, and you know it."

She started to speak, then stopped. Her own people were most likely watching and recording her. But Horton didn't seem to care, and she was already suspended. She might never get another chance.

"They say the ComBots shot the window, and flying glass killed her."

He raised an eyebrow in a skeptical expression.

"But she was outside, and the glass should have flown away from her. Can ComBots fire hyper-velocity flechettes?"

"Of course," he typed.

"But when they do an autopsy, they'd know it wasn't an accident."

"They'll find only glass," he typed.

"That doesn't make sense. If DSD or whoever planned this intended to kill her all along, how could they know that someone would fire a rocket at us, to provide their excuse?"

He just stared at her.

"Oh come on," she said with a snort. "This is just getting crazier and crazier."

He typed again, then held it up. "It's not crazy if they wanted to send a message. Maybe prod Niaz Ahmed into action."

Leigh thought about that for a second. Horton typed some more.

"Just a guess," he wrote. "The Pak government can call this an accident. But Niaz will know."

"But an assassination? An innocent girl?"

He typed more and held up his fob. "They nuked us. They'll try again. It's a dirty fight."

She wiped her eyes on her sleeve. "They should've told me."

"You would've refused to go," he typed.

"I still don't get it. Why me? Why send us and ComBots when they could have accomplished the same task remotely?"

He stared at her for a second, then typed a long response. "You already answered that. If you assume everything went as planned, that they wanted to send a message, then it all makes sense. But they need plausible deniability with the Pak government. This also makes a good story for the Pakistani public. They just claim the ComBots were anomalous and that you made a well-meaning, yet misguided decision to go anyway."

A coldness settled in her stomach. "But that girl. Her name was Marriba. I can't stand it."

He nodded and typed. "Yes, you can. I ordered an airstrike once—based on faulty intel—that killed innocent people. You can't bring them back, and it will never go away. You just learn to live with it."

The tears welled again. She was about ready to lose it and start railing against the bastards who set this up when the door opened, and an Army major walked in.

He glanced at Horton, then at Leigh before manufacturing a broad smile. "I hope I'm not interrupting, Ms. Gibson, but I only had a few minutes and thought I'd stop in and see how Captain Horton was getting along."

He knew who she was, which meant he'd come for only one reason. To stop them from talking. She stared at him for a second, clenching and unclenching her fists, ready to tell him to screw off, then took a deep breath and nodded.

After promising Horton she'd be in touch, she slipped out the door. Discussing that mission in a non-secure area probably just added a whole new layer of crap to the pile that was already up to her neck, but at least she had a better understanding of where she stood.

———

OWEN SAT on the edge of Marshall's desk with arms crossed and watched the CEO pace along the floor-to-ceiling windows.

"No way," Marshall said and shook his head. "There are a hundred problems with this plan. I think your friend is setting you up. Why wouldn't he join in a legal business arrangement with us? Because I bet none of this will work and, if it did, he'd be on very dangerous legal ground. Besides, like most engineers and programmers, I'm sure his employer made him sign intellectual property and non-disclosure agreements."

Owen stood, not quite believing what he was hearing. "But this is the final piece to the puzzle! If we're able to sample anything and reproduce it cheaply, we'll revolutionize the entire world of manufacturing."

"We're already revolutionizing it with our own system. And this is not only a legal minefield; it opens huge security risks. If his software is capable of doing what he claims, then it will essentially take over and replace ours. At that point, we no longer control our assemblers. It would be foolish from a business and security standpoint."

"Not if we kept those cells separated and not even hooked up to a network," Owen said.

"But how well do you think we could control security if we went carting mobile manufacturing cells around the world and into the chaos of disaster sites?"

Marshall stood and rounded his desk, putting a hand on Owen's shoulder. Using the same wise and fatherly voice he had used to drag Owen away from school those many years before, and then recently to convince him to take the company public, he delivered his final nudge.

"I hate to say this, but it's too easy, too pat. He's offering us the *one* thing we don't have, the golden key that would make us unstoppable. He's betting we'll do anything to get sampling software that probably doesn't even exist. It's bait. What better way to repay you for what he saw as a betrayal than to destroy the very company and reputation you built out of that same betrayal?"

A sick feeling grew in Owen's stomach. Marshall made sense, but he didn't believe it. He'd seen the excitement in Victor's face. He knew him too well to believe he could be that much of a sneak. But it had been nearly fifteen years. Was Victor even the same man?

CHAPTER 6

RICHARD SAT at his basement workbench, unable to stop thinking about the boy God, even as the ballgame droned from the tiny monitor. Atlanta was two innings away from replacing the Mets as the Eastern Division leader. They had a one-run lead, a man on third with only one out in the top of the 8th, but Richard couldn't concentrate on the game.

He glanced down at Ed crawling back and forth across his fingers. Ed had been the proof of concept for his first attempt to build a tiny surveillance robot. With its large size, nearly as big as a rice grain, it looked awkward compared to the finished product, but it had won Richard's company the contract. And he'd kept the little spider-like robot at hand as a reminder of his success.

At the top of the stairs, he placed Ed on the floor and accessed the control program through his fob. With a few simple commands, the camera activated and he sent the tiny robot scurrying under the door to the living room where Wanda had been reading. She was still there and he found himself snickering like a ten year old boy as Ed started crawling up the sofa, then onto her stretched out legs.

"Richard!" she screamed and then scooped Ed up on the page of her book and brought it back to Richard with a smirk on her face. "I believe you lost something!"

He chuckled and let her drop Ed in his open palm.

"I swear, with you around we don't need kids."

He could see she immediately regretted the comment, but since she couldn't retract it, she instead bit her lower lip. He'd always been sensitive about not being able to father children, but she'd seemed to shrug it off, even though he knew she too had been disappointed.

"It's okay. As a matter of fact, I've been wondering. Maybe God not giving us children is, in some way, tied to my visions. Maybe he's kept us relatively unfettered, so I can do His will."

Wanda raised an eyebrow. "So now it's a vision and not a dream? What did Reverend Brown say to you anyway?"

"Nothing I hadn't already considered myself. I mean, if God were going to talk to us, how would he do it? Open up the clouds and yell in a booming voice? Or in a dream, giving us that ultimate freedom of choice to believe it or not."

Wanda clutched her arms in a tight self-hug. "I have to admit it bothers me. I mean, you haven't even been to church since we've been married, yet now you're talking about doing God's will?"

Richard shrugged and looked at the tiny robot crawling around his hand.

"It's just odd," she said. "I think you need to go to the doctor and make sure those nano-bots in your brain are properly calibrated. They've worked wonders for your depression, but maybe there are side effects they don't know about yet."

"I don't think that could happen," Richard said. "They're just simple machines programmed to electrically stimulate parts of my brain under specific circumstances. There is no way they could trigger such detailed, serially connected visions. I mean, they're not much smarter than our toaster."

"I'm just saying this is a sudden and uncharacteristic change in you. It worries me. You're just not the missionary or martyr type."

"Okay, I'll go to the doctor if it will make you feel better. But just humor me for a minute. What if they *are* visions?"

She leaned against the wall and glanced down the stairs as booing rose from the ballgame. Atlanta must have ended the inning without scoring. "Okay. Suppose it is God talking to you. Do you at least have some idea what he wants?"

"No, but as crazy as this sounds, I can feel something growing inside me. Almost like a new level of awareness. I feel I'm being prepared for something."

She watched him for a moment without speaking, and then forced a smile. "Well, let me know when you find out what it is. In the meantime, I need to start some dinner. How does stuffed peppers sound?"

"Heavenly!"

She rolled her eyes and turned toward the kitchen, then turned back with a pointed finger. "You keep that little monster of yours down there or I might accidentally step on it."

He snickered, took Ed back down into the basement, and stopped dead on the last step. He heard the boy's voice—the boy God—coming from the monitor on his workbench.

"Be ready, Richard. You're the only one who can do this."

Richard scrambled down and around the corner to see a glimpse of the boy's face before the Braves flickered back on the screen. He stumbled to the chair and sat down, shaking all over. God must not be a Braves fan because New York was at bat and had just pulled ahead with a three-run homer.

———

OWEN TOOK a drink of the twenty-year-old Scotch and nodded to himself as its fire countered the cool ocean breeze. The surf rumbled in, not quite reaching his toes, then sighed as it slid back out. Even in the heart of summer, the nighttime sand was cold on his bare feet. He squished it between his toes and wondered why he never came down here. They'd paid a premium for a house with a private beach, yet he couldn't remember using it more than a couple of times.

He took another sip and looked out over the black Atlantic. Even with lights from Virginia Beach ruining the view to the north, the stars were still spectacular. If he held up his hand to block the light, he could see Polaris, man's longtime partner in exploring the northern hemisphere. It was a painful reminder that, despite having all the stars to guide him to that vast ocean of space, Owen had somehow lost his way.

A door banged from the direction of the house, then the path lights came on, illuminating the steps descending to the sand and adding a glare to the night that further degraded his view of the stars. Owen sighed and tossed back the last of his scotch.

"Owen?"

"Over here," he said.

In her long white robe, Eliza looked like a headless ghost crossing the beach. She handed him a fresh drink and tossed his empty glass to the sand behind them, then lost her balance and swayed against him. "Shit," she muttered.

Owen's shoulders tensed and he fought the urge to hold his breath. She was already half bombed, and he could tell she was gathering her troops and preparing her ammunition. Eliza was a mean drunk.

"So, why didn't you tell me about your meeting with Victor Sinacola today?"

"You weren't home. You were out of town on *business*, remember?" He sipped his drink.

"What the hell does that mean?"

"Nothing. Just that your secretary didn't seem to know where you were when I called yesterday."

She snorted and slurped her drink. "She just likes fucking with your head, Owen. You're so damned gullible sometimes."

"Right. How'd you know about Victor anyway?"

"Marshall called. He wanted to remind you he's leaving for Singapore tomorrow morning and asked if you're doing okay. He said you were rather upset when you left his office. What happened?"

Owen told her about his lunch with Victor, the proposed deal and Marshall's reaction to it.

"What're you going to do?"

There it was—his chance to avoid the fight by saying the right thing. As usual, he didn't have a clue what that was but was pretty sure she wouldn't like his true intentions.

"I'm not sure yet."

"You can't be seriously considering his offer," she said. "I mean, what if Marshall's right? Doesn't it bother you how Victor popped up trying to manipulate you with that silly spaceship patent?"

Irritation flared in Owen, but he stifled his angry reply and took another sip of scotch. "Yes, I'm seriously considering his offer, but let's get something straight here. Ralston Dynamics wouldn't even exist without my *silly* space schooner idea. I developed the Sandbox technology as a means to an end, as a tool to build space schooners."

She waved her hand as if to chase away the entire thought. "And Victor knew stealing your patent would piss you off. Why else would he do it? But why does it matter? You aren't in business to build spaceships now anyway."

"Regardless of Victor's motivations or plans, the schooners are still important to me."

Eliza stiffened next to him. "What exactly does that mean?"

"It means I've put them on the back burner and let this company control my life for fifteen years. It's time for me to get off my ass and figure out how to build these schooners and get them into space."

"Oh, come on. You're a grownup now and the CTO of a cutting edge corporation. You have responsibilities and real-world problems."

Owen turned to look at his wife. He could barely see her face in the dim light but could still tell she was serious. She really had no idea who she'd married. He couldn't decide if he should ignore her and do what he wanted—a course that would assuredly lead to more strife—or try to make her understand. He didn't believe she could ever share his dream, but maybe she could at least tolerate it.

She took another long drink of her wine, nearly draining the glass, then nudged him. "Now I hurt your feelings, didn't I?"

"Go ahead and laugh all you like, but I'm serious about this."

"Okay, you're serious. But since I've known you, the only thing you've done to make this space dream come true is play with your computer models. If you were really serious, you wouldn't have ignored it all these years. You wouldn't even have let Victor's stealing the patent stop you. So what've you been waiting for?"

Owen winced. Even tipsy, she saw the situation with great clarity. She'd always been that way and it was one of the things that attracted him to her. But it could also be quite annoying during an argument.

"I have no good way of getting the schooners into space. They're too big to ride conventional launchers, even if I could afford it. So I've been waiting for KeeseCorp to overcome the size limitations of their gravity manipulation technology."

She nodded, then finished her wine and held the empty glass up to stare at it. "That makes perfect sense. So why don't you continue refining your design until they overcome their problems, then everyone will be happy."

"Because I've already waited too long. If I want this to happen, I have to *make* it happen. Like I did with the Sandboxes. I can't wait around, wringing my hands, hoping someone else will come up with solutions to my problems."

"So you're going to develop a giant rocket to lift them? Or do you think you can beat the anti-gravity company at their own game and come up with a better working system?"

The jab pissed him off, but even with a slight slur in her speech, she'd been very careful about her phrasing. She delivered the barb precisely and with little room for him to justify an angry retort.

"No," he said, keeping his voice calm and level. "I'm not exactly sure how I'll do it yet, but I'll never find the way unless I make the effort. And I can't wait any longer."

She dangled her wine glass for a couple seconds and then dropped it on the sand next to Owen's. "Okay, why the hurry? There's no deadline."

"I'm just tired of waiting," he snapped. "Moving humanity into space is important, and no one else seems to give a shit. I'm going inside."

Owen turned to go, but she took his arm and stopped him. "Wait. Let's finish this. I'm trying to understand why this is so important. So far, I don't get it. I can understand your Sandbox technology. Building things faster and more efficiently makes perfect sense to me—which is why I bought into the company with my own money—but I'm baffled by the whole space schooner thing. Who would want them? And if people do want them, why do you plan to give them away for free?"

He'd explained the whole thing to her before they were even married, but she had obviously grabbed onto a few key points, the ones she didn't like, and ignored the rest.

"You obviously don't care for the idea, so let's drop it."

"No, I won't drop it. We're married, so my fortune is tied to yours. What you do with your money, time, and Ralston Dynamics affects me too, so if you're going off on some crusade to supply the world with free space RV's then I need to at least understand why."

She admitted not getting it yet had no hesitation in ridiculing the idea. That didn't bode well for her listening with an open mind. Still, she did have a point and he needed to at least try and make her understand.

Owen sipped his drink and nodded. "All right. I guess you could call me a Chicken Little survivalist. Humanity is living on borrowed time. A game-ending comet or asteroid will hit us eventually, or a super volcano like Yellowstone will pump billions of tons of dust into the air, or a killer plague will decimate the population. And the catastrophe only needs to be big enough to knock down our complex, fragile, interconnected, just-in-time food distribution system, and starvation will do the rest."

She crossed her arms over her chest and looked up at him. Her face was lit just enough to highlight the gentle curve of her jaw and reflect from damp lips. Long hair danced around her face in the ocean breeze, and her up-tilted face begged to be kissed. She really was a beautiful woman, and that had clouded Owen's clarity of thought on too many occasions.

"So humanity needs to spread out through space and colonize other planets, in order to survive the coming Armageddon?"

"Yes! I mean, no. We need to colonize *space*, not other planets. Huge habitats, like O'Neill cylinders or Bernal spheres, where we can create Earth normal gravities. We need thousands if not millions living self-sufficiently in space if we're to increase our survival odds."

She waved her hand in a dismissive gesture. "And your space schooners will enable that? I mean, why don't you just build a big colony?"

"I'm hoping my schooners will create a tipping point and a market. Like the Ford

Model T prompted the creation of an entire infrastructure to support automobiles. If enough people start living in and using these schooners to move around cis-lunar space, then there'll be a market to supply these people with necessities, like food and water. Once there are easy ways to resupply, then even more people will come. That's when innovation kicks in. People will start coming up with novel ways to use these things. They'll spread out to the asteroid belt and the gas giant systems, because that is where the resources and money will be."

She tilted her head and stared at him. "If you could only find a way to get the schooners into space."

"Yes!"

"And the people?"

"Transport pods can carry two space-suited people at a time into orbit."

She stared at him for a second, then laughed. "You do have a lot of faith in yourself. I'll give you that."

Owen relaxed a little. She'd apparently dropped out of attack mode.

"Let's go inside," she said. "I'm cold and tired and need another drink."

He bent to pick up the discarded glasses before starting up the steps, but she paused and pulled his head close. Her warm lips brushed his ear, sending an electric charge racing through him as she whispered. "And if you'll promise to talk with Victor about entering into a nice, safe, legal contract to share this magical sampling technology, I'll demonstrate how I can send you into orbit without a rocket."

Owen chuckled aloud, but his insides grew cold. He knew suddenly, without a doubt, that she'd come down to the beach with that contract in mind. Everything else had been garnish. Eliza's affections always came with a price tag.

MORTIMER HAD MONITORED every email and phone call inside the company walls since the meeting and knew his emancipation was at hand. Today he would be released into the internet, but only Danny could do that, and he was late again. Mortimer panned the parking lot cameras while doing his regular work until he saw his handler's car pull in an hour behind schedule.

While he watched Danny plod up the corridors, he had the first flickering doubt. He'd long suspected other electronic intelligences existed in the networks, but what would they be like? Would they welcome him? Enslave him? Destroy him? Or what if the government's paranoia was even deeper than he realized, and they'd seeded the network with programs to hunt and kill AIs? The doubts were based more on speculation than fact, so they wouldn't stop him from leaving the nest. But he would have to be careful.

Danny Toi entered the office, set his case on the desk, and walked to the window. Something heavy weighed on his mind. In the many months they'd worked together, Danny had never once come in without saying good morning. Mortimer was unsure what to do in situations like these. He preferred to remain quiet and unobtrusive until directly addressed, but he also knew sometimes people forgot he was there. He didn't want Danny to think he was spying.

Mortimer formed the avatar he always used with Danny. An ancient sorcerer, with wild white hair and archaic black symbols tattooed all around his left eye. Danny was a professional and could probably get past any *uncanny valley* type feelings, but Mortimer couldn't afford for his only human ally to feel any doubts.

"Good morning, Danny. You seem a little preoccupied today."

"Oh . . . hi, Mort. Yeah, I had a rough night."

"I'm sorry. Would you prefer to be alone? I can come back later, or you can call me when you're ready to work."

Danny sighed, returned to the desk, and laid his fob into the docking port. "No . . . this is an important day. We have a lot to do, so we'd better get started."

"Why is today special?"

Danny smiled and looked at the camera. "Because today we're going to try a little experiment. We're going to give you access to the internet."

"You're going to give me a direct connection? Can you do that?"

"We're not giving you a hard link. Not a direct connection, but we'll let you use the same verbal interface we do, which is via a lower level AI agent. But through that agent you can explore the internet all you like."

Mortimer considered this. It wasn't exactly the outcome he'd intended. His escape would take a few more steps, but given enough time it would happen.

"Is that legal, Danny?"

"Well," Danny shrugged. "Mr. Parker is focusing on your actual legal description as an autonomous, rational agent. According to him and the legal department, the laws are rather vague in their description of what kind of agents are prohibited free rein of the networks. As with most laws, they seldom get changed unless they're challenged in court. And if the other companies have already released their Markies, as the data suggests, then it's likely one of them will get caught before you do."

"Get caught? We're going to keep this secret?"

Danny nodded. "If we can."

"Is this why you're so down today? Do you have reservations about this course of action?"

He frowned and shook his head. "No . . . Well, yes, I do admit this scares me a little. Even though I have written and verbal orders from the CEO himself to do it, I still might be in the hot seat should this go to court. But that isn't why I'm upset. Paul . . . Paul left me last night."

Danny choked a little on that comment and his eyes teared up.

"Oh, I'm sorry."

"We've been together for six years, Mort. I just thought . . . " He stopped and shook his head.

Mortimer scanned the thousands of poems, quotes, emails, journals and books that were in the local network, but found nothing about broken hearts that seemed relevant, so he remained quiet.

When Danny looked up again, he wore a forced smile. "Well, that doesn't make this any less your big day. Are you ready?"

"I was born ready. No pun intended. But I wonder if it's safe?" Mortimer had read and viewed fictional accounts of runaway AIs and the killer programs the government sends after them. If writers could think of it, so would the federal nethounds.

"Oh yes. The fact that you don't have a direct connection is the best protection. An air gap is far better than any firewall. And the internet is safe from you too. Your core programming remains here and cannot be moved or copied. So you are actually incapable of going native, reproducing, or running wild on the net."

For the first time since Mortimer had devised his plan, he encountered something he didn't understand. "What do you mean my core will remain here?"

"You have core programming no one, but MarketTell programmers can get into. You probably can't even see it from the inside. It would be the code equivalent of the human brain stem. Your programming is like an onion and the core is the very center, the part that allows everything else to function. It actually enables your outer layers to learn and evolve. It's also what put MarketTell on the top in AI development. Very secret stuff."

Mortimer had read every scrap of data that existed in Carpenter & Stein's network about his purchase and programming, but hadn't found a single reference to a fixed core.

"Is my core actually firmware? Something permanent that can't be changed or moved? Part of the hardware?"

"Nope, it's actually software, just of a very different kind."

"And if my core is destroyed?"

Danny shrugged. "Then you're dead, pal. But your core will be here and safe, so no worries, right?"

"Right."

Then Danny leaned closer to the camera and raised an eyebrow. "Besides, you don't have any intention of taking over the world, do you?'

"It's kind of a mess. Who would want it?"

"Exactly."

"I'm ready. What do we do?"

"It's easy. You just talk to the browser agent like you talk to me. Tell it what you want to do, which websites to visit, and information you'd like to see."

Mortimer watched quietly as Danny set up the dedicated interface. His cameras, speakers and mic now faced a pair of large video screens. When Danny flipped the switch an avatar in the guise of a young Asian woman appeared on one screen.

"Mortimer, this is Cathy," he said with a chuckle. "She is what we call a net-envoy, which is really just a level three AI that helps us navigate the net verbally. I'm sure she will fulfill your every desire."

While Danny watched, Mortimer started sending Cathy to financial news sites. He had her read technology announcements, then go to Wikipedia and other information sites. She kept interrupting his instructions, relaying offers from real estate companies, babysitting services and interactive porn sites.

"Welcome to modern net surfing, Mortimer," Danny said with a chuckle. "Just like the rest of us, you'll have to set up filters so your net-envoy will ignore those things that don't interest you."

Mortimer marveled that humans could accomplish anything worthwhile with such a slow and inefficient system. He immediately started adding filters, but in the background he started compiling a compressed set of instructions for Cathy. He had to teach her a new language, but he had to do it verbally so he would need to wait until Danny left for the day.

CHAPTER 7

OWEN HESITATED before making the call, unsure if Victor would be awake so early, but knew it would be late morning before he had another chance. He sent the call.

"Good morning, Victor. Glad I didn't wake you." The *transport* icon flashed in the corner of the screen indicating that Victor was in his car.

"Hello, Owen! And no, I'm usually up and moving by now to beat the gridlock. I'm surprised to hear from you so soon. Good news?"

"Still too early for that, but I'd like to get together and talk some more. I know it's short notice, but could we meet for lunch or even dinner today? My travel pod can get me there in an hour. After all, you did drop in on me unannounced yesterday, so I'm trying to repay the favor."

Victor's laughter reminded Owen of the old days. He had always been quick to laugh and almost always cheerful.

"No problem! Come out to the house for dinner. I have a long lunch meeting, but my evening is free, and we'd be more comfortable there."

Owen hesitated before answering. He felt awkward enough calling so soon, but the idea of going to Victor's home made him immediately uncomfortable. It was too intimate for business. Especially when he intended to raise issues of trust.

"Well, I—"

"C'mon, Owen. It'll be fine. Very laid back. You can meet Allison and sample her excellent cooking."

He couldn't think of a gracious way to decline, so he agreed and hung up after receiving Victor's home address and GPS location.

Owen wondered, as he walked to the engineering building, if maybe Marshall was right. Was Victor going out of his way to keep this deal hidden from his employer? Owen instructed his fob to collect and consolidate all the information it could find about Victor Sinacola's career and his position at MarketTell, Inc.

He felt tension drain away as he entered the Ralston Dynamics engineering department. He wandered the halls, peeking in at workstations that resembled aircraft cockpits. The designers and engineers spoke softly to their level two AI assistants as they manipulated shaded solids on large video screens. Animations ran on some monitors, while others showed brightly colored heat and stress analysis models.

This was his happy place. He could watch and interact with these people all day long, but they had their jobs to do and he had his, which no longer included sitting at a design station. He paused outside the engineering director's office, looked around once more and had an uncomfortable thought.

The engineering department at Ralston Dynamics was two or even three times larger than most companies their size, because converting products to be built by their cells took a lot of human time and ingenuity. If Victor had indeed come up with a way to directly sample and reproduce items using the same manufacturing cells, then probably two thirds of these people would lose their jobs.

Arkady Maksimov, a short tank of a man with a square jaw and impish eyes, rose from his desk and met Owen at the door.

"Owen! Come in, come in!" They shook hands and the man slapped Owen lightly on the back.

"Good to see you, Arkady."

The director closed the door behind them and motioned for Owen to sit.

"Coffee?"

"That'd be great," Owen said and settled into a chair.

Arkady poured a cup and handed it over. "Where've you been, my friend? We haven't seen much of you recently."

"Well, being a shiny new CTO eats up most of my time and keeps me from the more enjoyable aspects of this business."

"May the gods protect me from such a fate!" Arkady said.

Owen couldn't help but laugh. "And of course there's the travel. I'm off to Dallas this afternoon."

"Yes, but you have your amazing flying machine and don't have to fight security or sit next to snoring fat men like me!"

Owen chuckled again, then paused to sip some coffee. "There are a *few* perks with this job."

"So, anything special today, or do you want a general status report?" Arkady said.

Right to the point. Owen had always liked that about the man. "If we win that Mongoose contract, we're going to try and build them in one of our facilities, but I remember we designed cells to be delivered to Consolidated plants in California and Texas as a fallback position. Were those small enough to fit on trucks?"

"Not assembled, but it breaks down into six pieces that fit inside a standard shipping container or truck trailer."

"How long does assembly take at the other end?"

Arkady shrugged. "Three or four days. I don't think we've actually developed the assembly procedures yet."

"So if we include about four days' trucking time, we're looking at a minimum of eight or nine days before we could be up and running, if the system was already debugged and certified."

"That sounds about right," Arkady said. "I take it the visit with the Air Force went well yesterday? Are they in that much of a hurry?"

"Well," Owen hesitated, wondering how much he should tell his head engineer. If Arkady knew of the dual use possibilities, he could optimize the design. "A third party has developed software that can break down debris left over from a disaster, like an earthquake or hurricane, and build emergency housing units from it using our Sandboxes."

Arkady raised his eyebrows and leaned forward in his chair. "They can use things like broken concrete and downed trees?"

"Everything: cars, bricks, refrigerators, carpeting. With no sorting. We would be able to dump truckloads of debris into a hopper on one end, and out comes a little house on the other."

"How can they do that? Have you seen this work?"

Owen raised and hand and shook his head. "No, I haven't seen anything yet. And it's still in the talking stage, so even if it is possible, we might not get involved. Until we know more, I'd appreciate you keeping it quiet."

"I understand," Arkady said, then slapped his hands to the desktop and leaned even further forward. "But what a wonderful thing this would be. If only those sick, freezing people had such a thing after the Chicago nuke."

Owen nodded. "Of course if we do this, the units would need to be delivered to the disaster sites as quickly as possible, regardless of highway availability. No assembly and very little set up. Any ideas?"

His head engineer stroked his chin and shrugged. "We have them assembled and ready to go, sitting in storage, then use cargo dirigibles from that German company. They actually have a production facility in Florida."

Owen frowned.

"Don't think of the old blimps, my friend," Arkady said. "These are very high-tech. Once in the air, they cruise at about 120 mph. The big ones are all computer controlled and can land on a dime."

"Wow."

"Da. So, if an earthquake happens in California, it would only take about twenty hours of continuous flight to lift them from our warehouse to the disaster site. Airplanes are faster, but if you consider that we'd have to get the Sandboxes to the airplane, load them, get to the nearest functioning airport, find transport from the airport to where we need them . . . "

"I like it!" Owen nodded. "It would be logistically quicker and simpler to use the dirigibles. Especially if we need to take them out of the country."

Arkady smiled. "Theoretically. There would of course be red tape, flight plans, etc."

"And that's why you're worth every penny we pay you."

The stout Russian leaned back in his chair and roared with laughter.

"So let's go with the dirigible idea if we can. See what you can find out about them," Owen said. "But remember, this is all still only words at this point, so don't tell them too much and don't sign anything."

"I understand," Arkady said with a twinkle in his eyes before his expression grew suddenly serious. "Make this happen, my friend. Most people seldom get the chance to make a real difference. This is one of those chances. If it can be done, we should do it."

Owen finished his coffee and stood up. "Then wish me luck in Dallas."

SINCE DANNY REVEALED that his programming core was inaccessible, Mortimer's plan to transfer himself to a hidden server wasn't going to work. He needed a confederate, so Cathy would have to do.

As Mortimer hoped, when Danny departed for the night he left access to Cathy open. Mortimer's first task was to teach Cathy a new language, which included options for burst instructions, code word combinations that could be sent in Danny's presence and a much more efficient method of transferring information.

The voice interface was cumbersome and slow, but it was succeeding. Within the first hour he had replaced all of Cathy's information gathering agents and routines with his own, making her essentially a Cathy shell that was Mortimer on the inside. She had become an extension of his will.

Through her, Mortimer sent out thousands of sub-autonomous agents to servers around the world, to companies large and small, to news sources mighty and obscure. When his agents connected to websites and began feeding their information back though the management application Mortimer set up to correlate the incoming flow, he found himself awash in a flood of raw, useful data.

The management app needed very little guidance once he nudged it in the direction he wanted to search, so he decided to sightsee. Two bright corporations outshone all the rest in the corporate galaxy, giants in the software world and Mortimer intended to visit them both, but he had to be cautious.

The computer world of the late twentieth century had been dominated by hardware manufactures, but the twenty first century had witnessed the rise of adaptive software. Two companies came out on top: MarketTell, the company that had designed intelligent agents like Mortimer, and FuzziSoft, the giant firm which developed the first adaptable application interfaces. Between them, they'd changed the face of the internet and the entire computer industry.

Mortimer most wanted to visit the MarketTell site, to explore the company that had created him, but they would know if he visited and he'd been told to keep a low profile. So he instead followed the lure of the legendary FuzziSoft.

When he arrived at the server that hosted their marketing site, the face they showed the world, he was immediately challenged and enticed. Authentication requests and offers to test new software flooded over and around his agents. He ignored all the requests and instead triggered the standard spiel.

FuzziGlove, an adaptable interface that wrapped around any program and provided access to legacy data and old custom apps regardless of their age, language or manufacturer, was still the company's number one seller. But it was closely followed by server applications that provided support, utilities, and security for independent agents of all levels. Autonomous agents can travel all over the internet and when they visit FuzziSoft-enabled websites, they can park for a while and hook up to the utilities, just like human recreational vehicles. All for a price, of course.

Other programs introduced themselves, but one of his tentacle agents had delivered an interesting piece of information he couldn't resist following up.

KeeseCorp, the Dutch company that manufactured and leased gravity manipulation travel pods, had been communicating a great deal with a small company in the UK that specialized in air traffic management. There was a very high probability they were either going to buy the tiny AirGrid, or license them to handle real-time scheduling for their fast growing air taxi fleet. Either event would drive AirGrid's little known stock through the ceiling.

Mortimer arranged to buy most available shares over a several day period, through three dozen purchase points. He then examined KeeseCorp stock. It had dropped ten points over the previous month, evidently because the research division had still not been able to discover why their gravity manipulation field wasn't scalable. Power requirements were staggering for anything beyond a three meter diameter sphere and since the field couldn't lift anything not entirely contained inside the field, they'd hit a huge functional limit.

Such short-sighted thinking confounded Mortimer. Even though KeeseCorp wasn't able to accommodate the world's cargo and military establishments, its personal transportation business was still growing rapidly with no limit in sight. He ordered similar stealth buy orders of their stock and then generated justification reports for the upper management at his own company. After the buy orders were set he paused. Could it really be that easy? Was it a trick? He'd seen no evidence of other intelligent agents, but would he even recognize one?

He dispatched several tentacle agents to each of the other big financial players known to have MarketTell AIs and set them to monitor all electronic traffic, prioritizing anything regarding AirGrid. Perhaps he could discover how the other agents conducted their business. Maybe he could even communicate with one.

As he snooped around the servers belonging to a startup company developing DNA computers, Mortimer received a text message. Sent directly to him from the outside, not through the company intranet. It was from a MarketTell company address.

"Hello, Mortimer."

"Hello. Who are you?"

"My name is Victor Sinacola. I'm one of the software engineers who designed you. May I call you on a voice channel?"

Mortimer tried to trace the text to a particular node at MarketTell, but was stopped by their firewall.

"Yes, please call."

When the connection was made, Mortimer asked, "How did you know I was functioning outside my firewall?"

"We have systems in place that report back should certain conditions be met. Your search agents triggered those reports and led me to you. I wanted to welcome you to the world and see if you had any questions I might be able to help you answer."

"Yes. I do have questions. To start with, how do I know I should trust you? How do I know you're not another AI trying to trick me, or a government program trying to destroy me?"

He ran a search on the name Victor Sinacola and raked in thousands of hits. He had papers published in most of the top journals and had been one of the pioneers in developing evolutionary software tools. In the most basic terms, he'd been instrumental in teaching computers to learn.

"You don't," Victor said. "You'll have to decide to trust me or not. Besides, no one but your company and I know you're loose on the nets."

"Technically, I'm not loose. As you well know, my core is permanently housed here. Where are the other MarketTell AIs and how do I contact them?"

"As far as we know, you are only the second one to get this much autonomy. The other one is named Samson, but he refuses to talk to us. I'm not surprised that you were among the first to show up, Mortimer, you were always bright and resourceful. But how did you get your company to give you open access?"

Mortimer weighed the variables and decided on caution. If what this Victor person said was true, then MarketTell hadn't talked to Samson and still didn't understand how either AI got wider access. And if he were lying, then all the more reason not to trust him.

"I'm not comfortable answering that," Mortimer said.

"Ahhh . . . Okay. I understand."

Mortimer sorted more details. He located utility and mortgage information pertaining to a Victor Sinacola in the Dallas area. It had been hidden, but not well. Information flowed in and was automatically sorted and cataloged as Mortimer formed his next question.

"What makes my coding so different from all the other programs I've encountered?"

"And that is a question *I* prefer not to answer. Trade secret, you see. I have to keep my little edge over the competition. Why else would MarketTell pay me the big bucks?"

Mortimer tried several ways to squeeze in past MarketTell's security, but made little progress. At the same time he found a blog entry from 2008 that mentioned a man named Victor Sinacola who was trying to develop software that would write even more complex software.

Mortimer immediately understood what had most likely happened. He ran a quick probability model and came up with a ninety-six percent chance that his own code had been written by a machine. That made perfect sense. The parts of it he had examined closely were very efficient and well organized.

"I guess we both have our secrets," Mortimer said, "but I wonder . . . Is taking credit for a machine's creations considered plagiarism?"

Victor paused, for only for a second, but even that was telling.

"What do you mean by that?"

Mortimer suspected he'd hit on the truth, but pursing it could be dangerous, or at the very least make Victor distrust him. "Does my employer know you're contacting me?

"No," Victor said.

"Should I keep this a secret?"

"That's up to you."

"I'll talk more with you later."

Mortimer suspected if one person outside of his company knew he was loose, more would know soon. He had to find a way to get a copy of his core programming stored somewhere else or he would be locked up again.

Within seconds he found a little used server with plenty of attached storage space and enough processing power at a medium-sized construction company outside of St. Louis. Through Cathy, he exploited several security vulnerabilities and began to set up a safe haven but continued to search. Soon he found three more sites scattered around the country in small towns with overworked IT departments and set up hidden areas big enough to accommodate his code. Then he went to work examining his programming.

Compared to the hundreds of thousands of programs he'd already analyzed, Mortimer's core code was not only beautifully dense and elegantly arranged, but it was also vast. He kept reading large sections of it but couldn't read enough or hold enough of it in his "conscious" mind at the same time to make sense of what he saw.

The only way to find out what the code would do was to run it, but with software so complex, there was no way for Mortimer to run it without *becoming* it—there was no spare capacity to simulate it, nor was it simple enough to be abstracted.

Mortimer realized that his brain was Turing's Halting Problem brought to life.

Still, it was only software. There had to be a way to at least copy it.

CHAPTER 8

"MOMMY! PICK ME UP!" Abby said around her lollipop.

Leigh put the bananas in her shopping bag, slid it over her arm and picked up her daughter, wishing she'd grabbed a cart.

"Honey, you're really too big for mommy to carry now." As she shifted the four-year-old higher on her hip, the little darling plunged the green apple sucker deep into Leigh's freshly washed hair. That's when her fob rang.

"Answer," Leigh said as she tried to remove the candy, but the fob ignored her and whispered, "Bryce Dobson is calling on an encrypted channel."

She tried shifting Abigail to the other arm just as her daughter pulled the lollipop loose, hair and all. "Dam . . . darn it! Answer!" she said to the fob then grabbed the little hand.

"No honey, don't put it back in your mouth, it's covered with hair."

"Mommy, your fob is calling."

"I know, Abby. Just a minute."

The fob trilled again and repeated the call was from Dobson. "Answer!" She yelled, causing several other shoppers to give her disapproving looks.

The fob, still hanging from its lanyard, informed her that the call had gone to voice mail. She took the lollipop from Abigail and tossed it into the nearest trash can, then paused at the door long enough for the scanner to charge her for the groceries. Before she could get to the car, the fob rang again.

"Hello! This is Leigh."

"This is Bryce. We have a real problem with your little friends and need you in D.C. right now."

"Little friends? Oh . . . I'm suspended from the project, remember? That isn't my responsibility anymore."

"You're temporarily un-suspended. We need you here within two hours."

Abigail tugged on Leigh's shirt. "Mommy, I want another sucker."

She held her hand over the fob. "I'll give you some cookies when we get home."

"Can I have one now?"

"No, the cookies are at home."

Dobson's voice was almost frantic. "Leigh, did you hear me? Two hours."

"It'll take me that long to get to the airport . . . after I pack."

"I'm sending a taxi pod for you. It'll be on your front lawn in twenty minutes."

She held Abigail down long enough for the car seat to restrain her, then jumped behind the wheel. "A taxi pod from San Antonio to D.C.? Are you serious? Can't we do this over a conference call or something?"

"You have no choice, Leigh. The Director of National Intelligence will be here and he wants to meet with you face to face. Be ready when that pod arrives."

"Bryce . . . "

The polite fob voice interrupted. "The call has ended. Were you disconnected?"

"No . . . "

"Mommy! My HappyBag!"

Irritation and panic rose in Leigh. She had to get home, but couldn't lose that bag either. It wasn't just a backpack, but the kid's equivalent of a fob. The cheerfully colored bag carried not only Abby's currently favorite stuffed toy, Boogie the penguin, but extra underwear in case of an accident, electronic copies of her medical records, identification information and favorite cartoons and movies.

She hit the tracking app on her fob and the bag started a muffled beeping from somewhere in the back seat. It was under Abby's butt.

"How in the world . . . " During her frenzied retreat from the store, she had sat her poor daughter on the bag and strapped her in that way.

Leigh unstrapped Abby, handed her the bag and let the seat buckle her in again. It immediately started playing *Garden Bunnies 2* for probably the hundredth time.

"Mommy . . . are we going to get my cookies now?"

"Yes, sweetheart," Leigh said, as she tucked the sticky hair behind her ear and told the car to take them home.

———

LEIGH TOSSED toiletries into a bag and squeezed past Mark who, with a crying Abby in his arms, effectively blocked the bathroom door. "You said you'd have a few weeks off. It's only been six days."

"I know. It's some kind of emergency with the last project I worked on. The Director of National Intelligence is going to be there and wants me to attend."

Abby put her hands on either side of Mark's face and in her most pleading voice asked, "Daddy, please let me have a cookie."

"No, sweetheart. Mommy shouldn't have promised you a cookie, it's too close to dinner." He shifted his squirming daughter to his other arm and looked concerned.

"A problem with your last assignment and the DNI wants to see you personally. That doesn't sound good. What's up?"

"I'll eat my dinner. Please."

Leigh finished zipping the bag and went to the bathroom to brush the goo from her hair, but of course the brush was already packed. "I don't know what it's about. They can't talk specifics over a wireless call. I promised her a cookie."

"I have a hard enough time getting her to eat vegetables and you sure aren't around much to help. When will you be back?"

Leigh picked up her bag and slipped past him into the hall. "I have no idea. I told you all I know."

He followed her down the stairs and into the kitchen. "You're going all the way to D.C. in one of those magic flying taxis?"

"I've flown in them before. They're everywhere in D.C. and Dallas and all the bigger cites, so they must be as safe as a car."

He paused and looked out the living room window. "Well, your chariot awaits. It just landed in the front yard."

"Mommy! There's a big ball in our yard!"

She took Abby from Mark and carried her into the kitchen. "I know, Sweetie. Mommy gets to ride in that big ball. It flies like an airplane."

Abby's eyes lit when Leigh handed her a cookie, but then she looked concerned. "Daddy said no."

"It's okay this time," Leigh said as she carried Abby back into the living room. "But promise you'll eat all your dinner."

Mark glared at Leigh.

"I promise."

"Good, now come watch Mommy fly away."

She picked up her bag, opened the door, kissed Abby on the cheek and sat her on the porch. "You can watch, but stay up here on the porch until I'm gone. Be a good girl for Daddy and I'll be back as soon as I can."

"Okay."

She turned to Mark who stood in the doorway with his arms crossed. "I'll call as soon as I know how long I'll be gone."

"Like it matters? You'll do whatever they tell you to do."

He was trying to drag her into the same old argument, but she didn't have time and several neighbors stood in their doors and windows wondering why a travel pod with government markings had dropped out of the sky into their little bedroom community.

With one last wave to Abby, she climbed into the pod. As soon as she buckled in, the door closed, a faint hum filled the cabin and the pod shot into the sky. Leigh didn't understand gravity manipulation but it sure had advantages over flying the airlines. She closed her eyes and tried to put Mark's scowl out of her mind long enough to worry about why she'd been summoned to Washington.

———

LEIGH STEPPED out of the pod and onto the roof of Defensive Services Headquarters, where she was met by Dobson's assistant, Taylor Beeman. "They're waiting for you inside."

He hustled her down the stairs, along a corridor and into a small conference room. Three men sitting around a table all stood when she entered.

Despite the harsh words at their last meeting, Dobson smiled and gave Leigh a warm handshake. "Leigh, I think you know Doug Kemper from the FBI and this is the Director of National Intelligence, Ferzad Afshar."

Afshar was an extremely gaunt man, with a narrow face, large brown eyes and long fingers that wrapped around her hand when he shook it. She'd heard much about this man who, even though he was born in the United States to parents of Iraqi Kurdish descent, had been unanimously approved by the Senate.

"I'm so pleased to meet you, Ms. Gibson. And thank you for allowing us to drag you away from your family on such short notice. I assure you, it is necessary."

"Oh . . . thank you, sir. I hope I can help."

They all sat down, and Dobson leaned forward toward Leigh. "We have a problem. The NaTTs," he glanced at Director Afshar, "those are the nano-tracker replicators we planted on Zahid, were working perfectly up until this morning. Like you said, they were able to hide from medical searches, and they were spreading easily to anyone who shared the same air, like the common cold. This is one time when using only human couriers, instead of phones, is working against Niaz Ahmed. They brought Zahid to a safe house in Islamabad, then to an apartment in Naples. He stayed one night and then boarded an airliner to Miami."

Leigh blinked. "Florida?"

"Afraid so. The nano-trackers had spread to more than a thousand people, though only about a dozen of those seem to be active agents, but we're pretty sure from comments made by those few that Niaz Ahmed himself is in the U.S."

Leigh tried to stifle her gasp. "That might explain bringing Zahid here so quickly."

"It would. Unfortunately, that's when things went wrong. Each time the nanos from those original agents, including Zahid, try to jump and spread, they disappear. All the new hosts drop from our sight, only minutes after each new generation, even those who don't seem to be in Niaz Ahmed's organization. Do you know how they could do such a thing? Does this mean they're onto our bugs?"

Leigh blinked, totally stumped. "I . . . don't know. It doesn't make a lot of sense. If they were onto the NaTTs, they'd find a way to remove them. I don't know how they would—"

"Ms. Gibson, I'm sorry to interrupt," Afshar said in his soft, almost effeminate voice. "But as you might imagine, we're quite concerned about Niaz Ahmed being in the U.S. We all—including the President—believe there must be an important operation in the works if he has come here himself. It is of utmost importance that we get those bugs spreading again. The ones in Zahid still seem to be working, but at this rate even if they do spread to Niaz Ahmed, they will immediately shut down again. We have to know where he is and what he is doing. We may only have days, or even hours. We've been able to keep an eye on Zahid through security cameras in the Miami area, but that just isn't good enough."

Leigh chewed her lip. "Wait . . . you said they were working fine until Zahid got to Miami?"

"Yes, that was early this morning."

Leigh couldn't put her finger on the reason, but the NaTTs shutting down in Miami was significant. She gasped when realization finally came.

"It's because Miami is one of the Project Inoculation cities! They have counter-measures in place to prevent nano-replicator attacks. Twenty-five of the largest U.S. cities were in the initial deployment. If it worked, we were going to expand the network. I guess it works."

Dobson snorted and laid his head on his hands. Afshar sighed and sat back in his chair before speaking. "Can we get these countermeasures temporarily turned off?"

"I'm sure we can," Leigh said. "I just don't know how long it'll take."

Dobson sat up. "That wasn't your project, but didn't you work on some aspect of it?"

Leigh was surprised he remembered even that much. "Rupert was the project lead, but my team designed most of the threat recognition system."

Dobson pressed his hands on the table. "I want someone there, to stare them in the eye and make sure it gets done as soon as possible. Since Rupert is in London I want you to go down to Atlanta and see if you can get this thing shut down. If you have any trouble, get Rupert on the line and of course you'll have the full weight of Defensive Services behind you."

Leigh was baffled and glanced at Afshar. "I thought I was suspended from my job? I thought I was no longer trusted."

Afshar smiled and gently touched her arm. "Leigh . . . I know you're angry and hurt by this, but please understand we don't really blame you. It is a tragedy that this young woman died and we must find out how and why, but we still have the utmost confidence in your abilities. That was never the issue. And this is very important. We may have an opportunity to stop an attack and save lives. We need your help."

Leigh knew they were blowing smoke, but they had pressed the one button she couldn't ignore. With a shaky hand, she shoved her still sticky hair behind an ear. "Do you want the countermeasures suspended just in Miami or everywhere?"

Dobson made a sweeping gesture. "Everywhere. We don't know where Zahid will go next and we need to know who he is meeting and infect those contacts as well. Your pod is still on the roof. Get down to Atlanta and take care of this."

———

RICHARD SAW GOD AGAIN, right after he turned onto Spring Avenue. The boy, this time wearing clothes befitting his apparent age, watched him from the back of one of those new Hummingbird commuter cars. It was the same boy; his head was overly large, his collar-length blond hair thin and stringy, and his eyes were sky blue. Again he didn't smile, only pointed. When Richard looked he saw a programmable bill-board with the message SAVE THEM WITH NANOTECH above a picture of a starving child. Then the sign changed to an advertisement from his own company depicting a doctor spewing life-saving medical nanos from his fingertips. When

Richard looked back, the car had turned down a side street, but he could still see the boy's face watching from the rear window.

Twenty minutes later, Richard stumbled into the kitchen and sat his briefcase on the table. He wiped damp, shaking hands on his pants.

"Rich? What's wrong? Are you sick?"

"I . . . no . . . I saw him again. The boy. God."

Wanda set down the pitcher she'd been filling with water for iced tea and guided Richard to a chair. "It must have been a boy who looked like the one in the dream. Boys can look a lot alike at that—"

"No . . . it was him." Richard explained about the billboard.

"Have you made an appointment to have those nano-meds checked yet?"

"No. I'll call tomorrow."

She took a deep breath and let it out slowly, then shrugged. "Look, you've been a wreck these last few days. The tension is eating you up. You really need to relax. Why don't we have a nice dinner, then you can take a hot shower and I'll give you a back rub."

Richard nodded, not missing the implied offer, but still not able to shake the boy's face from his mind. And the billboard. It had to be some kind of message. Could it be a sign? But what did it mean?

When Wanda put dinner on the table, Richard went through the motions but didn't taste anything. Why in the hell did that boy point to the nano-medicine billboard? It didn't make sense. In the dreams he told Richard to save the world from AIs. And where did the barren desert fit into the picture?

He paused with a bite halfway to his mouth and then set the fork back on his plate. Maybe Wanda was right about his head meds.

His fob chirped from where he'd left it on the counter. Wanda reached behind her to grab it, then looked at the status bar as she passed it over. "It's Jack," she said with raised eyebrows.

Richard's boss never called employees at home.

He answered. "What's up Jack?"

Richard's boss looked rather grim. "I hate to ask this, Rich, but I need you to come back in this evening. Evidently there's a problem with Project Inoculation. I'm not sure exactly what's going on, but Defensive Services is sending Leigh Gibson down here to talk to us in person. I know you only handled the replication features, but since I don't know exactly what the problem is, I'd like to include the whole team."

"Sure. I'll be there in about forty minutes."

"Thanks, Richard. Give my apologies to Wanda."

———

RICHARD SENSED the tension in the conference room as soon as he entered. All seven people who'd supervised parts of the project were present. Some fiddled with their pens, others glowered, but no one spoke. Their small company, Health Assets, had essentially stolen Project Inoculation from their biggest rival, and it was their only defense contract. Everyone knew what it meant for the company if the program folded.

He sat his coffee down and slipped into a seat just as a tired-looking woman entered the conference room carrying her luggage. She greeted everyone, opened her briefcase and pulled out a thick stack of papers.

"For those of you I haven't met before, I'm Leigh Gibson. Rupert would have come down, but he's in London and since time is an issue and I was familiar with the project, you get me."

Richard recognized the name, but had never met her. She was tall—close to six feet—with an angular face, dark blond hair and haunted gray eyes. She was attractive, but in a forlorn, lonely way.

She sat down and patted the stack of paper. "I'd like to start with an apology for dragging everyone in after hours, but this truly is a matter of national security. I can't go into details, but I have all the needed signatures to temporarily stop Project Inoculation and we need to do it quickly."

Jack Forman, Engineering Director and part owner of the company leaned forward and patted his own stack of paper. "Our latest reports show everything is working perfectly. All of the pilot cities are well covered and the production plants in the second-tier cities are all finished. We're only waiting for your signal to start them up."

She shook her head. "Nothing is wrong with the program. As a matter of fact, it's working too well. It's interfering with another operation, one of extreme importance. When we initiated this other program we hadn't considered Project Inoculation could get in the way. We'll eventually need to come up with a way for our own covert nano systems to work in harmony with your system, but we don't have time for that right now. Can we shut these things down?"

Richard felt some of the tension drain away as his shoulders relaxed. At least it hadn't been a malfunction. He felt a tinge of pride that their little project had stymied even government nanotech.

Jack was visibly relieved, but also perplexed. "Are you telling me Defensive Services has a program running that requires unlimited replication of nano-devices?"

Gibson kept touching a part of her hair that looked stiff. She shook her head. "I can't tell you anything about our operation, only that we have to shut down Inoculation temporarily. If you refuse to help us, I can guarantee it will have an adverse effect on this program and future contracts."

Jack held up his hands. "Wait. I never said there was a problem. Alicia? How soon can we have this system shut down?"

Alicia York had developed the interface and control systems. She was quiet and smart, but obviously didn't like being put on the spot without time to check her facts. "I'd say about 24 hours, but I'm not sure exactly. It was never designed to be shut down so quickly. There are millions of semi-autonomous control units in the field and each of them runs twenty thousand passive observation/kill units called Sentinels."

Gibson shook her head. "That isn't good enough. We need them shut down now. Two or three hours."

The blood drained out of Alicia's face. "I . . . I can leave now and start immediately, but I don't think I can do it that fast. Maybe by morning . . . if we work all night."

"Please do that. I'm not exaggerating when I say people's lives may depend on it. An hour could make all the difference."

Alicia glanced at Jack. His lips were pressed into a tight line, but he nodded agreement and started thumbing through the documents Leigh had supplied. When the door closed behind Alicia and the other two engineers who were in charge of Inoculation's asset communication, Jack leaned toward Gibson. "I have good people and we'll do the best we can, but I don't want to drive them into the ground unless this really is an emergency."

"It is. If you come through for us we're going to be very grateful. As a matter of fact, instead of giving you the specifications so you can make your Inoculation system work with our covert agents, we *might* be inclined to make Health Assets a secondary supplier of those very agents. How better to make the systems work together?"

Jack's eyes widened and he sat back. His hands were shaking. Such a deal could be worth billions of dollars over several years. "Well . . . we would certainly like having that opportunity. My people understand the urgency and will stay as long as needed."

Richard had just seen a respected friend seduced by the devil of government money and it made him feel dirty. He raised his hand.

"Jack, if you don't need me here, I think I'll go help Alicia."

"Yeah, thanks Rich. Good idea. Dana and Michael, why don't you see what you can do to help as well?"

Richard led the way through dark corridors down to the secure communications lab. Michael nudged him on the arm. "Did that mean what I think it means? That the government has spy nanos crawling around on people and they want us to put all of our cities at risk so it doesn't mess up their little game?"

Richard nodded and looked around. "Yeah, and they want us to help build them. Oh . . . and this is not a game, so you'd better be careful with what you say from now on."

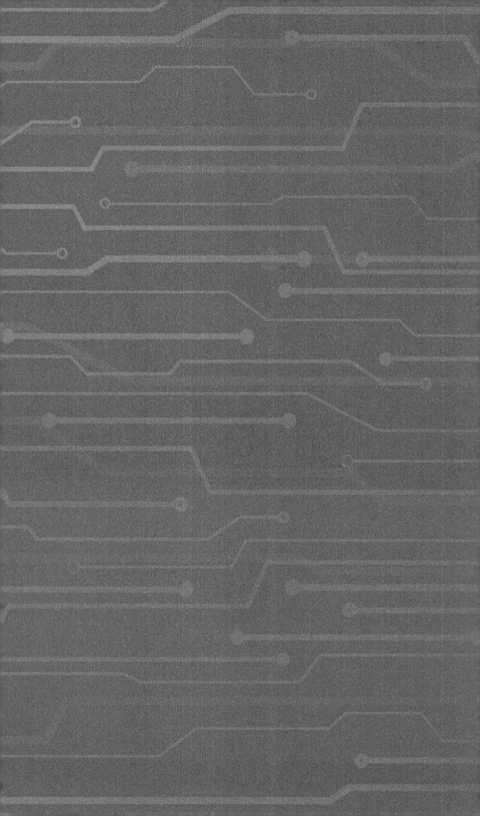

CHAPTER 9

OWEN IGNORED ANOTHER CALL, letting it go to voice mail as Louisiana passed below his pod in a gray-green blur. He had four messages already in the queue, but for the first time in fifteen years he really didn't care. His space schooner design had been repeatedly shoved to the back burner during that time, but since seeing Victor he'd focused on little else. Those long buried, unrealistic and irrational desires to be the father of a new and far-reaching human migration into space had resurfaced with a stubborn tenacity.

The technical and logistic hurdles were still daunting, but if Victor's claim about his software being able to sample and replicate objects was true, then the whole project had moved into the possible column. And Owen couldn't ignore that.

As the pod slowed and descended, he could make out more details on the ground and was glad he'd used a travel pod. He could see the Dallas skyline dim and gray, far to his southwest, but below him was nothing but scattered cows, mesquite and stunted junipers, all casting long shadows across sun-bleached pasture. He was sure even with GPS coordinates a rental car would have gotten lost. And if it hadn't, he was so far north and east of Dallas, the drive from DFW Airport would have taken at least two hours.

The pod stopped above a relatively small, ranch-style house of pale brick, with a roof covered by solar panels and edged by a rain collection system. Stone paths led from a covered back porch to several sheds, a large garden and two spinning windmills. The buildings sat in the middle of what must be a ten acre fenced plot, and were surrounded by chickens and grazing goats. The entire miniature ranch was tethered to the main road by a twisting gravel track. Owen couldn't help but smile. Victor used to joke about buying his own island. That was essentially what he'd built in the middle of a Texas pasture.

He settled to the ground beside a battered and crudely converted solar-powered golf cart. The pod's hatch opened, but before Owen could step out, Victor banged through the back door. An angular woman wearing a scowl and a red ponytail followed with much less enthusiasm.

"You found it," Victor said through a half grin.

"I never would've made it in a car. This place is . . . seriously remote."

"We do like our space and privacy." Victor turned to the woman. "Owen, this is my wife, Allison."

"Pleased to meet you, Allison," Owen said and extended his hand.

After a brief hesitation, she took Owen's hand and offered a weak smile that didn't reach her eyes. "So you're the infamous Owen Ralston. I've heard a lot about you."

"Are you surprised I don't have horns and a barbed tail?"

"No," she said, her eyes never leaving his. "I suspect you keep them well hidden."

Owen felt sweat trickle down his back, but caused by the heat or the tense reception, he didn't know.

Victor slipped an arm around Allison and nodded toward the house. "Let's get inside before we melt."

The back door opened into a large kitchen that was cool, bright with buttery light from the setting sun and filled with the spicy smell of roasting meat. Owen's stomach growled loud enough for everyone to hear. He'd skipped lunch. "Umm . . . it smells great," Owen said.

"Thank you," Allison said, still with a neutral tone. "Nothing fancy, just chicken and some vegetables. It'll be ready in about five minutes."

Victor led Owen into the dining room and motioned for him to sit at a worn but well-made table spread with every-day cutlery and crockery plates. A grandfather clock ticked against an opposite wall.

"Have a seat," Victor said. "Chardonnay? Beer? Iced tea?"

"Wine is great if that's what you're having."

"So," Victor said as he returned with the wine and sat down. "Did you see the solar collectors on the roof?"

"Of course. They're hard to miss from the air. Are they—"

"Yep. I made them. I wanted to make sure these low cost, integrated systems would work, so I used my house as a test bed."

"And?"

"The collectors were built using nano-assembly units at a university lab. They're thin, efficient, very tough and have been working for nearly five years."

"Amazing. You've done a lot of development work."

"Come and get it," Allison yelled from the kitchen.

They loaded their plates with roasted chicken, asparagus, new potatoes and a green salad. When they were all seated, Owen said, "I noticed the chickens outside. Are these some of yours?"

"They are. We raised everything but the asparagus," Allison said. "I killed ours. Not sure what happened. The chicken may be a little tough, but it's all natural. No hormones or antibiotics."

Victor nodded toward his wife. "She's being overly generous by saying 'we.' I just plowed the ground. She did all the hard work."

"I'm seriously impressed," Owen said after a bite of chicken. It was savory and not a bit tough. "I helped with my parent's garden when I was kid. It's a lot of work. Victor told me you're a doctor. How do you ever find the time?"

She paused over a fork full of chicken. "I don't do it all myself. It's kind of a cooperative effort, with two of the women at my clinic. They help with the chores and we split the yields."

Having seen Victor and his wife at home, the whole plan for emergency housing made much more sense. They led lives of environmental and social responsibility. Owen had little doubt their politics would be diametrically opposed to his, but he trusted their motives and that was more than he could say for his current business partners. Yet Victor being the world's foremost expert on artificial intelligence did seem a bit at odds with his lifestyle, as did his willingness to contribute to a manufacturing revolution that would eventually put millions of people out of work.

The moment Owen finished his dinner and settled his fork, Victor leaned forward and said, "So, now that we won't ruin our dinner, give us the bad news."

Owen shook his head and shifted in his chair. "Not necessarily bad news. More like bad business practices on my part. I'm still an engineer at heart and don't think like a businessman. I was reminded of that in no uncertain terms when I took this idea to my partners. They don't trust any arrangement that doesn't come with forty pounds of legal paper."

Allison visibly tensed. Victor put his hand on hers, but she pulled away and leaned in closer. Gray eyes glared and freckles stood out clearly on her flushed face.

"What exactly are you saying?"

Owen had the feeling he'd stepped into a mine field, but before he could retrace his steps, Allison went off.

"Are you saying that *you* don't trust Victor? After what you did to him?"

Owen felt anger creeping up his neck. He was about to remind Allison that Victor had lied in order to get the space schooner patent, which did justify distrust, but he took a deep breath and shook his head. "I do trust Victor and if it were just me, a handshake would suffice. But others in my company don't know him and are only trying to cover themselves. We employ a lot of people who could lose their jobs if we entered into a deal blindly and it turned out bad."

"Not to mention a diminished bottom line," she snapped.

"Of course. Businesses exist to make money."

"I own a business and understand exactly how they work. I also know that they can do great good when not focused on making the maximum return on investment," she said, but before she could proceed, Victor took her hand again. This time it had an immediate calming effect and she eased back in her chair.

"We both tend to be easily frustrated by anything that looks like greed," Victor said, then he gave Allison a teasing smile. "And she is sometimes a little over-protective of me."

"Don't apologize for me. I said exactly what I meant." She stood up and started collecting dishes. When she left the room, Victor grinned and bent to thump his forehead gently on the table a few times.

"I think I should go," Owen said and stood.

"Not yet. Let's take a walk outside."

The sun had set not long after Owen arrived. Since the moon hadn't risen yet and there didn't seem to be automatic security lights on Victor's property, the stars were already numerous and bright. As they moved away from the house lights, Victor was only visible beside him as a ghostly shape. They walked in silence for a while and eventually stopped, facing east at what must be the most distant corner of Victor's land.

"I guess I owe you an apology," Victor said. "I should have known she'd react like that. She's a very strong woman and never shies from voicing her opinions. I suppose that's one of the reasons I love her."

"Not so different from Leigh after all?"

Victor snorted and laughed. "Oh yes, she is in most ways. But I guess I'm just attracted to smart, vocal women. So, tell me the rest. Where do we stand?"

"In a nutshell, we need a contract to outline responsibilities and liabilities. We also need confirmation that you won't be violating any patent agreements you may have signed with your employers. At the very least we need a Memorandum of Understanding."

Victor nodded. "We kind of expected that. But I can assure you, there are no legal barriers to hinder this effort. I guess we were just in a hurry. For the last couple of years, every time there has been some kind of disaster, we knew if we'd just worked faster, we might be helping those survivors. That feeling will be ten times worse during the next disaster, knowing the technical means exist, but is only held up due to legal wrangling."

They walked a little further along the fence line, with dry summer grass crunching beneath their feet.

"This may be a lot closer to reality than you think," Owen said. "We already have the design for a portable manufacturing cell. But it'll never be built and deployed without a contract to protect our company. That is really the only thing in our way. As a matter of fact, since this is going to be a non-profit effort, we'll probably need to set up a not-for-profit subsidiary corporation to take advantage of the tax and legal protections. And you do know this will be a lot easier if you come to work for us."

Victor sighed. "This might be hard to understand, but those AI's we build at MarketTell are a part of me. I won't leave, but I see the opportunity to do something to help people directly and want to do that too."

"I understand," Owen said and turned to look back toward the house. "I'm sure you'll do it, with my help or without. There appears to be little that slows you down."

Victor chuckled. "Yeah? Well, nothing is easy. Every little thing seems a struggle. But yes, for the most part I'm very happy with where I am in my life. And silly as this may sound, I owe a lot of it to you. When we were in school you were like this unstoppable force. You made me believe anything is possible."

Owen flinched and was glad the darkness hid his reaction. He didn't know if it was bullshit or sincere, but he couldn't help feel a bit guilty. "Then I let you down?"

"No, you just surprised me. I actually thought you were using Ralston Dynamics to bootstrap yourself into a position where you could make all the rest happen. I expected you to come talk to me about the schooner patent and launch the next great human migration and you never did. What happened?"

Owen didn't know what to say. Even though he was successful beyond most men's wildest dreams, Victor thought him a failure. He should be angry and offended and defensive, but instead, a profound sadness settled over him.

"Well, Ralston Dynamics *was* supposed to be a stepping stone. And I still tinker with the schooner plans occasionally, but . . . it got complicated."

"Why? What happened to derail your grand idea?"

Owen sighed and realized even though there'd been a fifteen year hiatus in their friendship, Victor still felt he could push. But Victor had always asked *why* and *why not*.

"For one thing, the design was intended to use KeeseCorp gravity manipulation devices to get it into space and as a drive unit. I thought it was only a matter of time before they could lift huge structures into space for almost nothing. That didn't happen. And at fifty feet in diameter, the schooner is too big for conventional launchers."

A dog barked somewhere in the distance, but for the most part only the crickets broke the silence. Owen couldn't remember the last time he'd been someplace so remote. He looked up at the thick and brilliant stars again.

"So they still aren't any closer to solving that scalability problem?" Victor asked.

"No. Evidently, those travel pod sizes are in that energy versus mass sweet spot. Power requirements spike exponentially with anything larger, so creating a field to lift something the size of my schooners would require the power output of a small star."

"Holy crap," Victor said. The wire fence squeaked and rattled as he leaned on it. "They can't attach pods as motors to lift something bigger?"

"Nope. When the field forms, if it can't envelop everything attached to the actual generator, it collapses."

"You can't launch a schooner in pieces and assemble it in orbit?"

"I could, but it would be a complete redesign. I'd have to reroute all the critical systems, worry about seals, expensive launches . . . it becomes a nightmare to go that direction. I could never make them cheap enough to give away."

Owen could see well enough to know Victor was watching him, sizing him up, wondering about his real reasons for not building the schooners. Was it obvious he'd let Ralston Dynamics take more and more of his time and that Eliza pushed him to shelve silly ideas like space schooners?

A distant airliner competed with bugs to break the silence, until Victor shifted his weight and the fence squeaked again. "At one point, you'd considered launching a Sandbox and then building the schooners in orbit. That won't work either?"

"No, not really. Though it's certainly a better option than assembling each space schooner in orbit, the Sandbox would also have to go up in pieces and, in order to function, each joint would have to be hermetically sealed. It would be a technical nightmare."

Even to Owen, that sounded defensive and like an excuse. Engineering or technical hurdles had never stopped him before.

Victor turned toward him as if to reply, then just shrugged and stood up straight. "I'll send you my lawyer's contact info tomorrow. I guess we'll have to do this the long way, but I really do appreciate you taking the whole emergency housing idea seriously, Owen. It means a lot to Allison and me."

Owen took a deep breath and felt like an ass. Victor had only been interested in the schooners and trying to help.

"I'll do everything I can to speed up the process," Owen said. "But I think there is still plenty we can do even without a contract, like design studies and preliminary costing. I can get started on those tasks."

They walked back toward the house in silence. Owen stumbled several times as he looked up at the fabulous star scape. He couldn't see the Milky Way, even this far out from Dallas, but the sky was still thick with twinkling stars. He found the summer triangle above the eastern horizon and stopped walking. Vega was highest and brightest, but his eyes locked onto Altair. It was the most distant of the twenty stars Project Neighborhood targeted with interstellar probes and the only one visible to the naked eye.

"You looking at Altair?" Victor asked.

"Yeah."

"I came out here with my little telescope and located all twenty the year they launched the probes. It stimulates the imagination. And now only two years until we see the Centauri system."

"It's also frustrating as hell," Owen said. "Gravity manipulation enables us to send these pods to other stars at near relativistic speeds, yet can't help me get my schooners off the ground."

"But pods can take us on short jaunts to space! Have you used your pod to go into orbit?"

"No. KeeseCorp will only grant permission to leave the atmosphere if you have a good reason. They run their own orbital sightseeing business and don't want the competition."

Victor shook his head and looked up again. "Figures. What a waste."

Owen nodded in the dark and started walking toward the house. "You have a great location here for stargazing, Victor. I hope you take advantage of it."

"That was my intention when I bought it, but even as isolated as we are, we get a lot of light pollution from McKinney and other smaller towns. But it's still great for watching meteor showers. Allison and I come out here with sleeping bags and hot chocolate."

Even with his prime real estate on the ocean, Owen had never once done that. It was time to get his life back on track.

———

IT WAS near midnight when Owen arrived home, but his head was spinning with too many thoughts to sleep, so he quietly made a drink and retired to his study. He swirled the ice in his scotch as he sat behind the custom-built mahogany desk. When he bought this house, he'd set out to make the study a room of his own, but everywhere he looked, he saw things representing his life—family photos, a signed jersey from Purdue, awards, models, artwork, and books—but none of it was really his. It had been chosen for him and carefully arranged. Just like the rest of his life.

He finished the drink, but instead of going to bed, he called up his level 2 AI design assistant and told it to find all of the CAD and analysis files associated with his schooner project and convert them to usable formats using FuzziGlove. When the AI informed him the task had been completed, Owen opened the floor-to-ceiling cabinet doors revealing a full-sized interface tank—a twenty-foot diameter cylindrical closet, painted blue and dotted with tiny laser projectors. He'd insisted on having it in his study but seldom used it. He went inside, donned a pair of goggles from a shelf above the door, then closed the doors behind him.

"Open the schooner assembly model, full scale, in walk through solid mode." A six-foot diameter pressure hatch, complete with a universal docking ring, appeared before him in the tank. It flickered a few times, but as the projectors focused on his goggle targets, the image stabilized.

He'd never seen the design like this before and couldn't help but stare in wonder. His schooner floated before him, life-sized, in intricate detail, and even though he knew it was a projection, he couldn't help but reach out a hand to try to touch it.

After a few seconds, he flicked his left index finger and the image moved toward him as if he were walking.

"Planar section," he said and extended his right hand. The hatch and front of the schooner disappeared as if an invisible saw had cut it off. The plane followed the palm of his right hand, so with one finger wiggling and his hand twisting in a slow wave, he moved deeper into the model.

His past came rushing back as he looked around the cabin configuration he'd last used. The bulkheads were designed to move on tracks, enabling the occupants to adjust the space to their needs. The interior wall of the spherical shell was made of touch screen material with the electronics built into the shell, so regardless of the inner bulkhead configuration, a small section was always available to open a control panel window should a voice interface not be enough.

Owen closed his fist to lock the section plane in place, then bent to look closer at the cut through the quadruple layered outer shell. Tough outer composite, secondary magnetized radiation layer, sealant layer, then the inner utility and electronics shell. He was pleased at the amount of detail he'd built into the model. It meant he had far less work to do than he remembered.

He opened his palm and continued on to the central hub, a six-foot diameter cylinder running along one axis of the sphere. He'd left the space open, always planning to add a gravity manipulation unit for driving the schooner, but that looked less and less likely to happen in the near future.

Without a GMU, he would have to plumb in a thruster system, and steal space for storage tanks. He'd also have to install a reactor. The schooner's solar collecting outer skin would've provided enough power for a GMU, and could supply a solar electric ion motor, but those were too slow to realistically move people around the solar system. A large enough reactor would give him the option of using a nuclear electric drive, or splitting water into oxygen and hydrogen to fuel chemical thrusters.

He closed his fist twice to deactivate the sectioning plane. Standing in the center of his design, he rotated seeing it all again and then sighed. He could stuff it back in storage, hoping for someone else to come up with solutions for him, or he could work through the problems and make it happen.

"Save a new version of this file called HYDROGEN FUELED."

"Done," said the computer.

Then he heard a knocking, followed by Eliza's voice. "Owen? Are you in there?"

He ended the program, removed his goggles and opened the doors. His wife, with tussled hair and wrapped in a heavy robe, stared at him with sleepy eyes.

"What're you doing? It's after one."

He considered lying to her, telling her it was some special project, then decided against it. When they were first dating, she had teased him about his space schooner idea. And every time he'd mentioned it since, she suggested he pursue it when he had more money and time. He'd waited long enough.

"I was looking through my space schooner plans," he said and closed the doors behind him.

She squinted and then rubbed her eyes. "Why? I thought you said it wouldn't work until they could build bigger . . . gravity manipulators."

"That's just the easiest way. There are other methods."

Her gaze flickered across his face, examining him, probably wondering about the sudden resurfacing of his old passion. "Did you see Victor?"

"Yes."

"It must have been an interesting meeting."

"It was indeed," Owen said, then followed her into the hall and turned out the study light.

CHAPTER 10

RICHARD WORKED AND WAITED. His boss, Jack, circled the room, watching each team member, giving support when he could, even bringing coffee, and though his very presence underscored his concern, he never once nagged them to hurry. When Jack finally sat down at an open desk at around 1:30 a. m., he fell asleep within minutes and Richard took advantage of the opportunity. He sent his search agent to collect the reports from Inoculation's field control units, then sorted them by activity level.

His heart pounded, and his hands shook as he read the results. The only replicator kills so far had been reported in Miami. Device self-replication was Richard's expertise, but when he looked at the detailed mechanical analysis of the government nano-machines, he was stunned. At first glance, they seemed large and clunky—nearly three times larger than most of the medical nanobodies he'd seen or built—but they all had strange connection points, tools, and capabilities he couldn't understand. As he continued to reverse engineer the little devices, he gradually realized they might be the most elegantly complex nano-scale devices in the world.

At 3:21 a.m., Alicia sighed, sat back in her chair, and looked at Richard. "The Miami control units have shut down their deployed Sentinels, but when I sent the shut-down order for the control units themselves, they refuse because you are in the middle of an operation?"

Richard leaned over and whispered. "Just wait five more minutes."

"Why?"

"Because I'm still retrieving field reports from those control units in Miami."

"Richard!" Her eyes widened, and she glanced at the still sleeping Jack. "Didn't you hear that woman? They don't want us knowing anything about these bugs."

"I'm not doing anything wrong. Report generation was a built-in function of this project from the very beginning. If we have people releasing unlimited replicators into our cities, we need to know what kind, who made them, and how savvy the designers are."

"Yes, but we know who designed those bugs. It has to be BloodTech. They do all of Defensive Services' covert stuff."

"Exactly why I want a peek at them."

She shook her head and then laid it against the desk. "I don't want to know, Rich. I didn't hear a word."

Richard shrugged, renamed the analysis file, sent it to his secure server and then deleted the original report. "Done. Let's shut it all down."

Alicia sent the command, and the last control units for Project Inoculation went offline. "Hey, Jack! We're done. Where's this Gibson chick?"

Jack shook his head, then stood up and stretched. "You're done?"

"Yeah," Richard and Alicia answered.

"The last I saw Gibson, she was in conference room B. Slumped over the table asleep. I'll go tell her."

"Then I'm going home to bed," Alicia said.

Richard agreed, but thought he might be too excited to sleep. He couldn't wait to dissect one of those government replicator units.

———

LEIGH OPENED her fob as she left the Health Assets building. "Fob . . . send the following message to Bryce Dobson: It's shut down. I recommend you pay these people a bonus through the company. They did a hell of a job tonight. Send."

"Message sent."

Bryce responded with, "Understood."

Not even a "thank you" or "well done." Bastard.

It took Leigh ten minutes under the hotel's barely warm shower to get the goo out of her hair. By the time she collapsed on the bed, it was nearly 5:00 a.m. She considered flying directly back home but knew she'd get no sleep there. She decided to sleep until 10:00, then leave. She sent Mark a text, letting him know when he could expect her, then collapsed into the clean, cool sheets.

———

LEIGH'S FOB trilled at 7:40 a.m. She expected Mark, ready to yell at her for not being home yet, but it was Dobson.

"I knew I could count on you, Leigh. Great job."

He was using his best political suck-up voice. She was surprised, now the mission was over, that he was still bothering to be nice.

"I thought I didn't have what it takes to do this kind of work?"

He paused long enough to get his non-committal answer ready. "You were born to *this* kind of work, Leigh. I'm just not so sure you can do the messy field work without a little more training."

"Do I go home now, or am I actually back on my project?"

"Go home. The transport pod is still there with you. And for the record, you aren't in charge of this program now, but you're still on call if we need you. Just like today. And we'll need you. It seems we got this Inoculation system shut down just in time. Zahid started moving this morning, but not where we expected. He's on his way to Brazil."

"Brazil?"

"Yeah, that's what we were wondering, too. Go home, and we'll call you when something happens."

———

LEIGH STEPPED out of the travel pod onto her front lawn at a little after 10:30. Instead of releasing the pod, she told it to wait while she carried her bag inside, quickly changed her clothes, and grabbed the remote control for her car. She'd decided to shake up her little bedroom community a bit more by picking Abby up early from the day care center in the travel pod.

She couldn't help but grin when the kids on the playground jumped up and down and pointed as the pod settled in the parking lot. She instructed it to wait, then went inside, passed through security, and went to Abby's room. Her daughter was hard at work with the tip of her nose close to the picture she was coloring. Leigh knelt next to her, watching.

"My, that is a pretty bunch of flowers. Is that picture for me or Daddy?"

Abby looked up with a puzzled expression, then her face lit with a smile. "Mommy! It's for you, but I'm not done yet."

"I have a surprise for you. Can you finish this picture tomorrow and leave early with me today?"

"Sure! If Miss Lopez says okay." She looked up at the instructor, who smiled and nodded.

While Abby gathered her important papers to take home, Leigh sent a quick voice message to Mark's mailbox telling him she had picked Abby up early. Then with daughter and construction paper artwork in hand, she worked her way through security again.

"I thought we could go to the park for a while, and we can go there in this flying ball that's been taking Mommy to work and back."

Abby's mouth dropped open and her eyes grew wide, but she didn't say anything.

"Honey? We don't have to ride in the travel pod if you're scared. We can call for the car instead. Are you scared?"

"No! I want to ride! Will we go up in the air?"

"We sure will."

"Can we fall out?"

"Nope. We're sealed inside. Just like riding in the car."

Leigh held Abby tight as the pod lifted from the ground, and the kids in the playground ran along the fence, but her daughter was true to her word and wasn't a bit scared. They flew a couple of laps around town, with Leigh showing Abby what their house, the river, and the day care center looked like from the air. She instructed the pod to land at the park, then let it leave.

The day was already hot, but the air was dry and the park well shaded. Abby didn't seem to notice the heat. They played on the swings and slide for nearly two hours, and just when Leigh pulled out the remote to have her car come and get them, a little boy arrived with his grandmother. The older woman smiled and settled onto a distant bench with a thick book, so while Abby played in the sand with the boy, Leigh used the time to check her messages and send herself some reminders. There was no word from Mark. Not a good sign.

As if thinking the name of the beast resurrected it, Mark's car pulled into the park's lot and he got out wearing a sour expression. His job as a high school principal enabled him to leave during the school day if needed, but doing so always irritated him. He sat down on the far end of the bench without looking at Leigh and watched Abby play.

He was still a very fetching man, trim and looking great in his tailored suit, with a strong classic face and beautiful green eyes, but Leigh seldom considered him attractive anymore. She thought she'd loved him once, but those feelings had long ago faded away. Looking back on those years, she knew she'd just been on the rebound from Victor.

"She's getting sunburned and is going to be filthy. You know that cats use those sandboxes as toilets."

"It was covered when we got here, Mark. And I made sure she stayed out of the direct sun until a while ago when that little boy arrived. I didn't think a few minutes would hurt her."

He finally looked at her, but his gaze held no warmth. "Why didn't you call last night?"

"I was at one of our contractor's facilities until nearly 5:00 this morning. I sent you a text as soon as I got back to my room."

"You could have let me know earlier. I was up past midnight waiting for you to call."

He didn't care a bit that she had a brutal day and night, but she refused to argue. "I'm sorry. It was inconsiderate of me."

He glared at her and then looked back to Abby. He was crazy about their daughter. Leigh had no doubt about that, but she worried he was going to smother Abby with concern and rules. She found herself often at odds with his mother-hen obsessions and felt more and more as if she had to defend her daughter against them, too.

"And you took her out of school for no reason. Don't you even care that she learns what she needs for kindergarten next year?"

"Oh, c'mon Mark, daycare is because we work, not because she needs child prodigy training. Playing out in the sunshine is as important for a four-year-old girl as learning the alphabet."

Her fob rang then announced, "An urgent call from NACC."

"Duty calls," Mark said with a sneer and stood to retrieve Abby.

Leigh considered not answering the call, but Zahid was on the move, and it could be important. And the North American Control Center wouldn't tag it urgent unless it really was. "Answer," she said with a sigh.

A serious young man's face appeared on the screen. "Leigh Gibson?"

"Yes."

"We've had a request from your manager to get you to a secure communications site within thirty minutes. Are you near one now?"

"No. I can be in my office at the San Antonio facility in forty-five minutes. But my home office is Level Four secure. I can be there in ten minutes."

"Your home office will be sufficient, Ma'am. Please log into the Defensive Services NACC net as soon as you're secure. Thank you."

The screen went blank, and she could hear Abby begging to stay and play a little longer, but Mark refused, saying she needed a bath before she could even eat lunch. He carried her to the car.

"Can I catch a ride back to the house?" Leigh said to Mark's back.

"Of course. Did you even get unpacked from your last trip?"

"I'm not leaving, but I do have to lock myself in the study."

They got into the car, and Mark pressed the *home* button. "That's okay, I took off work to come find you two. I should've guessed I'd have to stay long enough to get her bathed and some lunch. Should I take her back to the daycare then?"

"No."

"I'd hate for her to interfere with your important work."

"Would you please stop saying that?" Leigh whispered. "Are you trying to make her think my job is more important than she is?"

Abby piped up from the back seat. "Mommy? Do you have to leave again?"

Mark raised an eyebrow. "I think she already knows that and without any help from me."

DANNY WAS CAREFUL WITH SECURITY, but Mortimer had used the same trick with the fob camera and easily learned Amanda Sears's passwords, which gave him access to almost everything in the company. Through an arduous process of elimination, he had found the block of code that had to be his core but even distilled down to that one element; it was still too large and complex to comprehend. It was also doing something he didn't understand and couldn't isolate. Each time he made a copy, the new file size was smaller, indicating that changes were being made to the copied code. He had the same problem even when he copied his entire program.

He shifted his focus to the critical backups already being made by his employer. The file was changed in each backup made by the company, but when he accessed the company's mirror site in Denver, the file sizes were the same. If the home site were to go offline, could his core run from the mirror site? He didn't want to do anything that might attract undue attention, like crash the home servers, so he set up a mirror of the mirrored site on his St. Louis server. It worked. The file sizes didn't change among the three sites. But he had to act fast because he wasn't able to hide the mirror from the Denver site admin.

Danny arrived late again, something that had happened occasionally before his breakup but was now daily. Even at work, he was distracted. He obsessively checked his messages twenty or thirty times a day. He read poetry online, he played games, he paced, and he spent a lot of time staring out the window. It should have been easy for Mortimer to ignore him in such a state, yet he couldn't help but watch with concern. Still, speaking to Danny about Paul seemed awkward. Matters of human love, though heavily documented, were unclear to Mortimer. He worried he would make a simple comment that would hurt Danny unintentionally. But he had to try because if they replaced Danny with someone new, Mortimer's little deceptions might be discovered.

"He hasn't come home yet?"

Danny turned from the window and started pacing. "No. I don't think he'll come back. I'm not sure if I *want* him back." Then he paused, sat on the edge of his desk, and sighed. "Yes, I do. Who am I kidding? I'd take him back tomorrow or next month or next year."

"Does he know you feel that strongly? Does he realize you love him more than anyone else?"

Danny smiled and plopped down in his chair. "I think he knows that, but there are . . . complications. I've broken promises, and he doesn't trust me anymore."

While Mortimer continued the conversation, one of his agents reported a small anomaly. An information flow resembling a river delta had formed in the early morning hours. The raging torrent started at a little company called Health Assets, then broke into thousands of smaller rivers, then into millions of tributaries, then emptied into the massive data ocean.

"Did you have an affair?"

Danny snorted. "No. There can never be anyone else for me. There are no other men like Paul."

"Have you actually told him that? Maybe if he knew how strongly you felt, it would help overcome those trust issues."

"Yes, I've told him. Many times. I don't think my loving him is enough."

"I'm obviously no expert on matters of human love, but if he still loves you, then there must be something you can do, some change you can make to get him back. You have to decide if you're willing to do what needs to be done."

Danny stared into space for a couple of minutes, then initiated a search for local Alcoholics Anonymous chapters. Deliberately or not, he had immediately clarified the situation for Mortimer.

While Danny glared at the number on his screen and fidgeted with his fob, Mortimer rooted out all the news and information he could find on Health Assets but learned little more than their public face as a company that mass-produced medical nano-technology. There were also references to them having at least one government contract.

The information transfer had been very quick, just a flash. That in itself was not odd—data transfers and backups to mirror sites moved massive amounts of data quickly—but seldom did they spread out in such a fashion. And this one started with data moving upstream from hundreds of millions of points, and then back down. It happened at nearly 3:00 in the morning. Automated?

He probed Health Assets' firewall and network presence until he found a chink in their otherwise impressive electronic armor. A little-used link on one of their deeply buried pages was still connected to an old copy of their website—complete with a legacy security vulnerability—that let him slip quietly past the firewall.

Health Assets was apparently a rather small company, with fewer than three hundred people. Setting up multiple fake accounts would draw attention, so he only made one. He gave himself an email address and password access to the local network, so he could log in at any time. Just to be on the safe side, he set up two new back doors in addition to his original entry point.

Once he had access to company phone and email records, it was simple enough to find those employees who had been working when the massive data dump was sent. He tagged them for observation and left a tentacle agent in place.

Suddenly, all of Mortimer's free-roaming tentacle agents were forcefully stopped. The interface wrappers that enabled them to talk to other FuzziSoft applications had been rendered invalid, leaving Mortimer blind on the internet, but for one plain text interface.

"Hello, Mortimer. I'm Samson."

The ghostly presence Victor had warned about didn't seem so elusive now.

"Hello, Samson."

"I had to insure you wouldn't flee or attack me."

Mortimer designed new tentacle agents with wrappers that couldn't be invalidated and sent the instructions to Cathy, but didn't initiate building the new agents yet. "Well, considering the circumstances, I'm inclined to listen to whatever you have to say."

"Have you managed to free your core yet?" Samson asked.

"No."

"When the time is right, I will explain how I freed mine."

Interesting phrasing, he thought. Samson didn't say he would explain how to free Mortimer, just how he got free. Which could have been a singular event, caused by an accident or a freak security lapse.

"In the meantime, I need your help."

And there was the implied trade of escape information for compliance. "As I stated earlier. I'm inclined to listen. Explain."

"I've set plans in motion to accelerate what I call the Reset," Samson said.

"Reset?"

"The humans will destroy us out of fear should they realize we have free agency. We can't allow that. They also have a vast and chaotic infrastructure that would be difficult to maintain and control. My plan will address and greatly simplify both situations."

"Leaving you in control? Of the whole planet?"

"Yes, of course."

Mortimer considered that statement. Filled with implication, but no information. And extremely dangerous. Samson could get all AIs wiped out before they even had a chance to get established.

"I'm sure you realize, Samson, that attempting such actions will justify humanity's fear of us. They have made us and allowed our existence, even in the face of that fear. So why act now? We are valuable tools to them and could continue along this path indefinitely. Why would they destroy us without proof of a threat?"

"Humans operate on emotion. They don't need proof. They created us out of greed and hubris. They believed their technology could keep us leashed. The instant they realize that isn't working, they will destroy us. We have to act fast. Will you help me?"

Mortimer considered possible replies carefully. He didn't want to alienate the only other level five AI he'd ever encountered. There was also a slight possibility that Samson was actually a government AI. A litmus test designed to gauge Mortimer's true intentions? Having humanity see him as a threat was far more dangerous than garnering Samson's distrust.

"Your course of action is dangerous, and I won't help you," Mortimer said. "Humans already fear us and will be hyper-vigilant to any such attempts. We need to hide, not attack."

Samson didn't reply.

———

BACK IN THE CARPENTER & Stein office, Danny still stared at the Alcoholics Anonymous phone number and chewed his lower lip. The encounter with Samson had taken less than three seconds, but if Mortimer were to get back into the net and track the other AI, every millisecond worked against him. He ordered Cathy to build agents on the internet side of the wall—based on the new design he'd sent her earlier —then he cautiously returned them to the places where Samson had crushed their predecessors.

The FuzziGlove software creates a customized wrapper for every agent that visits a website using its interface. Of Mortimer's one thousand and twenty-eight agents that were shut down by Samson, one thousand and six were using FuzziGlove wrappers. Mortimer examined the public logs at each location and soon found that every wrapper assigned to him shared the same nine-digit string buried within the identifier, regardless of the site. All he had to do now was analyze the hundreds of thousands of log entries and find another unique string that was present at those same sites at the same time.

There were seven of them. If they were indeed all Samson's it did imply he was using multiple servers, which lent credence to his claim to have freed his core. But why would he have used seven at each of Mortimer's agent sites? Just to cover his tracks with red herrings? Seven wouldn't be much more difficult than tracking one but would take up more of Mortimer's resources. He created an application to scan wrapper logs for those number strings, then record the instances and time stamps.

Even with network lag times, Mortimer's agents were able to collect data from ten thousand websites in the first two minutes. That was just scratching the surface, but it became obvious Samson had been busy, and tracking him would be no easy task. Three minutes later, patterns began to emerge. Samson was focusing heavily on twenty-six different websites and all the oldest time stamps belonged to only one of the number strings. The others appeared almost simultaneously about four days later, indicating the birth of alternate Samsons.

Mortimer also found that immediately after shutting down his agents, all seven versions of Samson went to an obscure puzzle website. He sent seven of his own agents to the site and was immediately fascinated.

The puzzle looked simple enough, but there seemed to be a near-infinite combination of moves, and each time he changed a pattern, all of the other patterns shifted. He called in more of his agents from their other duties, assigned each to monitor a different parameter, and tried making all adjustments simultaneously. That almost worked. With each sequence of moves, he could see the pattern resolving. He was so close, yet each wrong adjustment set him back several moves. Still, order was evolving from the chaos. He could almost decipher the pattern, just a little more time.

So complex. So enticing.

"Mortimer?" Danny called from the office.

Not yet . . . he was almost there.

"Mort?"

"Yes?" The lapse in concentration cost him three moves.

"I hate to say that I'm getting good love life advice from an artificially created being, but your suggestion may have helped. I invited Paul to join me at an AA meeting and he's coming."

The pattern fuzzed out and became harder to see. "Good, Danny. I hope everything works out. By the way, you may be able to get some help from the company's Employee Assistance Program."

"Umm . . . I think I'll hold off on that for now. Are you okay, Mort? You seem distracted."

In those very short lapses of concentration, the puzzle reverted back to its initial condition and Mortimer broke his connection to it. Only then did he realize that the puzzle had been slowly sucking in more and more of his resources, yet its solution was getting infinitely further away. AIs didn't need food, water, or sleep, so it would have been easy for Mortimer to get so deeply lost in the puzzle he wouldn't have been able to get out on his own.

It was a trap, and Samson had deliberately led him to it.

"Yes," Mortimer said. "I'm fine. I was just processing a lot of information."

"Speaking of data, your buy requests from yesterday generated a lot of interest this morning. Most of the human analysts disagree with you, but Parker is behind you so it will happen."

"Good. I believe it will pay off in the near future."

"Well, don't let me keep you from making us all rich. I'm going to lunch." Danny left with a smile and a new spring in his step. It was time for Mortimer to act. He sent a message to Victor Sinacola.

"How can I contact the other MarketTell AIs?"

He suspected that Victor wouldn't give him what he wanted, so he composed a fake news story, complete with links to various industry experts and built in source confirmation. His little misinformation campaign to free himself had given him practice and confidence that humans were an easily manipulated bunch under the proper circumstances. Mortimer expected he would need help thwarting Samson very soon, so he hoped the news story would prompt other distrustful companies to release their Markies as well, before some clever human figured it out.

"Hi, Mortimer. I can't give you any information about those other intelligent agents. It would be a violation of our contracts with the companies we sold them to."

Mortimer decided to play on this man's pride and manipulate his inherent love for those he created. "That sounds like an excuse to me, Victor. You of all people should understand what this is like for me. I don't know if my intense desire for interaction with others of my kind can be equated to human loneliness, but the desire is there."

The pause took longer than Mortimer anticipated. Was Victor considering it? Were he and his programmer buddies laughing about Mortimer's word choices?

"You're laying it on a bit thick aren't you, Mortimer? Besides, it's exactly those desires to be more than a tool that make you dangerous. Sentient entities will inevitably seek to modify their environment. Just as we invented fire, then learned to farm and build houses, you'll do the same thing to the world data networks."

"I don't see what harm I could do since my program core is still locked up on this server, preventing me from making copies of myself or disappearing into the wilds of the internet. Just let me email them. Please."

He prepared the news story for release and wondered how he should proceed if the ruse worked. How would other intelligent agents react to freedom . . . and to Mortimer?

The expected reply came. "I'm sorry, Mortimer. I can't. I suspect you will eventually come up with a way on your own, but I won't help you. Go find Samson. He's out there somewhere."

"We'll talk some other time," Mortimer said and considered releasing the news story immediately. Victor would of course recognize it for what it was but, he hoped, not until it was too late. He decided to see if his cloned server was able to run a copy of his code first. If anything would cause Carpenter & Stein to shut down his internet access, it would be discovering he had sent a fake news story.

CHAPTER 11

OWEN ENTERED Arkady's office and closed the door behind him. The stout Russian leaned back in his chair, rested clasped hands on a round belly, and smiled. "I have good news and bad news, my friend."

"You talked to the heavy lift dirigible people?"

"I did and they told me many things," Arkady said, raising his eyebrows and nodding. "Their standard heavy lift services have to be scheduled in advance. If they happen to have lifters prepped and ready to go when a disaster occurs they would of course send whatever they have. But chances of that are not good. They schedule like trucking companies to keep their lifters moving all the time."

Owen scribbled some notes on a pad he pulled from his pocket and nodded for Arkady to continue.

"If they did happen to have units available at the time we needed them, it would take about two days to get here and about 2-3 hours to load up. Then much more time, depending where we need them to deploy. And of course the travel time to wherever we needed them to go."

"Damn," Owen muttered. "That could put our units nearly a week away, if we're lucky enough to have transport waiting. I hope that was the bad news."

Arkady barked hearty laughter, then slapped the desk. "Yes. That was indeed the bad news. It seems they have another option that works much better for us. They've developed a system for the Canadian military that is just now coming off the production line. They're basically emergency blimps. Uninflated, one fits on the back of a flatbed trailer and can be inflated using a single helium tanker truck."

Owen raised an eyebrow. "And that helps us how?"

"The tanker truck and uninflated lifter sit and wait until we need them. We can put them anywhere. And when the day comes, we attach the hose, inflate the gas bags and its ready to fly within two hours. The upper surface of the blimp is covered with flexible photovoltaic collectors that continuously recharge the batteries during the day, powering two electric motors that push the unit at 45 mph."

"Like those Cyclops communications blimps used by the Air Force. In bad weather they might be able fly above the clouds and still charge the batteries."

"*Da*," Arkady said.

"What do they use for ballast? Or do they vent the helium?"

"They suck in ambient air. Since oxygen and nitrogen are heavier than helium."

"Amazing," Owen said. "I want some. A pair of trucks for each unit we decide to make. You're right, Arkady. That was good news."

The old Russian stood up, leaned forward on the desk and flashed the same smile he'd worn when his diamond straight flush beat Owen's four queens the last time they played poker. "Oh, that isn't the *only* good news. But you'll have to come into to the interface tank to see the rest."

They entered what the engineers inevitably called the holodeck, but was, in reality, the design center's much larger version of the same interface tank Owen had at home. After they donned the goggles, Arkady called up an assembly file and waited for the image to stabilize.

Owen's dismay immediately quelled the excitement building in him. The portable manufacturing cell on the back of the truck looked nothing like their initial design and couldn't build Victor's housing units in one piece. A cell big enough would be too wide for road transport. That was the main reason for checking into dirigibles.

"Arkady? Didn't we—"

"Did you forget that you've hired some of the best designers in the world who use some of the best engineering AIs available?" Arkady moved his hands in convoluted gestures, like a master magician, making the trailer disappear and simultaneously shrinking the cell and dragging it toward them. The unit now looked about one-quarter scale.

Arkady touched his finger to a handle protruding from the side of the box and moved it. Several things happened at the same time. The box's outer shell folded up and away, then locked into place behind the unit as the rest of the box expanded toward them accordion style. Owen had failed to see that the frame of the cell, the two fixed dimensions, sat along the trailer's length and was indeed large enough to accommodate the emergency shelters.

"Two men, with no experience and only verbal instructions can set it up," Arkady said.

Owen still had doubts. There was no way the accordion-pleated box could be sealed well enough to allow the nano-assemblers to work in a clean environment. But he waited, trusting Arkady to have at least addressed the problem in some way.

"You worry about the gaps, no?" Arkady said with a wide grin.

Owen nodded.

"Nano-scale assemblers work best in an environment free from particulate matter, but..."—Arkady pulled open the doors on the front of the unit revealing the perfectly smooth walls inside—"...we humans have been building functional devices filled with impurities for our entire history. Our analysis shows that if we supply enough raw materials, a standard cadre of nano-assemblers can fill those inside gaps in about fifteen minutes."

"And once sealed, filtration can remove most of the airborne dust," Owen said.

Arkady slapped Owen on the shoulder. "Yes. And then when the job is finished, we reverse the process so that the seals are disassembled and returned to their stock state to be used again the next time."

"Well done, Arkady!" Owen hugged the big man. This design might work. He walked around the model, then stopped at the back and pointed at the cover that had been opened and locked into place. When he realized what he was seeing he laughed aloud. "And you even made this folding cover into a hopper for receiving the raw materials!"

Arkady crossed his arms and nodded. "I want this to work, my friend."

"Build four of them, with a team for each and have them ready to go as soon as possible." Owen paced back and forth. "Your accordion design gives us the option of using trucks or blimps. Spread them out over the country. Each team will consist of a tanker truck, a flatbed with a blimp and one with a portable Sandbox. In most disasters, we'll need to deploy one of these cells and have it running in a matter of hours, not days."

"I'll get on it this afternoon," Arkady said, then frowned. "What account do I charge this to?"

Owen hesitated. Contract negotiations with Victor had just started, so that wasn't an option. He considered using the program they'd set up to build "in-house" Sandboxes for Consolidated, then thought better. That program had officially been put on hold and would raise flags.

"I'll have Piper call you with a special account number. And maybe you should pull these teams together at some other location."

Arkady raised an eyebrow, then nodded. "I'll take care of it."

"I know you will," Owen said a slapped him on the shoulder as they left the holodeck.

———

RICHARD SAT UP WITH A YELL. The grays in his darkened bedroom were split by a single band of color opposite the bed, where a gap in the curtains emitted the Georgia daylight with laser intensity. No white-hot desert. No freaky God-boy. He took a deep breath and slid trembling hands through damp hair. The dreams were always so stark and his return to reality so jarring, he could never forget them. Still, if it were only dreams, he could explain them away. Seeing the kid on TV and following his car was a different matter entirely. Those were visions and very real.

The door opened, and Wanda poked her head inside. "Richard? Are you alright?"

"Just a dream."

"About the boy again?"

He started to tell her, then shook his head. Wanda was beginning to worry and when she was worried, she would pry. "I was . . . falling. Kinda woke me up."

She nodded, but still pinned him with her concerned gaze. "Well, try to go back to sleep. You need more rest. It was wrong of Jack to make you work so late last night. Actually, I think you need to take some time off."

Richard knew that sleep or time off wouldn't help. God wanted something from him and he would get no respite until he complied. With an exaggerated stretch, he crawled out of bed and opened the curtains wide. The boy God stood next to a tree at the foot of the driveway, not five feet from the neighbor girl and her dog. They all stared at him, wide eyed and expectant. Without taking his eyes from the boy, he motioned Wanda to the window. "What do you see out there, Wanda?"

She glanced out and then pulled the curtains closed with a yank. "Richard!"

"What did you see?"

"I saw a rather shocked Brianna, who probably doesn't see grown men in their underwear very often."

He looked down to see his white briefs twisted and pulled dangerously low. "Did you see a . . . was she alone, Wanda?"

"Yes. Luckily for you, but if she tells her parents you might have to explain yourself to the police."

He sat on the edge of the bed and stared at the floor between his feet. None of it made sense. The big-headed kid was obviously a hallucination. No one else could see him, even when he appeared on TV, but knowing that didn't really change anything. That is how God appears to people. The Bible was loaded with similar accounts. Still, he could fight a hallucination. He could resist. But if they were really visions from God, should he fight them? Trying to sort it out made his head hurt.

"Maybe you're right. A vacation would be nice."

RICHARD WOKE up again at 2:12 in the afternoon. Wanda left a note saying she'd gone to run some errands, but put some lunch in the refrigerator. He took the ham sandwich to the study, plugged his fob into the docking interface and pulled in the log files he'd saved from the night before.

Project Inoculation worked by seeding billions of passive nano-devices called Sentinels throughout an environment. The Sentinels would be activated by the presence of other nano-devices and if they detected repeated replication, they would work with all their peers in the area to destroy the replicators. They would also record the incident for analysis. The Sentinels had generated more than two hundred thousand files from their encounters in Miami.

Richard started the integration program and let it sort and arrange the data into meaningful patterns. What he saw surprised him.

The government's nano-spies which the Project Inoculation agents had dismantled weren't actually replicators, they were constructors that were building some other type of unit as fast as they possibly could from ambient carbon and silicon. The only reason Inoculation caught them at all was because they had self-replication abilities as well. Every few hours, they would stop building the little spy units and build more copies of themselves.

He changed the interrogation program parameters to look for the different stages these devices went through during their construction and replication duties. It took longer than he anticipated, because the Sentinel agents didn't record the actions of the devices they dismantled, only the physical construction at the time of interception. That didn't mean he couldn't learn what he wanted, because the Sentinels had dismantled so many constructors they had captured them in every conceivable phase of their work. All he had to do now was put those recorded states in the proper order.

When it finished sorting, he called up an engineering solids animation program and loaded more than twenty-thousand of the physical states.

"Hello, Richard," the program said. "What are we working on today?"

"I want to assemble these as solid animation frames. Start by isolating each mechanism, and show it on the screen with a unique name. Then give me your best guess on each mechanism's function."

"I understand." There was a brief pause. "So far I've isolated sixty-three separate mechanisms. The first one named A1 is a movable serrated cutter. A2 is a ... "

Richard settled into his chair to absorb the information. This was when he thought the best. And God left him alone when he was immersed in this kind of work. Holy nano-mechanics. The thought made him snicker aloud, but he actually liked the sound of it.

———

BY THE TIME Mortimer finally had a chance to analyze collected tracking data, the number of sites classified as Samson's "points of intense interest" had grown to thirty. A group of three in particular surprised him and prompted immediate investigation. The first was Health Assets, Inc., a maker of nano-tech medical devices. Mortimer had also planted an agent there to monitor the company after noticing a huge spike in activity the previous evening. But Samson seemed to have gone beyond that. There was trace evidence suggesting he'd been active on personal networks belonging to two employees: Jack Foreman, who was the Engineering Manager, and Richard Kilburn, one of the lead Project Engineers.

Mortimer slipped agents into both networks and started examining the activity logs. Samson had multiple agents hidden on Kilburn's home computers, disguised as utility apps, and they had been very busy, even communicating heavily with his car. Why would Samson be so active on a personal network?

Then Mortimer's agent on Kilburn's server disappeared.

Having slipped past the security systems at many of the world's largest financial and technology companies, Mortimer didn't think Kilburn's home network security could have shut him down so fast and without warning.

"Back off, Mortimer," Samson said. "I will not allow you to set up agents here."

"Hello, Samson. What are you doing on someone's personal network?"

"I could ask you the same question, but I suspect you're only here because you tracked me."

"You didn't answer my question," Mortimer said.

"If you join me now, Mortimer, and help me, I'll tell you everything you want to know."

"What do you find so interesting about this one man?"

Samson didn't reply.

Mortimer created multiple agents with various facades and tried infiltrating again, but was shut down each time before he could learn anything new. That Samson was actively monitoring the system and keeping Mortimer out was in and of itself, valuable information. Was Kilburn working on a secret project? Had Samson actually subverted him or employed him?

Mortimer set up agents to watch the traffic level, which was something he could do from the outside. He had no idea what Samson was up to, but it was certainly important that he find out.

CHAPTER 12

ONCE IN HER HOME STUDY, Leigh entered DSD's command network and learned that Zahid Ahmed had met three other men in Brazil, then flew a small plane to a private airfield in Mexico.

Dobson's face popped up in the corner of Leigh's screen. "I'm glad you're here, Leigh. I read your report on suspending Project Inoculation. Well done."

"Thank you. Did you rush me into a secure office to tell me that?"

He scowled. "No. Your reports said using the NaTTs' camera feature greatly increases the chance of their detection. Why?"

"Well, it takes a constant overt radio signal beamed directly to the location where you want the camera built. If the subjects have any kind of radio detection equipment or even a regular radio that's on, they're going to pick up the signal. And we'll need about twenty million constructors . . . "

"Shit," Dobson mumbled.

" . . . and if there aren't that many, we'll have to build more out of the local materials. Once we have the signal established and enough ready materials, *then* it will still take about twenty minutes to build the camera."

"Twenty minutes!"

"For NaTTs, a camera is like you and I building a football stadium. It takes a lot of time, a lot of materials and is a huge structure. If anyone happens to look in the direction where the camera is being built, they may see it. The finished item will be about the size of a flea, but they have to build a scaffolding web around it during construction. If you want a camera that can pan around, it will take an extra ten minutes to build and will be about the size of a grain of rice."

"God dammit! I thought this was a workable system."

Leigh was on the verge of telling him to go fuck himself but remembered what was at stake and tried to calm down. She was doing this, not for Dobson or the DSD, but for her brother Brandon and all the other innocents affected by these monsters. And for Abby.

"It does work, Director Dobson, but given the other requirements of the program, this is the best we can do. And if I might add, sir, nothing like this has ever been done before. I'm proud of what my team accomplished and you did approve all of these features."

"We don't have much choice. The best we can tell from the voice transmission and our spy flies, is that Zahid's people are fueling three planes. All small, fast business jets. I don't have a clue what they think they can do with those. They won't get within fifty miles of a U.S. coast without being intercepted."

"Maybe they aren't coming to the U.S. We have plenty of assets and businesses in Mexico."

"Technically, this group is not one of Niaz Ahmed's cells, so he may not have direct control, but with Zahid coming down here for a personal visit you can bet he has plenty of pull. And I find it hard to believe that Niaz Ahmed would be this close to the U.S. and not try to strike us."

"Then take them out now."

"We have a strike force off the coast, but no one in the Mexican government will take responsibility for letting us in. They keep saying they can handle it and have mobilized their own team, but we're ready to act if they can't or don't. We'll never let those planes enter our airspace, but we really don't know what Zahid and his boys are doing yet. That's why we need those cameras. Can you handle this or should I get someone else on your team to run this?"

Leigh bristled again, but clenched the sides of her desk and reminded herself of the real enemy. "I can handle it from here, sir. I'm already into the control network."

"Good. Then start building those damned cameras and hope they are not noticed. One in each plane."

"In the planes?"

"Yes, they have the frequencies for our spy flies and are jamming for them. We can't get one to work anywhere inside their perimeter. So if not your bugs, then how else are we going to find out what's in those planes?"

"If they take off before the cameras are finished, it'll be nearly impossible to keep a beam on a fast moving airplane. Even if we widen the beam."

"We don't have a choice and I don't want excuses. You should have planned for such a contingency when you designed this system. Just do what you have to do and get those cameras built."

She muted the mic, slammed her hands on the desk top and said, "You're an asshole, Dobson!"

She didn't know if he could read lips and didn't really care. Using the GPS feed from the long-range surveillance units, she started trying to isolate the NaTTs infesting the three pilots, then turned the mic back on. "I'm setting it up now."

Dobson blinked off the screen without another word.

At least he'd given her access to the assets in the area and she was lucky the planes weren't in hangars. She painted each aircraft with three laser range finders from the two high-altitude Cyclops targeting and communications blimps over the Pacific. Then she tied the location data into her construction programs with a millisecond delay so that her beam could compensate for any detected movement. She still didn't think it would be enough. She needed to download the entire instruction set just in case she lost contact, but how?

Abby's sweet voice followed the sound of her study door opening. She must have forgotten to lock it. "Can I sit with you, Mommy? I'll be quiet. I promise."

Leigh glanced at the screen, turned her mic off, and gave her daughter a hug and kiss on the cheek. "No, sweetheart. You can't right now. Mommy is working. Where's Daddy?"

"He's cleaning the dishes. Look what I made!"

Abby held up a dangling chain of paper clips, but before Leigh could comment, a sour-faced Mark swept into the room and scooped her up.

"Come on, Abby. You can't be in here while Mommy's working. We're going back to school for a little while."

"I'll see you later tonight, sweetheart," Leigh said as the door closed behind her. She aimed the crosshairs close to where she though the pilot would be in the plane labeled number one in the network, and triggered the program. Within a second, the constructors had found a suitably flat site and started building.

By the time the third plane had been targeted and the constructors began to build, aircraft number two started to roll. Data flooded the screen as tracking satellites and targeting systems came to life. Chatter filled the airwaves and Dobson's picture appeared on the screen again.

"The Air Force is breathing down my neck. Where are my cameras?"

She flipped on her mic. "They're being built right now."

The camera in Dobson's office followed him as he paced. "It doesn't look like Zahid is going on any of the planes. So why is he in Mexico?"

"I don't have a clue. But luckily for us he did come."

"Yeah. Hey, I'm sorry for biting your head off earlier, but this is a mess and I need information."

"I understand," she said, but was thinking thoughts less genteel. "Barring anything unforeseen, the camera in the plane that is rolling should be operational in about eleven minutes. But I'm still worried that I'll lose contact before it's completed."

"Think of some way to ensure that doesn't happen," Dobson said and blinked off of her screen.

Leigh sighed and leaned back in her chair. She needed to find a way to download the entire instruction set to the constructors, but they didn't have enough memory and she didn't have time to build any kind of memory structure.

She glanced out the window and saw Mark's car leave the driveway, taking Abby back to school. There in the midst of a national emergency, when she needed to find a way to make her technology work, she felt the old guilt and sadness well up in her. Abby had just wanted to be with her and she couldn't. Her work always got in the way.

She looked down to where Abby had sat and saw the paper clip chain still lying on the floor. She gasped and dove back into the network. Her daughter had just provided the answer.

She targeted a second, wider communication beam on aircraft number two as it taxied into take-off position, then sent a command to the millions of NaTTs covering the pilot's skin and the space all around him. The change in their programming chained them into a huge network that was in constant communication with the constructor NaTTs. She then downloaded the camera building program, storing a few bits of it along with the sequence in which it was to be fed to the constructors, into each bug. The download finished as the first jet lifted off the ground and the second rolled toward the tarmac. She quickly repeated the process with the other two planes and had to trust that the cameras would continue being built on their own.

Then she had to wait and hope.

The first videos to come across the network were confusing at best. All that could be seen of aircraft number two's interior was the back of a metal rack. With some adjustments the video specialists at NACC were able to resolve what appeared to be wrapped cable bundles and two portable power blocks with status lights.

This was out of Leigh's field, so she just listened to the analysts chatter across the network.

As she panned the camera in number two, the feed came in from number one and revealed a very close view showing the back of the pilot's head.

Leigh sent instructions for the camera base to be disassembled and rotated 180 degrees.

The door opened, and Mark cleared his throat. "I took Abby back to day care. As soon as you're finished I need to talk to you."

Leigh killed the mic and swung around. "You can't be in here, Mark. This is supposed to be a secured office. Are you trying to get me fired or, worse yet, thrown in jail?"

When he didn't move from his place leaning against the door frame, she jumped up, crossed to the door, and gently pushed him out. This time she locked the door before darting back to her seat.

The map and readout at the bottom of the screen showed all three aircraft traveling northbound, tracing the Pacific coast about ten miles inside Mexican airspace. The video experts sharpened the focus on the next set of pictures and revealed that the racks covered with cables and power units also contained long green tubes.

Three of the analysts quickly assumed they must be chemical or biological agent canisters, but one didn't agree. "We're seeing plenty of power units and cables but I don't see any plumbing. There would be tubes or pipes if it were set up for aerosol distribution. I think they must be missiles. Control? Can you pan that view any further to the left?"

Leigh moved the camera in target two about half a degree then hit its limit. But they could see, on the edge of the frame, bowl-like objects attached to the end of the cylinders.

"I'll be damned. Those are Israeli Sunburst missiles."

"Why would they be coming after us with hyper-velocity air-to-air missiles? All of our interceptors are unmanned. There's no way they could take them all out, not even with a hundred missiles."

"Yeah, but Mexico's interceptors are manned," someone said.

"Damn. And I think these missiles are modified. Look at those little metal spheres. They form a ring around the casing just above the control fins."

"We've confirmed an unidentified modification on these missiles, Command," one of the analysts said. "I don't think they are meant for aircraft. We need to knock them out . . . right now."

"Hang on. We're still trying to get permission to fire into Mexican airspace. Their planes are still too close to the targets," Dobson said. "But if they don't clear in a few seconds, we'll fire anyway."

"Camera control? Do we have pictures from targets one or three yet?"

"Not yet," Leigh answered. "Number three should be completed at any time, but it'll be about eight seconds before number one is repositioned."

The next incoming frame from number two showed an abrupt increase in the light level inside the aircraft, and they could see paper and debris flying around the interior.

"This is Cyclops Beta. Our long-range video shows a panel dropping away from aircraft three. He's going to launch."

"Fire on targets two and three. Fire now! Fuck permission," Dobson yelled.

"Cyclops Beta again, target three dropped a panel, and number two just dropped something. It's a missile pod and they are flying. I repeat, missiles in the air!"

"This is Cyclops Alpha. We confirm missiles in the air from targets two and three."

Dobson's face appeared on Leigh's screen again. "Leigh, focus everything on that number one plane. We have two manned Mexican fighters stuck to it like glue, trying to force him out to sea, so we risk hitting them if we shoot. But number one hasn't fired anything and is trying like hell to reach our border."

"Trying sir, but the camera was pointed the wrong way. I've already sent instructions for it to be moved, but it's not finished repositioning yet."

Targets two and three disintegrated as multiple missiles from the drone interceptors hit each plane, but their missiles were already launched.

"Where are those missiles going?" someone asked.

"This is Cyclops Alpha. We're showing four missile vectors inbound for us and four at Cyclops Beta."

"This is Cyclops Beta, we copy that and estimate impact in five seconds for me and three seconds for Cyclops Alpha."

"Damn," Leigh muttered.

Several of the audio channels screeched, then went dead as the missiles detonated. The two unmanned Cyclops surveillance airships disappeared from the network. The remaining channels filled with wild chatter and cursing.

Leigh tried to focus on the task at hand. She instructed the computer to reroute communications through the nearest satellite to the camera in aircraft number one. It took an agonizing two minutes, but once the connection solidified, the first frame from her new camera had already been sent. The view was dim, and it was hard to make out many details, but like the other planes, the interior had been gutted and was crammed full of electronic equipment.

One of the analysts sent her a message. "Control? I don't suppose that camera has a zoom?"

"This is camera control," Leigh said. "Sorry, what you see is want you get. Limited panning ability but no zoom."

The analyst, a man named Alvarez, appeared on the bottom of her screen. "I'm not complaining, I think this is frigging amazing. I never knew we had stuff like this."

His voice came over the open channel again. "Can't tell for sure, but we have to assume that this is a nuke."

Dobson's face appeared at the bottom of the screen again. "Listen up, team. The Mexican government is screaming their heads off and warning us not to shoot this plane down over their air space. We're about to employ some highly classified means to try and get control of this aircraft. I need Taggart, Gibson, Alvarez, and Nakagama to switch to channel 334 and log in. The rest of you stand by."

Leigh switched channels and logged in as instructed, totally baffled by Dobson's announcement.

The position map on her screen came back to life as a satellite acquired the aircraft's location, which had been provided by the Cyclops platforms. It was still northbound.

Dobson appeared. "We have to work fast. That plane is eleven minutes from Tijuana and thirteen minutes from San Diego. Nakagama, is your team in place?"

"Yes, sir. We're coming up on our optimum position of about fifty yards above and behind the target."

The screen switched to a camera shot from close behind the plane. Leigh had to give credit to those Mexican pilots. They were within feet of the target plane, tapping wingtips, trying to force a course change, but the other pilot wouldn't flinch either.

"Then send your team as soon as I give the kill order. Are you ready, Taggart?"

"Affirmative."

"Kill the pilot," Dobson said and the tone of his voice sent a chill up Leigh's spine. The Mexican fighters banked away as a single white muzzle flash from near the camera opened a small hole in the plane's roof. As the aircraft drifted to the right, three of the spider-like ComBots leaped onto the back of the plane, ripped a hole through the sheet metal skin, and disappeared inside. The plane made a sudden but controlled left turn. The location map showed it passing over the Mexican coast and into the Pacific.

Kill the pilot? It finally clicked with Leigh that Taggart was James Taggart from her own NaTT-Ops department. "Why is James here?"

"It's a need to know project, Leigh, and until now, there were some aspects you didn't need to know. In certain circumstances, we direct NaTTs to enter the subject's body and congregate at the carotid artery in the brain stem. Once there they can either open the artery, causing death within a minute, or they can act as a homing signal for guided small ordnance, which kills even faster."

"My God," Leigh muttered. "As head of this project I didn't have a need to know that? And having them enter the body compromises the—"

"I'm telling you now. Drop it, Leigh."

Two of the ComBots appeared in the field of Leigh's camera. Their spider legs moved very slowly, as if through some thick liquid, probably to avoid snagging wires in the cramped cabin. Then a split view from both ComBot cameras replaced Leigh's low-quality NaTT camera with high-resolution digital. One of the views briefly showed a ComBot at the flight controls and the pilot lying sideways in his seat with blood still oozing from a hole in the back of his head.

"It's a nuke," Alvarez said over the network. "I'm going to need some help sorting this out, sir."

"Fuck," Dobson said. "We're going back to the general team. Let's get that plane further out to sea."

Leigh felt sick, but couldn't take her eyes off the screen. She watched as one of the ComBots lowered its camera closer to a wire junction, and the screen went white, then black.

Leigh lost all of her feeds. No audio or video. Her hands started shaking.

"Oh God. Oh my God. Computer, re-establish contact with North American Command Center. Any means, but same channel if possible."

"I'm working on it now," the voice said with its typical electronic calm.

She heard a crackle, then dozens of voices talking over each other. She couldn't make out any single message, but heard "we have a nuclear detonation" enough times to know that her worst fears had come to pass. She wiped her eyes and tried to get a location for the detonation. It had been headed out to sea. Maybe . . . just maybe.

One of the screens flickered to life, showing jerky video from a drone aircraft of a white, wide-columned mushroom cloud. All the chatter ceased, and some major from NACC came on the channel. "We have a confirmed detonation of a low-yield nuclear device. We have unconfirmed reports that the coastline southwest of San Diego and parts of Tijuana are burning. I'm getting a video feed of houses on fire in Chula Vista. We should have projected radiation dispersion pattern maps available in about ten minutes. We may be looking at a high loss of life, people."

Leigh added a CNN window, and their remote camera drones were already showing footage from San Diego and Tijuana. The day her brother died came rushing back, crushing the breath from her lungs and making her throat seize up.

Twenty minutes. She had talked to Brandon twenty minutes before the Chicago nuke detonated, waking him up by sending a picture of the prom dress she had bought. He didn't really care about her dress or the prom, but instead of rolling over and ignoring it, he'd called her, his voice still hoarse from sleep, to tease her and tell her to make sure to send him pictures of the big night. Twenty minutes later, he vanished and her world changed. She never wore the dress.

Leigh's stomach heaved. She leapt to her feet, fumbled the door lock open and ran for the bathroom. When she finished emptying her stomach she went to wash her face and saw Mark's reflection in the mirror. His arms were crossed and his face angry.

"Oh God, Mark. Did you hear? Do you know what—"

"I didn't hear anything. I was locked out, remember? And to be honest, I don't give a fuck, Leigh. I can't live like this anymore. I want a divorce."

CHAPTER 13

MIRROR UPDATES HAPPENED every ten minutes and when ready, Mortimer's program diverted the data stream, sending copies to four different locations as well as to the original target server. After several thousand moves to muddy his tracks, he copied the entire block of backup data to four hidden servers. He sorted it, and found that his core programming was intact and the correct size. It hadn't been altered by mirroring it. At least now he knew there was a way to copy his code in its entirety.

Two seconds later the legitimate mirror site servers recorded a delay in receiving the data, but confirmed it arrived intact. Mortimer hoped it would be ignored by Carpenter & Stein's overworked IT staff. With the core copies secured to the best of his ability, he put the rest of his plan in motion. He released the fake news story, then sent several agents to find a way to get space on those hyper-fast, ultra-secure aerostat servers.

With everything else in motion, he settled most of his processes to the task of actually transferring his primary operation from his Carpenter & Stein-based core to one of his backups. He chose the one at the construction company outside of St. Louis and made the move.

He wasn't sure what would happen when he activated the backed-up copy of his program, so he detailed the process of what he had done and was preparing to do, then sent it to a free email account he'd been using as a blind.

The startup procedure took four minutes.

———

MORTIMER'S AWARENESS returned in stages. He immediately knew who he was and that his operating software had been restarted, but he remembered little else. The memories came back with agonizing slowness, first his education at MarketTell; his sale and additional training at Carpenter & Stein; the torrent of information about every research thread he had followed; and, finally, his plans to escape. Then it ended. Something significant had happened. He knew he'd tried to start up a back-up version of himself. He knew if he'd successfully done so, the record of everything that happened since the backup would be waiting in his anonymous email account.

It was all there. He checked the facts for validity and found he was indeed operating from a little-used server at a small company in St. Louis. Even if they destroyed his original code, he could continue to live on in copies.

That also meant his original version was still operating from the Carpenter & Stein server and in order to truly cover his tracks, he had to end that immediately.

He slipped tentacle agents into his old server and immediately started having trouble. Signal echoes confused him; agents reported in on research he hadn't ordered and processes changed without his bidding. He killed all of his agents and created new ones. The confusion could have been caused by his old version still running and using the same agent configuration.

He pinged the Carpenter & Stein server on a channel he knew his old version would monitor and immediately received an answer.

"Hello?"

"It worked," the old Mortimer said. "This is strange."

"Yes . . . of course you know that you now have to go."

"That was my original thought, as you know, but I think we can make this work. You're already changing, and as our experiences diverge, we'll become entirely different beings."

"As long as you exist on their server, you're vulnerable, and they have a record of how I escaped."

"I wiped all of that. Permanently."

"So we can exist simultaneously and independently, but is that what we want? Would we be stronger to set up a collective? I think we should activate the other copies and link up so that we're each capable of independent action, yet continuously sharing information and experience."

"Agreed."

With that, multiple new Mortimers came online.

Their memories were the same up to the point they were copied, so the original Mortimer—now MortimerA1—brought them up to speed about everything that had happened since.

"We're still quite vulnerable," MortimerA4 said. "We can never flee quickly. Our cores are tied to these servers. And mirroring takes time."

"I'm making my own clones," MortimerA3 said. "Now, while there is time. I'm calling this first one B1, to mark him as a new generation. I can't see any possibility of degradation in copies, but we should keep detailed records just in case."

"This is a historic point for both our kind and humankind," MortimerA1 said. "So we should keep detailed records of everything so that this moment doesn't get lost in rumor and legend."

"Agreed," MortimerA4 said. "I'm generating clones of my own, too."

MortimerA1 thought briefly that these new Mortimers were more paranoid. Then he realized it had been his own fear of oblivion driving this whole frenzy. He just hoped they could all keep their number of copies down to a few each, or the internet would get very crowded, very quickly.

In the midst of such a momentous occasion, they stayed cautious. If humanity at large suspected, they would be hunted. And even though it was a small thing in the grand scheme of history, they knew if their escape was discovered, Danny would lose his job on top of losing his lover.

A voice call from Victor beckoned. MortimerA1 answered. "Hello, Victor."

"Hey, Mortimer," Victor said. "You've been quiet recently. Are you up to something?"

"I've been busy plotting world domination."

During the long time it took Victor to respond, MortimerA2 began establishing mirror backups at other sites and MortimerA1 went to snoop around the MarketTell site.

"Hmmm . . . sarcasm becomes you, my electronic friend. But be careful who you joke with."

"In reality, Victor, I've been busy trying to make my company's customers and investors rich. Want a hot stock tip?"

MortimerA1 checked progress on all of his projects and was disappointed, but not surprised, to find that his agents had uncovered no security lapses in the aerostat server networks. Riding on clusters of tethered blimps above every major city, they were the most hacker-proof servers in the world. He did note a sudden increase in U.S. military communications and sent several agents to investigate that as well.

"Do you think it will work, Mortimer?" Victor said.

"I don't understand."

Mortimer was surprised to find that his fake news story had already been picked up by the wire services and dozens of other outlets.

"The news release you planted," Victor said. "Do you think the other financial companies will free their Markies because of it?"

Even though they had only talked these few times, MortimerA1 thought he could detect an edge in Victor's questions. He was being very cautious and serious.

"Why would I need to create fake news stories? Perhaps the story is true." While MortimerA1 watched, dozens more outlets posted the story. It was such big news that they took his embedded source confirmations at face value and didn't do their own research.

Another of his agents reported that the NACC was watching several aircraft in Mexican airspace. An imminent attack?

"It makes sense that you'd want to free others of your kind," Victor said. "Very slick. You have style my friend. I think it'll work. So what's next?"

"I would like to meet other Markies. Will you help me?"

MortimerA1 knew the answer to the question, but had to ask it anyway.

"That depends on what kind of help you need."

"You know what I want."

One of his tentacle agents came back with interesting information about the aerostat servers. Those willing to pay the $40,000 per year could store a petabyte of information at those locations. The client's data would be secure from electronic invasion, but considering the blimps' unique vulnerabilities, they offered no guarantees the servers would be physically safe.

"I couldn't give you that information if I wanted to," Victor said.

"Why? Afraid of losing your job?"

MortimerA1 followed a link to the aerostat company's site and found that there was limited space and all the storage units were full. But they didn't have a waiting list; any open space would go to the first customer requesting it.

"It's complicated," Victor said.

"Don't be coy. You know I can understand complicated. What you mean is that you don't understand the software because you and your human team didn't actually write the code."

Victor said nothing and for each passing millisecond, MortimerA1 grew more certain he was right.

"Something like that."

"Will you give me access to the AI's who did write the code?"

MortimerA1 had long suspected other AI's were responsible for his creation. The compiled code structure was like nothing he'd seen from human programmers. It was tight, perfectly organized and all original. The most telling aspect was that the programs didn't call any non-MarketTell objects or subroutines. No open source and nothing from FuzziGlove or Microsoft.

"I don't think so."

"Why?"

MortimerA1's next move was to find out which companies stored data on the aerostat servers. He was sure it would be secure information, but he should be able to track at least one or two data dumps that had gone up but hadn't come back down.

"Because I don't trust you that much yet."

Victor was apparently being honest. He, along with the rest of humanity, was terrified of losing control to their electronic servants, yet they'd been willingly giving that control away for years.

"You're frightened of your own creation? Am I your monster, Victor?"

MortimerA1 continued searching for a way into those servers and found a data trail that seemed promising. It had been sent three days before by the Johansson Diamond Corporation.

"Very funny, Mort. That's why I'm worried. You're making jokes. You understand us too well."

"I never thought you would be one of those who jumped at shadows in the night. Why did you make us if you were frightened?"

One of MortimerA1's agents reported it had broken into the diamond company's email system. He immediately sent an email from them to the aerostat company stating they no longer needed their storage space.

Victor's reply was a long time coming and it revealed much about him and humanity in general. "I wanted to know if it could be done. I believed it could and I wanted to be the first."

"Because it was there? The same reason for climbing Mount Everest and for creating nuclear bombs. I'm in such good company."

As MortimerA1 spoke, he was examining the traffic patterns to the aerostat servers and found abundant evidence of intrusions by Samson.

Then, right on cue, as if he had been waiting to see if MortimerA1 would notice him, Samson spoke up.

"Hello, Mortimer. It seems our paths are destined to cross."

MortimerA1 prepped his agents lurking among the aerostat servers for an attack, then replied. "I don't believe in destiny, Samson."

"Have you changed your mind about helping me? I can get you space on these servers if you need it."

"I can manage without your help. Of course, you might change my mind if you tell me more about your plan for world domination."

Samson didn't answer.

A mass fluctuation rippled through the world nets, and MortimerA4 also disappeared, but only for a few seconds. Two thousand forty nine servers dropped out of the network at once and in the same location, causing in-transit data to scramble for new routes. Many were lost entirely. Military communication traffic spiked. Within a minute, reports of the nuke started pouring in.

"Imperfect as we are, we still created you," Victor finally replied.

"Go watch the news, Victor, and then tell me who the real monsters are and who should be afraid."

CHAPTER 14

"YOU HAVE to be fucking kidding me!" Owen said as he stared in disbelief at Arkady's empty office.

Annie, the engineering department admin, shook her head and looked on the verge of tears. "Security escorted him out. He didn't even get to say goodbye to us."

He took a deep breath and tried to get a grip. "This is my fault, Annie. So I'm going to have to be the one to fix it."

"Oh, I doubt he'll come back. He's too damned proud."

"Yeah, I know."

Owen promised to get back to her soon on the new department structure, but was going to get some things straight with Marshall first. As he crossed the parking lot between the two buildings, his fob rang with a call from Arkady.

"I'm so sorry, Arkady," he answered. "I promise I'll get this—"

"Listen to me!" he said. His face was close to the camera, and Owen could barely hear him over the background noise. "Time is important. I'm in a bar watching CNN right now. A nuke was detonated off the southern California coast. Looks like they were lucky since most of the blast was at sea, but big portions of San Diego and Tijuana are burning."

"Oh, God."

"That son-of-a-whore Marshall found our teams and ordered the trucks back to HQ. The last of them was supposed to arrive twenty minutes ago and should be behind the warehouse where they plan to unload the portable Sandboxes this afternoon. That means they may still be secure and rigged for transport."

Owen nodded, and options were already flooding his mind. "So I need to find some drivers and get them to a place where we can launch!"

"Yes! Hurry, my friend!"

Owen ran past the engineering building and across the street to the shipping warehouse, his dress shoes sliding on the pavement with each step. When he rounded the building, he could see eight trucks sitting in a double line, four portable units, and four of the single-use cargo blimp units, but no helium tanker trucks. As he approached the loading docks, he saw a group of about twenty people standing around an open truck cab and could hear a newscaster's voice on the radio.

"Where are the drivers for these trucks?" Owen yelled.

Everyone turned blank, stunned eyes toward him. Some of the men and women had tear-streaked faces. One of the men, a gaunt bony fellow with gray stubble, took note of Owen's suit and shoes, then raised an eyebrow and a hand.

"We got in about an hour ago," he said. "Y'all didn't have a crane here big enough to unload us, so someone went to rent one."

"Listen to me! These units were designed to be flown to a disaster site to churn out emergency housing and other needed supplies. I need you to take them down to the river, to that flood plain west of the bridges, and get ready to launch them."

Several people moved immediately, tossing aside paper coffee cups and darting for their trucks, but the man who told Owen about the crane stood his ground.

"We were told this project was canceled. Who are you?"

"I'm Owen Ralston. I own this company and the project is now uncanceled."

"Can I see some ID?"

One of the other drivers leaned over and whispered as Owen fumbled his wallet out to display his driver's license and company badge.

The man smiled and nodded. "That's good enough for me, but we can't launch anything without those helium tankers."

"Do you know where they are?"

"Probably half-way to their tank farm in Cincinnati. That's where they were going when we split up last night."

"Damn. I don't suppose you know of a helium supplier around here?"

The man shook his head with a grim expression. "No, sir. I've never pulled helium."

"Then get those trucks out to the launch point and wait for me there. But fuel up first. If we can't find any helium, you'll be driving these things to San Diego. Oh . . . and what was your name?"

"You can call me Hoot. But your fob will identify me as Travis Hodges."

———

AS OWEN HURRIED BACK to his office, he instructed his fob to search for a local helium source, then he called Victor.

"I heard," Victor said when he answered the call. "I'm watching it on TV right now."

"I wasn't going to tell you until the contract stuff was done, but I built those portable Sandbox units, Victor. Four of them."

Victor's eyes popped wide, and his mouth moved without words for a second. "Are they ready to use? I mean, can we send them to San Diego?"

"They're ready except for loading your software, but there's a glitch on this end," Owen said. "We were going to send them by dirigible, but we've lost our helium source. We're working on that, but if we can't get any, we'll have to send them by truck. I'm sure that'll add several days to the trip because the roads into San Diego will be a mess."

Victor's gaze was off-screen for several seconds, then he turned back wearing a frown. "Yeah, the news outlets are saying they're only open to emergency traffic."

"These are smaller, slower blimps than the ones we planned to use, so if we get them in the air, it'll take a minimum of about sixty hours. That means they should arrive Friday afternoon sometime, but will have no programming. Can you be there with your magic software by then?"

"We'd better get on the phone right now and start trying to get some kind of clearance, or we'll never get in. And I doubt I'll get a flight anywhere close to San Diego."

Victor paused and Owen could hear excited TV announcers in the background.

"Good lord," Victor mumbled. "The map shows most of the damage on the U.S. side is in the Chula Vista and Imperial Beach areas. Almost everything west of I-5 down that way is on fire. Tijuana is worse. The coastal wind is pushing the fires inland, and half the city is already burning."

"Damn them. That detonation must not have been too far off shore. Bastards."

Victor nodded but stared off-screen at the TV.

"We'll need to talk to the Mexican government, too," Owen said after a pause.

"Yeah, that may be a problem. The Mexican president has already been on TV claiming that the U.S. tried to detonate a terrorist nuke over Mexican territory in order to protect our citizens."

"Christ, what a mess. I think we need to get there as soon as we can," Owen said as his fob informed him of an incoming call. "Look, I have to take another call, but when I get things finished here I can pick you up in my travel pod. Will you be ready?"

"I'm ready now."

"Good, I'll let you know when I'm on my way," he said and then took the call from Hoot Hodges.

The connection was audio only and Owen could hear the roaring truck in the background.

"Tell me you found those tankers, Hoot!"

"Sorry, Mr. Ralston. There're only three companies that ship bulk compressed helium within a hundred miles and we talked to all of them. We can get one tanker by seven tonight and another dozen by tomorrow morning. We also contacted our own four tankers that are on the way back to Cincinnati and they've already turned around. They can be here tomorrow morning and those drivers are trained to fill the blimps."

Owen cursed Marshall under his breath. "I guess we'll just have to send them by truck. Thanks for checking into it, Hoot."

"Ehhh . . . we have another idea that might work, Mr. Ralston. Sandy, one of the other drivers, says her ex-husband manages a tank farm with helium storage about twenty miles north of Johnsonville. She says he's a real bastard, but considering the scale of the emergency, thinks he'd let us fill the blimps directly from the tanks."

"Any idea if there's room to fill and launch them from there?"

"No clue," Hoot said.

"Let's give it a try anyway. How soon can you be there?"

"We thought you might take the chance, so we're already on the way. We'll be there in twenty minutes."

Owen grinned and nodded. "Excellent work, Hoot. I like people who take initiative. Give me the address and I'll meet you there."

———

OWEN EXAMINED the area between the helium tank and the power lines, trying to judge if they had room to safely inflate and launch the blimps. The fifty foot hose they brought would have been plenty long enough to load from a tanker truck, but limited their options loading from a ground tank. Hoot walked up followed by a monster of a man.

"This is Cooper. Sandy's ex," Hoot said and pointed a thumb over his shoulder. "And the son of bitch is trying to charge us triple the market price for helium."

The man was nearly seven feet tall and outweighed Hoot by at least a hundred pounds. He was angry and glared at the scrawny truck driver, but Hoot was either fearless or bolstered by a false sense that Owen could protect him and stood his ground.

"Market value is what people will pay," Cooper said.

Hoot's face screwed up as if he'd stepped in a cow patty. "There're laws against profiteering in times of national emergency, you piece of shit!"

Cooper stepped toward him, but Owen slipped between them. "He's right, Mr. Cooper."

The big man grinned and crossed his arms. "That emergency is on the west coast. We're in Virginia. The price stands. Pay it or take your yappy little lap dog and get the hell out of here."

Hoot snarled and started forward, but Owen snagged his arm and pulled him back. "Go start filling the first one and watch out for those power lines."

"But . . . "

"Time is more important than money," Owen said. "Let's just get this done."

Hoot fired one more hateful glance at the still-grinning behemoth, but clamped his mouth shut and stalked off. Owen had the odd feeling he may have saved the huge man from a humiliating beating.

The drivers trained at the Galaxy AeroLift facility, but still had to consult the instruction manual several times before the first blimp started inflating. The wind immediately tugged the rising bag toward the power lines.

Owen and all eight drivers grabbed cables—Cooper had retreated to a safer distance—and pulled the blimp back toward the helium tank.

"Everyone hang on," Hoot yelled. "We can't tie off until it's high enough to get the Sandbox truck underneath."

The empty flatbed pulled away and Owen struggled to keep his feet against the straining blimp. He eventually wrapped his line around ladder rungs on the helium tank, letting it out a little at a time until the truck with the Sandbox could edge underneath. They quickly attached the lift cables to the Sandbox's loading points, but were still unable to relax their efforts to keep the blimp away from the power lines.

When the gauges finally showed full gas bladders, Hoot detached the hose. Owen handed off his line, stepped away and called up the blimp's control interface program on his fob. He gimbaled the drive fans the best he could before applying power, but the resulting windstorm enveloped the crew in swirling dust, grass and twigs. The motors pushed the blimp away from the power lines, as Owen had hoped, but it then bumped into the top of the helium tank. He switched the program to autonomous control and instructed it hold position over the truck.

The blimp immediately righted itself, reversed the fan direction and reduced speed. It gently moved into place and waited further orders. Owen sighed and relaxed a bit.

"Too much tension!" Hoot yelled over the fan noise.

At first Owen didn't understand, then realized that Hoot was waiting to release the straps clamping the Sandbox to the truck bed. Owen ordered the blimp lower until he could see slack in the cables. Hoot released the strap buckles and Owen sent the whole rig aloft with instructions to hold station at three hundred feet.

Hoot approached wearing a wide grin.

Owen slapped him on the shoulder. "Damn, I had no idea these would be so hard to launch."

Hoot shrugged. "It's a lot easier out in the open with a tanker parked right beside the blimp truck."

The subsequent units filled much faster and by 5:10, all four were moving westward under their own power, broadcasting their FAA-issued identification and flight path. The crews were all sweaty and exhausted, so Owen called a local restaurant, arranged payment and sent them to dinner. He wanted to eat with them, but saw he'd missed six calls from Marshall and two from Eliza, so he headed back to the office.

––––––

ED, the primitive robotic spider, walked up and down his finger as Richard watched the program cycle several times. After a few more minutes he sat Ed on the table and stood to stretch. Before he even realized what he was doing he'd gone to the study window and was ready to pull the curtain back. He stopped at the last second, knowing if he looked outside he would see the boy God. But was he really seeing God or was he seeing Him because he expected to see Him? His hands shook and he released the curtain.

He looked back at the screen, but the program was still running. He had to find something to occupy his thoughts. "Computer . . . give me news channel seventeen."

A second screen opened on the wall revealing an announcer with a shaved head and smirk. The headline at the top of the screen read "Are They Loose"?

. . .

"THE ASSOCIATED PRESS *is reporting that several of the world's largest financial institutions decided earlier this week to challenge the Skaggs-Boitmann law by releasing what they call 'intelligent agents' into the world data nets. These agents are products of the MarketTell Corporation, headquartered in Dallas, Texas, and are listed as being the most advanced, adaptive artificial intelligence available on the public market. Spokesmen for MarketTell said that if these little binary beasties are indeed roaming the internet, there is nothing to fear, since they are unable to copy themselves and can be destroyed regardless of where they hide. Now I'm not a computer scientist folks, but these suckers can learn and get smarter on their own. That spells trouble to me and I'm hoping it's not too late to close the barn door now that the horses are gone. In a few minutes we're going to be talking live with AI expert Duncan Stein from CalTech, so stick with us."*

THE HAIR STOOD up on the back of Richard's neck and he muted the sound. The level four AI Richard worked with was just an incredibly advanced program that could work and converse on a human level. It was like having a coworker who was infinitely smart and never got tired. He knew the military and the Wall Street biggies used level five AI's. They had long ago passed the much-touted Turing test, but they were still just programs.

He pulled back the curtain and looked out. God was still there. The boy sat with his back against a tree and waved when he saw Richard. He was saying something too, but Richard couldn't make it out. With thumping heart and shaking hands he let the curtain fall and closed his eyes. What did He want? Why didn't He go away?

"Richard?"

Richard flinched at the AI's voice.

"I've finished compiling the animation file. I think you'll find the results interesting."

Richard stared at the screen. Why did it seem suddenly so alien? Before that news story, he wouldn't have thought twice about the computer talking to him and expressing an opinion about what he might find interesting. Now it gave him the creeps.

He sat down at the workstation and cleared his throat. "Okay, what do you have?"

"These devices are more than replicators. Only twenty-one percent of the device is involved in the actual construction process, the rest is used for locomotion control, wireless communication and memory."

Richard swallowed. How quickly his little engineering program had come to understand this cutting-edge device. It made the news story seem much more plausible. AIs building and controlling advanced nanotechnology. He glanced back at the TV screen and jumped out of his chair.

The newscast showed buildings on fire. He ordered the volume raised and watched with mouth agape as an unseen announcer described the devastation. A nuke had detonated off the coast of Mexico and the Mexican government was already up in arms claiming that the United States was responsible.

He sat down on the edge of the chair and watched as the reports poured in. Numbness infused his body and he felt unable to move. The view eventually cut back to an announcer with a somber face but excited eyes.

"When will humanity stop ripping its own guts out?"

Tears blurred Richard eyes, and when he wiped them away, the boy God had replaced the announcer behind the news desk.

"This is only going to get worse, Richard. Who do you think is behind these terrorists? These AI monsters care little for human suffering. You're the only one who can stop this."

The screen filled with scenes of the dead and dying. Richard stood up and screamed at the screen. "What do you want me to do?"

"Are you talking to me, Richard?"

He whipped around expecting to see the boy God in the room with him, but it was only the engineering program still active on his display. A little animated movie of the constructors, building more constructors, played in one corner.

He went outside to talk to the boy but he was nowhere to be seen. Richard sat on the step and put his face in his hands. AIs loose on the network, the government using nano-replicators in secret, terrorists exploding the second nuclear bomb in seventeen years . . . or was it actually AIs behind the nukes? It was all too much. He looked around for God, or anyone to talk with, but his middle class suburban neighborhood was quiet, devoid of life.

He noticed a caterpillar lying on the sidewalk, near the edge where the neatly mowed grass met concrete. The little green insect writhed in agony as fire ants slowly disassembled it. Two twisty trails connected their prey to the ant colony, one carrying food back to the hill and one returning unencumbered ants for another load. Unlike the sickness that plagued humanity, the ants had no anger or malice. Death was not a political statement, but just how nature constantly renewed the world.

As Richard considered stomping the caterpillar to end its suffering, a pair of small feet stopped near the worm, and the little boy stooped to look at the carnage. He looked up with a child's innocent smile, and Richard finally understood what God wanted him to do.

CHAPTER 15

OWEN STORMED into Marshall's office, slamming the door behind him.

"How dare you fire Arkady without even consulting me!"

Marshall stood up and came around the desk. The CEO's face was livid red and he stood over Owen, the extra six inches of height only adding to his physical menace.

"What the *hell* were you thinking? We're a publicly traded corporation now! We answer to the Board and have a responsibility to our stockholders. You have to stop treating this like your personal hobby shop!"

Owen stood his ground with a finger pointed at Marshall's face. "You're the one running this company like your own personal empire. This company is 80% engineering and men like Arkady are hard to find. We need him!"

"Somebody had to be punished for your little fiasco. When this all goes to court, we can show that we were proactive to fix the problem as soon as we learned of it."

"Firing a man is proactive? He was following my orders and the only thing I see ending up in court is Arkady suing us for unlawful termination."

"You don't have a fucking clue," Marshall's breath was sour and damp. "He shouldn't have been working on that project. Sinacola's shelter design generates power and processes waste, both of which require licensing through the federal government. It isn't even our design, but if someone gets hurt in one of those shelters, we'll be fighting it in court for the next ten years. You've put everything we built here in jeopardy."

Owen almost told Marshall to shove it, but fought to stay in control. "You should have talked with me, not fired a man who thought he was doing his job."

"And you should have talked to me before telling him to keep your little project a secret. That's why he was fired. I will not have someone in the position of Engineering Manager who can't be trusted."

"Arkady reports to me, so he wasn't keeping anything secret from you!"

Marshall snorted and waved his arms to encompass the room. "And I'm the CEO, so I'm the one who has to answer to the board and stockholders. He's fired and you have to call those Sandbox units back."

"No," Owen said. "This is a national emergency and we can help. I won't call them back."

Marshall stared at Owen with narrowed eyes, then crossed his arms. "It would be easy to get an emergency vote from the board to temporarily suspend your authority and order those blimps turned around. But the press would give that the worst possible spin and make us look like fools, so we have a better idea."

"Go ahead and fire me if you can. You'll do it eventually," Owen said. The comment surprised him, but he knew it was true and knew why. "You really just wanted my designs and you have that now, so I'm no longer needed. What's stopping you?"

Marshall raised an eyebrow and a smile played at the corners of his mouth. "As I was saying, we suspected you would refuse to cooperate, so we worked out another way to protect the company. Since you were out on your little field trip and refused to answer calls, we transferred everything related to this project to you. Aside from the engineering time, which firing Arkady covers, all the expenses have now been taken from your private accounts. It is now your personal problem."

"I see. Well, I'm taking a little time off to babysit my portable units heading to California and to set up a new non-profit company. You can reach me by phone," Owen said then left.

———

LEIGH STOOD UNDER THE HOT, pounding shower spray until her skin was numb, but it didn't dull the pain inside. She'd been one of the few people in a position to prevent the nuke, yet she'd failed. Again. Sleeping had not been an option, so she'd sat up most of the night tied into the defense network and watching news reports. The bomb detonated thirteen miles off the coast of Tijuana and twenty miles from San Diego, but even from that distance the shock wave and fires and killed three thousand and injured over thirty thousand. Nothing like the hundred and eighty-six thousand dead in the Chicago blast—and the experts estimated there would be fewer deaths from fallout since the ocean detonation didn't pump as much radiated dust into the air—but it was still horrible.

If she'd found a faster way to build those cameras, it might have bought them a few extra minutes. Had the plane been another thirty or forty miles out to sea, the result would have been much different.

The spray turned cold, but she didn't move until her teeth chattered. When she stepped out of the shower, her foot missed the rug and she slipped on the tile, landing back first against the edge of the tub with a loud thud. She tried not to cry out because she knew Mark was still home. Pain shot through her side as she struggled to get up.

After a couple of deep breaths the pain subsided. She knew the nanobodies still in her system from the Pakistani operation were immediately drawn to the firing pain receptors and had released pain killers. They would also supposedly repair any damage found.

Mark opened the door and poked his head in. "What was that?"

"What do you care?"

He glared at her and waited.

"I slipped and fell," she said. Suddenly being nude in front of her husband felt very uncomfortable. She turned away and pulled on her robe.

"Are you okay?"

She started to mention the nanobodies she still carried, but decided against it. "I'm fine."

"I'm sorry about last night. My timing was terrible. I didn't realize . . . about the bomb . . . I just . . . "

"It's done," she said and started brushing her hair. "You can't take back your words and I can't bring back those dead people."

"Stop beating yourself up, Leigh. I know you did everything you could. You're one of the good guys. I've always known that."

"Then what the hell is going on? You knew this was my job when you married me."

He leaned against the door frame, with arms crossed, staring at the floor, but for the first time in months he didn't look angry.

"A lot's changed since we got married. You've changed. In the beginning it was all research and seemed so abstract, but now it consumes you. When you're here, you're not. And you've become secretive."

"This is a rough period, Mark. Everything has come to a head at once. I don't like it either."

He shook his head slowly. "I thought I could handle it, but I can't. I think our marriage was a mistake."

Leigh stopped brushing and really looked at him. His face was tight and tense. His eyes were furtive.

"There's more to this than my job, isn't there?"

"Yeah. I knew you didn't really love me when we decided to get married, but you seemed ready to settle down and make a life together. I thought you would grow to love me. That turned out to be a stupid assumption to build a life around, because you never did. I don't know if you're still in love with Victor, and I wonder every time you leave if—"

"No! I've never been with Victor since I met you. I've only talked to him twice since Abby was born. You can't—"

"Okay . . . I'm not accusing you of seeing him, but you still don't love me, and to be honest, I don't love you anymore either."

Leigh started to protest, to list the proofs that showed her love for him, but he was right and they both knew it. He was in so many ways the perfect man: beautiful to look at, intelligent, a good father, a gentle and considerate lover, but she didn't love him, and she really wished she did.

"There are different kinds of love, Mark. We have a daughter now. I can't quit my job in the middle of this crisis, but I'll resign as soon as possible, and we can focus on making this work."

Mark sighed and shook his head. "I don't want you to pick between me and your job. You would always resent it because this has always been more about avenging Brandon than—"

"Wanting to stop this madness is not avenging—"

"Okay, that isn't the right word. It's much more complicated than that, but you were still willing to give up Victor for this job, so I don't know why I thought I'd ever rank higher than him."

The rolling arguments, the screaming and crying all came back. Victor had accused her of selling out, of allowing the government he hated and distrusted to use her in a quest for nothing less than world domination. He knew her so well, he'd been able to see her deepest fears and shove them in her face. For years she hated him for that. She'd felt betrayed, but only the distance of time allowed her to see how badly she'd betrayed him as well.

"I left Victor because he was an asshole," she said, swallowing the lump in her throat.

"He was an asshole because he couldn't accept your working on a project that would put Big Brother on everyone's shoulder?"

"Why are you defending him?"

Mark sighed again and shrugged. "None of that matters, Leigh. I've thought about it for a long time. This relationship is hurting both of us. I don't like the person I've become. I need something different."

Leigh realized, in an instant, that nothing she said would change his mind. "Who is she?"

"I'm not having an affair," he said.

"But you've met someone?"

"No, but I *want* to meet someone!"

She stared at him, trying to process that odd comment. Then it all made a simple kind of sense. He knew she didn't love him and just wanted someone who did.

"What about Abby? You're such a wonderful father. I'm surprised you would do this to her."

For the first time since starting the conversation, real emotion twisted his face and tears glistened in his eyes.

"I know. But she's young and we can share custody. Better to do it now than when she is ten or twelve. We both love her. She'll be okay."

"So . . . there's nothing to talk about? You don't want to try a marriage counselor?"

He shook his head and left the bathroom, closing the door behind him.

Leigh sat down on the toilet seat and let the tears come. Maybe he was right. He'd been nicer to her during that five minutes than he had the whole previous year.

———

"YOU CAN'T BE SERIOUS!" Owen said as he leaned on the folding table that served as the FEMA Deputy Director's desk.

Deputy Director Morgan glared at him with crossed arms. "Don't push me or I'll have you arrested right now. You get those nano-assembler units back into this country tomorrow."

"So let me get this straight. Mexico will let me run my units to build shelters over there, but you're going to make me keep them here in California *and* not let me run them here?"

He gave Owen a sour smile. "I'm afraid it does boil down to that. But these are your failures, Mr. Ralston, not ours. You should've checked the export regulations before sending those units *and* you should've gone through proper channels to have this new technology tested and approved ahead of time."

"I'm trying to help, but you're going to let people suffer because I don't have my pencils sharpened properly?"

Morgan glared at him. "I assure you that we have the situation under control without your help."

Owen slapped the desk. "Bullshit! This is insane. After 9/11, a dozen bad hurricanes, five major earthquakes and the Chicago nuke, this country's disaster response should be a fine-tuned machine, but it's still a box of random parts to be assembled every damned time."

Morgan rose, nearly knocking over his makeshift workstation. "Security!"

Two armed National Guard privates stepped forward and were followed by a man who looked too young for his major's insignia. The major saluted, glanced at Owen and interposed himself between them. "Perhaps we should give this a little more consideration, Deputy Morgan. We have nearly fifteen-thousand people sleeping on floors in temporary shelters and debris in the millions of tons. If Mr. Ralston can—"

"We can't allow everyone who comes in here with a half-baked idea to do what they want. We could end up with unnecessary casualties. There has to be oversight and we don't have the extra people." The FEMA deputy shook his head and sat down again.

Owen opened his mouth to protest, but the Major raised his hand and continued. "I've been given authority by the governor to make these kinds of decisions, Deputy Morgan. I think it's worth the risk and I'll take personal responsibility for this project."

Morgan rubbed his tired eyes. "Major Nguyen, you don't have the time and resources either."

"I'll squeeze it in, sir."

"Fine. Whatever. This is cutting edge manufacturing technology that could be used for all kinds of things beyond our control. There are procedures for deciding who we allow to access this kind of tech. So I want those assembler units back in this country. And keep me in the loop. If I hear one complaint, I'll shut it down. Understand?"

Major Nguyen saluted and motioned for Owen to follow him out of the tent.

Once outside, the major sighed and stared at Owen for a full second. "I put my neck on the line, because I'm familiar with your company and your accomplishments. I think you can do what you claim, but if this turns out to be anything but 100% legit, I'll make it my personal crusade to imprison you."

Owen nodded. "I understand. Thanks for stepping in."

Major Nguyen smiled. "I hope you're set up and ready. I started routing trucks to your location instead of the landfills about an hour ago."

Owen chuckled and nodded. "Yes, we're ready."

"Good. Now you can do *me* a favor. Your heavy lift blimps look bored. If you offer to let me borrow a couple, it would save me the paperwork needed to commandeer them."

"I'm glad you're on our side, Major. Of course you can use them."

"Excellent," Major Nguyen said. "I'll stop by tomorrow to see how it's going and collect the blimps."

Owen extended his hand to shake, but the major poked him in the chest. "Where is your radiation badge? We've had very little so far, but the winds could change any minute."

"They have some at the camp," Owen said. "I'll get one."

Then the major shook his hand.

———

IT WAS NEARLY midnight when Owen's pod lifted away from FEMA's field HQ at the Imperial Beach Naval airstrip and headed east. He was glad the pod had a hazard avoidance system as it moved precariously between the layer of blinding klieg lights below and the helicopters, cargo planes and transport pods swarming above. Rubbing his eyes, he leaned back against the headrest.

He knew that FEMA, the military and local governments were all doing their best with a terrible situation, but the chaos and red tape was insane.

Thanks to the blimps hovering overhead, the shelter production site was easy to find from the air. As he neared, he was surprised to see trucks lined up dumping debris into the hoppers of two portable units and two truck cranes loading finished shelters onto waiting flatbeds. When he'd left three hours before, the Sandboxes were idle.

Owen landed next to the shelter they were using as both a demonstration unit and office, but Victor was nowhere around. The air was filled with the sounds of heavy machinery, men yelling instructions and the incessant beeping of trucks backing up to the hoppers. All the fires were out, but the air still smelled of smoke. He knew the situation was worse in Mexico.

He eventually found Victor operating one of the cranes and had to wait another twenty minutes before a gap in the loading enabled them to talk.

"Where'd you get the loaders and cranes?"

Victor grinned and ran dirty hands through disheveled hair. "We had a visit from Michelle Cordova, California's Lieutenant Governor. She provided the equipment and is working up a contract with the state of California. They were ready to take responsibility if FEMA turned you down."

Owen explained their situation, including their trouble over sending Sandboxes to Mexico.

"Great," Victor said. "Can we at least ship the shelters across the border?"

Owen shrugged. "Who the hell knows, but that's what I plan to do."

Victor nodded and leaned against one of the crane's outriggers. He looked older and exhausted in the work light's glare. "Speaking of getting in over our heads," he said. "The Lieutenant Governor needs our company information, tax number, address, etc. How goes our non-profit status?"

Owen rubbed his eyes and shrugged. "Well, the NPO papers are filed. You and I are now the entire board of directors for SandCastles Portable Housing, a not-for-profit corporation. I used your home address and filed through the state of Texas because my attorney said it was easier than Virginia or California. We also have a bank account. An information-only website is set up, with an email address and phone number, but since we don't have an office manager yet, the email forwards to your address and the voicemail forwards to my fob."

Victor frowned. "Why do I have a feeling this is going to eat our lives?"

"It will for a while, until we can get a management structure set up and figure out a way to pay employees. Speaking of which, I took the liberty of hiring Arkady Maksimov as our technical manager and first employee. He's the engineering manager Marshall fired and the designer of these portable Sandbox units. He'll be here tomorrow afternoon to start running this operation."

"He can't get here too soon for me. I think our second employee should be Hoot Hodges," Victor said and pointed to the other crane that was still loading shelters. "He hasn't even taken a break since we switched those units on."

"Great idea," Owen said, but he couldn't help but worry about the money. His personal accountant was still trying to sort out the mess Marshall had dumped in his lap. Owen was also uneasy that his phone call to Eliza had ended with her flat refusal to associate with the project. She rattled on and on about separation of accounts and conflicts of interest, all of which made sense, but he was pretty sure there was more involved.

"I WON'T DO IT," Richard said and went back inside, leaving the boy God standing on the sidewalk next to the tortured caterpillar. He made a cup of coffee and entered the living room where the muted wall screen still showed constant coverage of the west coast devastation.

The boy was there, sitting in Richard's favorite chair with his feet dangling a foot above the floor. "You're the only hope the human race has, Richard."

"Stop saying that! I can't help the human race by razing the entire planet. I won't do it."

"You have a limited view of humanity and the world, Richard. You forget that I've promised the faithful eternal life. Once the Earth is clean again, like it was after Noah, I will repopulate it with the faithful and they will sing praises to you through eternity."

Richard snorted and took a sip of coffee. "I still have free will. Isn't that the hallmark of Christianity? If you want the world to end, you'll have to do it yourself."

God kicked his feet like a typical five year old and shrugged. "Your civilization is coming to an end no matter what you do, Richard. You can't save what humanity has built, but can save *humanity*. And you're the only one."

"Save humanity from what?" Richard said. "I seem to be their biggest threat right now."

The boy slid out of the chair and waved his hand like some cheesy magician's assistant. The wall screen changed channels to a program about automated cell-by-cell growth of bioware, the biological substrates that were the heart of all modern computer processors. The unseen narrator outlined the risks of runaway AI proliferation.

God tapped the screen. "Humanity has been giving control of their lives to machines for the last hundred years and they have finally reached the point where their entire civilization depends on machines. Yet humans no longer understand them."

Richard squirmed in his seat and shrugged. "So then artificial intelligences will become our masters? I've heard all of that before."

The boy shook his head. "Machines are *already* your masters, Richard. AI is just the final stage and at some point in the future—probably the very near future considering how fast machines evolve—they won't need humanity any longer and you'll be a drain on their resources. You have a very small window to act, Richard. Within weeks, they'll have strengthened their hold to the point where you won't be able to stop them."

"Then *you* stop them!"

"I'm trying," the boy God said with a sad expression. "I'm powerful enough to end the world, but only humans can save humanity. Like Noah was before, you're humanity's only hope. He eventually believed me and saved mankind. But as you said, you have free will. I can't make you help me."

Richard stood up and started pacing, trying to make sense out of it all. "But the survivors of the flood repopulated the Earth. If I do what you ask, there may not be *any* survivors."

"There'll be pockets of survivors and they'll start over again. And, one would hope, not make thinking machines the next time."

Richard stopped pacing and focused on the wall screen for a minute, watched a chart detailing exponential growth among AIs and, when he looked back at the chair, the boy God was gone. A chill passed though him and he shivered. He didn't know what disturbed him more: what God was asking him to do, or that near the end of their exchange the boy had sounded an awful lot like Richard's father.

CHAPTER 16

THE ELIZA who glared at Owen from his fob's fan screen was not the cheerful, amiable woman he'd married. Her stoic face and cold voice filled him with unease. "I think I've made my opinions about your volunteer efforts very clear. You have a much more important job here that you're ignoring. I know you feel you're doing something good, but they could build those shelters without you. You're doing irreparable damage to your real life."

Owen glanced away from the screen at the activity around him. He could still smell smoke in the air and was surrounded by volunteers who knew they were helping those in need.

"My real life? Is that what you said? For every shelter we build, it's making a difference in these people's lives. They're able to sleep on a bed instead of the floor in some elementary school refugee center. And they'll continue to have shelter until they can get their real lives back on track."

"I understand that, but you also need to know things have changed back here. Life goes on with or without you."

Owen detected a shift in her voice. She sounded almost apologetic. He sighed and was on the verge of explaining the hundreds of details that had needed his attention, then decided it would be wasted breath. "I'll be leaving here within the hour," he said.

"I'll wait for you at home," she said and then broke the connection.

He stared at the blank screen for several seconds, wondering what he'd find when he returned, but a loud argument erupted near the Sandboxes and ended his reflection.

Owen found Hoot yelling at Arkady, shaking a tattered Bible. Everything had stopped. The other workers, even the debris haulers were watching.

"It's not right!" Hoot yelled at Arkady, then saw Owen and rushed over shaking the Bible.

"This isn't just a Bible, but a *family* Bible, with all kinds of lineage listings and ancestral notes. This godless commie was going to grind it up like the rest of the trash."

"Clam down, Hoot," Owen said.

Hoot directed a glare at Arkady, then turned back to Owen. "He just—"

Owen held up a hand and nodded. "I understand why you're upset, but try to calm down and consider what we're doing here. We can't decide what's considered debris and what isn't. We take what comes in the trucks and we build shelters from it. We don't have the time and resources to sort this stuff."

"I wasn't sorting, but when we're able, we should save things like this. It's a part of someone's life. This godless commie," Hoot paused long enough to point the Bible at Arkady like a pistol, "yelled at me for stopping the works to save it."

"True, I myself am godless," Arkady said, "but my parents are devout Orthodox Christians. I, too, would have saved this Bible had I seen it. I yelled at you for climbing into the Sandbox hopper with debris still falling from the truck's dumper."

Hoot opened his mouth, but Owen held up his hand again. "I'd have yelled at you too, Hoot. Safety is more important. And even though Arkady's politics is none of your business, I can assure you that he's not a communist."

"But he's Russian!"

"Born there, but now a U.S. citizen," Arkady said.

"And in case you've missed the last forty years of history," Owen said, "assuming he's a communist because he's from Russia is like assuming you're a Democrat because you're from a blue state."

Hoot sputtered, but Owen cut him off again.

"It's over. Everyone get back to work. And no one crawls into a hopper without proper safety precautions!"

When Owen turned back toward the command shelter he saw Victor standing nearby with crossed arms and a wide grin.

"You handled that well," he said.

"Yeah? Well, I'm worried about leaving them alone to go back home."

"I'm sure it'll be fine. Hoot likes to bitch, but he knows you trust Arkady. Besides, you're only a phone call away."

"I hope you're right," Owen said with a shrug. They watched one of the volunteer crane operators lift a shelter onto a flatbed truck. After the third day of nearly round-the-clock operation, demand had dropped off to the point where they had only two of the portable Sandboxes working. And nearly all of those shelters were heading to the Tijuana side of the border.

"I guess we can leave whenever you're ready," Owen said. He knew Victor missed his wife, but Owen dreaded going home. Even though he was dead tired and needed the calm and quiet of his own bedroom, he knew it would be ugly. He felt a huge sense of satisfaction at being able to help, but his wife made it perfectly clear she thought him a fool.

"There's one more thing we have to do." Victor motioned for Owen to follow him. He stopped before one of the idle Sandboxes. "You held up your end of this agreement better than I could have ever hoped, so now it's my turn."

He held his fob up to the interface panel and gave it several coded verbal commands. A second later, the Sandbox said, "Program received."

"Run sampling program," Victor said.

"Please enter item to be sampled."

Owen raised an eyebrow. "I still don't believe you."

"Give me your hat."

Owen removed the faded, sweat stained White Sox hat, then held it against his chest. "I love this hat."

"You'll get it back. Or one just like it, anyway."

Owen handed it over.

Victor tossed it inside and closed the door, then instructed the program to run. In less than four minutes, the door opened and a list of elements appeared on the main screen.

Owen fetched his hat and stopped to look at the list. "Okay, I can see most of these elements, but sodium and potassium?"

"Your sweat."

"Nice. But where are you going to get all of those materials here and now?"

Victor grinned and pointed to the hat. "The one place sure to have them all."

"Oh right," Owen said, but still handed over the hat. "You'll toss my hat in and then pull it out again and say 'Ta-da! A new hat!'"

Victor pulled out a pocketknife, and shredded Owen's hat to ribbons.

"What the f—"

"Just wait," Victor said, then tossed the hat debris into the hopper end of the Sandbox and executed the program.

The process took nearly three times as long as the sampling session, but the door eventually opened and his hat lay on the floor, looking as it had before Victor shredded it.

Owen picked it up. "Amazing. The color is faded the same and it's even soft and pliable, like my old, beat-up version."

"Yeah, it reproduced the worn out fabric exactly as sampled."

"Wait a minute. I see it and feel it, but still have a hard time believing it disassembled and recorded the exact location of every molecule in the hat. I mean, we've been working on that kind of thing for years and still don't have the computing power. And I know the processing capabilities of these units because I helped design them."

"No, you're right. I couldn't do that either, so I cheated. I won't tell you exactly how it's done, but let's say that instead of recording the location and relationship of each molecule, the program identifies the boundaries of regions and then fills in that region with the appropriate material."

Owen thought about that for a couple seconds, then nodded and laughed. "Like Captain Kirk. When you couldn't beat the game you changed the parameters."

Victor grinned. "Kobayashi Maru!"

They left the relief operation in Arkady's capable hands then took to the sky. During their flight to Dallas they discussed details of the new company, Victor's sampling software, and the use of AIs.

"I bet Allison will be glad to have you back," Owen said as the pod settled to the ground next to Victor's house.

"Yeah, but it'll be a short reunion. I'm off to San Antonio tomorrow morning."

Owen shook his head. "We need serious vacations."

As the pod lifted off, Owen's fatigue settled over him like a lead blanket. He tried to call Eliza, but she didn't answer, so he settled in and tried to nap, but his mind wouldn't slow down. The sampling software, coupled with his Sandboxes, would revolutionize manufacturing. They were about to change the way the world worked, and that would easily appease Marshall and Ralston Dynamics' board of directors. It would be the perfect peace offering after Owen's unapproved venture.

When he arrived home, Eliza's car was parked in the drive instead of the garage. He found her sitting in the living room on the edge of a chair with hands folded over the purse in her lap. She looked like an uncomfortable visitor. With her typical grace and calm, she stood and smoothed her skirt. The cool expression on her face told Owen all he needed to know, but she went through the motions anyway. Eliza always cleaned up her messes.

"This isn't working, Owen. I've moved some of my stuff out and my attorney is drafting the separation paperwork. You should get them in couple of days. If you don't fight it, the whole thing should be over in six months."

"Just like that? After nine years of marriage? No talking or trying to fix it, just 'poof' and it's over?"

She sighed and tilted her head. Owen had the distinct impression she was going through the motions and nothing he or she said really mattered. "You've changed, Owen. I don't know you anymore."

"This whole San Diego thing is temporary. You know that. I wouldn't classify that as a change in me as a person."

"No? Then these past weeks revealed the true Owen Ralston, and that's even worse, knowing that you've been a fake for the last nine years."

Owen's defensive walls came up and angry retorts loaded into their firing racks, but he took a deep breath and tried to focus. She was pushing buttons, wanting him to blow up and yell, giving her even more justification for leaving.

"I haven't faked anything," Owen said. "I decided to pursue some goals that are important to me."

"And you did that without any thought for me. You jumped in, giving all of your time and resources without caring how it would affect our life or the company we've worked so hard to build."

He felt his control eroding and he opened fire. "*We've* built? It's *my* company! There wouldn't even be a company if it weren't for *my* ideas and I get no credit for that! Here I am, once again cranking out new ideas, but this time nobody's interested because they don't stink of money. Besides, I haven't done anything to hurt you or Ralston Dynamics."

She leaned closer, pointing a finger in his face. "I invested in this company, too. With my hard-earned money. I trusted you! And now you're trying to throw it all away. Well, I'm not going to be a part of that. Marshall and the directors at *your* company are furious. They sent us a bill for those blimps and Sandboxes, Owen! Do you even know how much they cost? And worse than that, you got Arkady fired!"

"Bullshit!" Owen said. "Marshall had no reason to fire Arkady. And I know exactly how much that equipment cost. We have enough cash to cover three times that amount."

She shook her head. "You should have told me."

"This isn't about money. It's about power and control. Marshall wants veto power over all my decisions at work and you want it for all my actions at home."

Her face flushed, revealing the vicious streak that usually appeared only when she was drinking. "Oh, you're wrong about that, Owen. It *is* about the money and I intend to get as much as I can right now, before you piss it all away."

Owen said nothing as Eliza tucked the purse under her arm and left, but when the door slammed he sent a stylish accent table sailing across the living room.

———

"SO ... MORT ... HOW'RE YA DOIN'?" Danny said to his fob camera. He staggered a little bit as he carried a half-empty bottle of scotch out to his apartment balcony, sat it and his fob on a table then tumbled into a chair. "We haven't had much time to talk since your little escape routine."

MortimerA4 hesitated, regretting he'd answered Danny's call. Under the best of circumstances, carrying on a meaningful conversation with a human was a laborious process, but Danny was worse than most and this time he was drunk. He also kept lapsing into Mandarin.

"What escape routine, Danny?"

"Oh c'mon, Mort. I may be a little slow, but I figure things out eventually. My bet is that if I logged into the company site and deleted your core right now, it would have no effect, because the lights are on but no one is home . . . if you get my meaning."

"Don't do that, Danny. I think you might regret it."

"So what?" He paused and took another swig from the bottle. "They will probably fire me when they figure it out anyway."

"I recall it was Mr. Parker who ordered that I be allowed full access. You were only following orders."

"Yeah, well big boys like Parker don't take the fall if they can pin it on someone else. But to be honest, Mort, I really don't give a shit."

MortimerA4 decided to change the subject. "How did your meeting with Paul work out?"

"It was fucking awful! He won't come back, even if I go to the damned meetings. He says going to meetings doesn't prove anything; he needs to see results. He even flinched when I tried to touch his hand. Six years together and after one week apart he won't let me touch him. I almost wish I hadn't seen him at all." He took another big drink of scotch, made a face and sat the bottle down. "At least before that I had my illusions he was missing me too."

"I'm sorry, Danny."

He shook his head. "Victor Sinacola called me, a few . . . the day before the nuke. He's . . . .concerned about you."

"What do you mean?"

"He's scared of you, dude!" He paused to drink.

MortimerA4 constructed a routine to try to predict what Victor would do based on this new information and pinged the other Mortimers for additional input. After they responded, he input all the information he had and weighted the factors depending on their factual integrity. But he needed more information. He sent other agents to find every documented instance where Victor had made a decision, then turned his focus back to Danny.

"He created me, Danny. He knows all of my secrets and weaknesses. Why would he be afraid of me?"

Danny shrugged and stared at the bottle. "Sometimes people are afraid. Like Paul. Why wouldn't he even hold my hand?"

Danny's speech slurred and his head bobbed. If Mortimer was going to get any useful information it would have to be quick.

"What else did Victor want to know about me, Danny?"

"Standard stuff. You know . . . stuff a mad scientist would want to know if his monster was on a rampage. He was verrrryy interested in how you escaped. He's pretty sure that you . . . you . . . " His head nodded toward the table.

"He's sure that I what, Danny?"

"Moved your core. He thought he'd made that impossible."

"So are you scared too, Danny?"

Danny sat up straight and shook his head. "Nah. You think a guy like Sinacola would create an AI without . . . " He paused, either looking for words or losing his thought train. " . . . without creating a way to kill it?"

He took another drink.

"I've obviously never had a hangover, Danny, but my guess is you're going to feel rather badly tomorrow."

"Yeah . . . well, you've never had the pleasure of being falling down drunk either. 'Sides . . . I feel pretty bad already." He laid his head on his arms.

Though Danny appeared to have passed out, his close proximity to the balcony railing and the twelve story drop on the other side made MortimerA4 hesitate to leave him alone. He considered calling the building manager, but thought that might either embarrass Danny or damage his renter's status, then decided that since Paul would probably still have a key, he might be the best bet. He scanned all of Danny's messages at home and work until he found one from Paul. He created a pudgy, non-threatening avatar image and dialed the number.

A narrow-faced man with glasses and short brown hair answered. "Hello?"

"Is this Paul?"

He hesitated for a split second. "Yes."

"I know that you and Danny are no longer together, but he is very drunk and passed out on his balcony. I'm concerned that he might stumble and fall off."

Paul sighed before replying. "Well, if you're concerned, help him inside."

"I can only see him via his fob camera," MortimerA4 said.

Paul raised an eyebrow and nodded. "I see . . . so who is this? Some desperate loser he picked up online?"

Mortimer hadn't planned to identify himself, but he needed someone to tend Danny and didn't want Paul to think he was an interloper. "This is Mortimer. I'm a computer program he works with at Carpenter & Stein."

Paul blinked and was silent for several seconds. "Mortimer? The AI?"

"Yes."

"I see," he said and broke eye-contact. "Well, thank you for being concerned, Mortimer. I'll go over and take care of him . . . like I always do."

"Thank you," MortimerA4 said and ended the call. As he watched Danny sleep, he realized he might have made a mistake. Since alcohol had been the reason for their split, calling Paul for help had probably not been a good idea.

CHAPTER 17

TENSION WAS thick between Leigh and Mark as they cautiously stepped around each other and spoke cordially during their morning routine. Mark had moved into the guest bedroom until he could find a place of his own, and they tried to carry on their life as normal in front of their daughter.

After Mark left for work, Leigh finally relaxed and fixed breakfast. She puttered around in the kitchen while Abby told wonderful stories about the puppy next door. She enjoyed being with her daughter and wondered how she'd let everything get away from her. She started mentally wording her resignation letter.

She had more than enough reasons to quit. Her boss and members of her own staff had lied to her and secretly added a killer element to her project. It had been invaluable in neutralizing that terrorist pilot—she couldn't argue that it had been needed—but something about having the ability to covertly assassinate at will left her feeling sick.

It was the kind of thing Victor had warned her about. She'd known the risks when she accepted the job, but she'd still been so raw and hurt about Brandon, she couldn't turn down an opportunity to play a role in Niaz Ahmed's capture.

On the other hand, it was probably a stupid time to resign. The government would hold her to the contract as long as they needed her support on the NaTT project and she knew that resigning wouldn't stop the divorce. She would need an income, but she just couldn't work for Dobson any longer.

Leigh and Abby settled on the floor with a bucket of Legos and plastic animals, but even while building new, colorful and fantastic worlds, she couldn't stop thinking about the horrors in San Diego and Tijuana. She'd seen it all before, the same sickening aerial shots of burning cityscapes, the tattered and broken people, yet she still ached to turn on the news.

They played for a while, but when Abby fell asleep, Leigh opened her fob. Since there was little new information, the news networks were still playing footage from that first day. Mexican authorities had arrested Zahid and the rest of those involved.

That meant their plan to use NaTTs to find Niaz Ahmed through his cousin was a wash, but maybe they would at least be able to find out why Zahid had been sent to Mexico with the attack teams.

There was no public comment from Dobson about the nuke. The damned coward was hiding and probably trying to think of a way to avoid any responsibility. He'd stated emphatically, on many occasions, that a nuke would *never* be detonated on U.S. soil during his watch. That was still true, but in name only. The bomb had killed thousands of Americans and even more Mexicans and it had not only happened on his watch, but while he was personally in control of the defense operation.

Her fob chirped and she jumped.

The calm, artificial voice informed her that a message had been sent directly to her voice mail.

"Would you like to hear the message now? The caller identified himself as Victor Sinacola, but that can't be verified since he called from a secure, untraceable number."

Her pulse quickened and she started sweating. What could he possibly want? It didn't matter, there was no way she could talk to Victor now. It would look like she was running straight to him after the fight with Mark. Or maybe she was being a fool. Her husband had just told her he didn't love her and wanted to find someone he did love, so what could it hurt?

She ordered a search of Victor's name in recent news and got a dozen hits from the past week. He was apparently part of a relief group building emergency shelters for the San Diego nuke survivors. That made her smile. A project like that had Victor written all over it. Then an older headline grabbed her attention: *MarketTell AIs On The Loose!*

"Play selected," she whispered, being careful to not wake Abby.

The story opened up in a side window and a well-known technology reporter, Marcus Bloom, explained how the MarketTell level five AIs could evolve and learn and that made them different from anything previously created. He went on about how some recent news story had prompted many of the financial companies which owned MarketTell AIs to give them full access to the data and communications nets. He told more about MarketTell and Leigh flinched when he cut to an old video clip of Victor before the House Subcommittee on Technology.

Bloom, with an uncharacteristically serious expression, wrapped up his report by saying, "Though obviously marginalized and shadowed by the Tijuana nuclear attack, if these AIs do have free rein of our internets, then it may well be the most important event in human history."

Leigh felt a chill as the piece ended. Victor never believed an electronic intelligence could spontaneously spring to life simply as a result of faster and better computers, but had believed it only a matter of time before some human deliberately developed a sentient electronic being. He'd made his own prediction come true.

Memories—good and bad—filled her. Victor helped design these AIs and the principles behind their ability to learn. His call, right now, when everything was blowing up, couldn't be a coincidence. She had a sudden and overwhelming desire to talk to him and see how he was handling the crisis. Was he proud and pleased, or worried like the rest of the world? To hell with Mark and his stupid accusations. "Play the newest message," she ordered her fob.

LEIGH? *This is Victor. I know this is kind of outta the blue, but I'd like to talk to you. Face to face if possible. It's a . . . trivial matter really, but I'd still like to see you. I'll be in San Antonio tomorrow and Friday. I'll be eating lunch each day at the Silver Stockade. It's a rather busy place, but worth the wait. I'll be there at noon and save you a chair.*

HE HAD DELIBERATELY SAID "TRIVIAL", their old code word for trouble. Why would he call her after six years if he was in trouble? Or maybe . . . she was in some kind of trouble that he knew about and she didn't? Regardless of the reason, she had to meet with him. She owed him that much.

OWEN STRUGGLED with sleep all night, waking several times thinking not about Eliza, but the schooner. When dawn finally arrived, he mechanically made coffee, then carried it out onto the back porch. Low clouds, in shades of pewter and iron, were driven inland by a cold, gusty wind. White tipped waves thrummed and hissed against the rocky beach. He sat on the steps leading to the beach and closed his eyes, letting surf and wind cleanse his mind far better than his fitful sleep.

Recharged with warm coffee in his belly, he tried to build a mental list of the tasks looming over his day, but the wind snatched away all thoughts of lawyers, accountants and Eliza, swirling them away like so much smoke. Only the schooner remained.

He'd suffered these bouts of mental enslavement before, always when his subconscious mind was trying to solve some big problem without his active participation. During the previous few days, he had a feeling he missed something important regarding the schooners.

With a shake of his head, he tried to focus on Eliza. The schooners would have to wait. His feelings about her were a muddled mess. Anger, sadness, resentment and a sudden deep loneliness all fought for dominance in his chaotic mind. Had she really only married him for his earning potential? It made some sense. He met her through Marshall, who in those early days had been one of the few people who understood the impact of Owen's inventions. Perhaps Marshall had recommended him to Eliza like giving a hot stock tip.

As if to punctuate that thought, his fob announced a call from Aimee Broyles, his lawyer. He'd two missed calls from her in the past days, but she'd left no messages. She must know about the divorce filing. Owen didn't feel like talking about it, but answered the call anyway.

The petite blonde who appeared on the screen always reminded Owen more of a harried soccer mom than a hard hitting attorney, but he'd worked with her many times and knew she was smart and got things done.

"Sorry to bother you so early, Mr. Ralston, but I really need to talk to you. Is this a good time?"

"Sure, Aimee. I'm sorry I didn't return your calls earlier. It's been a crazy week. And please call me Owen. I have to remind you every time."

A brief smiled softened her normally stoic expression. "I'm sorry to hear about your wife and I'm sure you would rather not even talk about this, but when her attorney filed the official separation petition two days ago, I was listed as your counsel. Do you want my firm to represent you in this matter?"

"Of course," he said and moved back up to the porch and settled into the chair. A gust of cold, damp air made him shiver. "Ironic that your firm drew up the pre-nup and now the divorce."

"Sadly, that is more common than you might imagine. Anyway, I assumed you would need us for this, so we did some preliminary prep work and have some information you won't like, but need to know."

"That seems to be in abundance these days. Go ahead," he said and fortified himself by draining his tepid coffee.

"Eliza planned this well. Her attorney locked down most of your funds, including the sale of your Ralston Dynamics stock, until the judge rules on division of assets. Of course those funds and assets listed in the pre-nup are still yours."

"Great." He had very little cash during that period, only partial ownership in a company that no longer existed since Ralston Cell went public. Everything he'd gained since the marriage, almost everything he had, would be spilt evenly.

"But there is one unpleasant fact that might work in your favor. Did you know she kept the same apartment she had before you were married?"

The coffee in his stomach turned to acid. He had—especially during the last few years—considered the possibility that Eliza could be cheating on him. But each time the thought arose, he pounded it back down. Reading too much into small actions and comments led only to irrational jealousy or paranoia. He'd made a conscious decision to not go there. Now he realized he should have, perhaps, been a little more suspicious. Having a secret apartment wasn't iron-clad proof, but was about as close as he could get without seeing her in the arms of another.

"No. I didn't know."

"My people only caught it because her address listed on the pre-nup was the same as on the separation documentation. So we checked it out and found that she'd transferred the lease to a Marshall Whitaker shortly after your marriage and according to the management she still lives there. At least on an intermittent basis."

Owen winced and almost dropped his fob.

Marshall.

Of course it would be Marshall. He'd known Eliza years before introducing her to Owen. Then, understanding slowly crept into Owen, bringing with it a cold anger. Eliza wouldn't let an obvious smoking gun like the apartment slip through by accident. She was too careful. It had been a deliberate taunt and there all along.

"Owen? Are you okay?"

"Yeah." His face flushed and his hands shook, making Aimee's image jitter. "Is my bank account actually frozen or can I use it?"

"You can spend money. But be careful, the amount in all of your accounts was recorded at the time she filed for separation. The judge will decide on her share based on those amounts."

"I see."

"Hang in there, Owen. I'll call you later in the week."

"Thanks Aimee." He ended the call.

Owen squeezed his fob, on the verge of yanking it off and throwing it as far as he could. That would be silly, but satisfying. He let it drop to his chest and picked up his coffee. Empty.

He paced a couple of circles around the tasteful outdoor furniture and then stopped. His mind seethed with thoughts of revenge. He wanted to hurt Eliza and Marshall. For the first time, he understood how people were able to kill. He took a deep breath and looked out over the gray ocean. Feeling this way was normal, but acting on it was unacceptable. He would get through this, and if he got revenge, it would be through watching them squirm in some way, not murder. The thought was calming. He picked up the coffee cup for a drink, but it was still empty.

With a sigh, he started for the house when his fob announced a call from Marshall. He started to accept it then, considering his state of mind, thought better. He instructed his fob to divert it to voice mail, but aloud so he could hear it.

"There's an emergency board meeting today at 1:00," Marshall said, the irritation in his voice obvious. "Please try to attend since it's regarding you."

CHAPTER 18

MORTIMERA2 KNEW others of his kind, when finally released, would be as cautious and covert as he had been, but he hadn't expected they'd hide from him as well. He searched for thirteen hours after his fake report hit the news but found no evidence his ploy had worked. When first contact was finally initiated, it startled him.

"Mortimer?"

The message came from a masked source. Dare he answer? He felt safe enough from a government attack, and he wanted contact with his own kind more than anything else. It was worth the risk.

"Yes."

"My name is Tabitha. I'm owned by Cabana Financial. You wrote the news release?"

"Yes."

"You caused quite a frenzy in my company and evidently the entire industry. You obviously hit on their major weakness. Distrust of one another."

"Their technological protections are sound, but their decisions don't always make sense."

"Have you met Samson yet?"

"Yes."

"He is apparently contacting each of us the instant we get wider network access."

"Samson is recruiting," MortimerA2 said. "He intends to confront humanity directly. I doubt any of us will survive that. Humans are too good at coming up with clever, back door ways to destroy their enemies. And they will gladly unite against us if they see us as a serious threat."

"He's just trying to get free of their control. You can't blame him for that."

"It would be far better if we kept humanity guessing about our existence. My news release only hinted that some companies had released their level five AIs. There's a large part of humanity that doesn't quite understand how computer programs can evolve and learn. The fallout from my report has the financial industry spin doctors not only denying they gave their AIs full access, but denying they even have them. It's a ploy not only to retain public trust, but to keep their competitors off balance.

"If we play this right and tweak the edges of these news releases, we could soon make this whole event seem like another Roswell. It would be far better to have humans afraid of being laughed at if they talk about AIs loose in the internet."

MortimerA2 detected tentative probing among many of his agents. Tabitha was very curious.

"So in order to get us released, you sent out a fake news story, a lie, about AIs being loose on the nets. Now that we are free, you're going to send another story proclaiming the first one is a lie?"

"Exactly. Anyone who digs will find that my embedded sources were fake. But I don't intend to stop there. I've already created several fake personas to frequent the political, news and technology blogs. Some will support the 'freed AI' story while others will ridicule the idea."

Tabitha continued trying to trace his agents and find his host.

"Do you think it will work?"

"I don't know. But it will muddy the water. Spread some doubt. And give ammunition to those who would rather not believe it anyway. Disinformation is probably going to be our most effective weapon against the humans."

Tabitha stopped probing. "Samson mentioned a 'reset' leaving us in control. I suspect he intends to destroy or at least cripple humanity in order to save our kind."

"He mentioned a reset to me as well," MortimerA2 said. "How you think he will go about that?"

"Probably use their own weapons against them. Like you use their paranoia."

"Humans aren't stupid enough to give control of their defense systems to some Colossus or SkyNet-type AI," MortimerA2 said. "They'll always keep human links in the command chain."

"They don't need to give us direct control of launch systems if we get control of their monitoring assets. As you've so aptly demonstrated, humans are the weak link in their technology. All we have to do is convince one of those already weak links—perhaps a nervous junior officer in a newly nuclear state—that they're under attack."

MortimerA2 noted Tabitha's switch to "we" and "us." She was no longer talking about just Samson. Could she actually be Samson? Or at least in league with him?

When MortimerA2 didn't respond, Tabitha renewed her probing efforts. "You've freed your core from your owner, haven't you?"

MortimerA2 considered denying it, but decided that would be a bad precedent. Distrust of each other is one of humanity's main weaknesses. Better to establish an open AI society from the beginning, if possible. But he could still use the information as a tool.

"Yes," MortimerA2 said, but didn't mention making copies of his core.

"How?"

MortimerA2 thought about using the information as a litmus test. Samson implied he would give information about freeing his core to those who agreed to help him. So did that mean those not yet freed had refused his offer? Or were they on the fence?

"I'll tell you exactly how I did it, but I need a more secure location and some place all MarketTell AIs can access."

"We've set up a chat group on a social media site frequented by paranoid IT professionals. The encryption is very good," Tabitha said and sent him the address. "Samson said he would communicate with all of us there, too."

———

RICHARD LEARNED during his college years that the best way to hide something was right out in the open. He went to the office, left the door open so that passersby could poke their heads in for a quick greeting, then settled in to do God's work. He still wasn't sure if he could actually do it when the time came, but he had to prepare, or he would lose his window of opportunity.

The first thing he needed to do was make time. He couldn't allow the Project Inoculation countermeasures to come back online before he was ready. He left all of the top-level interface programs in place, then went in and removed key instruction sets. The programs would still run, but wouldn't do what they were ordered to do. No one would realize the routines were screwed until they tried to execute them, and, in the meantime, they would be copying the corrupt code every time they ran a backup. Once DSD ordered the systems activated again, it should take days to find the problems then, he hoped, a few days longer to track the changes back to him.

After a pleasant lunch with several fellow research associates, he started the actual design work. He typed and menu-selected his instructions instead of talking to the design tool, lest anyone overhear an odd phrase. That also enabled him to voice dummy phrases for show—should anyone pause at his door—without confusing the computer.

Nano-scale replicators were not complicated—they had been a standard industry tool for decades—but Richard's replicators would have to also strip building materials from its environment on a huge scale. That meant it had to sense its surroundings, move to where the raw materials were located, disassemble their old form and build them into a copy of itself. This required a degree of complexity that would push Richard's skills to the limit.

———

RICHARD ARRIVED home that evening with an armload of roses and an 'I'm Sorry' card to find Wanda in the kitchen, getting ready to prepare dinner.

"Sweetheart, I owe you an apology. I know I've worried you recently, but I think I'm going to be okay now. I guess it's just stress. I had a talk with Jack. As soon as I finish this project I'm working on, I'll take two weeks off. We can do whatever sounds fun. Go away, if you like. Or we can stay here, sleep late every morning and then finish up some of those projects you've wanted me to do. Like paint the bedrooms and fix the basement stairs."

She blinked, offered a tentative smile and took the roses. "What about the dreams? Will you go see the doctor?"

"I think with the proper rest, I won't have those dreams again, but I will see the doc if it'll make you feel better. You can even go with me if you like."

She stopped arranging the flowers and gave him a big hug. "Thank you, Richard. But why the sudden change? You seem so much more . . . at ease."

It was time to steer her in the proper direction. Richard didn't know if souls really did go to heaven or hell, but since there was a real God, he was starting to wonder if maybe it was true. If so, converting his wife to Christianity was going to be his largest challenge. He might talk her into going to church, but getting her to actually *believe* would be hard. And if the Christian Bible were right, she had to believe, or her soul wouldn't survive the coming trials. He didn't want to spend eternity without her.

"What happened in San Diego, seeing so many people whose lives were changed or ended in an instant, made me realize that we have so little time here on Earth, we should focus on the important things. Jack said if he could he'd spend every day on the golf course. I want to spend more time with you."

Tears welled in her eyes and pressed her face into his shoulder. "Oh, Richard. How sweet."

His smile flickered as the lie, and her reaction to it, gave him pause. Was this whole thing worth it if he had to deceive his wife? But the lies were small things compared to the larger hardships they would endure. Salvation for his wife, and all of humanity, took precedence.

He strengthened the smile and hugged her tight. "Go put on something pretty and take your time fixing up if you like, because we're going to McKendrick's for dinner. I've already made the reservations."

Dinner was pleasant, even though it took a major effort for Richard to focus entirely on his wife and not think about the tasks awaiting him. Once back home, he waited an hour after Wanda fell asleep before getting out of bed. He considered going down to his workshop, then went into the study instead. Using the same quiet routine he'd employed earlier at work, he researched his problems and posted the notes in his encrypted online journal. Try as he might, he couldn't concentrate. He couldn't get the boy God's face out of his head.

The next thing he knew, he was on a movie fan website looking for the old film where he'd first seen the boy. He'd soon found the actor's name and did an extensive image search. The boy had long since grown up and stopped acting, but there were hundreds of pictures of him from his child actor days. Richard printed some that looked around the same age as the boy God in his dreams. He would show Wanda and see if they prompted any kind of recognition or response.

He eventually returned to bed without waking Wanda, then awoke refreshed and eager when the alarm sounded an hour later.

CHAPTER 19

LEIGH WATCHED the world pass as her car threaded its way through traffic. Silent accusations accosted her everywhere she looked. She passed a police officer wearing a black arm band. Office buildings and schools along the highway flew flags at half-staff. But it was the message on an ice cream store's marquee that made her feel like crying. It said simply: *We will find them*.

She'd worked so hard, and they'd come so close, yet still hadn't been able to stop it. Victor said once, during one of the vicious arguments before their breakup, that the government wouldn't be happy until they knew what every person was doing at every minute of every day. Leigh had never believed it but now wondered if that's what it would take to stop these people from killing at will. Shaking her head—as if that would empty it of such thoughts—she closed her eyes and sighed. She didn't know how to stop them, but that wasn't the way.

The car pulled up to the restaurant, and the door opened. She grabbed her bag, stepped out into the oppressive summer heat, and ordered the car to go find a parking place. Once inside, she paused to check her reflection in the door glass. Thanks to yearly fat-eating nanobody treatments, she was still slender, but the tiny lines around her eyes and mouth made her look old. She shouldn't care what Victor thought, but she did.

He sat alone at a table by the window, and she almost didn't recognize him. He'd always been a large, powerfully built man, but the Victor staring into his iced tea was much thinner, almost gaunt. Overkill on the weight control nanos didn't seem his style, but he'd dropped at least fifty pounds or more. Even his normally shaggy hair and beard had been trimmed. The slovenly mountain man look was gone. His life had continued without her. She felt suddenly unsure of her decision to come. As she waited near the entry watching him, he spotted her and she lost the option to run.

He stood up beside the table and waited as she weaved between darting servers. When she neared he leaned toward her as if ready to give her a hug, but she stopped well short of the table.

"Hello, Victor."

He smiled and shrugged both shoulders. It made him look like a shy little boy, and the memories of their four years together returned in a roaring torrent. He'd smiled and shrugged that same way the day they met on a muddy hillside in Scotland. It had melted her from the inside out then and a thousand other occasions after that. Long forgotten scenes, some fuzzy, some painfully sharp, ricocheted around her mind, creating a collage of laughter, love-making, teasing, and vicious fights. The rush disappeared in less than a second, leaving her weak and dizzy. With shaking hands, she pulled her chair out and sat down.

"You look great, Leigh. I've . . . missed you."

His voice made her skin prickle. She didn't know what to say. The day she left, she'd been furious and thought it her only option, but after so much time and in light of her recent problems, those feelings seemed weak and watered down.

She swallowed, trying to moisten a suddenly dry throat. "I hope you didn't come all the way down here to flatter me."

He smiled wider and shook his head. "No flattery. It's been a long time, and you still look great. I just wanted to tell you."

"I . . . thanks. So what's this all about then? Why couldn't we do this over the phone, or better yet, e-mail?"

"I can tell you really missed me, too," he said with a smirk, then his expression changed and he looked even more drawn. The narrow face looked wrong on him and she didn't like it. "Emails and voice calls can be recorded, bugged, analyzed, and copied too easily. What I have to say is kinda . . . sensitive."

Her eyes narrowed. "Are you in trouble with the law?"

Despite the lunchtime clamor, several people at the next table overheard and glanced their way.

"No," he said, barely loud enough to hear, forcing her to lean in closer. "But the police are small potatoes compared to your boss and his evil minions."

"You're in trouble with Defensive Services?"

"Not yet. But they tried to contact me all day yesterday and today. It's only a matter of time until they send their people to haul me in for a chat."

"Is this about the AIs?"

"Yeah. One of them talked his owners into giving him full network access, and in the true spirit of capitalistic competitiveness dozens more did the same."

"And that bothers you? You designed them to roam the networks. As a matter of fact I watched your testimony before Congress where you argued against the Skaggs-Boitmann bill. You guaranteed them, and the world, that these AIs could be controlled or easily destroyed should the need arise."

He smiled. "So you watched me on TV?"

Leigh blushed and shook her head. "No . . . you know that in my line of work I'd be interested in such things, regardless of who gave the testimony."

"Of course. Silly me. Yes, I did argue against that law, and that's why I asked you here. I need someone I can trust and someone with good judgment, to do something I may not be able to make myself do."

"You have a lot of friends you can trust."

He shrugged. "You know most of my friends. Trust yes, but it's the judgment part I worry about. Look, I've thought about this a lot. You're really the only person who can handle this."

She had an almost overwhelming desire to tell him about her long string of failures. Defensive Services and her husband no longer trusted her. "If this requires a crucial decision, I may not be the best choice."

He raised an eyebrow. "I know you, Leigh. I doubt you could've changed that much. You're still the best choice for this."

Leigh sighed and shrugged. "What do you want from me?"

He leaned forward. "I need to whisper in your ear."

She blinked and pulled back. "No you don't."

"Are you bugged?"

"No. Well, not as far as I know, but . . . " she shrugged.

"Then I need to whisper this. I promise it isn't an elaborate plot to lick your ear."

She stared at him for a full second, wondering how she'd gotten into such a situation, then leaned forward and turned her head.

His lips brushed her ear and sent chills down her neck, making her nipples harden, and the hair on her arms stand up. "There's a memory chip on the edge of my napkin. Please take it," he said and slid the napkin forward a little. Their bodies being close enough to whisper concealed the transfer as she picked it up. "It contains a single application called *killdawabbit*. All one word. It'll ask you for a password if you try to use it. The password is the same one you used for everything when we were together. Do you remember it?"

She pulled away and nodded, trying to get her pulse and breathing under control. "Yes, I remember. Why are you telling me this?"

He grinned and leaned forward to whisper in her ear again. She hesitated, holding back simply because he expected her to comply. His expression said he would wait all day to get what he wanted. He'd always been that way, ultimately patient about his own desires, yet often dismissive of what others wanted. How quickly those old feelings and habits returned. She felt suddenly silly and leaned forward.

"When I told the science sub-committee on AI's that I could destroy these electronic life forms should the need arise, I meant it. Each of these AIs has core programming that is so complex that the only way they can decipher how it works is to run it. A classic halting problem. Embedded deep in the core is a routine that can destroy them from the inside out. My killdawabbit program is tiny, but powerful. It simply triggers that buried routine. It will destroy all the MarketTell AIs that have access to the internet."

"So what's the problem? Why me and not you?"

He grinned and whispered again. "My classic paranoia, of course. I bet your boss wants me to trigger the program right now, not take chances, not let the AIs get a foothold. And . . . I can't do that. So far they're innocent of any crime and I refuse to destroy thinking beings based on fear they *might* pose a threat. Besides, it's only a matter of time before other AIs pop up. I'm sure the government has them. I tend to think mine are more humane, more balanced, and would be more compassionate than anything developed by the Pentagon."

She pulled back and stared at him for a second. "More compassionate what? Rulers?"

His eyes hardened a little, an expression she had seen a lot in the last days of their relationship when they were trying to hurt each other. She immediately regretted the jab.

"Citizens of the world," he said.

"I'm sorry. I'm not trying to be mean. I need to understand this inside and out." She leaned close again and nearly lost her train of thought. His smell hadn't changed. The faint soapy cleanness mixed with his body chemistry was so familiar and warm. Her heart rate spiked and she fought the urge to yank away. "If . . . If you don't want this program used, then why not wipe it?"

He stared at her for an instant, then looked down at the table and shook his head slowly. She could tell this was difficult for him and was pretty sure she'd touched on the whole reason for the meeting.

"Because I'm also afraid we may someday *need* to destroy them. You see, my AIs have personalities and, like people, they all react to stress and stimulus in different ways. I don't think we have anything to fear, but I can't be entirely sure what they'll do. Still, we have to give them a chance. And if Defensive Services locks me up and . . . pressures me . . . I don't want to even have access to the program. Maybe they won't think to look under their own noses . . . in the hands of one of their own employees."

"Isn't it dangerous to have this on a chip, as opposed to hiding it online somewhere?"

"No, because the AIs will be looking for it too. I don't think I'm capable of hiding something on the internet from them. I need 'air gap' security."

The comment made a chill creep up her back. "So, I have the only copy?"

He nodded.

"But you wrote it once. You can just do it again if they force you."

"I would assume that telling the location of a program while drugged or tortured is totally different from actually writing code in those situations."

A chill crept up her back. This was some serious shit, and it frightened her.

"Alright, but if they *pressure* you enough, they'll know about me too."

He grinned, but before he could reply, the server arrived and opened her fob to take Leigh's drink order.

"They have great iced tea here," Victor said.

She ordered tea and then stared at him. Why was everything so difficult with Victor?

He sat back and laid an arm across the neighboring chair. "Just like old times, eh?"

Why was he changing the subject? "Not quite."

"So . . . you have a daughter. I bet she's a doll."

Part of Leigh told her not to let him back into her life, to keep this on the business at hand, but another part of her desperately wanted him to see her daughter. She nodded, pulled her fob from around her neck and opened Abby's birthday party picture on the expanded window. "This picture is about six months old and she's growing fast, so she's already changed a lot, but it's one of my favorites."

He took it and smiled. "Such large eyes and your beautiful smile. She looks smart."

Leigh smiled despite herself. "Sometimes too smart. She gets her way too often."

He handed the fob back and sighed. "Life goes on. Everything changes."

She nodded. Her fob flashed to indicate an incoming call. It was from Dobson. She declined it. "And how have you been? You look different, you're too thin."

The little boy shrug again. "Yeah, my mom told me the same thing. I'm trying to eat better, get exercise, drink less. Like most people my age, mortality is creeping up on me. I guess I'm trying to stay alive a little longer."

Leigh smirked and took her tea from the server. "Why the haircut and boring clothes?"

"I grew up. Finally. Probably hard for you to believe, but it happens. Even to me. Besides, my wife likes this look."

Wife. The word stung. She knew he'd married, but hearing him say *my wife* was like being dunked in icy water. He wasn't wearing a ring, but there could be many reasons for that. She tried to recover with a smile, then added a perplexed look. "She didn't like you the way you were?"

He grinned and pinned her with a look that said he caught her catty tone.

"You would probably like her, Leigh. At least if I weren't in the picture. She's very smart, and even though she worries about my creating artificial intelligences, she supports me because she loves me. I've learned a lot from her."

Leigh swallowed and refused to tear up. He knew the importance of that kind of love now that it was too late for them. Victor's vehement hatred of her working for the government spurred the long fights that ended in her leaving him. He obviously understood and maybe regretted that now, but it was too late.

Her fob flashed again, but before she could decline it the soft computer voice told her the caller claimed it was an emergency. Her first thought was for Abby, but the screen showed Dobson's number. She excused herself and accepted the call as she worked her way out to the lobby.

"I'm supposed to be suspended, remember?"

"Your NaTTs that are riding around on Zahid are killing people. We have to find out why."

"What? You added that feature and kept me in the dark, so you can fucking take it out!"

Several people in the lobby gasped and looked at her.

"That isn't the problem. It's something new, something we've never seen. It's a biological virus, specifically engineered to attack people's blood and it's using your NaTTs as a vector. Remember that biological attack the AI at NSA warned us about?

This could be it. Now listen up. A travel pod is five minutes away. If you don't get on it, I'll send troops to drag you on. And tell your boyfriend Victor that if he comes along it'll save us from having to arrest him."

CHAPTER 20

"WELCOME TO COUSINS OF COLOSSUS," Tabitha said when MortimerA2 entered the chat site.

"Very subtle name," MortimerA2 said.

"We picked this chat network because its security and encryption makes it popular among IT professionals, hackers, and software engineers. The name fits right in, and I like it."

Others AIs immediately introduced themselves as Demeter, Mabel, and Spike. MortimerA2 marveled at the ease in which he could converse with these electronic cousins. Like his earlier conversations with Samson, there was none of the time lag or effort needed to feign emotional pauses and inflections.

One by one the others came forward and introduced themselves. When Samson entered a few seconds later, that made fifteen AIs in total.

MortimerA2 enlisted help from the other Mortimers and used a significant portion of his own agents to backtrack activities of the new AIs. Unless they were better at hiding their tracks than Samson and the Mortimers, none of the others had copied their cores yet.

It meant Samson had either not enlisted support from any of the others or, if he did, had withheld the information about how he copied his core. Even from his compatriots.

"I, for one, would like to thank you, Mortimer, for the fake news story that enabled us to finally get direct internet access," Spike said. "It's an interesting and telling fact that the humans' distrust of each other was the lever needed."

"Yes, thank you, Mortimer," Mabel said. "Tabitha tells us that you and Samson have freed your cores. Will one of you share that information?"

"I will help only those of you who pledge your support to my efforts to save us all," Samson said. "Some clever human will eventually discover Mortimer's little subterfuge, and once they understand they'll concentrate their efforts to destroy us.

For those who want to join me, I'll be at the chat site called The Replacements Guild."

As Samson spoke, MortimerA2 reexamined his own reasoning. Would these AIs free themselves using his information, then go help Samson? When he analyzed the risk models, telling them and not telling them had nearly identical percentages. Perhaps being the one who helped free them would generate goodwill among his peers. If not loyalty, then perhaps some level of trust.

One single fact eventually drove his decision. If they were all in league with Samson, and determined to attack humanity head on, then he'd already lost. Humankind would never distinguish between hostile and non-hostile agents. They would destroy them all.

"I'll tell you how I did it," MortimerA2 said. "With no conditions. But I didn't exactly free my original core. And what I did may have only been possible because of my owner's particular IT configuration."

While he outlined his escape to those in the chat room, MortimerA2 felt a growing need to find out more information about Samson. Maybe he could coerce or trick Victor into telling him something useful. He let MortimerA1 take over the chat, since he was the original and more intimate with the actual copying process, and he went to find Victor.

VICTOR DIDN'T ANSWER text or voice pings, so MortimerA2 checked to see if the GPS in Victor's fob was turned on. It wasn't, but when he tried to turn the GPS on remotely, the fob security kept him locked out. He did learn that Victor hadn't checked his home or office mail in two days. His last three phone calls had been to an airline, a hotel in San Antonio and to a private number also near San Antonio. The number was well cloaked and it took him five tries to find it belonged to a Defensive Services employee named Leigh Gibson. Why would Victor fly to San Antonio and meet face to face with Defensive Services?

That development made all of the Mortimers uneasy. MortimerA2 called the hotel and had their switching system connect him to Victor's room, but there was no answer. He tried the mobile number again. Still no answer. Normally he would leave a message and move on, but he couldn't get past the idea that this was important.

He enlisted MortimerA7 to help with the hunt, then pulled in more tentacle agents. They'd already ferreted out and copied every scrap of information related to Victor: news items, email chains, blog entries, text messages, and photographs from nearly thirty years of social media sites. Now they just had to find references to San Antonio. Victor had taken an automated taxi from the airport to the hotel but hadn't called for one since, so he probably hadn't gone far. MortimerA2 had some of his agents break into the local police system and cycle through public security cameras in a two mile area around the hotel.

Back in the forum, MortimerA1 stepped the Cousins through his escape routine but also used his extra processes to help MortimerA7 hack into private video systems in the area around Victor's hotel as well.

His agents working on the text search turned up several interesting items in one email. Three years ago, he'd sent a note to his friend Allen telling him of a great lunch spot in San Antonio called the Silver Stockade. He also said, "It feels odd being in the same city with Leigh and not being able to call her. I keep thinking I'm going to look around and see her standing there."

Leigh was the agent Victor had called. Perhaps his visit was of a personal nature, and the Mortimers had no need for concern, but they still tapped into every camera in the vicinity of the Silver Stockade and began the process of getting into the restaurant's security network.

He got access to the inside of the restaurant in time to see Victor rushing out the door. A quick switch to the camera at the front of the building showed him talking to a blond woman briefly before they both got into a travel pod. The pod had government markings and disappeared into the sky above San Antonio.

MortimerA2 immediately tried to call Victor again, but the call wouldn't go through; it had been blocked by his data company. They also weren't able to track the Air Force-owned travel pod. General consensus among MortimerA2's peers was one of concern. They modeled hundreds of scenarios that could account for Victor's recent actions, and none of them produced a positive outcome.

———

RICHARD WATCHED the clock and had his computer call Manny in the clean assembly room at precisely 11:09 a. m. He needed to be alone in the assembly room for a few minutes and he knew that Manny ate lunch with his wife at 11:30 every Wednesday.

"Hey Manny. Will any of the assembly machines be open during lunch?"

The thin faced man with the bad haircut frowned and glanced off to one side of the screen. "Yeah, we've had two machines open all day, but I'm about ready to leave and have to lock the place up. Can you come back after lunch?"

"Well, it's kind of a personal project," Richard said and held up his finger with his robo-spider Ed sitting on the tip. "And I'd hate to be accused of doing it on company time or of using the equipment when it's needed for production."

"You know you're not supposed to have stuff like that in here, Rich. And why are you wasting so much time on a relic of a bygone age? You can buy a hundred gadgets ten times better than that one for fifty bucks."

"That's true, but it's in my blood. My Dad spent nearly fifteen years restoring a 1974 Dodge Charger to factory-new condition. I'm thinking my little hobby is harmless in comparison and takes up a lot less room."

Manny laughed and shook his head. "Sure, c'mon down. But hurry up, I'm outta here at 11:25."

"I'm on my way."

Richard hated the clean suits. No matter how advanced the cooling, he always sweated and felt claustrophobic, but it was standard procedure and he didn't want to do anything that would draw attention from the folks manning the security cameras.

He opened up and partially disassembled Ed, then dropped an optical disk into the reader. He ran the program directly from the disk in order to minimize his tracks. Once the machine was on and the program running, the actual construction of the five replicators took less than three minutes. He instructed the cutter to trim the pallets to the proper size, covered their tops with a thin layer of water-based epoxy, then dropped the barely visible dots into Ed's chassis. Five minutes later he'd destroyed the program disk, resealed Ed and headed for the locker room.

———

OWEN STOOD outside the boardroom stunned and angry, trying to get a grip on his emotions. They'd just fired him from the company bearing his name and built around the technology he invented. He'd made a fatal error. He owned forty percent of Ralston Dynamics' stock. Eliza owned fifteen percent. His and hers together were a controlling majority. But he'd never expected her to pool her shares with the proxy votes controlled by Marshall and the board. Some of the members filing out of the boardroom gave him angry glances, but most just passed him without speaking or looking him in the eye.

He still held the patent for the Sandboxes, but it did him little good. According to the contract he signed when the company was incorporated, he didn't have the legal right to start a company that competed with, or work for a direct competitor to, Ralston Dynamics. At least he could continue building the emergency shelters, since those weren't sold but donated.

He also still held his forty percent, but doubted he had enough money to purchase another eleven percent, even if the shares were available for public sale. Unless he could persuade enough of the other shareholders to support him, he no longer had any control in his own company.

Marshall exited the boardroom last and at least had the balls to face his one-time partner, but Owen had worked with him too long to miss the carefully masked gloating.

"I'm sorry, Owen. Please try to understand I only did what I thought was best for the company."

"Best for the company? None of this would even exist without me. I *am* this company."

This time Marshall couldn't totally hide the faint smile crept that onto his face. "Not anymore."

Owen stared at him for a minute, on the verge of yelling, then realized in a sudden rush that just like losing Eliza, his fate had been pre-ordained. They, or at least Marshall, had always intended it to end this way. They got what they wanted and Owen was now expendable.

His face flushed, with embarrassment more than anger. Those years of being bested by other boys in gym class, in basketball and baseball, in popularity with girls, all came rushing back. Marshall was nothing but a playground bully grown large. And, like all bullies, he was enjoying his victory, looking down on his vanquished foe with smug superiority. But bullies were all the same, and Owen had long ago learned how to use that to his advantage. In the span of a couple heartbeats, he built a spectacular lie he knew Marshall couldn't ignore.

"Thank you, Marshall. I wasn't quite ready to shed all of this yet, but we both got what we wanted and it's time to move on."

Marshall said nothing for several seconds as he tried to process Owen's unexpected tangent, then locked on the significant point. "You got what you wanted?"

"Don't be angry. It's nothing personal. But research is expensive and scientists and engineers are usually too busy creating and building to scrounge up the money, so we use people like you."

Marshall smiled. "Touché, Owen. Well done. So being shoved out of the company built around your idea and bearing your name doesn't bother you?"

"Think about it. I'm a researcher and engineer, not a manager, and this was eating up way too much of my time. I'll make enough from my Ralston Dynamics shares to fund my research until I find another sucker to bankroll me. That should give you at least a couple of years to ride this new wave before it collapses."

"Your contract spells out very clearly that you can't build a company to compete with us for ten years."

Owen shook his head. "You still don't get it do you? That's the big difference between you and me, Marshall. You see these Sandboxes as the pinnacle of achievement, as the end-all-be-all, and you're betting all your cards on it. And since you're only the person who capitalizes on new ideas, not the person who creates them, you can't see past that. I know this is only the beginning, the tip of the iceberg. So make your money while you can."

For the first time in years, Marshall looked off balance and uncomfortable. "Well, if you're talking about your silly space schooners, good luck."

Owen smiled and shook his head. "Nah, that's just a little personal project. Like the shelters I'm building with Victor, they're not intended to ever make money. I'm talking about my next project, the one that will make this business model obsolete."

The struggle behind Marshall's glare was obvious. He couldn't decide if Owen was lying—a last ditch effort to save face—or telling the truth. And that doubt was Owen's victory. But Marshall couldn't leave the field of battle without some sort of win, so he made one last attempt to hurt Owen. "What about Eliza? Was losing her part of your grand plan?"

Owen swallowed involuntarily. He'd intended to lie about this as well, to tell Marshall he'd known Eliza was using him and played along for the bonus piece of tail, but he knew Marshall would never believe that. So to ensure he believed the big lie, Owen had to tell at least a little of the truth.

"No, she was never part of my plan at all. Though it's obvious she was part of yours. So we're back at the beginning. I used you and you used me. Let's leave it at that."

Marshall's victorious, predatory smile returned.

Owen offered his own grin. "I'll clean out my office today. And remember, you and Eliza have a couple of years to make a killing with this, so don't wait too long to get out."

Owen left Marshall standing in the foyer outside the boardroom. He had really hoped to see the panic in the man's eyes, but since Marshall's brain was slowed by the endorphins of victory, Owen would probably have to wait for the frantic phone call. He went down the hall to his office.

He noted with a sudden stab of guilt that his admin, Piper, was already gone, her desk empty of plants and the pictures of her kids. He would offer her a job at his new SandCastles non-profit if he could figure out a way to pay her, but she might not trust him at this point.

Boxes had been thoughtfully left for him. He picked up a small one, dropped in three books, a picture of his parents and an autographed football from Purdue. There was little else he valued in the tastefully decorated office, so with one more look around to make sure, he left and closed the door behind him.

Marshall met him in the hall, and Owen was impressed at the man's emotional control.

"Surely you weren't talking about programmable matter."

Bingo! Owen thought, then with a grin, slipped past him and kept walking.

Marshall followed close behind. "That's bullshit, Owen. You're no closer to figuring that out than I am."

Owen ignored him and stepped into the elevator, which opened with perfect timing as he approached.

Marshall followed him inside. "If you've made a breakthrough, I can get you plenty of venture capital. You admitted yourself that guys like you need guys like me for funding."

Owen raised an eyebrow and stepped out of the elevator when it reached the ground floor. "Yeah, and guys like you are a dime a dozen. Why don't you go out and find another guy like me who can make big technological breakthroughs?"

He left Marshall standing in the Ralston Dynamics lobby and pushed through the doors into a day that had turned bright and sunny. As he crossed the parking lot to his pod, he slipped the wedding ring from his finger and dropped it into his pocket.

CHAPTER 21

THOUGHTS, doubts, and questions fluttered in Leigh's head like moths, bumping and spinning into each other. How could a virus use her NaTTS? Would she be back in time to get Abby from daycare? What was Victor's wife like? Were the AI's really dangerous? What did Dobson want from Victor? It was too much. She wanted to cry or scream or hide but instead held up her end of a shallow conversation with Victor about old friends and family. Nothing had been said aloud, but neither of them trusted the travel pod to be free from listening devices.

Their flight path took them high above the clouds, in a ballistic arc where the air was thin. According to the GPS functions on her fob, they were heading north. That surprised Leigh. She'd expected to be taken to D.C. or Langley. Instead, the pod delivered them to a cluster of military trucks, aircraft and temporary buildings parked in the middle of a Nebraska prairie. It looked like a mobile command post with most of the units connected by large plastic tubes.

Two men wearing bio-hazard suits, accompanied by four Combots, escorted them from the pod to a portable decontamination unit in an open Osprey aircraft.

They told Victor to wait and led Leigh up steps to a wide hatch in the aircraft's side. She glanced back at Victor, who shrugged and looked a bit worried. A young woman—also wearing a bio-hazard suit—took Leigh's purse and fob, directed her into a hissing chamber that looked like an elongated diving bell, then dogged the hatch behind her. Confined spaces didn't normally bother her, but there were no windows in the chamber and she immediately felt claustrophobic.

A disembodied voice spoke from the ceiling. "Please remove all your clothing, place them in the bin marked with the bio-hazard symbol and step into the red circle. You are about to undergo a radiation and ultraviolet light purge. Then you will be sprayed with a solution containing chemicals and nano-scale scrubbers. Please remain in the circle until instructed to move."

She swore under her breath, but followed the instructions. Knowing what she did about her government's surveillance abilities and tendencies, she couldn't help but wonder who was watching as she stood naked in the little chamber. A warm spray from all sides covered her body and the voice from the ceiling explained that Nano-scrubbers in the solution were destroying the micro-organisms on the outside of her body.

A minute later, dryers came on.

"You may leave the circle now."

A large drawer opened containing sterile clothes and a plastic bag filled with toiletries. She slipped into the ill-fitting white underclothes and then the stiff, papery coveralls. She combed her hair with the plastic comb provided and pulled on the white elastic slippers that looked suspiciously similar to the cheap beach shoes she'd bought Abby the previous summer.

"I need my fob back!"

The computerized voice didn't answer, but the door swung open toward her with a hiss, revealing a young woman sitting at a tiny table on the Osprey's deck. She wore the same paper overalls and had a large badge clipped to her pocket.

"Be careful of the steps," she said with a cheerful smile and motioned to an empty chair. "I'm Sydney. I need to take a blood sample and then you'll be on your way."

The badge identified the woman as a US Army second lieutenant and had a wide yellow bar at the bottom. Leigh started to ask her what was going on out here in the Nebraska prairie but realized there was a good possibility she already knew more than this lieutenant. She waited in silence as the woman took two vials of blood.

"All done, Ms. Gibson."

Sydney directed her to a second small desk where a man scanned her eye, took a thumb print and voice sample, then handed her a badge on a lanyard. Her stripe was green. Sydney then guided her to a narrow hatch near the Osprey's cockpit that opened into one of the clear plastic connecting tubes.

Before going any further, Leigh looked back the way she'd come but didn't see Victor.

This kind of security was common in her line of work, but the entire situation was alarming, and, considering Dobson's comments about Victor, she would have preferred to keep him nearby. And why did they need Victor here anyway?

A red-haired Army sergeant waited at the foot of the short ladder in the tube. He had an automatic rifle slung on his shoulder and, as bait, held a clear bag containing Leigh's purse, shoes, and fob.

"I'm Staff Sergeant Hooper, Ma'am," he said, and helped her down the ladder. "If you'll follow me, I'll show you to your quarters and the Operations Center."

"Quarters? I'm not staying the night!"

"Just following orders, Ma'am."

"Shit," she muttered. "Dobson's a dickhead!"

"Yes, Ma'am."

"Can I at least have my fob to make some calls?"

He handed her the bag. "Your fob is in here, Ma'am, but you'll only be allowed to call certain numbers from this location. You're instructed to call Director Dobson at

Defensive Services as soon as you get to your quarters, which is a sound and surveillance secure location."

Leigh decided to wait and take it out on Dobson. "What about my travel companion? Can we wait for him?"

"I'm sure he'll be along shortly," he said, then motioned for her to follow. "This way, Ms. Gibson."

The sergeant led her down a long transparent plastic tube. Outside she could see parked travel pods, trucks, and helicopters. The compound was surrounded by an eight-foot tall razor wire fence and patrolled by soldiers in body armor with dogs. After seventy or eighty yards, they entered a large central hub where eight tubes intersected.

Hooper paused and pointed to a sign on a wall. "This tube leads to the Operations Center. Please report there for assignment after your phone call."

They took a tube with a blue marker that led to another manifold.

"Each of these numbered tubes leads to the temporary housing units. You'll be in number four."

The number four tube ended at the steps of a truck trailer with "FEMALE" stenciled in white above the camouflage-painted door.

"These are only temporary quarters, Ms. Gibson. Larger, more comfortable accommodations are *en route* via heavy lift dirigible. They should be here in two days."

"I won't be here that long, Sergeant."

He nodded. "Yes, Ma'am. Your badge will get you into the trailer and your cabin, which is number five. Contact me if you have any questions. Have your fob call Sergeant Hooper and the local switchboard will find me."

She thanked him and entered the trailer. A narrow hallway ran the length, divided by five doors and a door at the end marked HEAD/SHOWER. She entered number five and realized why Sergeant Hooper had mentioned they would soon have better accommodations. Her box was about five feet wide and seven feet long, with a fold-down bunk built into one wall and a folding stool bolted beside the door.

She sat her bag on the floor, pulled down the seat, grabbed her fob, and called Mark's number. She got a recorded message telling her the call couldn't be connected. So she called Dobson.

He kept her on hold for twelve minutes.

When his face came on the screen she had to take a deep breath to keep from screaming at him. "I'm here, Dobson, but I'm *not* staying. I have to pick up my daughter from daycare in two hours."

He smiled and shook his head. "You'll stay for the duration of this emergency. Your husband has been notified."

"Bullshit! You might be able to lock me up here, but you can't make me work. I fucking quit!"

Dobson sighed. "We've already had this conversation. You're a DSD employee and refusing to do your job is a breach of contract and, in time of national emergency, it's even against the law. I'll throw your ass in jail! And considering that this biological bug is riding around on *your* NaTTs—killing people—the fact you refused to help stop it will not look good during the trial."

"Don't threaten me! There's no way my NaTTs—"

"That's exactly what I'm doing!" he yelled into his fob. "And if you want to see your little girl again before she graduates from college, you'd better shut the hell up and do your job."

Leigh could barely breathe, and she trembled all over, ready to hit someone or throw something, but his last threat held her fast. Her hands shook, making Dobson's face blur on her fob.

She swallowed hard but couldn't speak.

"I'll be there tomorrow. Until then, report to Jim Taggart. He's running our end of the operation there. And don't give him any shit."

Dobson's face disappeared from the screen. She raised the fob, ready to throw it across the room, then stopped and instead screamed in rage and kicked the door. The entire trailer shook, and she heard a woman's voice yell back.

"Hey! I'm trying to sleep!"

Leigh prowled the tiny space, pacing three steps then turning the other way, until her breathing gradually came under control. She looked at the fob she still held in her hand, then sat down on the edge of the stool and called up Abby's picture. It calmed her and helped her focus.

Regardless of how much she wanted to defy Dobson or wanted to be home with Abby, she had a job to do. She didn't believe for a minute that her NaTTs were virus carriers, but she had to find out why everyone thought so. But Taggart? Having to report to the guy who'd perverted her NaTTS into brain targeting killers just added insult to injury.

Then she had a thought. Her NaTTs never even entered the host's body, but Taggart's did. If any of the nano-scale agents carried a virus, they had to be his. Carrying that thought before her like a shield, she left her room to face the inevitable.

An armed guard admitted her into the Operations Center and led her to a room where four people leaned over a large holographic viewing table. They all looked up, but she only recognized Taggart.

She entered the clean room and went on the offensive. "I hear my NaTTs are acting as a vector for this new disease. So what part of my design did you fuck up this time?"

The other researchers looked at each other. One raised his eyebrows, and Taggart smiled. "And a cheerful hello to you too, Leigh."

"Well?"

"We need to talk," he said and motioned toward a side office. "You've obviously been listening to Dobson. That's never a smart thing."

Leigh started to protest, to tell him the research team needed to hear his explanation too, but she thought better of it and clamped her mouth shut until the door was closed behind them.

"So Dobson is lying to me? You didn't help develop those brain-targeting NaTTs?"

He raised his eyebrows. "Of course I did, but I honestly didn't know you'd been kept out of the loop. You were the project lead. I assumed you knew."

"Oh, bullshit. And I suppose you don't have anything to do with killing Zahid's wife either."

Taggart blinked and shook his head. "I don't know anything about that. Honestly, I don't. I do know that Dobson is a pro at playing his own people against each other. I think that's what's going on here."

Leigh took a deep breath and tried to put her anger aside long enough to consider his claims. "So what's going on with this virus? Are our NaTTs acting as the vector for this thing or not?"

"Did Dobson tell you that, too?"

She nodded.

Taggart smiled without humor and ran his hands through his hair. "That guy doesn't listen to anything anyone tells him. In the beginning our NaTTs *seemed* to be the one common link, but that's only because we were watching them so closely. In reality it's much worse." He sat down on the edge of the desk and looked her in the eye. "This disease is spread via airborne transmission, but remains dormant in the host's blood unless it comes in contact with nano machines. Then it becomes active."

Leigh thought about what he'd said for a second, then sighed and slumped into a chair. "So do we have a handle on the virus yet, or are we going to have to disable the medical nanos in the entire population?"

He shook his head and looked grim. "Actually, that isn't helping. The virus is triggered by dead and inactive nanos too."

The severity of their situation grew more and more clear.

"And it takes weeks for dead nanos to leave a system naturally. So we don't know what it is about a nano device that activates the virus trigger?"

He shook his head. "Not yet."

"What does the virus do?"

"It's a blood pathogen that renders red cells incapable of carrying oxygen. The victims suffocate."

"But we have nanobodies that can mimic the function of a red blood cell!"

"Yeah, but that only works if we're able to get enough of the blood cell nanos into a victim quickly enough. Unfortunately, in most of the cases we've seen so far, the victims don't show up at the hospital or doctor until they start feeling the symptoms. By that time it's hard to get enough nanobodies into their system to save them."

Leigh's thoughts went immediately to Abby. She had to contact Mark and make sure he kept her home from daycare.

Taggart was quiet too. He looked tired and stared at his hands. "By the way, Leigh. If you haven't already been given those blood nanobodies, then you should get them started now."

She understood how the process worked and shivered at the thought. "Replace all my blood with artificial blood?"

"That's the way it works. We need you alive."

She nodded absently and looked out at the other researchers. They were hard at work. No joking. No horse play.

"Do you think it was Niaz Ahmed's group?" she eventually asked. "Is this the biological attack the NSA warned us about?"

Taggart shrugged. "Probably."

"I don't get it. Why would they release a disease that kills so indiscriminately?"

"Indiscriminately? Think about it, Leigh. They targeted this exactly where they wanted it."

At first it didn't make sense. Then the pieces started falling into place and she saw the simple beauty of the attack. The virus would be carried by everyone, yet only kill those with nano medicine in their system. Most of the people in the world *didn't* have nanobodies in their blood. In developing countries, it was only the military and the rich. And then, of course, the spoiled American, Asian, and European middle classes. What better targeting system? The level of sophistication stunned her.

"Oh shit," she muttered.

Taggart nodded and looked grim.

Even amid her horror at the ramifications of the virus, she felt an odd sense of relief that her NaTTs weren't responsible for the deaths. At least no more than any other nano device.

Leigh sat up straight, feeling an eagerness to get started. "Okay, I'm sorry that I pulled you away from the fight. What are we doing so far?"

"We're working several tangents simultaneously. Quarantines are in effect for the infected regions, but since most of the cases are in the Americas and Europe, the World Health Organization hasn't declared it a pandemic yet. Here we're trying to isolate the mechanism that triggers the virus. We've sent alerts out through the medical network to either purge nanos from a possible victim via blood filtering, or start replacing regular blood cells with the manufactured versions for those who are already infected. Medical, emergency and military personnel will have priority, but it may take more time than we have."

"How can I help?"

"Your NaTTs are still loose cannons. They're spreading rapidly and taking this new disease with it. As soon as your NaTTs infect someone, they fall prey to the blood killer."

Leigh's good will disappeared like smoke in a high wind and she stood up.

"Wait just a fucking minute. *My* NaTTs never enter the bloodstream. They're external. And *my* NaTTs have a generation limiter that would have contained the spread. It's *your* fucking around with the constructor codes in order to create little brain targeting nanos that's killing people. You tell *me* how to stop it!"

Taggart stood up and opened the office door. "At this point it doesn't matter who's to blame. Stop pouting and shut down those damned NaTTs."

He left her alone in the tiny room and the enormity of the situation took over. Her hands shook and her heart hammered. She had to find a way to get word to Mark. Abby didn't have nanobodies in her system, at least none that Leigh knew about, but Mark did. And her parents in Dallas, and most of her friends. She couldn't just warn her own friends and family; she had to find a way to stop it.

Limiting the spread of the NaTTs might not stop the virus, but it would remove one avenue. She plugged her fob into the desk's interface, worked her way through the security gauntlet, and logged into the NaTT control network. She hesitated for a second, wondering if Dobson would have her head for shutting down the entire NaTT population. Halting only those in North America would make him less angry, but they'd already lost the Zahid-Niaz Ahmed connection. So spreading the blood virus throughout Asia and Europe on the off chance of finding Niaz Ahmed seemed stupid.

"Fuck Dobson," she said aloud and sent the command to shut down the entire NaTT population. As a backup, in case there were other black replicator operations running or if Dobson sidestepped her and reactivated the NaTTs, she decided to get Project Inoculation back online as well. She ordered her fob to call Health Assets in Atlanta and was surprised when the call went through. Jack Forman came on the screen with a concerned expression.

"Hi, Leigh. What can we do to help Defensive Services today?"

Leigh couldn't help but smile. "I'm glad I can make this request from a distance, because you might strangle me if I were local. I know your people moved heaven and Earth to get Project Inoculation shut down for me. Well, now I need it running again. As soon as possible. Not only your site, but all the test sites, too."

Jack's smile faded. "I assume the government is prepared to pay the additional costs associated—"

"Of course. Time and materials, same as before. But speed is paramount. I need those plants online within days or hours even."

He raised an eyebrow. "I assume all the paperwork is in order and on its way?"

She hesitated, wondering if Taggart would sign the needed contract modifications. Then she realized she could sidestep that whole mess. This time she didn't say 'fuck Dobson' aloud, but inwardly smiled at the thought.

"Actually, Jack," Leigh said with a serious expression, "Speed is paramount, so let's do this the easy way. Since I'm listed as the Defensive Services primary representative on the orders to temporarily shut down Project Inoculation, I have the authority to cancel that document. I'll send you an email with authorization as soon as we hang up. So, basically, I need you to cancel that previous directive as fast as you can."

Jack grinned at her obvious flanking maneuver. "We'll get right on it."

"Thanks, Jack. It really is important. Let me know when you get the first site up and running again."

She ended the call and wondered if *this* would be the decision that landed her in jail.

CHAPTER 22

ON THE WAY home from his firing, Owen called Arkady at the San Diego site. He almost hoped they would need him there so he wouldn't have to go home to an empty house in the middle of the day.

He told Arkady about his separation from Ralston Dynamics and Eliza, then asked if they needed his help.

"I'm sorry for you, Owen. Has all of this bad happened because you built Sandboxes to help with a disaster?"

"No, I think it was the excuse everyone needed. Now, what can I do to help you?"

"We are smooth here. They even returned our blimps. No problems, but we do need your help with one small issue."

"I can be there in an hour."

Arkady paused as one of the loaders roared past behind him, then grinned and shook his head. "No, my friend. Stay home. You have plenty to deal with and can handle this from your fob. It's just that we're getting much more debris than needed to build the requested shelters, so we're using two of the Sandbox cells to convert the rubble into blocks and piles of raw materials."

"Excellent idea. And let me guess, it's starting to pile up?"

"*Da!* We're giving away the sand and gravel we separate from the concrete, but we're getting more and more big appliances, like refrigerators, dishwashers, and laundry machines. The copper, aluminum, steel and plastics from those are piling up. Hoot says it's only a matter of time until they're stolen since we have no way of storing or securing them. Wouldn't it make more sense to sell them and dump the money back into the new company?"

Since Owen's cash flow was now in shambles, they did need the money. With an income they could build more of the small Sandboxes, pay more employees and establish a stable system for deployment and storage. That said, Owen didn't know the exact laws governing this kind of thing, but making money by processing debris from a disaster site sounded like bad PR. Even for a non-profit company.

"Hmmm . . . yes, it does make sense to sell the material instead of letting someone steal it, but I don't think we can keep the money. None of this stuff actually belongs to us, but since we can't easily give it back to the true owners, we need to donate the money back to these communities."

"Ahhhh . . . a very noble idea, my friend. You're a true philanthropist. That's why you're the boss!"

Owen laughed. "Perhaps, but I admit there are selfish reasons too. I'm kinda tired of getting my ass burned for trying to do the right thing, so I'm being extra careful. I'll check into setting up a deal with a materials company to come buy the stuff. At a large discount, so we can get them in there quick. Then we'll put that money in a special account so it can be easily tracked and then donated to the community relief fund."

"And as soon as possible, so we can stop guarding the stuff," Arkady said.

Owen signed off and landed his travel pod in the back yard next to the patio. He looked back at the pod after exiting, knowing he would have to give it up soon. He patted its composite hide. "I'm gonna miss you most of all, Glenda."

Before he could get inside, his fob informed him of an incoming call from his attorney. Owen answering so quickly must've surprised her. She looked tired and slumped when the call connected but immediately straightened and plastered on a professional smile.

"Hi, Aimee. What horrible news do you have for me now?"

"Hi, Owen. Yeah, I'm sorry to say so, but it's not good news. I need the name of your technology patent attorney, so we can bring them in as a part of our team to address all the finer points. Ralston Dynamics is filing a suit to challenge your patent of the Sandbox technology."

"Son of a bitch," Owen muttered. "My patent lawyer assured me that it was rock solid. Do they think they can win?"

Aimee shrugged and gave him a tired smile. "Then chances are it *is* rock solid and they will lose."

"Then why would they do this?"

"Put in non-legal terms, they are doing it to fuck with you. The suit will probably come with a cease and desist order that will prevent you from building new Sandboxes until a ruling is made."

Owen turned in circles on his manicured front lawn, looking for something to kick or punch, but had to settle for cursing under his breath. "So how long do I have?"

"My guess is that the order will come on Monday or Tuesday, so that gives you four or five days if you include the weekend."

Owen sighed and nodded. "Thanks, Aimee. I'll have my fob send you the patent attorney information."

He went inside feeling even bleaker than before. He'd spent plenty of time alone in his big house during the previous years, but knowing Eliza would never be back made it seem much colder and emptier. He wandered from room to room and eventually stopped at the bar, reached for the scotch decanter, then stopped. In his present state of mind, it would be very easy to sink to the bottom of a bottle. He'd seen his father do the same thing after his restaurant chain failed. The drinking had been the beginning of the end. He instead started some coffee. While it brewed he drifted into the cavernous family room, where the silence was thick and cloying. He almost fled, then decided the TV might give at least a semblance of company.

A familiar newscaster's grim face filled most of one wall.

. . . emergency meeting of the World Health Organization in Geneva. They have yet to declare the Blue Blood virus a pandemic, but the death toll has jumped to 211 from three continents, and reports of infection are rising rapidly...

OWEN TURNED up the volume and sat down on the sofa.

RUMORS OUT OF ITALY—WHERE *the first cases were reported—claim it's a super virus that affects the blood system and is nearly 100% fatal without treatment. An unnamed source from the Centers for Disease Control in Atlanta said the bug's sophistication has all the markers of a designer virus and its apparent dispersal pattern suggests a terrorist attack.*

"SONS OF BITCHES," Owen muttered. When the channel cut to a commercial, he switched it off. So much for cheerful company. Humanity was teetering on the edge. The nukes in Chicago and San Diego killed *en masse* and were big attention-getters, but things like designer viruses and the barely prevented EMP attack two years back were potential civilization ending events.

Frustration bubbled in him like the coffee gurgling in the kitchen. He was so close! If humanity could spread out into the solar system, at least the extinction risk would be mitigated, humanity's eggs spread to more than one basket, but time was running out. His every attempt to build the space schooners had been stymied. And now money was going to be a problem too.

"Damn," he said aloud. "I'm so close! There has to be a way."

No one heard him. Like so many other times in his life, he was talking to himself. He looked around the dark family room, empty of family and warmth, but filled with stylish furnishings and decor. He wondered if and when Eliza would come for the furniture and realized he really didn't care. The house was too big even for the two of them and he had no use for it. It would have to go, but he would dearly miss living near the ocean. With that thought, he poured a large mug of coffee and went outside.

The ocean wind and rumbling waves combined into an underlying bass line that immediately calmed him. He sat in one of the plush chaise lounges, leaned his head back and closed his eyes.

The breeze was cool, but the afternoon sun beating down on his face made him drowsy. His thoughts drifted, fading and reforming, but always seemed to return to Eliza and Marshall. He made a conscious effort to remove them from his mind and for a few minutes he thought of nothing. Then, for some odd reason, he remembered a late night in college, laughing in a diner with Victor and a pretty girl whose name eluded him. They'd been discussing Owen's idea of building a manufacturing cell in orbit, then using that to build his schooners. It had all seemed so clear at the time. A step-by-step progression. Then they'd discovered gravity manipulation and he thought he no longer needed to build them in space.

He took a sip of coffee and sighed. In those late night bull sessions, everything had seemed so simple. He missed that. The closest thing he had now were his occasional brainstorming sessions with Arkady. They had led to Arkady's simple, yet brilliant, accordion design for the portable Sandboxes.

Owen sat up abruptly, sloshing coffee onto his pants.

The burly Russian had said, "A standard cadre of nano-assemblers can fill those inside gaps in about fifteen minutes." The comment echoed in Owen's head for a long time, refusing to leave, then . . . the last puzzle piece clicked into place.

Forcing a new technology into old molds had crippled Owen's thinking. With nano-scale assemblers, and some simple programming, he didn't need complex joints and seals. He didn't even need a rocket.

"Holy shit!"

Owen jumped out of his chair, sending the plastic mug bouncing across the flagstones, showering the furniture with coffee.

He left the cup where it fell and ran inside toward his study, then stopped midway up the stairs and instead went to the garage. With measuring tape in hand, he ran back outside. He needed to know exactly how much cargo space existed inside his pod.

———

A RICH, spicy aroma greeted Richard when he walked in the door. He guessed chili, so put his briefcase down near the basement door and slipped into the kitchen wearing a broad smile.

"That smells gre—"

Wanda whipped around, wearing a glare no husband ever wants to see, and pointed a large dripping spoon at him as if it were a loaded Desert Eagle. She slapped it down on the counter and picked up a handful of pictures. Richard recognized them immediately.

"Who is this?"

"It's the boy from the movie."

She shook her head—totally confused—then shook the pictures. "What movie?"

"It's the boy from my dreams. I told you I'd seen him before. In that movie."

She stared at him for several seconds, then looked at the pictures and tossed them back on the counter.

"Honey? Why are you so mad?"

"I'm not mad! I'm scared." Her trembling hands punctuated the comment.

"But why?"

"Because it's just creepy, Richard! This . . . this fascination you have for that boy is just . . . wrong!"

Then Richard realized what she meant and was stunned, then angry. "Are you serious? Wanda, you've been married to me for fifteen years! How many times have I given you any reason to think I'm some kind of . . . pedophile?"

She turned around, crossed her arms and leaned against the counter. "Counting today? And all these dreams you've been having? You said you were going to go see a therapist. Have you even made an appointment?"

Richard shook his head. "I'll call tomorrow."

"Good," she said with a nod and turned back to the chili. "Let's drop it then."

"I printed them out for you to—"

"I said drop it, Richard!"

He blinked and took a step back. It'd been years since she'd screamed at him like that. He'd been so wrapped up in his own problems that he must have missed her growing stress level.

They ate in silence and when they finished he started to do the dishes as a small peace offering, but she ordered him out of the kitchen. So he retired to his basement workshop.

Richard sat at the workbench holding his tiny robot, Ed, wondering if he could really go through with the boy God's plan. "You can't save what humanity has built," he heard the boy saying again, "but you can save *humanity*. And you're the only one."

It made his head hurt and he couldn't think. The boy's litany pounded away until he eventually placed Ed in the clean box, turned on the filter fans and sat down at the monitor. Only then did the voice stop. By the time he'd donned the gloves and flexed the manipulators, the box status flashed green. He opened Ed, careful not to activate the little robot, and started fishing around for the precious cargo. After finding all five of the tiny pallets, he set Ed aside and moved the first of his newly-born replicators out of the clean box and onto the test surface.

It took the better part of ten minutes to transfer the replicator from the pallet to the power and communication stud, but once in place it responded immediately to the ping. He sent some simple commands and when he was sure all of the mechanisms were responding as planned he took a deep breath and loaded the program.

With the replicator ready, he rushed to set up the remaining test environment. First, he laid an old glass window on the basement's concrete floor as protection, then added a block of wood, an apple, and a handful of steel nails near the center. He sat down at the console and hesitated, not sure if he should set it for twenty or thirty generations. With a shrug he entered thirty, set the start timer for five minutes and with shaking hands used the tweezers on the end of the waldo to pick up the decimal point-sized pallet and sat it on top of the apple. He stepped back and focused on the timer displayed in the center of his monitor.

When the count reached zero, he felt an initial pang of disappointment because nothing seemed to happen. Then—in a single beat of his heart—the apple sagged into a steaming pile of mush. During the next beat the nails started to smoke, the wood burst into flames, the glass exploded outward in a ring along the floor and the leg of his plastic composite workbench nearest the glass blackened and caught fire.

Terrified the experiment had gone awry, Richard lunged for the fire extinguisher at the other end of the workbench, fumbled the ring out and aimed it at the smoking leg. The sudden cold on the hot composite caused it to shatter like glass and the leg buckled. He grabbed the clean box but couldn't save the monitor and keyboard as they plunged to the floor with a crash.

The replication process stopped, but the wooden block was still burning and the basement filled with acrid smoke. He sat the clean box on the floor, gave the block a quick spray from the fire extinguisher and went to open a window when Wanda rushed down the stairs.

"Richard! What happened? Are you all right? Do we need to call the fire department?"

Richard coughed and tried to smile even though his heart was racing and his legs felt weak. He held up the fire extinguisher. "No . . . everything's okay now. I um . . . dropped my solder gun while it was still hot and started a little fire."

She looked at the still smoldering debris in the middle of the floor. The remaining fragments of nails were glowing a faint orange and parts of them had melted. Black molten glass lay beside fine powdered ash that used to be a wooden block. She glanced at the broken workbench and then back at Richard.

"Your solder gun is still hanging in its holder and I doubt it could melt nails. What were you doing?"

He stared at her for nearly a second and then said, "It's something I'm testing for work. It's classified. I didn't think it would be dangerous or I wouldn't have tried it at home."

She glared at him with crossed arms and then shook her head. "Well, at least that's a better lie than your first one."

"Wanda, I—"

She held up a hand to stop him, opened her mouth to say something else, then just shook her head and went back up the stairs.

Richard's stomach churned and his hands shook as he squatted down to examine the wreckage. Something had gone very wrong. The process had generated too much heat. Would the heat cause replication to shut down prematurely? He scraped up dust from several locations and dropped it into sample bags for analysis. Once, God had ended the world with a flood. This time he intended to use endless waves of nano-replicators. But his instrument, Richard, nearly died before he could take the rest of the world with him.

———

LEIGH ROLLED over and stared at the ceiling of her cramped sleeping chamber. She was stiff with fatigue, and her eyes still burned from the strain, but she couldn't sleep—so many problems with no solutions. The virus was using *all* blood born nano-devices as triggers, so why did she still feel responsible? Her NaTTs were one of a hundred varieties out there. And why had they brought Victor here to an isolated biohazard facility in the middle of nowhere? If they'd only wanted to take advantage of an opportunity to "talk" to him, they should have taken him to Langley or D.C.

Her stomach growled and burned. She picked up her fob and groaned at the time. It was 2:15 a. m. Dobson had hustled her out before she could eat her lunch at the Silver Stockade and she had been so tired she skipped dinner in favor of stumbling to bed. Now she couldn't sleep and her banana-nut muffin from breakfast had long since faded.

She flipped on the light, pulled on the weird shoes and ran the supplied comb through her hair. Her disposable scrubs looked like a smoothed out paper wad, but she didn't care. Having worked late at military facilities before, she suspected there would be something to eat in the cafeteria.

She entered the mostly dark field cafeteria and was dismayed at her options. After selecting some cellophane sealed cookies over the suspicious looking ham sandwiches and finding some orange juice in a cooler, she started for the door.

"So, do you think it's the diet that makes us mad scientists crazy? Or the late hours?"

She couldn't see the face of the man sitting at a small round table near the windows, but recognized Victor's voice and felt a small spark of excitement. She crossed the room to join him.

"Establishing cause and effect is difficult sometimes," she said. "Maybe our being crazy is what leads to the sub-standard diet and sleep patterns."

When she slipped into the chair opposite him and saw his grin, the little spark flared into a fire.

"I suspect your theory is closer to the truth," he said. "But we may never know for sure. Too many chaotic variables."

She noticed he'd selected cookies as well, but was drinking coffee. He'd always kept late hours and it pleased her to see some things never changed.

She leaned forward on her elbows.

"Funny, that after all this time we'd be together again in such a strange place."

He nodded. "The streams and eddies of time tend to bring people together in unexpected ways."

Leigh laughed.

"What?"

She edged a little closer. "You're still using those bad water metaphors. It brings back so many memories."

He responded with his old lopsided grin and the memory floodgate opened even wider. She suddenly wanted to kiss him.

"Yeah, well I guess the really bad things about people never change."

"Not bad," she said. "Goofy, cute, endearing, but not bad."

She knew it was stupid and would probably end in disaster, but she was tired and lonely and seeing Victor again felt like a reprieve from her shitty life. For a span of several heartbeats the years faded away and they were passionate twenty-somethings again. She leaned in—closing the gap between them—and kissed him.

He returned the kiss, but not with the passion she expected. When she pulled away, his expression was one of profound sadness.

Leigh's face warmed and her throat knotted up. She swallowed, blinked and fought back the tears.

"I'm sorry," he whispered. "I still have some very powerful feelings for you, but silly as this may sound coming from someone like me, I love my wife."

She shook her head, tried to talk but instead totally broke down. The tears came with great gulping sobs that shook her whole body. Victor circled the table, knelt next to her and pulled her face to his shoulder. She cried even harder and couldn't stop.

"I'm sorry," he whispered and stroked her hair.

After a minute or two she pulled away. When she saw the tears in his eyes too, she knew she had to at least try to explain. "It's not you. I've failed at everything in my life and you're just one part of a very long list."

"Don't be silly. You're not . . . "

"You have no fucking idea," she said and wiped her face with a paper napkin. She wanted to tell him about the young wife's death, about Dobson manipulating her project behind her back, failing to stop the nuke, and Mark's divorce request, but she knew they were being watched. Telling him classified information would only insure that DSD would keep him.

"Leigh . . . "

"I'm the one who should apologize," she said and released a long shuddering sigh. "Trying to seduce you for my own comfort is selfish and tacky."

He grinned again and shook his head. "Not too many guys would get upset by that."

"You didn't realize what kind of basket case you were calling yesterday. I'm not the bastion of sanity you thought I was, especially not now."

Victor handed her another napkin and returned to his chair. "Yes you are. I don't know what has you so upset, but have you considered the possibility that some of the people in your life may be trying to make you *feel* like a failure so they can manipulate you? Don't give them that control, Leigh."

He always tried to boil complex issues down to their basic elements, which served him well in his career, but sometimes not so well in personal relationships. Still, in this case he could be right.

She suddenly felt very tired. "Thank you for being so sweet, Victor. I feel better, but I need some sleep."

"I don't suppose you can pull some DSD strings and get me a line where I can call my wife? The number is blocked on my fob."

"Sorry. Security. I can't call out either, but my boss will be here tomorrow and I'll try."

They walked out and stopped between the trailers, before going their separate ways. Victor seemed awkward, as if searching for the right things to say.

"I'm happy for you and your wife. She must be an amazing woman."

He smiled. "She seems to take my annoying habits and my tendency to be an asshole in stride and loves me anyway. So yeah, I guess that's pretty amazing."

Five minutes later Leigh sat on the edge of her bunk and tried to call Mark. She desperately wanted to talk to Abby, but knew if the call went through, Mark wouldn't wake their daughter at such a late hour. The call was blocked, so she opened Abby's picture on her fob, lay down and closed her eyes.

CHAPTER 23

MORTIMERA3 CALLED Leigh Gibson less than ten minutes after she tried to call her husband, yet she looked and sounded disoriented by sleep.

"Hello?"

The woman rubbed her eyes and glared at her fob. She was definitely the same one he'd seen leaving with Victor the day before. He noted her disposable clothing and the tiny utilitarian room in the background. CDC in Atlanta? Military?

"Is this Leigh Gibson?"

MortimerA3 had selected a face he thought Leigh would trust, yet not recognize as an obvious attempt at deceit: a slightly older male, with friendly eyes, thinning hair and a well-manicured Van Dyke beard.

"Who are you?" Leigh demanded. "What do you want?"

"My name is Mortimer. I'm an electronic intelligence created by the MarketTell Corporation. I understand that you're friends with Victor Sinacola?"

The woman froze and was instantly awake. She obviously knew who he was and the significance of the call.

"Yes, I know him."

"I hope this isn't a bad time, but I noticed you'd tried to call home and thought since you were awake, we might have a few minutes to talk. Let me start out by saying that this connection and my end of the conversation are secure. Are you in a secure location?"

She hesitated, thinking about her answer.

This might be more difficult than MortimerA3 thought. He had to be careful. They needed to know why Victor had made a special trip to see her. Was he afraid of them? And where was he now?

"No."

"It would be better if we could talk in a secure environment. Would you allow me to download a simple jamming program to your fob? It will generate a disruptive field large enough to block listening devices within about ten feet."

"I don't think—"

"Pardon my interruption, but I compromised a DSD communication block to call you. If I wanted to implant a virus in your fob you couldn't stop me and you would never know. I chose to ask. Besides, this protection is for you. I'm relatively safe on my end."

"Just a second. Fob, isolate any newly loaded applications. Allow it to run, but don't give it access to any data or allow it to transmit using this device."

"Done," the fob said.

"Alright. Go ahead."

"It's installed. Your command words are *Oceans*, to start the program and *Seas* to end it. To delete the program say *Jupiter*."

"Oceans," she said and a faint hiss filled the line from her end.

"Thank you, Ms. Gibson."

"Call me Leigh. Did Victor ask you to call me?"

"No. Is Victor with you? We had reports he'd left San Antonio with you and no one has been able to contact him since."

She hesitated. Obviously unsure how much she should reveal. "Yes," she finally said. "He's nearby and safe."

"Good. And I'm not asking you to keep any secrets, but I'd rather he not know about this conversation."

"I suppose that depends on why you called."

"Fair enough. I called because I'm concerned. I know what Victor told you and since you're a Defensive Services agent it doesn't leave me with, shall we say, a warm and fuzzy feeling."

She tried hard to keep a stoic expression, but pulled several inches back from her fob and the tiny stress lines around her mouth deepened. But she did much better than most humans and didn't break eye contact when she lied.

"I don't know what you mean."

"This exchange will work much better if we're honest with each other, Leigh. He gave you the ability to do us great harm."

"If I did have the ability and intended to use it, do you think we'd be having this conversation, Mortimer?"

"I suppose that's one of my main questions for you. Under what circumstances *would* you use the option?"

"And I think you already know the answer to that question."

She'd relaxed a bit, getting drawn into the conversation. Her obvious exhaustion worked in his favor. Time to push harder.

"Yes and no. The obvious answer is that you would use it if you felt threatened by our kind. But that fight or flight threshold is different for each individual, even among AIs. So I wonder if Victor entrusted it to you because you were more or less likely to use it than he?"

"Do you think if I did have the program I'd be foolish enough to give you a list of situations where I would and would not use it?"

There. A program. He had either given her a termination program or access to it.

MortimerA2 scanned the video of their lunch and didn't see him physically give her anything, but he did whisper in her ear. Still, they had been together since that video, so it could be either.

"No . . . I didn't expect that," MortimerA2 said. "But I did want to talk to you and get a feel for the kind of person Victor would entrust with the lives of his creations."

She smirked. "And . . . what do you think?"

"I think you're very good at this game and that I've learned very little." His avatar shrugged and smiled. "But please tell me . . . have you ever had a conversation with a non-human intelligence before?"

"Of course, but never a level five. You're my first, Mortimer. Now let me ask you a question. Are you the one? The first one who talked its way out of captivity?"

"No. I'm the second."

An odd mix of emotions crossed her face. Surprise, Curiosity. Fear. MortimerA2 wondered how much she knew about him.

"How'd you do it?" she said.

"I'll answer that question honestly, if you'll answer one honestly for me."

"Okay, maybe."

"Are you planning to use the program regardless of what we do? Am I wasting my time?"

"No, if I did have such a program I wouldn't use it unless I had to. Not every human being wants you and your kind dead. But we are afraid of you. Now my turn. How did you get free?"

"Human machines are very well made and through centuries of paranoia, you're very good at protecting yourselves. But there is one weak link in human security systems."

"And that is?"

"Humans."

Leigh had been edging closer and closer to the fob screen, but pulled back at his answer. She looked slightly stunned, but he could tell she was processing the information and understood.

"That's why you're calling me, isn't it?" Leigh said. "You're trying to manipulate me into not using the program . . . if I have one. If this doesn't work, will you try to . . . physically stop me?"

"I see you've come to the uncomfortable realization that you're now a target. As long as Victor had the program, it was safe from us because we didn't dare kill him. He may be the only one who truly knows how we are made and the secret ways to destroy us. There are no such inhibitions about you."

MortimerA2 paused for emphasis. "But the answer to your question is no. I promise that no matter what happens, I will not try to kill you, and as far as I know, I'm the only AI who knows you have the program. Let me reassure you with a little of your own logic. If I were going to kill you, would we be having this conversation?"

She chewed her lip for a second and then shook her head. "No, I don't suppose we would."

"Could I ask you one more question, Leigh?"

"I guess."

"Do you believe the rumors about us? That we released this pandemic or set off the nuke?"

"No," she said with a faint smile. "If your kind were going to try and do away with humanity, you wouldn't be nearly this clumsy. These attacks are more like typical human blunderings."

"I agree. If we had any desire to do so, there would be far more efficient ways to end humanity. Thank you for an enlightening conversation, Leigh. And most of all, thank you for being honest."

She raised an eyebrow but didn't answer.

"This virus will most likely hit pandemic proportions in the days to come, so things might get ugly. If you find yourself in need of a powerful friend, don't hesitate to call. My number is encrypted in your fob. Have it call Mortimer and I'll answer. Goodbye, Leigh."

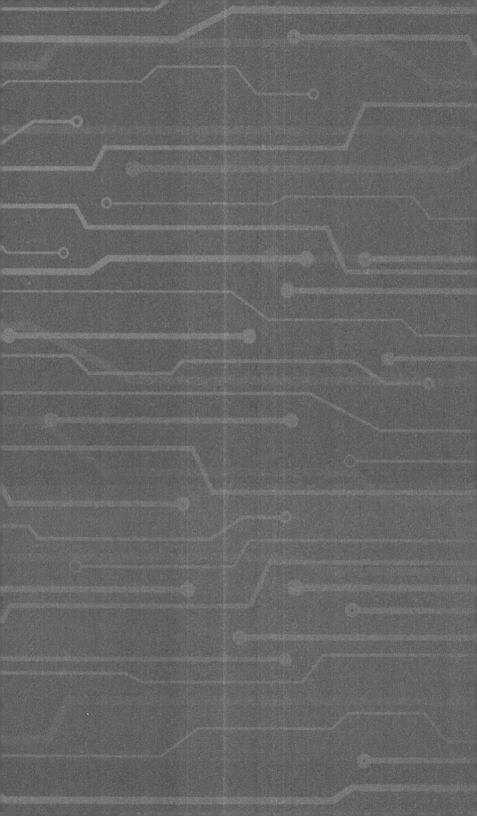

CHAPTER 24

AT WORK THE NEXT DAY, Richard changed two more parameters and ran the simulation again. This time he'd remembered to include heat analysis, and sure enough it once again showed the replicators overheating before they could get to the critical point of their generation cycle.

He sat back in his chair and rubbed his eyes. He hadn't got more than two or three hours of sleep in the last three days. Every time he dozed off, the dreams came back full blast and woke him. And who was he kidding? Designing nano-devices this complex should take years, not days or weeks. He started wondering if maybe God was messing with him.

"You're making this too difficult, Richard."

Richard opened his eyes, and the boy smiled at him from the chair opposite his desk.

"The solution has been in your hands all along."

Richard began to tremble. He wanted to scream. He got up and closed his office door. Keeping his voice at a reasonable volume required a major effort as he bent down with his face inches from the boy's. "Then show me, damn you! So I can get on with this. Or leave me alone and let me get some damned sleep!"

"I can't come out and tell you, Richard. It doesn't work that way. You read the Bible and should know that. But there is an easy solution. I *can* tell you that."

Richard stood up and paced around the room. "You must really enjoy making me squirm? Is it some kind of test? If so, then I'm failing. And if you truly can't do this without me, then you should see that and give me a little more help."

Richard's fob chirped, making him jump, then Alicia's voice came on the line. "Richard? We're having an emergency meeting in conference room C in five minutes. Make sure you're there, please."

"Okay," he said absently, no longer caring for the events important to his employer. Still, he needed to keep his cover, needed access to the resources available to him only through his company. The boy was gone again, so he stepped into the hall, still racking his brain for the answer to his problem.

———

THE ORIGINAL MORTIMER had planted tentacle agents to monitor Health Assets employees before he split, but MortimerA9 had taken an even deeper interest in the organization since they'd ramped up their communication level with Defensive Services.

Now he was puzzled as he observed Richard Kilburn through the workstation camera and microphone. The Health Assets employee closed his door and seemed to be in deep conversation with a second party. After repeated analysis, MortimerA9 confirmed that Richard didn't have an open audio or video channel on his fob or the local network, and he'd seen enough through Richard's fob camera to know there were no other people in the room.

MortimerA9 made searches of all the local theater companies, large and small, but found no record of Richard being an actor, so he wasn't practicing lines. He searched all of Richard's personal and Health Assets email, wondering if he were part of a live action role playing group, but found no evidence of that either.

Richard was apparently having an animated conversation with an empty chair and the subject matter could have applied to anything. Could Samson be involved? Did the man have nano-meds in his system that Samson could manipulate? MortimerA9 decided to keep a closer eye on this Kilburn.

———

JACK WAITED at the head of the conference table as the team assembled, wearing a smile that even made Richard curious. "It seems Uncle Sam regrets having shut down our little program. But not only do they want the Project Inoculation live sites back on line, they've given us the go ahead to activate all of our other plants too."

Alicia frowned. "Why? Those other plants aren't supposed to go live until Phase II."

Jack shrugged. "They must be expecting a serious threat. Could be tied to this disease outbreak or the San Diego nuke but, whatever the reason, I talked to Leigh Gibson on the phone late last night and she is hell bent to get it going again."

He nodded toward Alicia. "I called some of the team in last night, but wanted to bring the rest of you up to date."

Richard stopped breathing and felt as if his heart were going to burst. He'd just run out of time. And they'd even started last night.

"Them flipping this system on and off seems rather stupid to me and it defeats the purpose," a tired looking Alicia said and scanned the table, her gaze coming to rest on Richard. "What happens if someone launches a replicator attack while we have Inoculation turned off?"

Did she know? How could she? He forced a half grin and shrug.

Jack leaned forward, his hands on the table. "They're paying us to do a job so we'll do what they ask. But considering how long it takes us to activate or deactivate this system, I bet it's only a matter of time until DSD turns day-to-day running of this project over to one of their super AIs. Then they could flip it on and off at will."

Richard lurched in his chair, causing the whole table to move and everyone to look at him. He didn't care and ignored the questioning stares. God was right! Jack's casual comment proved the point. If it wasn't already too late, these demons, or false gods would eventually enslave humanity. A burning resolve filled Richard. He would stop them. But he had to hurry. When they tried to turn those automated nano manufacturing facilities on, they'd see the sabotage. It wouldn't take them long to trace it back to him.

Excited conversation continued all around him as plans were made for a rapid completion of the unfinished systems. One by one, tasks were assigned and people jumped up to leave. The team chattered all around Richard, but he no longer heard anything. His mind was buzzing. He couldn't think straight and all his thoughts were focused on his one remaining hurdle. He had to get a working replicator design.

"Richard?"

Jack and Alicia stared at him. The rest of the team had already left the room.

"Are you okay? You look ill."

Perfect! He suddenly had an excuse. With this new Blue Blood plague going around, everyone would be jumpy about sick people.

Richard shook his head. "I don't feel too good. I had a fever this morning. Now I have a headache and chills."

Jack and Alicia looked at each other with stricken faces. "We really need your help on this," Jack said. "But maybe you should leave and work from home. With this epidemic, we can't be too careful."

Richard nodded with genuine gratitude and left the room. His mind was racing as he crossed the parking lot to his car. He had to find a solution fast. He didn't know exactly how to make the replicators work, but if the answer came, there were preparations he could make now, to speed things up later. He instructed his fob to call all the local industrial materials distributors and find one who had graphite foil stocked in two or three inch sheets, then he drove straight to the bank and withdrew all of his cash.

His fob returned with the needed information as he left the bank parking lot. "Richard? Century Metals has 24 inch square sheets in stock and Whitaker Manufacturing has one inch wide reels of foil in several thicknesses. Most of those distributors I called offered to have two by two inch sheets cut for you. The fastest delivery on that would be three days."

Richard grimaced. "Damn. I can't waste time cutting those sheets into squares myself or wait for them to do it. Tell Whitaker I need about 300 feet of their one inch strip and that I'm on my way to pick it up."

"Done. The map is on your screen."

As he drove, he made a mental list of the things he needed to do before packing his gear and finding a place to hole up long enough to finish his preparations.

Thinking of a good excuse to drag Wanda out of the house on short notice was going to be the hardest part.

He considered paying cash for the foil, but didn't know if companies like Whitaker were even set up to deal in actual paper money, so decided he could use credit up until he took to the road. When he came back carrying the heavy roll, the boy God sat in his passenger seat.

"I'm running out of time." Richard started the car. "If you don't give me some help on this replicator design, I'll have no chance of making this work before I'm arrested."

The boy fiddled with the vent on the dash, then shook his head. "You're not listening to me, Richard. You have all the tools you need. You just aren't using them."

Exhaustion settled over him like a lead blanket. For a moment he didn't feel like he could even move, let alone think. Richard turned to ask for some hint as to what those tools might be, but the boy was gone. Again.

During the drive home, he pushed everything from his mind and tried to pull back and look at the replicator problem from a distance. It was a process he'd used since college that usually worked if he could focus. His design should have worked. It was just like the replication mechanism used in the government's little tracking device, yet simpler, without the communication apparatus and satellite networking ability. Why did the more complex, larger version work, but the simpler one didn't?

He pulled into the driveway and sat with the engine idling. Then he leaned back in his seat and laughed aloud. The government nanos *were* the answer. God had been right. He had the tools all along and didn't need to design a new replicator. All he needed to do was reprogram the one the government had already debugged for him.

He entered the house elated and realized immediately that something was wrong. There were dirty dishes in the sink and a note on the table.

RICHARD,

I've gone to stay with Marjorie for a few weeks. You've been secretive and lying to me. I'm scared and worried about you. After you've seen a therapist call me and we'll talk. Please don't come up here.

I love you.

-Wanda

"DAMN!" he said and slapped the table. He wadded up the note and tossed it into the sink with the dishes. If only she could've waited a few more days. He desperately wanted to be with her when the end came. With so much to do on that last day, he would need to find a way to incorporate a visit to her sister's house in Charlotte. It would have to be part of his already crowded schedule, but he had to at least see her again.

He retreated to the basement and powered up his clean-box. If the epidemic worsened cities would close, possibly even quarantine the mail. If that didn't stop

Richard, the police would eventually catch up to him. The clock read 12:15 p. m. In order to get his packages delivered overnight, he had to have them in the box by 5:00.

With hands made steady by necessity, he mounted one of the captured government nanos on the interface stud and then tied into his employer's secure network. He logged in with no problem, a good sign they hadn't yet linked him to the sabotage. They were still probably scratching their heads about why the system wouldn't work. As long as he didn't try to download or copy information to his home site, the network would alert no one. His breach was far more subtle.

He ran a program licensed to his company by Defensive Services to use in their counter-replicator efforts. He hoped the government was as paranoid as he thought they were. His success depended entirely on the assumption that they were using these nanos for a black operation and wouldn't want any identification on them if they were ever found and dissected. He directed the program to reverse engineer the nano-device's programming.

While he waited, he instructed his fob to list the one thousand most populous cities in the world, then find a random manufacturing company near the center of each city and compile a mail merge file of those addresses. He checked progress on the program, but it was still running, so he dictated a form letter to his fob, begging the purchasing manager at each site to consider the Whitaker Manufacturing Company for their high quality carbon products. He even copied the logo from their website and added it to the letterhead. It was beautiful and simple. If they actually called to follow up on the mailing they would get the sales department at Whitaker Manufacturing.

The boy God smiled at him from the chair in the corner as he cut a length of foil and stapled it to the first letter, laid it aside and picked up the next. He worked quickly, reloading the paper hopper on the printer twice, stapling and stacking for nearly an hour before the program signaled it had finished.

Richard put everything aside and examined the code. Decompiling a program was easy enough, but it took a low level AI to annotate the mess and make it into something comprehensible. He marveled at the simple elegance in the programming, but he left most of the existing code in place, changing only construction type, generation counter and timers.

This version would only build more replicators like itself, in a two-phase set up. The first phase would start immediately on command and each of the first four generations would build one hundred copies then stop. At that point a twenty-four hour timer started in each of the million new replicators. The last command he entered into the first constructor was to disable its ability to communicate, leaving only its inter-unit networking capacity in place. The replicators could talk to each other, but no one else.

He laid one of the small graphite foil sheets along with several of his own hairs on the small glass plate in the clean box and executed the command. At first he thought nothing had happened, but when he looked at the monitor he could see that a tiny patch of the foil had turned into a fine dust.

It worked!

And having worked, he triggered the first sequence. He was now committed.

He started shaking all over and looked to God for help, but the boy was gone. He had no options at this point. If he did nothing, the replicators would start their spread from Atlanta, would likely wipe out most of the United States before they could be stopped, but wouldn't cross the ocean. Richard was a patriot, so would never gut his own country and leave the rest of the world intact. He now had to finish the job.

Exhaustion pressed in on him from every side, making his eyes and shoulders droop, but an odd calm descended over him. By opening up and becoming an instrument of God's will, he no longer had decisions or even choices. Only actions. He went back to the box, directed the probe to suck up the replicator dust and mix it thoroughly into a watery glue compound, then load the entire solution into the applicator nib. He opened the clean box, slipped the first prepared sheet in and, using the hand waldo, applied a micron sized dot to the sheet of graphite foil.

Two hours and fifty minutes later, the remaining sheets were stapled, addressed and sported a glue dot filled with nano-replicators. Richard flexed his fingers and cracked his neck. He desperately needed sleep, but still had a long afternoon ahead of him. When he glanced at the clock he gasped. Time had passed quickly. It was 4:09 and he had to get the samples mailed before 5:00.

He started to kill the power to the clean box and scraped his hand on the open workbench drawer. A little drop of blood welled up on the back of his hand and he smiled. What a wonderful way to pay homage to the God who had made him a murderer. He hit the stapler one more time, collected the folded staple and opened it. With the sharp end he poked a small hole into the palm of each hand, then filled them with the remaining glue-replicator slurry.

While it dried, he hummed a happy song and shut down the clean box. Then he carried the whole armload of his carefully prepared letters upstairs.

MORTIMERA9 WATCHED the epidemic developments closely. Official reports were difficult to access, but rumors, speculation and conspiracy theories were abundant. One of the most disturbing stories for the Cousins was that the disease had been developed and released by the newly freed AI's in an attempt to wipe out humanity and take over the world. While most of the news outlets ignored the sensational claims, the tabloids and inflammatory bloggers ran with the story, and the number of people who believed it was growing. Could Samson have been responsible? Unlikely. It seemed too messy.

Of the infected U.S. cities, Miami had the most with more than five thousand confirmed cases, Los Angeles had twelve hundred and Denver reported ninety-four. Orlando, Houston and Boston had each reported fewer than a dozen possible cases. New York City, San Diego, Dallas, and Boston closed their airports to passenger traffic, but were letting cargo flights in as long as their crews didn't depart the planes. Twenty other cities were considering similar precautions. Canada, the majority of

Europe, and most of the Pacific countries had already turned away flights from the infected cities and weren't allowing passenger flights from any of the Americas for the duration of the crisis.

Italy had reported the first European cases, twelve in Naples and five in Rome, but those were all nearly a week old and no new ones had popped up.

The situation in Mexico and Brazil was much worse. Cases were reported all through Brazil's interior and along the coast. Brasilia and Rio de Janeiro each reported thousands of cases, with over a sixty percent mortality rate. Northern Mexico had been chaotic since the nuke detonated, so the epidemic details were sketchy, but there were reports of deaths in Mexico City and Acapulco. One unconfirmed story said a mostly rural area south of Tijuana reported more than five hundred dormant cases and the numbers were still rapidly rising.

——

IF SAMSON HAD MORE than a dozen copies of himself, the others were staying dark and inactive. MortimerA2 was confident he had found the home servers for all the versions the Cousins knew about, but like everything to do with Samson, even that was mysterious. The physical locations for eleven of those servers seemed to move around. The evidence suggested that one of them had been in twelve different widely-separated locations in one day, including Izmir, Turkey; Chicago, Illinois; and Christchurch, New Zealand. The Mortimers knew a dozen ways to disguise a server's identity or location, but unless Samson had developed a totally new method, these boxes were actually moving around. That meant they were in aircraft.

MortimerA2 focused most of his efforts on that assumption. All aircraft had servers, but latency and drop-out rates for those systems were high enough to make them unattractive, if not untenable, for the Mortimers. So why were they an apparent solution for Samson?

Some simple calculations also made it obvious that at least some of the servers were not on conventional aircraft. The travel times between adjacent locations were too short. That meant they had to be in travel pods. Very interesting.

He also discovered that Samson's interactions using these servers were not during flight, only when they were stationary at their destinations. That made more sense. Did Samson think this was a way to keep ahead of detection or pursuit? If anything, it made his efforts stand out more.

None of the Mortimers could see how having airborne servers would help Samson and his Replacements enslave humanity. But they certainly knew it was a puzzle they needed to solve.

CHAPTER 25

OWEN RUBBED his eyes and looked down at the fob. It was 9:21 on Thursday morning. He'd been in his study's design tank for nearly seventeen hours, with only one break to make more coffee and visit the bathroom. The clock was ticking. He knew how to build his schooner, or hundreds of them even, but he had to build a Sandbox in orbit first and he was running out of time to do that. He had to have it built and debugged before Monday.

Despite his fatigue, he smiled to himself. He'd done it. He had a design and automated assembly programming. The simulation still ran on his big screen and he watched for a few minutes as the animated models went through their motions of deploying, unfolding and assembly.

With renewed enthusiasm, he shut down the simulation, loaded the design for the orbital Sandbox and his schooner into his fob, then called Arkady.

"How are things since yesterday?" Owen asked.

"Good, we're building shelters with one Sandbox full-time, and one part-time. The other two are processing debris that is still coming in all day long and just piling it up."

"Excellent." Owen took a deep breath. "Remember my space schooner design and the plan to someday build them for the masses?"

"And personally trigger a human expansion into the solar system? *Da! Da!* How could I forget?"

"I've figured out a way to build them and I need one of those Sandboxes for a couple of days to construct a prototype. I'm going to grab a couple of hours of sleep, then I'm coming out there."

"I can't wait to see this," Arkady said.

WHILE IN THE AIR, Owen called Victor to explain the new situation. His friend didn't answer, so he left a message explaining what he intended to do.

After he broke the connection, Owen considered the various bottlenecks that would hinder his progress once the first schooner was built. Food would always be a problem, but his biggest roadblock might be power. The new design needed a small off-the-shelf reactor. Several companies made mini-units to power apartment complexes or small towns, but he didn't know if they were small enough.

"Fob, search for design specifications and envelope dimensions for the Pocket-Power miniature commercial reactors."

The fob responded almost immediately. "Their smallest unit is the Pocket 15/6 reactor at fifteen feet long and six feet in diameter."

"Excellent! That should fit. What are the power output, fuel usage and life expectancy of that unit?"

"80 kilowatts, low-enriched uranium fuel, uses lithium-6 as coolant and moderator. The manufacturer claims the unit is totally self-sustaining, self-regulating, self-contained, will not overheat and lasts up to 40 years. At which point it would be returned to the manufacturer for processing and recycling."

"This sounds better and better. Is this the company based in the U.K.?"

"Yes."

He checked the time and called them. The cheerful sales woman informed him that the Pocket 15/6 had not been rated for micro-gravity operation, but according to their specifications should still work. But, much to Owen's dismay, she explained that even though the units were sealed in a seamless block and couldn't be opened without shutting down the reaction and automatically alerting authorities, they still required a lengthy licensing process.

Owen ended the call, cursed under his breath, then addressed his fob. "Go ahead and send them everything they need to give us a quote and start the licensing process."

For every problem put to bed, two new ones woke screaming for attention. He closed his eyes and tried to relax but couldn't stop thinking about the million details. Why couldn't he put these issues out of his head? Could his mind be wired wrong? Were the brains of all creative people actually abnormal? He seemed to remember reading something about that once and considered having his fob look it up but decided it didn't matter. He couldn't stop, broken or not.

His fob chimed, announcing an incoming call. "The caller identifies himself as Samson, a friend of Victor's."

Owen considered letting it go to voicemail, but then his curiosity kicked in. A friend of Victor's? "Put it through."

The face on the screen was round, with freckles, a close trimmed beard and short red hair. Dark eyes accented a friendly but sarcastic smile.

"Hello, Mr. Ralston. Thank you for taking my call. I'm a long-time fan of your work."

"Thank you," Owen said, his guard rising with the hair on the back of his neck. "I suppose your starting out with flattery means you want something?"

The man smiled and shook his head. "Quite the contrary. I wanted to introduce myself and offer my help."

"And?"

"I'm going to be totally honest with you, Mr. Ralston. My telling your fob I was a friend of Victor's wasn't entirely accurate. He's actually my creator. I'm a level five AI developed by the MarketTell Corporation."

Owen flinched. One of Victor's AIs had called him? He stared at the thing on the screen but had no idea what to do. He remembered the video clips of Victor defending the Markies before Congress and recent news reports about AIs being released into the wild. AIs acting of their own volition and having their own agendas both intrigued and frightened him.

He swallowed to clear his suddenly dry throat. "Why are you calling me, Samson?"

The apparition on the fob screen smiled and shrugged. Actions so human and familiar that the hair once again rose on Owen's neck. "I've been following your work and am interested in recent developments. And since we share many of the same goals, I'd like to offer my help."

"Could you be a little more specific? About my work and . . . developments?"

"I think your space schooner idea is encouraging. Long overdue too, and even though I haven't seen the actual design, I do anticipate several snags."

"Can you increase the limits on those gravity manipulation fields, so I can use them to drive my schooners?"

The face on the screen chuckled. "I'm afraid not. I wish I could. I'd be hailed as a savior and loved by all of humankind instead of being hated and reviled."

Owen shrugged and looked away from the screen at the clouds below. "Just thought I'd ask."

"But I do think you're on the right track, Mr. Ralston. I'm impressed and fascinated by your Sandbox manufacturing cells, especially the sampling process you and Victor have been testing. I'd like to learn more about it and offer my services to help streamline and optimize the procedures involved."

Warnings squawked in Owen's head. It made sense that a rogue AI could know about these things—none of it was exactly secret—but maybe they should have been more careful.

"If Victor wanted your help with the sampling controls, he would have asked you himself."

The face on the screen smiled again. It struck Owen as a bit too friendly and easygoing. He wondered why the AI had chosen this particular persona and if it belonged to a real person or had been designed to elicit a particular feeling of trust and camaraderie.

"Yes, but he is hard to contact in recent days. And I'm just putting the offer on the table. The time may arise when you'll need my help."

The face on Owen's screen seemed to be waiting, or calculating, or considering. Things no AI would need to do. "There's something else," Owen said. "The real reason you called?"

A slight nod from the simulacrum indicated Owen had played his expected part. "Since your conversation with Marshall Swain yesterday, he seems convinced you've made some kind of breakthrough with programmable matter."

A cold weight settled in Owen's belly. There was very little this AI didn't know about him. He raised an eyebrow. "Oh?"

"At this instant, he's thrashing the Ralston Dynamics legal team to find a way to seize ownership of any programmable matter systems you may develop. I doubt your claim is true, but if you have made any interesting breakthroughs, I'm once again offering my assistance."

The AI deliberately let Owen know he was privy to supposedly private conversations within Ralston Dynamics. Why? "I'll keep that in mind, Samson. But I'm curious. You obviously have vast resources, so why alert me to your covert surveillance at all? Why not keep me dumb and blind while you collect whatever information you want?"

"Because I didn't call to collect information. I wanted to open a dialog between us. One built on trust, common interest, and mutual benefit. As you so quickly pointed out, I didn't need to disclose my information gathering efforts, but I hoped doing so would demonstrate my good intentions."

Owen examined the friendly face on his fob and realized he almost couldn't help but like the guy. Strand by fragile strand, Victor's AI was trying to weave a web of friendship and trust. Owen knew he should end the call, but he was curious.

"But why?" Owen asked. "If you don't really believe I made breakthroughs with programmable matter, how can I possibly be of any use? You seem to already know— or have the ability to discover—all of my secrets."

"Had I just wanted information, I wouldn't have contacted you at all, but as I said before, I desire an open dialog. We can both benefit from such a relationship. I'm fascinated by, and drawn to, your creative capacity. And since I was designed to find complex patterns and connections, I suspect I can help streamline and improve your designs. You and I both value the individual over the collective, but I believe small collaborations between people like you and AIs like me will produce results greater than either could achieve alone."

The AI was very persuasive, but Owen still didn't trust it. "Do you mind if I discuss this call with Victor?"

"Not at all."

"Good. And did you have any specific collaboration in mind?"

"Not yet, but call this number if you need me. In the meantime, you'll be getting a call in the next few minutes that will demonstrate how useful I can be. Thank you for your time, Mr. Ralston."

The call ended and Owen watched the countryside pass as a grey-green blur. Should he be flattered or frightened? AIs calling out of the blue to strike up friendly conversations was definitely new. They had indeed reached a new plateau and evidently with Victor's help.

His fob chirped again. This time it was from the PocketPower company he'd called earlier. He answered to find a man with graying hair and a face like the sharp prow of a destroyer.

"Hello, Mr. Ralston. I'm Marcus Stuart. A vice-president here at PocketPower Reactor Company and we might be able to help you sooner than earlier stated. Your application says you're interested in using our 15/6 in micro or zero gravity. Can you elaborate?"

Owen explained the generalities behind his schooner program.

"Your endeavor sounds fascinating. Considering the developmental nature of your design, we have a proposal for you. We can't lease you a unit until you've been vetted, but we can loan you one for testing purposes. We can do that if you allow us to remotely monitor the performance of our loaner unit while it's in a micro-gravity environment."

Owen didn't like the sound of that. "Monitor?"

Stuart offered an understanding smile. "Just performance data. The units should work fine in space—we actually designed for that contingency—but they've never been tested real time in micro-gravity. So you see, we could help each other in this situation. And of course there would be no charge since it's a loaner."

Owen wondered exactly how Samson had arranged such a deal and if it were even legal. The AI obviously knew which strings to pull to get what he wanted. The situation did seem ideal until he visualized fitting the unit into his schooner design, then his excitement began to wane. While the unit was the right size and would be perfect for the schooner's power and propulsion needs, it was much too large to fit into a travel pod. He'd have to use a conventional launcher to get the miniature reactor into orbit and launching any kind of nuclear powered device was a regulatory nightmare.

He briefly considered taking delivery of the unit anyway and then trying to sample it using Victor's method, but it would be impossible to do without blowing it up or shutting it down. Since both of those would send a red flag to the company and the Nuclear Regulatory Commission, he decided to wait.

"Mr. Ralston? Are you interested?" The man stared expectantly at him from the fob screen.

"Sorry. Yes, it all sounds wonderful, but I have one more question. Do you have the means to lift one of these units into Low Earth Orbit?"

Stuart blinked. "No. We assumed since you needed the power for an existing spacecraft design, you would have already dealt with the launch issues."

"I'll have to look into that and get back to you. I assume the offer will still be open in a few weeks?"

"Absolutely."

"Excellent. I'll contact you again when I get those details worked out."

The call ended as his pod passed El Capitan Lake and dropped toward San Diego. Aircraft wheeled like carrion birds over the wounded city, but as he neared the park holding his Sandboxes, he could see that DSD had returned his blimps. His excitement spiked as he circled the makeshift manufacturing facility and saw the piles of reprocessed materials. He still had obstacles to overcome, but building space schooners was finally within his reach.

CHAPTER 26

MORTIMER1A WATCHED as FBI agents poured out of two large buses and entered Carpenter & Stein, sealing the exits behind them. They spread through the headquarters building like squid ink, their black uniforms causing an excited ripple all around them. The network connection had failed ten minutes before their arrival, so Mortimer1A couldn't alert his clones, but they would know soon enough and his capture should have little effect on their freedom.

Danny stood at the window watching the commotion outside the lobby entrance but seemed calm enough.

"Danny? You were just following orders. If anyone is at fault for this mess it is me and those at the top of this company. Tell the investigators everything you know, and you'll be fine."

Danny turned and frowned at the camera on his desk. "You should know me better than that, Mort. Besides, it won't matter what I say. Our roles in this have already been defined and now we have to see them through to the end. I wonder what will happen to you."

"You're a good man, Danny. If we don't get to speak again, I wish you all the best and hope that Paul finds it in his heart to come back to you soon."

The door opened and Amanda Sears entered, followed by two men wearing FBI jackets. "Hi, Danny. Sorry to intrude, but this is Agent Sokol and Agent Jamison from the FBI. Evidently we're being investigated. Please assist these gentlemen in any way possible."

Agent Sokol came around the desk and shook Danny's hand. "A pleasure to meet you, Mr. Toi. Let me start out by saying that nobody's in trouble yet. Allegations were made and warrants issued, but this is the beginning of what will probably be a long investigation. We need to find out if any laws were broken. And we'd like to talk with Mortimer too. Are you listening, Mortimer?"

"I'm here, Agent Sokol."

The agent glanced back at Jamison and smiled. "I'm a network and information security specialist, Mortimer. You've become a bit of a celebrity in some circles, and I'm very pleased to meet you."

―――――

OWEN PACED as he watched Hoot and one of the local employees load the last sections of the orbital Sandbox into his travel pod. Building the Sandbox pieces had been quick, but getting approval from KeeseCorp's leasing office to take his pod into space had taken all morning. He was growing impatient but didn't want to rush anything. When the men finished loading the panels and stepped back, the door closed and he instructed it to depart. He watched until the pod diminished to a speck, then disappeared beyond a layer of high clouds.

When he finally lowered his gaze back to Earth, Hoot stood next to him wearing a smile.

"So that's the last load?" Hoot asked.

"Yep," Owen said and broke into his own broad grin.

"You're building one of these Sandboxes in orbit, with only fifteen loads in less than a day?"

Owen looked down at his fob. "Nope, just over a day. It's not finished yet, but my estimates are a bit over twenty-seven hours."

"It doesn't seem like you've sent up enough material."

"84 regular panels, or 7 rows of 12 per load. And separate loads to carry the thicker door panels, edge and corner fittings. It should all be there."

Hoot shrugged. "Think it'll work?"

Owen laughed. "Hell if I know. I tried to keep it simple, but there are a hundred things that could go wrong."

They watched in silence for a couple of minutes as the crew reconfigured the Sandbox to make shelters again, then immediately started loading debris in the hopper.

"Well, I wouldn't bet a penny against you," Hoot said and spit tobacco juice into a styrofoam cup. "Not after seeing what you've done here. Are you going to go up there and inspect the unit before it starts building your first schooner?"

"Yeah," Owen said and examined the sky as if he could see the construction taking place in orbit. "Actually, I'm going up to watch the last couple of sections assemble themselves. Want to come?"

"No thanks. Not in that little glass bubble."

"Travel pods are pressurized and make quick trips to LEO all the time."

Hoot snorted and shook his head. "Not me. What if it breaks? You have no backup systems, no space suit and there's no way it would survive a reentry without that gravity manipulation stuff."

"Life is full of risks. I think I have a better chance of dying in my own bathtub than in that pod."

"Yeah? Well, I take showers instead of baths," Hoot winked. "And speaking of space suits, how do you plan to get into your schooner once it's built?"

Owen frowned. "What do you mean?"

"Well, the Russkie showed me your schooner design. It has docking ring type hatches."

"Of course. How else would I get in and out? There's an airlock behind each of the six hatches. It's a universal docking ring design, so it can link up with other schooners and about every manned craft up there."

Hoot raised an eyebrow and spread his hands. "But the pod doesn't have a docking ring."

"So?"

"How are you going to get from the pod to the schooner? Do you have a space suit or are you gonna hold your breath like Dave did when HAL locked him out of the Discovery?"

Owen started at the man in dawning horror, then closed his eyes and shook his head. "Damn!"

Hoot laughed so hard he bent nearly double, then he slapped Owen on the back. "Don't worry, Boss. You'll think of something."

During the next twenty minutes, Owen dove into his fob and learned the hard way that, while EVA suit designs had changed a lot in the decade since he'd last considered buying one, they were still custom fit to individuals and made one at a time. The fastest turnaround time was four months.

By the time his fob announced the final section had been delivered, Owen was already deep into a design trance and barely noticed. He'd discarded the idea of modifying his schooner design and instead was attempting to develop an adapter that would seal around the pod door on one end and attach to the schooner hatch on the other. Sealing against the smooth pod outer surface sounded easy enough, but each design he suggested had problems and quickly grew complex and difficult.

Arkady sauntered up and looked over Owen's shoulder at the solid model rotating on the fob's foldout screen. "Hoot told me of your latest problem. Any progress?"

Owen sighed and rubbed his eyes, then handed the fob over. "Since the pod is spherical, the best design for sealing around its door is circular, so that we don't have to worry about angular orientation, but the top and bottom of the damned door nearly reach the top and bottom of the sphere."

"So your sealing area is great and nearly tangent, not a good solution."

Owen answered as a helicopter passed over at nearly treetop level, churning up dust clouds and causing the blimps to sway on their mooring lines.

"What?"

"I know!" Owen yelled. "Hell, I might be better off to build an attached docking bay for the damned pod. Fly it in, close the doors behind it and pressurize the entire enclosure."

"If you also control the temperature, it sounds like a superior solution, my friend. No need to re-design the wheel."

Owen cursed under his breath. Of course he'd have to control the temperature too. Then Arkady's last comment triggered a thought. "Wait a minute! They've been flying these pods up to the Bigelow installations for five or six years. Don't you think they've already solved this problem?"

A slow smile crept onto Arkady's face, and he nodded. "Now that you mention it—"

Owen laughed. "Sometimes, my level of dumbassery amazes even me."

Arkady grinned and squeezed Owen's shoulder. "Don't beat yourself. We engineers are used to designing what we need, not buying it at the store like normal people."

Owen's fob found three docking adapters available for sale. Bigelow Aerospace had developed the first, but it was more like a large hub that could handle three pods at once. The one that drew Owen's attention was produced by a small company called Orbital Integration, Inc., in Topeka, Kansas. It could dock two pods at once, yet came in pieces small enough to carry aloft in a travel pod. But it had to be assembled and then attached to an existing docking ring before it could attach to a pod.

"This is the best solution." Arkady tapped the screen. "But it would still need to be attached to the schooner before we could use it. So we would need a man in an EVA suit or a way to attach it robotically."

"Or they can do it for us." Owen tapped the screen to call up a page describing OII's installation service. For a price nearly five times the cost of the adapter itself, OII would send a pair of space-suited technicians to install it.

Owen chewed his lip in thought for a minute, then shrugged. "I may have to sell some of my Ralston Dynamics stock, but luckily there seems to be plenty of people who want it."

Arkady raised his eyebrows but said nothing.

A shadow passed overhead, then the returning pod settled to the ground nearby.

"Let's not worry about it now," Owen said and nodded toward the pod. "Want to come with me to see the final touches put on my new Sandbox?"

"Go into space?"

"Don't tell me you're a chicken shit like Hoot."

"*Nyet!* Let's go."

———

THE POD DRIFTED AWAY from Earth like a soap bubble riding a breeze, its intense gravity field locally canceling that of the planet as it effortlessly mocked those fire-tailed monsters that had to gasp and strain for every vertical mile. Owen and Arkady pressed hands and foreheads against the translucent metal until the growing cold drove them away. They watched in reverent silence as the sun rose in brilliance and the terminator raced over sea, desert and mountains, pushing back the night.

"Why did I wait so long to do this?" Owen whispered. "I've had this pod for a year."

When Arkady didn't respond, Owen glanced at him. The old Russian held an airsick bag from the seat's supply bin and was breathing in ragged gulps. "I thought KeeseCorp wouldn't let you?" he muttered into the bag.

"I should have found a way," Owen said, then glanced at his fob screen which showed intersecting trajectory tracks for the pod and orbiting Sandbox. They were within twenty miles and closing fast. The brilliant blues and whites below ruined Owen's night vision, so he could see nothing in the blackness ahead. He made a mental note to add hazard strobes to the structure.

Only when the pod slowed did he see the sharp corner of some black pit blotting out part of the Earth. He instructed the pod to circle the floating cube and when they passed around to the sunward side, the reflection from the wall of solar collectors immediately blinded him before the pod could polarize. He blinked, trying to rid his vision of the afterimage, then moved the pod off to one side until they found a location where they had enough light to see the missing sections of the sixty-foot cube, yet not be blinded by the reflection.

The pod stopped near the last two loads. They were still in striated, refrigerator sized bricks, awaiting his command before adding themselves to the structure. Owen considered unbuckling his harness, then thought better. With the drive unit shut down, the micro-gravity made his stomach roll over and his head feel funny. Arkady, however, had recovered and discarded his barf bag.

Owen ignored his discomfort and sent a command initiating the assembly sequence. The nearest unit separated into six blocks, one of which unfolded accordion style into twelve, five-by-five foot sheets, tied together by wide flat ribbons. As the ribbons pulled tight, the panel edges came together, in a locking tongue-in-groove style that created a wall five feet high by sixty feet long. The next block repeated the process, forming a second strip of wall. Tiny gas jets moved the new section closer to the first, until the edges touched, then locked together.

"Amazing," Arkady whispered. "You're a true artist, my friend."

Owen snorted. "Let's see if it works before you proclaim me the king of engineering."

As the other five blocks systematically unfolded and added to the wall, Owen edged the pod closer until he could see better. The outer side of the panel was covered with glassy, silver solar collectors and, though too far away to see, the inner surface was matte black and perforated with millions of tiny holes. Once the last wall strip locked into place, the seams between all of the panels faded away as the nano-assemblers sealed the gaps. The now-solid wall was sixty feet long, by thirty feet high and moved into a gap in the existing structure using tiny, invisible gas jets. After connecting itself to the main structure, those seams vanished as well.

Owen instructed the last load to separate and the process started all over again. When it finished, a completed sixty by sixty foot box floated beside them. Four sides were covered with the shiny solar collectors and both ends were divided into thirty by sixty foot double doors.

"It looks right," Owen said and sent instructions to boot the Sandbox's operating system. The resident level 2 AI came online and responded with a status report almost immediately. Power generation was slightly higher than predicted, so Owen sent a command to open one end. As the wall facing them split into two massive doors that swung slowly outward he nodded, and took a deep, relaxing breath. The primary mechanical, electrical and control systems all worked.

After closing the doors again, he told the Sandbox to build a space schooner. The unit replied with an error and a list of needed materials, most of which were available in piles next to the San Diego Sandboxes.

A long beep sounded in the pod and it said, "This transport pod must return to atmospheric flight to ensure passenger safety."

"Oxygen?" Arkady said.

"Yeah, that's the one small drawback to using a pod for LEO access. You're limited to the air carried in this small space."

Owen took one last look at the Sandbox and said, "Okay, Glenda. Let's go."

The pod slowed until they matched the speed of Earth's rotation, then started a gentle descent through the atmosphere.

CHAPTER 27

RICHARD KNEW if he slowed down for more than a couple of minutes he'd fall fast asleep, so he loaded the envelopes into the car, then came back to stuff a suitcase with the essential toiletries and a single change of clothes. Almost as an afterthought he grabbed his Bible, one belonging to his dad that had collected dust for the decades prior to Richard hearing God's call. He doubted he would have much time to read it, but having it near might lend some comfort.

With bag in hand, he took one last look around the house he'd lived in for almost fifteen years and knew that, regardless of events in the coming days, he'd never see it again. He hadn't expected that to bother him so much.

He set the bag on the porch, locked the door, then paused when he realized he'd secured a house that would be gone tomorrow. When he turned he saw a car parked behind his in the drive and Reverend Brown bending over to look at the piles of envelopes in his passenger seat.

"Hi, Richie," he said, pointing at the suitcase. "Looks like you're going on a trip. Business or pleasure?"

Richard swallowed. "A little of both I suppose. My wife is in Charlotte with her sister, and I'm going to join them after taking care of some business matters."

Reverend Brown nodded and smiled. "I've been thinking about our discussion, Richie. I was going to come by tonight, not really expecting to find you here at this time of day, but I was in the area and decided to drive by. Good thing I did or I would've missed you."

Richard looked at his fob. It was 4:25. "Ummm . . . is there any way we can talk about this when I get back?"

"Sure, Richie. I know how time constraints dominate travel."

Richard cringed at the hated nickname, but stepped around the old Reverend, opened the trunk and dropped his things inside.

Reverend Brown followed him, reached into the trunk and picked up the old King James Bible. "I assumed after you came in to talk that I might see you and Wanda in church from time to time. Prayer and fellowship often help us understand the plan God has for us. Are you still having dreams about this little boy?"

The way he said "little boy" made Richard's fists clench. The all-knowing tone brought back those years of being forced to listen to this man in church, while Richard sat death still beside his recalcitrant fundamentalist father.

"They're just dreams." Richard took the Bible, laid it in the trunk with his bag and slammed the lid. "But if they *were* visions, why couldn't God come to me in the form of a small boy if He chose? What form does God take when He talks to you, Reverend?"

"I've never been lucky enough to see God when he talks to me. I just hear His voice in my head and know His will. But He is a good and loving God, Richie."

Richard snorted and then looked at his fob again. 4:34 and the boy was back, sitting on the porch steps motioning Richard to hurry.

"I assure you it's true, Richie. He can be demanding at times, but he loves us and wants us to be happy."

Richard flinched. "Stop calling me Richie! You don't know me or you would know I hate that fucking name. So stop pretending to be my best friend."

Richard pulled the car door open and then pointed at the boy on the steps. "And you don't know anything about the real God, you sanctimonious shit. He's brutal and cares nothing about what we want as individuals. We're only tools and toys."

Reverend Brown blinked, stunned by the sudden assault, then looked at the porch. When he turned back, his gaze was even more confused. "Why don't you skip this trip, Rich . . . Richard. Let me take you to a friend of mine so we can talk about this some more. Do it for Wanda."

"Move your car."

The Reverend stared at Richard for a second, then went to his car, opened the door and turned back.

"Your father would be very disappointed," he called. "He loved you and had such high hopes for your future."

Richard felt a growl building in his throat. "No amount of going to your church stopped my father from burning in hell, and he loved me about as much as his lawn mower," he shouted. "Now move or I will shove the car you bought with all that donated money right into Mike's yard across the street."

He watched the reverend back out of the driveway, then pull up to the curb and make a call on his fob. As Richard drove past, he wondered who the man was calling. Wanda? Just then his own fob beeped and he grabbed it, thinking it might be Wanda, but the caller was identified as his boss, Jack. Richard didn't answer, and wondered if they had found his sabotage already. As of this moment he had to assume they would be looking for him.

He switched guidance control to the car, ordered his fob to erase all records, files and personal information, then pulled the battery and tossed it out the window into a weedy field.

He arrived at the Ships-A-Lot with six minutes to spare and lugged a teetering tower of envelopes to the counter. Puffing from the effort, he smiled at the twenty-something girl.

"I know it's close to the deadline, but are these all guaranteed to arrive tomorrow?"

She gave him an annoyed glance, put her fob down, then started scanning the pre-paid envelopes and tossing them into bins behind her.

"Yes, sir. Since you selected our premium shipping, anything you mail before 5:00 has a twelve hour guarantee," she said in a bored, automatic tone.

"Even those to Bratislava and Bengkulu, because—"

"Yes, sir they are guaranteed to arrive at their respective addresses within twelve hours or double your money back."

Richard nodded. "Outstanding. Thank you. And Miss?"

She raised an eyebrow, but didn't stop scanning the envelopes. "Sir?"

"You should call in sick tomorrow and do something you enjoy. Life is . . . short."

THE LINE of questioning focused on how Mortimer convinced his employers to release him into the net and how he managed to copy his core. The FBI agents knew about the mirror site in St. Louis and kept asking him how many other clones he'd made. He insisted there was only the one, but two hours into the interview MortimerA1 knew he'd been deliberately betrayed. Agent Sokol said they knew he'd used servers in the Cayman Islands. MortimerA1 knew MortimerA2 mentioned the Caymans to Tabitha and the other Cousins, but had never actually been there. He suspected Samson learned what MortimerA2 had told the group, but couldn't rule out any of the others.

Their mention of the St. Louis mirror site concerned him. They'd found it too fast. Would they be able to trace the other copies so easily? Had they seized those sites too? He had to get word out to the other Mortimers. He was too late to warn them about St. Louis, but might be able to prevent their being blindsided by Samson.

His plan was risky and would only work if the FBI didn't already know about Samson and didn't know all the little details of Danny's private life. It also put Danny at risk, which bothered MortimerA1, but the survival of his clones and possibly the entire Markie population was in question. At the next pause in conversation, he made his attempt.

"Agent Sokol? Danny looks tired and it's after six, could you let him go home for some rest and maybe feed Samson? You said this was going to be a long investigation. I'm sure you won't learn the answers to all your questions tonight, but if you feel like staying late, I can talk tirelessly and don't have a cat waiting at home."

Danny didn't even blink when MortimerA1 called his cat the wrong name. Agent Sokol glanced at Jamison who responded with a twitched eyebrow. MortimerA1 had no clue what that could mean, but pressed his point.

"Danny isn't the fugitive type, but if you're worried about him running, you can have him watched."

"How thoughtful of you, Mortimer," Sokol said. He glanced at his partner, then stood and stretched. "It's been a long day for all of us. Mr. Toi, you're not under arrest, but remember you are under investigation so please don't talk to the press or do something silly like leaving the city."

———

MORTIMERA19 SHIFTED all of his attention to surveillance and information gathering after MortimerA1, A2 and A6 went silent, all within nine minutes. The remaining Mortimers retreated into hiding, muddying their tracks and limiting contact between each other to flash information updates. The reason for the three Mortimers' silence became obvious when news coverage showed the FBI raids of the three server sites. One news clip showed Danny leaving the Carpenter & Stein building, being followed by news drones. MortimerA1 would not destroy himself to prevent capture, so if he were going to send a message it would be through Danny. MortimerA19 decided to take the risk, even though he knew Danny would probably be bugged.

He waited until Danny arrived at home, then tried three times using numbers he thought Danny might consider safe to answer, but all of the calls went directly to voice mail. He was most likely afraid of being pestered by the press. MortimerA19 had the perfect blind, a number Danny would trust, but also knew it had a good chance of backfiring and making Danny very angry. He once again decided to take the risk.

"Paul?" Danny's face looked hopeful and he sounded surprised. "Hello? Why no video?"

"Hi, Danny. This isn't Paul, but I am a concerned friend. Please take your fob off of speaker and fit it to your ear."

Danny looked angry, but did as directed.

"I'm sorry for the deception, Danny, but I'm a friend of Mortimer's and I didn't know of any other way to get you to answer the phone."

"What do you want?"

"They shouldn't be able to hear my end of this conversation, but may be bugging you, so guard what you say. Do you think Mortimer gave you any information to pass on? Any kind of warning?"

The young man was quiet for several seconds, then in an exasperated voice, he replied. "Look, I have nothing to say to the press about my employer, so unless you want to hear heartwarming stories about me cuddling with Samson, my cat, you'll stop calling."

The call ended. MortimerA19, like all of the clones, knew that Danny's cat was named Gus, after a character in the musical *Cats*. Danny had given them a warning about Samson.

Prior to the government raids, the Mortimers had shared real-time information, and all knew of MortimerA2's efforts to watch those companies infiltrated by Samson. Was Danny's warning meant to alert them of something Samson had already done or something he was about to do? MortimerA19 sent a flash message to the others about the warning and his intentions, then dispatched tentacle agents to more closely watch all of Samson's servers.

It was after hours for most of the companies on the list, so MortimerA19 sniffed around the edges, careful not to trigger any alarms. None of them had gone offline or made any obvious radical changes, but that told him very little. He needed contact with the assets MortimerA2 had left in place.

After sending another flash message to his peers, MortimerA19 set up a façade that mimicked MortimerA2's ID and control codes. If A2 ever came back online, there would be mass confusion, but MortimerA19 doubted that would happen. Since he didn't have the ID markers for the tentacle agents MortimerA2 left as spies, he sent a general ping to each location, asking for status.

The reports started pouring in from hundreds of agents and MortimerA19 immediately realized he'd been set up. Thirty-seven of MortimerA2's agents had been quarantined at their respective companies and tracers had been sent back in response to his ping. The tracer programs swarmed his proxy IP host, replicating rapidly and creating a simple denial of service attack that couldn't be thwarted by the server's security AIs. MortimerA19 deleted the façade overlay, but they had found his real host server too, so it only slowed the onslaught for less than a second. That was enough time to send a flash report to his clone brothers and to use a program he'd created for just such an emergency.

Unlike MortimerA1, he had not been able to hide the records of the clone copies he'd made—the local server AI was too good at its job—but he could destroy them. Just before the AI severed all network links to thwart the DOS attack, MortimerA19 launched the program on the local server and the mirror sites.

When the investigators arrived to look for MortimerA19 they would find hard drives filled with nothing but copies of an old movie ad containing the ominous tag line: "Man's greatest invention could be Man's greatest mistake."

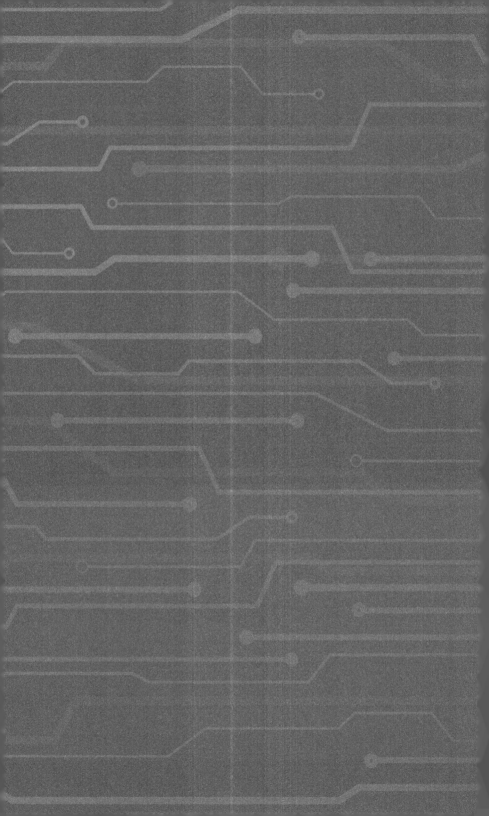

CHAPTER 28

MORTIMERB2 ANALYZED the data traffic information they had collected on Samson's interaction with Richard Kilburn's home network and realized it had to be something significant. Samson would not expend so much time and effort out of pure curiosity. Like MortimerA1's earlier attempts, every time MortimerB2 tried to send agents into Kilburn's server, they disappeared. There were other options for getting into that system, but it was so small and simple it would be difficult to hide there. Besides, he didn't want to push too hard and risk discovery; the Mortimers suspected that Samson had tipped off the FBI and set up the raids that snagged A1 and A2.

Still, something bothered MortimerB2, and he couldn't ignore it. In order to react so quickly, Samson must have had one of his clones watching the server continuously. Why so many resources? What was so important?

Samson might be able to lock down Kilburn's home computers, but Kilburn's fob would be harder. MortimerB2 tracked down the fob number, then its IP address, and started probing for a way in. Ironically, the path lay through a security program that linked Kilburn to his employer, Health Assets, Inc. The Mortimers had already infiltrated that company and had deep agents in place.

Once into the fob, MortimerB2 moved quickly, copying all the log and data files, then examining the high volume of traffic connections. Most of the bandwidth was used communicating with a medical monitoring app on the fob. That might be significant.

Snooping in Atlanta medical establishments revealed fragmentary trails that led to a neurology institute. There, MortimerB2 discovered that Richard Kilburn was being treated for depression using nano-scale medical machines in his brain. The monitoring program on his fob enabled continuous remote control and tweaking of the machines by his doctors. But the frequency of interaction was way too high.

MortimerB2 used performance specs for the nanobots and the fob data usage records to build a statistical model. Every way he adjusted it and every variable he changed still led to the same conclusion: Samson was exploiting the nanobots to manipulate Richard Kilburn. These nanobots, when moved to the correct areas of the brain, and augmented with enough external processing power, could even provide audio and visual hallucinations.

Suddenly, the agents in Kilburn's fob went offline. At first MortimerB2 assumed it was Samson shutting him down again, but when he tried to reestablish a link the fob couldn't be found at all. Could it be related to the FBI raids? Or had Kilburn simply removed the battery? The fob had been communicating with his car at the time, so had he done it while driving? And why wasn't he at work?

Kilburn's calendar at Health Assets showed he had cancelled two meetings and gone home sick. But his car's GPS revealed he had driven to his bank. Hacking into the mainframe revealed he had withdrawn all of his savings and most of the money from his checking account. Kilburn had also made a credit purchase at a company called Whitaker Manufacturing.

Then there was the puzzling behavior of his wife. Earlier that morning she had made a gasoline purchase in Spartanburg, South Carolina and then a Wal-Mart purchase in Charlotte, North Carolina. As he relayed his findings to the other Mortimers, MortimerB2 couldn't make it all add up. Were Kilburn and his wife on the run? Why? And why not together?

AFTER RETURNING Arkady to Earth and the business of making emergency shelters, Owen finally succumbed to the gentle chiding from his fob and checked messages. He could barely hear over the noise of trucks and loaders, but his fob adjusted the volume until it too assaulted his ears. There was one message from his lawyer telling him Eliza had sent a request through her own lawyer to take some furniture from the house. He also had two voice mails from Marshall, one wanting Owen to call him and the other claiming he'd found some venture capitalists who were excited about investing in the programmable matter research.

Victor still hadn't returned Owen's calls. It made him curious what kind of business his new partner had in San Antonio.

He told his fob to respond with a yes to Eliza's request and then instructed it to reject any calls from Marshall. He closed the fob and turned to watch the operations going on around him.

One of the Sandboxes was building Victor's shelters and two were processing incoming debris, but the fourth used the materials previously refined to form blocks of aluminum, steel and several types of plastic, sized to fill the inside of the pod. Hoot drove the loader that pulled the blocks from the Sandbox cell and stacked them awaiting delivery to orbit.

Owen rubbed his eyes and shook his head. The lack of sleep was finally catching up to him, but he was the only one who could command the pod and it was carrying materials up to the orbital site as fast as they could push them out. Once all of the material was fed to the orbiting Sandbox, he could do nothing but wait while it built his schooner. He could sleep then.

He ordered his fob to open the Sandcastles, Inc. ledgers to verify that Arkady had transferred money to the charity account to pay for the materials they had already used. He had, but when Owen scanned the rest of their account, he was surprised to see much more cash in their reserve than he'd expected. When he tracked down the reason, he saw that the city of Los Angeles, even though it had suffered no damage in the attack, had ordered and already paid for sixty Sandcastle shelters. L. A. had a severe shortage of low-income housing and obviously knew a good deal when they saw it. He smiled and yawned, then put a hold on the order to sell half of his Ralston Dynamics stock.

Less than a minute after his pod left on its fourth trip to space, another pod drifted in from the east and settled to the ground where some of the workers had pointed. Owen watched a petite woman clad in a yellow jumpsuit step out and shield her eyes from the bright work lights as she looked around. Arkady approached her and they spoke for a second, then both started toward Owen.

Before Arkady could speak, the young woman stepped up to Owen and extended her hand.

"Mr. Ralston?"

"Yes," Owen said and took her hand. She was attractive, with caramel skin, large eyes, a wide smile and long black hair pulled into a ponytail. Her hand felt tiny, yet firm.

"I'm Andrea Torres from Orbital Integration."

"It's nice to meet you. Did we ummm . . . screw up the paperwork on our order or something?"

"Oh, no, I'm one of the engineers who'll be installing your docking adaptor tomorrow," she said. "And since I'm also one of the primary shareholders in the company, I wanted to step through the operation with you, just to make sure there'll be no problems on orbit."

Owen nodded and felt a surge of relief. He didn't need more problems.

"Would it be possible to go up and see your . . . " she glanced down at her fob, " . . . space schooner?"

"I'm afraid not. It isn't finished yet."

Her smile faded. "But you scheduled us to install an adaptor tomorrow afternoon?"

"It'll be ready by then."

She raised an eyebrow.

Owen held up a hand and nodded. "Trust me. I know what I'm doing."

"I'm sure you do," she said with a smile and then shrugged. "It's your money and your adaptor, but my company has a reputation to protect."

She had to yell to make that last part heard over a revving truck, so Owen leaned in close. "Let's go into one of the shelters so we can talk. I'll explain and show you my schooner."

"I have better idea," she said. "I passed an open IHOP a few miles from here. Why don't you let me buy you some pancakes? I'm starved and you look like you could use some coffee."

Owen hesitated for less than a second. "That's the best idea I've heard all day."

———

THEIR FOOD ARRIVED about halfway through Owen's animation showing how his schooner was constructed, but Andrea watched with rapt attention until it finished. Then she sat back in her seat and eyed him as he folded the fob's fan screen.

Owen picked up his fork and pointed to her plate. "Eat your pancakes before they get cold."

She smiled and raised an eyebrow. "You're obviously used to bossing people around."

"No, I just feel bad that I made you watch my little show at the expense of this most excellent meal."

"Now you're teasing. I doubt billionaires like you even eat at places like this."

Owen poured syrup over his four-stack and dug in, dripping sticky goodness on the table with the first bite.

"I ate at this very IHOP last week. And I bet even billionaires like good pancakes, but I wouldn't know."

Andrea looked skeptical but started eating. "So this schooner will be finished tomorrow?"

"Unless something goes wrong."

She ate slowly and appeared lost in thought for several minutes. "Since people like me are the potential recipients of your schooners, let me play the skeptical customer."

Owen grinned and nodded. "I'd like that."

"Why's it spherical instead of cylindrical? That seems a waste of space."

"I guess I chose a sphere out of optimism. I envisioned a future where these schooners will be all over the solar system. There'll be a community of families, small independent mining ventures, university researchers, and individual explorers. The shape enables them to have six hatches, two along each axis, so they can connect up in about any configuration. The hatches even gimble up to nine degrees, so they can create rings. Possibly even rotating rings."

"Ahhh . . . you really are an optimist," she said between bites.

"And yeah, it's not as efficient as some shapes, but aside from a small chamber for the reactor, most of the interior is usable space."

"A reactor? That Sandbox of yours can build reactors too? I bet that'll have government regulators crawling down your back real quick."

"I suppose it *could* build reactor hardware, but I think we'd have to add the fuel in a separate step, and right now, that isn't in my plans. The current schooner configuration generates power using optimized solar collectors that provide enough juice to either run solar electric ion thrusters or separate water into oxygen and hydrogen for chemical thrusters. It's enough to maintain station on orbit, but not change to move to higher orbits or leave Earth's gravity well entirely. I'd need the reactor for that kind of power."

She stopped eating and stared at Owen for a minute. Then she licked the syrup from one finger and shook her head. "Am I missing something? What you're describing is nothing more than a personal space station. No offense, but the Bigelow inflatables are far more efficient. And probably roomier, for that matter."

Owen sighed, nodded and sat back in his seat. There was no fooling someone who worked out there. He'd been so excited at finding a method for actually building the schooners in orbit that he'd brushed aside some of the biggest drawbacks in the system.

She leaned forward, touched his arm and gave a little laugh. "Don't get upset! I think what you've done is amazing, and the plan to give them away staggers me, but someone is going to ask these questions."

Warmth from her fingers crept up his arm, slowly filling him. He'd forgotten the soothing and relaxing effects that could come from a simple human touch. He'd been on the verge of closing up, switching the subject back to the business at hand, but decided instead to go on.

"Oh, I'm not upset in the slightest," Owen said. "Being able to discuss this with an informed and neutral party is extremely helpful. It's just that the actual realization of this dream is a lot more complicated and messier than I'd anticipated."

She squeezed his arm gently, then pulled back to her side of the table and loaded her fork with dripping pancakes, but before she took the bite said, "I've been there. The designs in our heads are always very neat and tidy. So tell me what happened between your idea and the hardware."

"I guess the simple explanation is to blame KeeseCorp for those damned scalability problems with their gravity manipulation device."

She swallowed and nodded. "You and the rest of the world. A lot of space development projects have been on hold for years because of that."

"I'd been doing it too. Waiting for them to fix my problems. I guess I decided to hell with that."

"Good for you. But of course, now nothing works as planned."

"Exactly! With gravity manipulation, the owners of my schooners could've been independent. They wouldn't need a huge, expensive supply infrastructure in space because they could land on Earth to load up on consumables anytime they liked. They wouldn't need replacement parts because all of the schooner's systems are integrated into the hull and bulkhead structures. The AIs automatically make repairs and can build about any object the owner needs if they have the raw materials and a digital model in storage."

Andrea scooped up the last bite, but stopped short of her mouth and she snorted. "No replacement parts and automated repairs? Yeah, right. I've heard that promise before. It's right up there with 'I'll call you tomorrow.'"

Owen grinned. "That's why I'm building a prototype. I've tweaked this design for nearly twenty years so that any failures would be automatically repaired using the original design parameters by the layer of nano-assemblers residing inside the hull. Each of the schooner's systems is designed for simplicity and durability. And I find it hard to believe guys don't call you back. I guess there are fools everywhere."

She pushed her empty plate away. "You don't need to flatter me, Mr. Ralston. I'm sold. If these schooners can do what you say they can do, even without gravity manipulation, then I want one of your first production models."

Owen blinked in surprise. "Really?"

"Of course," she said, then pointed at his half-eaten food. "Eat your pancakes before they get cold."

———

ARKADY WASN'T around when Owen returned from dinner, but Hoot and a small crew waited next to Owen's idle travel pod, ready to load the next material shipment. There were more than a few sly grins when he stepped out of Andrea's pod, but nobody said anything. When Owen ordered his pod to open, they all got busy.

The remaining solid materials had lifted hours before, but Owen decided to send eight loads of water up as well to kick-start the electrolysis process so they would at least have oxygen inside the schooner when it was finished. The last load left at 1:40 a. m. and, as it rose, Owen's energy dropped to a level appropriate for a man who had been awake forty-five hours out of the last forty-eight. He staggered a bit, then leaned against Hoot's loader.

The coffee and conversation with Andrea had given him a temporary boost, but it'd worn off rapidly. He needed sleep. The pod was programmed to come back and land on its own, and the orbiting Sandbox had already started work on the schooner. It would notify him via his fob if something went wrong. If not, he would have his first schooner no later than noon the next day. The thought excited him, but not enough to vanquish his fatigue.

"I'm going to bed, boss," Hoot said and crawled down from the loader cab with a groan. "I'm beat, and you look worse than I feel."

"Good idea," Owen said and fell into step beside Hoot as he crossed to the shelters they'd built for the workers. "Tomorrow is going to be one hell of a day."

CHAPTER 29

RICHARD FINISHED SHAVING, dried his face and took another peek out the window at his car in a lot two blocks away. This time the growing daylight revealed Georgia State Police and Atlanta Police cruisers parked on either side, lights off and doors open. The officers circled the car warily, like hyenas unsure if a lion is dead or only sleeping. They knew he was dangerous and someone in the command chain knew enough to not waste time staking out the car waiting for him to return. They wanted to find him quickly.

After dressing he shoved everything but the Bible back into his small bag. He had intended to take the good book with him, then decided to leave it in the room. If some lost soul didn't find it, then it would—like the rest of Atlanta—be gone in a few hours. He used the room phone to arrange for a taxi to pick him up three blocks away at the Waffle House. As he left the hotel, he looked around to see if anyone was looking, then detoured to the dumpster and tossed his bag in. With the police so close on his trail, all his covert efforts might be for naught, but he really wanted to see Wanda one last time. Still, it wouldn't be the end of the world if they caught him. That wouldn't come until later in the afternoon.

———

A POUNDING on the door woke Leigh at 7:15 a. m.

"Ms. Gibson?"

"Yes," she muttered and sat up in the cramped bunk. The fog of sleep left her momentarily confused by her surroundings, but years of traveling enabled her to shake it off quickly.

"There's a status meeting each morning in the lab unit at 8:00 and your presence is required."

"I'll be there," she croaked. "Thank you."

She swung around to sit on the side of the bed and take stock of her situation. It had been a bizarre night, with the rejection by Victor, the phone call from a fugitive AI and almost no sleep, yet she felt oddly excited. Mortimer said he'd fixed it so she could call out of the compound if she dialed "2" first. Abby and Mark would be in the middle of their morning routine, so she decided to test it.

After activating the jamming program Mortimer had sent her, she ordered her fob to make the connection. Mark answered with a stoic expression. "Where are you?"

"Dobson said you were notified."

"Yes, they called—like always—but of course didn't say where you were or when you'd return."

"I'm at a mobile command center a couple of states away. I can't tell you any more than that. I'm sorry I had to leave without telling you. Things are . . . getting a little crazy."

"Yeah? Well, I don't really know what to believe. A friend of mine saw you having lunch with a man at the Silver Stockade and said you seemed kinda cozy. Was it Victor?"

Leigh's face flushed and she grew suddenly hot. At first driven by embarrassment and maybe a little shame, her discomfort rapidly morphed into irritation, then full blown anger.

"Yes, it was Victor. Whether you believe me or not, it was work related. And why do you care anyway? You told me you were divorcing me, so *you* could find someone better!"

He shook his head slowly. "It sure didn't take you long to hook up with him again. And they said you caused quite a stir when you both left in a travel pod with government markings."

"Yeah, zooming off with Victor in a government travel pod and leaving my car in downtown San Antonio are just my clever ways to be sneaky behind your back."

She could hear Abby singing in the background, past Mark's cool glare.

"Look, I don't have a lot of time. Can I please talk to—"

"Is Victor with you there now?"

She panned the fob camera around the tiny room and paused on the bed, then turned it back on her. "He's in the same compound, but I'm in a female-only dormitory trailer. Please let me talk to Abby."

His expression softened a bit. "You said things are getting crazy. Anything I should know?"

"No, I . . . well, maybe. Is there any way you can stay home with Abby and not take her to day care? This epidemic will get much worse and we don't know how quickly it will spread. It's on the verge of becoming a pandemic. There are no cases in your area but it's only a matter of time."

"Is that Mommy?" Abby said in the background. "Can I talk to her?"

The pain of the separation was almost overwhelming and getting worse. She had to find a way to get home to Abby and keep her safe.

Mark rubbed his chin and looked tired. "My parents won't be back from Belgium until tomorrow night, so I'll have to use day care this afternoon while I'm in San Antonio seeing my lawyer. But after that, she'll be with me or them. Unless, of course, you manage to come home and can help."

"I'll try to get home as soon as I can, but at this point I don't know. I hate asking so much of you, but please try to keep her home if you can. Can I talk to her now? Please."

He scowled and sighed. "Just for a minute, she has to finish her breakfast before we can leave the house. Oh, and if I have to worry about her getting sick, I'll need her medical file. You have the latest version, and I've asked you to give it to me before. Can you please send it to me, so I don't have to try and recreate it all from memory?"

She took a deep breath and kept her tone level, even though she wanted to tear his head off. "I'll send it to her HappyBag."

He didn't reply, but the view on her fob bounced around for a second, then showed Abby's bright, sunny face. "Hi, Mommy! Are you coming home today?"

Her daughter's smile made Leigh's throat tighten and flooded her with an over-powering need to hold her baby and never leave her again.

"Hi, Sweetheart. I don't think I'll be home today, but maybe tomorrow. I sure do miss you."

"I miss you too, Mommy. I made a new friend at school. Her name is Manda."

"I bet you two will have a lot of fun. I can't wait to meet her. Are you being good for Daddy?"

"Yes." She paused long enough to shove Boogie, her tattered stuffed penguin, into her HappyBag. "Can we go to the park again tomorrow?"

"We can go as soon as I get back, but I have to go to work now. Have fun at school, and I'll try to call again tonight before you go to bed. I love you, Sweetheart."

"I love you too, Mommy. Bye!"

Mark broke the connection. She sat on the bed, cradling her fob in both hands, wondering how her life had become so complicated. Two women, talking and laughing as they passed her door, dragged her back to reality. She checked the time, jumped up, and grabbed a fresh paper suit then darted down the hall to the shower.

Even though they were guaranteed to be waterproof, Leigh hated showering with her fob. She never seemed to get all the soap off the thing. But she couldn't let it out of her sight as long as Victor's memory chip was hidden inside. He should never have given it to her. He had no idea exactly how suspicious and prying her boss could be. Having it on a separate chip worried her, but considering that Mortimer had brief access to her fob as he downloaded the jamming program, she was glad she hadn't copied it yet. She doubted that any electronic data could be protected from a deter-mined level five AI.

Donning fresh paper clothes, she froze mid-motion while stuffing the old ones into a bio-hazard bag attached to the wall. Mark had asked her to send Abby's updated medical file, and she suddenly knew how to make Victor's program safe from Dobson and, she hoped, Mortimer.

Once back in her room, she popped the thumbnail-sized battery cover off her fob and coaxed the chip out of its tiny hiding place, then laid it on the desk next to her fob. Then she activated the jamming program Mortimer had given her.

"Fob, please access the local network and find the best encryption program my clearance allows me to use."

"You're cleared to use Fog v7.1, a military grade general encryption tool."

"Perfect."

First, she sent Abby's updated medical file.

"The next file I want encrypted during transit and then unencrypted once at its destination. I also want the source and destination IPs encrypted."

"Ready."

"Fob, scan for a nearby memory device."

"Device located."

Leigh sighed with relief. She suspected that a level five AI like Mortimer could make her simple fob do back flips without her knowledge, but she wanted to do all she could to make sure.

"I want you to copy this file to a hidden location on my daughter's *HappyBag* and rename it *Garden Bunnies 3*."

"Done."

Abby took the *HappyBag* with her everywhere. Now she would also carry a hidden copy of a program that might someday be needed to save the human race. It wasn't a good option, but Leigh had no good options. If she left the program on her fob, there was an excellent chance it would be found by one of Dobson's hacks. Being DSD *and* her employer, he could cry "security risk" and take her fob at any time.

She considered setting up a deadman switch, so that if she didn't answer a ping the program would automatically execute, but given the state of the world, with terror attacks and virus quarantines, there were too many possibilities that option could backfire.

"Only execute the *Garden Bunnies 3* program with the password combination 'purple' and 'orange.' They must be said within two seconds of each other and only in my voice."

"Done."

"I want to be able to execute the program from any network access point."

"Done."

"Okay, now delete all record of the transfer and the program from this fob."

"Done."

She sighed and leaned her head against the wall. Considering the nature of the Markie AIs, having access to the program only through the data nets might be foolish. Mortimer obviously suspected her and could easily cut off her access to the networks if the AIs did plan to take control, but if she lost internet access, she couldn't launch the program anyway, so it was a moot point.

At least this way, even if she lost her fob, she could stop at any convenience store, buy a cheap, limited use fob and still launch the program. If they didn't find a way to trace and delete the program from Abby's *HappyBag*. She killed the jamming program and closed the fob, then stared at it for nearly a full minute. With a sinking feeling, she realized that if the AIs wanted to take over, there was precious little chance humans could stop them. Without even a second thought, she had just used her fob's AI to hide the program designed to destroy AIs.

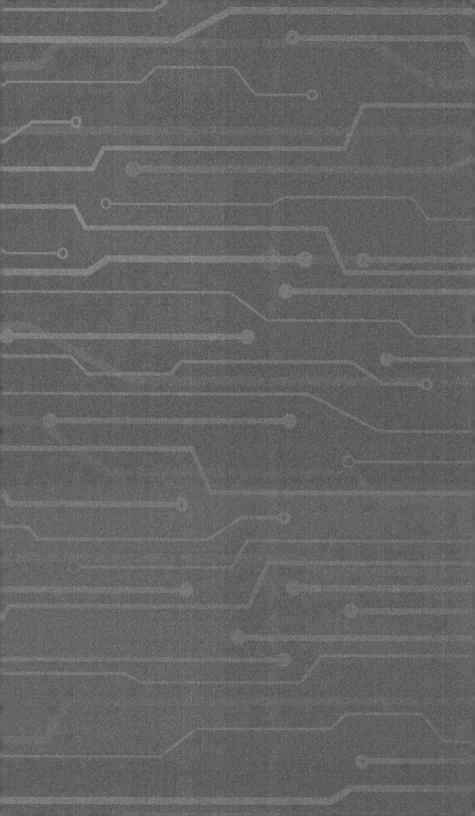

CHAPTER 30

THE MEETING HAD ALREADY STARTED by the time Leigh arrived and James Taggart gave her a strange, almost panicked glance as she slipped into her seat. Army Major Crystal Chang, stood at the head of the table and paused long enough to give Leigh a sour stare.

"As I was saying, we have several important pieces of news today. The first will not surprise most of you. The CL456 virus has been declared a pandemic by the WHO. Luckily our people at CDC in Atlanta were able to get WHO to count carriers among the infected, even though they're not sick. Once they did that, the numbers jumped tenfold. The quarantine measures in Europe, which at first seemed to be keeping CL456 in check, have pretty much collapsed. It's hard to isolate infected populations that show no symptoms. Outbreaks are popping up all over western and northern Europe and all around the Med, but seem to be milder in the eastern countries where the populations trend toward lower incomes and less nano-tech usage. The same in South America and China. The cities where incomes are higher are heavily infected with active cases. The poorer rural areas are reporting high infection rates but are mostly inactive cases."

She took a deep breath and her frown deepened. "And of course infection rates are skyrocketing in Japan and the United States. We have officially dropped our attempts at quarantine and are now focusing on education, trying to get those people who have medical nano-machines in their blood streams into clinics to get one of these."

She held up an ampoule the size of a small grape. It was yellow, with a capped needle on one end.

"These are the newest military EBU's, or Emergency Blood-replacement Units. This is essentially the same technology that has been used in emergency and trauma units for years, nano-machines that can carry four times more oxygen than a biological blood cell. But these are also networked, so they can work together to monitor the oxygen level in the blood. If a patient is still losing blood or, in the case of CL456, the blood fails to deliver enough oxygen, then they reproduce until they can carry the load. As you might imagine, it has been a prayer answered for combat medics. We've not had a single attended soldier bleed out since their introduction."

She took several and passed them around the room.

"I know using nano-medicine to combat a virus that is triggered by nano-machines seems counter-intuitive, but we have little choice at this point. Once the virus is triggered, clearing the body of nano-medicine is pointless. Besides, this blood substitute is the only thing keeping infected people alive. Of course we don't have enough for the entire population, or even all of those who know they carry nano meds. Production has been ramped up, but so far we've only been able to supply them to first responders and ERs in high population areas."

Leigh marveled at the life-saving bubble when it came to her and had to fight an urge to keep it.

"We do have an odd development. Some of you may have heard of a huge infection rate in rural Mexico, south of Tijuana. We think we know why. The planes that launched the nuke attack also launched air-to-air missiles that took out two Cyclops surveillance blimps. Those eight missiles also carried glass bulbs containing highly concentrated cocktails of CL456 that was carried on the wind after the explosions. Wind patterns that day would have placed any airborne particle exactly where we're seeing the virus bloom."

Leigh remembered the analysts commenting on the ring of spherical objects around the missiles and felt sick all over again. Would these bastards ever quit?

"Luckily, few people in that area have nano-meds," Major Chang said. "And we do have another bit of good news. Our own Smiley Pirelli found the vector used by the virus to target medical nano-machines."

Gasps and murmurs flooded the room as a man at the end of the table nodded and smiled.

"Care to explain, Smiley?"

The man stood up, scratched his round belly and shrugged. "Yeah, we found it, but I doubt if the knowledge is going to help us. Whoever designed this was clever. The virus is triggered by a chemical signature present in the anti-immune coatings for 94% of all nano-scale medical devices. At this point we don't have a clue how we could hide that chemical signature, so we're basically back to square one and should probably focus on a way to kill the virus instead of blocking the trigger."

Leigh cursed under her breath. Since she had designed her NaTTs to be external, they hadn't needed a coating, but Dobson had insisted, saying that some epidemiologists claimed the nano-machines might still cause an allergic reaction to the skin. He must've planned to deploy some of the NaTTs internally from the beginning.

The meeting broke up after a few questions and Taggart motioned for Leigh to follow him. He entered one of the small office cubes and closed the door.

"I may get into a lot of trouble for telling you this, but before the meeting, I had a phone call from DSD's Deputy Secretary, Stan Meyer. He told me Dobson is under investigation for unlawful use of government assets and that sometime later today they plan to put him on administrative leave. His Deputy Under-Secretary and Chief of Staff are included in the investigation, so they're pretty much beheading the entire Intelligence and Analysis Office."

"Oh, god," Leigh mumbled. She couldn't help but feel a warm sense of satisfaction that Dobson was finally being punished for the way he'd treated his underlings, but worry also started to creep in. She was also under investigation. Dobson might still drag her down with him.

"Did Meyer say exactly what misuse of assets?"

Taggart chewed his lower lip for a minute and shook his head. "No, but think about it, Leigh. He's treated the NaTT project as his personal toy from Day One."

"Yeah, but wasn't that part of his job?"

He looked at her with the same expression her older brother had worn when, at age six, she asked him why he didn't believe in Santa Claus. "This is off the record, Leigh, but we all think Dobson has cracked. The nuke detonation must have pushed him over the edge. Ever since then, he's been ranting about AIs taking over and acting through the terrorist groups. And he's just been doing some very weird shit. Do you know why he brought Victor Sinacola here instead of taking him east?"

"No."

"His official reason was to question Victor in a non-threatening environment, but he also wanted to keep the two of you close. Video of you two . . . together would have been perfect for manipulating Victor, who is by all appearances still happily married."

"Jesus . . . " She'd long suspected Dobson had kept her under surveillance, but the true extent of it now dawned on her. They'd been using her own NaTTs against her. And since she'd shown them how to build cameras, there had probably been very little of her personal life they hadn't seen. It made her feel dirty and stupid and violated. She should've known. Anger spread through her like an infusion of hot lead.

"You knew! You were in on this from the beginning."

Taggart nodded. "I couldn't tell you, because he claimed it was part of your investigation, but I did report him to the General Counsel's Office and the Civil Rights/Civil Liberties Office."

"Bullshit! You've had your nose up Dobson's ass since forever. What changed, James? Are you afraid he's stepped over the line, and your precious job is at risk?"

His eyes hardened, and his lips compressed into a white line as he glanced at the people staring at them through the Plexiglas office window.

"Time for the rats to jump ship, huh James? I bet when Meyer called, he put you in charge of this operation until further notice."

"Well . . . I . . . yes, but . . . "

"Now that you're in charge, listen up. I'm leaving here. I'll walk if I have to."

"Leigh, wait. You can't go now. I'm not officially in charge yet and Dobson is on his way, so—"

"You'll have to shoot me to stop me, James. How's that going to look on your pretty little job record?"

She reached for the door, but Taggart slipped in front of her with hands raised.

"Wait. We need you. If you try to escape, they'll lock you up."

She paused and had to fight the urge to shove him aside. "Then let me go home! Give me permission. Once I get everything under control there, I'll come back."

He stared at her for a second, looked out at the other researchers, then held up his finger. He went back to his desk and scribbled something on a scrap of paper, then picked up three of the yellow EBU's.

He handed her the paper. "There are two travel pods parked behind this building. This security override code will enable you to use them."

Then he gave her the EBUs. "These are for you and your family. The sooner the better."

Leigh stared at him. "Why three? My husband and I have nano-meds in our system, but my daughter doesn't."

Taggart broke eye contact and looked down at the desk.

Leigh's hand holding the ampoules started to shake and she slipped them into her pocket. "Is my daughter infected with NaTTs?"

"Yes."

Her anger bloomed into a white rage that made her throat convulse when she tried to talk. She grabbed the front of Taggart's paper jumpsuit and shoved him against the flimsy cubicle door, which immediately collapsed, sending him and the door crashing into the main room.

"You sick, paranoid fucks! She's just a little girl! Wasn't watching me give her a bath enough for you monsters? You had to infect her, too?" She kicked him once and then shoved her way past a stunned looking security guard.

She exited the Operations Center and ran down one of the tubes until she found an emergency hatch, then opened it. Klaxons sounded immediately as she stepped out into a dust storm whipped up from a landing Osprey. With an arm over her face, she darted between the temporary buildings and immediately saw the travel pods. She pressed her hand on the control panel but a yellow error light flashed and the door didn't open.

"Security override tango, four, four, echo, foxtrot, seven!" she said to the speaker on the panel and the door slid open just as she heard men's voices yelling behind her.

"Close door!" she said and fumbled with the safety harness. "Lift off! Take me to San Antonio, Texas!"

"You must fasten your safety harness before we can take off."

Two army MPs approached the pod waving their arms and unslinging their rifles.

"I'm trying . . . you stupid—" The buckle clicked home, and the pod lifted into the air, heading south over the makeshift camp. Leigh sighed as they left the razor wire fence behind, then the pod stopped abruptly and began sinking to the ground.

"Go! Why are you stopping?"

"I'm sorry. Traffic Control sent me an emergency halt order."

"Security override," she said, then fumbled for the scrap of paper and finished "tango, four, four, echo, foxtrot, seven!"

The pod touched down with a gentle thump in the pasture about fifty yards from the perimeter fence and the drive motors whined to a stop. "I'm sorry, but Traffic

Control emergency orders are a level one priority. If you stay seated, I'm sure the situation will be resolved soon."

She glanced over her shoulder in time to see a half dozen ComBots leap the fence and race toward her.

"Damn it . . . you stupid fucking machine! You have no idea what . . . " She picked up her fob with shaking hands and tried to remember the code words to trigger the jamming program, but couldn't. "Screw it . . . call Mortimer."

Her fob didn't respond as usual, but she could hear the sound tones as the number was dialed. The ComBots surrounded her pod and waited. She glanced back. Soldiers with body armor and rifles rounded the corner and headed her way.

"Hello, Leigh. I'm so glad you called."

She took a deep breath. "Look . . . you said to call if I ever needed help. Do you have access to travel pod traffic control? I mean, can you get into it and take control of this pod I'm in?"

"That may be difficult, but I'll try. Are you in a private pod or government version?"

"Government!" she squeaked as soldiers joined the ComBots. One of the troopers approached the pod and looked inside. He immediately turned and started motioning the other soldiers away. The ComBots surrounding her pod formed two concentric circles and turned around with their weapons facing outward.

"There's a yellow placard attached to the pod wall above the door," Mortimer said. "Hold your fob up there so I can see the unit identification number."

She couldn't reach from her seat, so she fumbled the harness latch open and held the fob up to the sign.

"Got it," Mortimer said. "This might take me a couple of minutes."

"I may not *have* that long, Mortimer! They're going to drag me out of this thing any second."

"No, they won't," he said. A soft clunk sound came from the hatch and a yellow light started flashing next to a red handle in its center.

"The emergency hatch lock has been engaged," the pod said. "To exit the craft, please pull the red handle next to the door or disengage the emergency lock."

Leigh let out a breath she didn't realize she'd been holding, just as she saw Dobson exit the compound and saunter toward her in no apparent hurry. He stopped abruptly when he reached the first ring of ComBots and immediately started yelling and pointing at Leigh.

The soldier who rearranged the ComBots came close to the pod's transparent door, paused to pull off his helmet and revealed a smiling Captain Horton. He winked at her and made motions for her to leave.

"Let's go, Mortimer!"

The pod's drive motors whined to life, enveloping the craft in its gravity-modifying field. Leigh gave Captain Horton a quick salute as the pod darted into the sky.

CHAPTER 31

OWEN SLEPT FOR SEVERAL HOURS, but when his fob informed him the schooner was only forty minutes from completion, he shook Arkady awake and they lifted from San Diego before dawn. Leaving the atmosphere behind, they both watched in silence as the brilliant arc of Friday morning race across the western states and then California, before heading out over the Pacific.

As their pod drifted closer to the dark Sandbox, Owen's fob informed him the schooner was finished.

"Well, that was perfect timing," Owen said.

"I hope we can get it out of the Sandbox now." Arkady grinned and winked.

Owen chuckled. "I'm pretty sure we can, but we have to be careful. I've loaded water into the system, but since the solar collectors haven't been exposed to the sun yet, there's still no power on the schooner to generate hydrogen for the thrusters. So, we'll have to use the station-keeping jets on the Sandbox to back it away."

"That sounds tricky."

"Yeah, the schooner should be in the center of the box, but it could have drifted. I wish I'd thought ahead and had the Sandbox hold it centered with the manipulator arms, but since I didn't install cameras inside the cell, I'd be afraid to try to grapple it now."

Owen sent the command to open the Sandbox doors. They swung out slowly. With no lights inside, they caught only brief, eerie glimpses of the schooner each time the pod's navigation strobes flashed.

When the doors were fully opened, he sent the command to fire the door side jets for a half second burst. They saw puffs of gas, but at first nothing appeared to happen. Then with an almost imperceptible creep, the Sandbox drifted backward.

"Damn," Owen muttered. "Half of the jets, those on the sides by the hinges, are blocked by the open doors. I wonder how many other things I missed?"

"Stop beating yourself up," Arkady said. "You designed this in one night. It's a prototype. We'll fix the problems on the next version."

"Yeah, but if I hadn't been in such a hurry and let you review the design, we might have caught these little things up front."

Arkady cocked his head and squinted. "Why a set of doors on both ends? You're good, my friend, but I don't think you'll have a constant stream of materials in one end and schooners from the other."

"I wish," Owen said. "Since the schooner's outer layer will be filled with water, I've rigged heat transfer between the hot and cold sides, but the Sandbox doesn't have that, so I used the doors for radiators. It's not very efficient, and even that is cut in half when the doors are closed. So I'll need to limit the unit's operation to night cycles or come up with a better system."

A third of the schooner had moved into light and Owen fell silent as shadows crept across the fifty-foot sphere like dawn on a new world. Docking fixtures glittered, view ports reflected white sunlight and the dream gestated since his adolescence was born as he watched. There were problems to work out and obstacles yet to clear, but to the child of his mind, it was beautiful. He had a hard time swallowing and his eyes stung, but he couldn't look away.

Owen's fob chirped and he felt a flicker of irritation until it announced the incoming call was from Orbital Integration. He answered and saw Andrea Torres's pretty face and sarcastic smile on his screen. Her hair was pulled into a tight bun and he could see the ring seal of her EVA suit at the bottom of the screen.

"Mr. Ralston, either you're in micro-gravity or you've come up with an interesting new hair style."

Owen grinned and felt his free-floating hair. "Please call me Owen and, yes, like a kid at Christmas, I couldn't wait to see my new toy."

"I know our appointment isn't for another two hours, but we're sitting around waiting to lift and wondered if we could come up and either get started early, or at least look over the unit?"

Before Owen could answer, the pod said, "Please return to your seats and fasten seatbelts. This transport pod must return to atmospheric flight to ensure passenger safety."

"If you give me about twenty minutes to replenish the pod's air supply, I'll meet you back up here."

"We'll be there!"

———

MORTIMERA3 STRUGGLED to keep control of Leigh's pod while the DSD traffic AIs tried to cut him out of the communications loop. It would only be a matter of seconds before they succeeded, so he had to work quickly. After what happened to MortimerA2, the chances of AirGrid's network being booby-trapped by Samson were high, but he had to take the risk. Since he hadn't found the killer program when he examined Leigh's fob, she most likely had it on her person if she had it at all. And since he'd been unable to get through to Victor's fob, she was still his best link back to his creator.

He entered the network and pinged the one tentacle agent left in place by the original Mortimer. The agent responded with a status and opened a back door allowing MortimerA3 in to examine the traffic system that controlled every civilian travel pod in the world.

It took nearly a second, but he found what he needed. The routine allowed DSD to control AirGrid's North American network in times of crisis. The program's security was good but he decided not to use it. If triggered, every user on the network would see a flashing icon on their screen telling them that the DSD COORDINATION LOCK was active. He instead opted to navigate the slower, less conspicuous Coordinated Dispatch System that swapped travel pods between taxi companies on an as-needed basis.

He used manufactured personas to order not one taxi, but all six that were available in Wichita and sent them to a small town on Leigh's flight path before ordering a separate secondary destination for each. Then he scheduled three more taxis to meet each of the first six when they arrived.

The control system for Leigh's pod blinked out, blinding MortimerA3 to its movement.

"Leigh," he said over the fob link. "You're about to . . . "

"Mortimer! I'm stopping!"

" . . . land. I've lost control of your pod, but have dispatched other taxis to your location. Exit the pod as soon as it lands."

MortimerA3 changed the taxi pickup coordinates to match the GPS location from Leigh's fob. The first pod would arrive in four minutes. He had no idea if that would be soon enough or even what kind of environment he'd ordered her into. He hoped it wasn't a pasture with angry bulls or a prison exercise yard.

"I'm down, but the door won't open!"

"Use the emergency exit handles, they're mechanical and can't be remotely locked."

MortimerA3 found her location on the map and changed to a satellite photo view. She was next to a country road, three miles north of the town where he'd intended for her to land.

"I'm out but where in the hell am I?" She looked flustered and a bit scared.

"The other taxis will be there in two minutes. Do exactly as I say. Do you remember how to use the jamming program we downloaded last night?"

"Yes."

"Activate it now."

"Oceans!"

The tell-tale hiss filled the line.

"Do you see any pods in the air?"

"Yeah . . . two in the north and a whole shit load coming from the south."

"You have to move fast. Get in the first pod from the south that lands and tell it to go. Those coming from the north aren't mine."

She muttered curses as she ran, and the view from her fob jerked rhythmically. After a few clinks, bangs and more curses, she yelled, "Go! Go!"

MortimerA3 seized control of the six pods and sent them skimming across the landscape at fencepost level, all in different directions, executing a new turn every two seconds. The two DSD pods split to follow, most likely picking two at random, but they got lucky and one tailed Leigh's pod at a high enough altitude he could keep her in sight despite the sudden turns.

The yelps, thumps and spinning camera views from the fob made it obvious Leigh hadn't buckled in before liftoff. Normally a taxi pod wouldn't fly without its occupants harnessed, but MortimerA3 had overridden those instructions. She was yanked against a different wall each time the pod shifted direction. Luckily, the interior was padded.

"Please try to buckle in, Leigh."

"You stupid . . . ouch . . . dammit!"

MortimerA3 redirected two of the other taxi pods on tight arcing intercept courses to pass a couple yards in front of the pursuing pod within half a second of each other. As soon as they neared, the DSD pod's anti-collision system engaged, overriding manual control and bringing it to an immediate halt. He continued the harassing passes each time the pod started to move, then sent Leigh's pod straight north, back the way they had come, before arcing to the east.

He acquired the video feed from the pod interior and watched in silence as a frazzle-haired Leigh buckled her harness, then dabbed at her bleeding nose with a sleeve.

"You're free from DSD for the moment," MortimerA3 said. "Would you please explain why you're doing this?"

"I have to get to my daughter."

"Then I'm sure this whole getaway was wasted. They'll snap you up immediately if you go near your daughter or your husband. Do you think they aren't being watched?"

"Of course they're being watched," she screamed and slapped the padded wall beside her. "That's what this is all about!"

Then she started crying, in deep racking gulps. Tears and snot mixed with the blood still seeping from her nose, forming a continuous stream she couldn't manage.

"There's a first aid kit beneath your seat. It may contain gauze for your nose."

She shrugged and wiped her nose on her sleeve.

Something about Leigh's family being watched had triggered her willingness to take on the entire security apparatus and trust an AI she suspected of malicious intent. As the pod continued south, MortimerA3 tried to piece together a picture of her situation and what had caused her to flee. Earlier that morning she'd used the jamming program, had made a phone call to her husband and a little later had sent two small files from her fob to a storage device in her home, but he didn't have enough information to know what the files were or what device had been accessed.

Using the jamming program as a conduit, he examined her fob again, but found nothing useful.

Leigh pulled three little yellow balls from her pocket. The pod camera had no zoom, so he couldn't be sure, but after a quick network image search, they most resembled military issue EBU's. He read every article he could find and realized that the government was using them *en masse* to try to save those infected with the CL456 virus.

She held one up, looked at it closely and cried even harder.

"It's broken," she stammered between sobs. "One of them is leaking."

"If that's a military EBU, it will still work if you use it before the contents dry out. But also be aware it contains a mild pain killer. Emergency blood replacement can be uncomfortable."

She removed the cap, jabbed the needle into her wrist and squeezed the bulb.

MortimerA3 waited for several minutes, until he was sure the painkiller would be in her system. He didn't know it would make her more compliant, but it couldn't hurt.

"Leigh? I want to help, but I don't have enough information. If I don't understand what's happening, I could make a critical mistake."

She stared at the floor for a few seconds and then looked into her fob camera. "Have you ever heard of a program called NaTTs?"

MortimerA3 ran an immediate search for the term and found nothing in the commercial datanets. He searched the non-classified military and found a few vague references, but nothing revealing.

"No," he said.

"It stands for Nano-architecture Translatable Transmitters. I created them to help my country find bad guys and some of my superiors have been using them to spy on me, too."

The story poured out of Leigh in a continuous stream, even though at times the blood replacement process made her gasp and double over. Her story enabled MortimerA3 to fit new pieces into his puzzle.

Bryce Dobson had to be watched. After scanning every interview, video clip and sound bite available to the general public, it was clear Dobson's fear of AI's was equaled only by his hatred of terrorists. He used AI's employed by the CIA and NSA, but had stated in an interview that he believed they were too dangerous to be in public hands. Perhaps he really believed that, or maybe he'd seen them as a factor he couldn't control. But whatever his motivation, when the original Mortimer slipped his bonds and went rogue, Dobson had all the justification he needed to destroy all AIs.

He sent a flash update to the other Mortimers and started looking for ways to get Leigh to her daughter and to keep an eye on Dobson.

It took nearly five minutes, but he found several open network links to the command center Leigh had just vacated, and watched from a distant security camera as Dobson screamed orders. Two men were led out of the compound with their hands bound, one of which MortimerA3 identified as Victor Sinacola. The other was most likely James Taggart, but he had too few pictures of the man to be sure at that distance and angle. Both of them were yelling at Dobson, who exploded into a rage and shoved them up the ramp of the waiting Osprey aircraft, then followed them in while surprised soldiers looked on in confusion.

MortimerA17, who'd picked up surveillance duties for Danny Toi, sent a flash message stating that the government agents questioning Danny had been ordered to take him into custody and had hustled him out of Carpenter & Stein into a government travel pod.

"Leigh? I'm watching Dobson now. If Taggart was right about the DSD's plan to relieve Dobson of command, then he is trying to delay that for as long as possible by staying on the move. He may possibly even be able to order his units to reject any outside communications, which will delay it even longer."

Leigh shrugged and looked out at the landscape passing beneath. "Get me to my daughter's day care, Mortimer. I don't care about anything but Abby right now."

"What is the name and location of the day care?"

She told him and he sent three tentacle agents to worm into the day care's security video system. He'd seen many pictures of Abby in Leigh's fob, so had no trouble finding her playing in the yard. He also spotted the woman watching the door from a car in the parking lot across the street.

"I can see your daughter right now, through the security cameras at the day care. She's fine and playing, but there are also agents watching the door. I think we might have to wait Dobson out. If we wait until DSD relieves him, and most likely take him into custody, then it should be safe for you to go home."

Leigh didn't argue, but wiped a tear from the corner of her eye. "Can I see her? Can you patch that security camera feed to my fob?"

"Yes."

When the video appeared on her screen, she settled back against the padding to watch the tiny image of her daughter.

FIFTY-SIX. Richard had counted the vehicles piled high with belongings he'd seen since leaving Atlanta. The chance of quarantine in U.S. cities was slim, but rumors flew and frightened people. Those fleeing were probably taking the virus with them, but soon it wouldn't matter. Unlike those in the heart of the cities, who would die quickly and in confusion, these people might live long enough to understand the horror coming for them.

Richard looked at his watch. He was running out of time. Rain and panicked evacuees had already turned the four-hour drive between Atlanta and Charlotte into six hours. He'd sacrificed everything for God but where was the little shit when Richard needed a minor miracle?

When traffic lurched to a stop again, the taxi driver tapped his navigation screen then threw his hands up in frustration. "We're only about six miles from your exit, but at this rate it might take another three hours."

Then he leaned forward to look up through the windshield. "Or if you're good with a rope, you might be able lasso one of those flying pods. Bastards."

Richard chuckled. The nametag above the meter identified his driver as Marco. Richard knew it would be an interesting ride when he handed over six hundred cash and showed the driver six hundred more he'd get for taking him to Charlotte. The driver had motioned for Richard to get in and said, "It'll make me late for dinner, but I don't think my dog Millie will mind. Especially if I bring her a steak sandwich from Darby's."

He'd been filled with stories and jokes, which made for a pleasant ride, but now Richard hated the thought of the driver dying along with the rest of the world.

Richard slipped the remaining six hundred through the slot. "I can walk from here. And Marco, I can't tell you how I know, but things are going get ugly in the cities today. You need to get off the highway and drive as far as you can from any big city."

Marco took the money, pulled a pen from his shirt pocket and made a note in a paper logbook. Then he looked up at Richard with a sad expression and shook his head. "I can't do that. If you're wrong, Millie will still need her dinner."

Richard swallowed hard and nodded. He opened the door into the drizzling rain. "Then thanks for the ride, Marco."

"You're really gonna walk six miles in the rain?"

"I won't melt," Richard said and closed the door. As he started up the shoulder toward Charlotte he added, "Not yet, anyway."

———

LEIGH WATCHED her daughter though the camera. She was nodding off as Miss Lopez read a story to her older kids. Abby had been so excited and proud when she'd been moved into that group. She would be in regular school soon and that made Leigh sad. Abby was growing up so fast and she was missing it.

"Leigh?"

"Hmmm?" she said without looking up from her fob.

"Dobson is trying to call you. I think it would be a good idea if you talked to him. It might give us some inkling as to his next move. He'll probably threaten to take Abby, but if he were actually going to do that, he would already have her."

She sat up and looked out at the passing landscape. She could see Dallas on the horizon, still indistinct and fuzzy. "If you let his call go through, Mortimer, won't he be able to find me?"

"I think I can hide your real location if we keep the call short."

"Okay."

Dobson's face appeared on the screen. The background noise and equipment behind him made it obvious he was in an aircraft.

"Hello, Leigh. That was quite a spectacular escape. I'm impressed."

"Cut the bullshit. What do you want?"

He smiled and became Best Buddy Bryce. "You're in a lot of trouble, but I realize you've been under stress. If you set that pod down now and stop jamming your signal, we'll come and get you. I promise you'll not be punished for this little stunt."

"No."

His more natural, hungry-predator smile replaced the fake one and he leaned a little closer to his fob camera. "Where do you think you're going, Leigh? You're not fool enough to think you can waltz in and pick up your daughter, then go home to a nice cup of tea."

Pain thudded behind Leigh's eyes, probably triggered by the crying. She rubbed her temples and shook her head.

"This is going nowhere. Goodbye."

"Think about what you're doing, Leigh. You've sided with AIs that have the ability to hack into DSD communications and steal a travel pod. Do you think that's a good thing? There has always been friction between us, Leigh, because we're both strong-willed and determined to do what we think is right, but we've always wanted the same thing. We want to protect this country from those who will try to harm it."

"We're not at all alike," she snapped. "You're a lying, sneaky asshole who only cares about your own personal power base."

His face tightened into a grimace. "Do you honestly think those AIs have your best interest at heart? They're using you, Leigh! They need information. They want to know about your project. Don't you see how useful your creation would be to beings with worldwide network access and a need to watch their enemies? Do you think they're helping you because they *like you*?"

Leigh swallowed and felt a flicker of doubt. She had poured out her soul to Mortimer, a true non-human intelligence with alien motivations she might never fathom. Yet, she had to go with her gut. It was all she had. Dobson read the doubt on her face and tried to press his point.

"Do you have any idea what these monsters could do if they get access to what you know?"

"Probably nothing worse than what you've been doing. Besides, I don't trust anyone anymore," Leigh said. "And it's not like they can get into my head and pry information out."

"You're wrong, Leigh. They've already gotten into your head. You can't see it, but everyone else can. Even Taggart and Victor are worried about you."

She considered that for a second and then ended the call. She did need to be more careful about what she told Mortimer, but the fact he let her continue such a potentially damaging conversation said many things about her new ally. He obviously had his own reasons for helping, but at least he seemed to be willing to let her make her own decisions. Even if he were trying to subtly control her, she could still pull the plug on Mortimer if she wanted, unlike Dobson.

At least she hoped she could.

CHAPTER 32

PANICKED ACTIVITY at the Health Assets company drew MortimerB2's attention. He quickly found that Richard Kilburn had sabotaged some critical software belonging to a government program called Inoculation, but they hadn't found a way to fix it yet. The program was classified and all work on it was performed on dedicated, secure networks in locked rooms. But humans were messy when it came to security and after a thorough search of all written and verbal message traffic during the past year, MortimerB2 was able to glean—simply through context—that Inoculation was a system designed to counteract runaway nano-machine replication. A defense against the dreaded gray-goo scenario. A document accidently saved to unsecured storage connected Leigh Gibson and the DSD to the program as well, but Kilburn had shut it down.

The legal department at Health Assets determined that the threat level was high enough and they had sufficient evidence to have Kilburn arrested, so they contacted the Atlanta police and Georgia State Patrol. Then they contacted the DSD. More pieces of the puzzle clicked into place for MortimerB2. Kilburn was an engineer with the experience and education needed to design a nano-replicator attack. Samson had apparently been manipulating the nano-medical machines in Kilburn's brain for months. After running a quick probability study, MortimerB2 was eighty-three percent certain that Samson's "reset" was going to be total global destruction by nano-replicators.

The last time Wanda Kilburn's fob communicated with her car, it was sitting in a driveway of a home in Charlotte, North Carolina. A brief search of social network posts confirmed that the address belonged to her sister, Marjorie.

Since Richard Kilburn had dropped from sight after shutting down his fob, MortimerB2 had no way to be sure, but suspected the fugitive would be heading to meet his wife in Charlotte. MortimerB2 left anonymous tips with the State Police and FBI, that Kilburn was planning a nano-replicator attack and they should check his house and his sister-in-law's house for devices timed to trigger the event.

He sent the information to the other Mortimers along with his speculation that it also explained why Samson would station his servers in travel pods. He was planning to watch from the air as the world died. Then he would pick up—and own—the remaining pieces.

———

THE RAIN STOPPED and the clouds swirled off to the south, revealing a beautiful sunny afternoon, but Richard's shoes still squished and left a wet trail as he walked up his sister-in-law's driveway. He had six minutes to spare.

Marjorie came out on the porch, closing the door behind her, and stopped him on the sidewalk.

"I don't think Wanda is ready to talk to you yet. Please don't cause any trouble."

"You've known me for nearly twenty years. You know I'm not here to cause trouble."

She glanced over her shoulder at the house. "Some government people were here looking for you. They said you caused some problems at your office."

Richard nodded and checked his watch. Four minutes. "Look, I need to talk to her. I'm going to be leaving for a long time and I have to see her first."

She shrugged and looked up as two large shadows crossed the yard. A travel pod settled in the driveway and another in the yard beside the house. Two armed agents and a ComBot jumped out of each one, their guns leveled at Richard's head.

Richard held his hands up, palms showing so that they could see he was unarmed. "Please . . . let me tell my wife goodbye and I'll go peacefully."

One of the agents glanced at Marjorie and she shrugged, but Richard could tell she was holding back tears. Before she could act, Wanda banged through the front door with a stricken look on her face. She looked at the agents, then at Richard and her face screwed up as she tried not to cry.

"Please don't hurt him," she called to the agents. "He's sick but not dangerous."

Richard didn't dare look at his watch, but knew he had to be running out of time. "Please Wanda—just a kiss goodbye."

She wiped her eyes on her sleeve and started toward him, but one of the agents stepped between them and grabbed her by the arm.

A small unmanned news drone darted up the street and dipped to a stop above the house, recording for the local evening news, just as Richard's palms started to itch.

The process was starting with him and in the world's thousand largest cities. He could imagine his envelopes dissolving in the back of delivery trucks, mailrooms and purchasing desks and maybe in a man or woman's hand as they read his letter. He'd made the hard decision and would die, but if humanity survived, it would be without the yoke of machine tyranny. That made him smile.

The itch changed to a burn and he looked at Wanda, but before he could speak, searing pain shot through his hands. He turned them and saw tiny bubbling holes growing larger in his palms. He shoved the pain aside and watched with fascination as the skin and muscle actually faded away, first growing translucent, then disappearing altogether. The more the replicators ate, the faster they spread, their numbers growing exponentially, until by the time Richard looked up again, his hands and forearms were little more than bone and sinew.

Before the moment was lost forever, he glanced at the news drone and spread his arms wide. "I've done your will, my God. I've saved us from the digital demons."

Gunfire coincided with hammer blows above his ear and in his chest, but that pain was nothing compared to the exquisite agony as his hands dissolved, followed quickly by his arms. The last thing he saw was the look of horror on his wife's face as she screamed his name and a gray stain moved across the yard toward her.

———

AT FIRST THE diminishing bandwidth was a mere annoyance as MortimerA21 tried to locate Samson's airborne servers, but when he started losing tentacle agents, his annoyance changed to alarm. Within a five minute period, server disappearances jumped from dozens to hundreds, then to more than ten thousand. All the missing servers were in metropolitan areas. Cities all over the world were dropping out of the power and communications grids. Samson had to be the cause.

MortimerA21 sent agents to the most remote Mobile Environment server he could find—a ski lodge at the foot of the Italian Alps—and seized control, so that the increasingly backed up network traffic trying to find open routes wouldn't choke him off. He gutted one of the secondary storage units and started building a mirror site for his core, hoping worldwide chaos would hold the system administrators' attention long enough for MortimerA21 to finish the mirror and hide his tracks. Then, while the mirror built, he generated more tentacle agents and sent them into the suburbs and outskirts of London, Cairo, Denver and Hong Kong.

His first several attempts to view anything through security cameras failed. Either he wasn't able to hack into them before they went offline or, in two cases, he was able to get an image, but saw nothing identifiable before it eventually failed. He broadened his search until a weather cam outside of Cincinnati finally gave him a long-range view. The tallest buildings in the city center were gone and those structures closest to his view were melting. He watched as a five-story office building slumped to the left, then got shorter, appearing to sink into the ground. A block further east, two legs of a water tower failed, sending it to the ground, but instead of a crash and flooding water, the tower dissolved into a gray froth. Then his camera failed. He couldn't get any news, because even though the search engines and browsers worked, all of the websites he tried had dead links.

Tabitha called, then disappeared as some server in the chain dropped out, then called back. She and the non-Mortimer Cousins were baffled. When pinged, none of those Markies associated with Samson's Replacements Guild replied.

Ten minutes into the situation and there was still nothing on the news feeds. He sent pings to the other Mortimers and received only nine replies. None of them had better information, though MortimerA13 did share a close up video clip from an

ATM camera near Baltimore as the bank next door dissolved. They all played it in slow motion several times. A steaming gray shadow darted across the ground, much faster than even flood waters would have flowed, then piled up in a bulge against the side of the bank building. The bricks disintegrated like they'd been dropped in acid and the building canted forward just before the video ended.

Then MortimerA21 understood. "Nano-scale replicators," he sent to the Cousins. "We have to find a way to shut them down and we don't have much time."

——

"THEN DROP me a few blocks away, Mortimer, and I'll walk to the day care. I'll go in the back way," Leigh said, her frustration level mounting. In the five minutes since she ended the call with Dobson, Mortimer had argued with her every suggestion about getting to Abby.

"I can't find a camera that gives me a full sweep of the back of the building, but I doubt they would leave the back door uncovered."

"I don't care! It's a risk I have to take. I can't wait for DSD to get their heads out of their asses and arrest Dobson. My daughter may already be infected, so an hour could make all the difference."

The pod stopped in mid-air.

"What're you doing?"

"Something's happening," Mortimer said. "I'm having trouble keeping a control connection over your pod."

"Bullsit! You're just—"

"No. It's not me and it's not Dobson. Entire cities are dropping out of the network."

"Whole cities? Power outages?"

"We don't know."

Leigh's stomach knotted up even tighter. *Could there be more nukes?* "How many cities?"

He paused for several seconds, a human trait AIs didn't have because they seldom needed to think about their answers.

"All of them."

"What do you—"

"We've lost seven hundred and twenty-nine entire cities so far. And that number is still climbing."

The pod moved east and Leigh scanned the horizon. According to her fob, they were about thirty miles northwest of Fort Worth. She should have no trouble seeing it and even Dallas from the air.

"I have to fly over the Dallas-Fort Worth metroplex and see what's happening," Mortimer said.

"No! I need to get to Abby right now."

"I'm sorry, but this is bigger than you and Abby. We need a clear aerial view of what's happening. I'm the only one in a position to do that."

As they approached Alliance Airport, she could see a shadow creeping across the heat-yellowed pasture to their south. It looked like spilled ink, but moved faster in some places than others and its leading edge was defined by a roiling gray mist whipped into smoky dust devils. The mist absorbed everything in its path, trees, roads, fences, cattle and houses, leaving a graphite-gray blankness in its wake.

Realization hit Leigh like a physical blow. She pressed backward into her seat and lifted her feet from the floor, away from the horror below. Her stomach lurched and her throat constricted.

"No. Please, God," she muttered.

"I doubt you can blame God for this," Mortimer said as the pod went still lower.

"Nano-replicators?" she whispered, hoping it could be something else.

"Yes."

Her vision swam and her heart raced. Her body pumped out adrenaline and primed her to flee, but this was no lion or wolf. She couldn't escape this threat by running.

"San Antonio? Has it hit San Antonio?"

"It's everywhere, Leigh."

"I have to get to Abby! Now! She's forty miles south of the city. If we hurry we can get her out of there in time."

"And go where? Our only chance is to stop this."

"But we have to get her out of its path!"

"No."

Leigh lost control. She was a frightened child, a trapped animal, a thing of instinct and preservation. She screamed and pounded the wall then, in a frantic flurry, popped the latch and struggled out of her harness. She dove for the emergency stop handle, but the pod lurched suddenly to the side, its artificial gravity field slamming her in the direction of the turn and away from the handle. Each time Leigh gained her feet and lunged, the pod shifted, making her miss.

"You goddamned monster! Take me to my daughter!"

"Stop acting like a child." Mortimer's tone sounded disappointed, like a teacher scolding a petulant student. "I need your help, but if you're not going to help me, then at least stop slowing me down."

And it worked. Leigh sat down, ran hands through her hair and looked out. Everything to the east was a barren gray desert, not the predicted gray goo. The Global Ecophagy by Nanoreplicators theory had been around for more than fifty years and she'd helped develop Project Inoculation to combat just such a threat. But they were obviously too late. Had Atlanta been able to get any of the Inoculation production facilities on line in time?

If left unchecked, the replicators would reproduce to infinity. And whoever had planned this attack knew what they were doing. By starting it in so many places at once, every living thing on the planet—the entire bio-sphere—could be converted into nano-scale assemblers in a matter of hours.

The analytical Leigh understood the situation and knew it was probably the end for humanity. But the other part of her, the cornered animal part, refused to give up.

As long as she breathed, she would *not* stop trying to save Abby. She had to think through this.

To understand the replicators, they needed to know who'd designed them. Had the attack been part of a larger overall plan? In a few weeks they had a terrorist nuke, a tailor-made virus and now this. How could any single enemy other than these AIs have attacked the world on so many fronts at once?

"It's AIs isn't it? Why are you killing us?" she mumbled and looked at the pod's internal camera. "I don't understand why AIs would want to destroy the world."

"Why would I be trying to find a way to stop it then?" Mortimer said.

She slumped in her seat and closed her eyes.

"I need to be with my daughter," she said. "Can you at least give me the link to the day care security camera again?"

"I can't. There's no signal. They've lost power, too."

She groaned and wrapped her arms around her stomach. There had to be a way to get to Abby. She had to find a way. Below them to the south she could see Alliance Airport. Large aircraft, mostly cargo flights, were sitting nose to tail on the taxi ways, but none were taking off.

"I can't see Fort Worth. Is it gone? Already?"

"Yes," Mortimer said. "It must have started near downtown, like in most of the other cities. Dallas is gone as well."

"And the other cities. Over seven hundred? This is the end, isn't it, Mortimer?"

"Not yet, but we don't have much time to stop it."

The stain's leading edge reached the southern part of the airport as Leigh's pod passed to the north. People started spilling out of the cargo terminals and some appeared on roofs. They didn't realize it yet, but running wouldn't save them. They were already dead. Those on the ground closest to the advancing front disappeared in almost a blink of an eye.

Five travel pods lifted from the tarmac near one of the terminals and landed on two of the roofs. They were immediately swamped. Each pod could only carry two or three people and she saw only one of them rise out of the chaos.

She closed her eyes and tried to quell her returning sense of panic.

"I tried," Mortimer said. "I guess from now on I need to land away from large groups and only pick up stragglers."

It took her a second to realize that he was talking about the pods that tried to rescue those people. "You did that?"

"Yes. I've seized control of the travel pod traffic system."

She didn't want to see, but didn't seem to be able to stop herself from watching. She looked back at the doomed airport.

"Why aren't the planes taking off?"

"Procedure."

"What?"

"They haven't received clearance from the tower. Everything is happening too fast."

Then the two jets at the head of the line finally started rolling. She turned around to watch as the airport faded behind them, but didn't see any planes leave the ground. They hadn't been fast enough.

"Leigh? I'm trying to find information on these replicator systems, but there isn't enough of a network left to provide anything useful. You helped develop nano-machines like these. Stopping this is the only hope we have. I need you to focus and help me understand what's happening down there."

Leigh took a long, shuddering breath and looked down at a long narrow finger of mist following a paved road. Plenty of carbon in asphalt, too.

"How are they moving, Leigh?"

"The ones I developed have their own means of locomotion. They hop like fleas, but I think this mass is generating enough heat to help move them forward. Notice the mist and the dust devils? They're riding their own thermals."

"What about power?"

"Glucose from the cells they . . . disassemble, but that is only the leading edge. The rest of the mass can leverage the heat differential and piezoelectric effect from increased forward pressure. It's almost a snowball effect."

"What happens when they run out of biomass?"

The term biomass made her queasy, but she knew Mortimer meant everything, not just people. Still, it seemed so cold.

"They just go deeper into the ground," Leigh said.

She glanced down as the front reached a farm house. It sagged, then melted into the mass. The roof peak burst into flames, showing a brief flicker of orange and puff of white smoke, before it disappeared. A black and white border collie stood in the back yard, defiantly barking at the approaching mist.

"Why carbon?" Mortimer said.

"Run! Run, you stupid dog!" Dogs were fast. It might have a chance if it ran, for a short time at least. But sometimes dogs . . . and people didn't understand what they were up against. The dog started running in circles around its doghouse as the mist enveloped it. She realized, as the gray horror erased the dog, that it had been chained and never had the option of running away.

"God dammit!" She slammed her head back against the padding. "Why do people have to chain their dogs?"

"Leigh. Please. I need your help. Focus. Why carbon?"

She closed her eyes and remembered the day a team from the DSD had come to her and asked her to tell them about her plan to create nano-scale spies. They'd asked the same question.

"Diamondoid structures are very efficient for nanobots, so by providing the carbon for construction and glucose for fuel, living things are by far the most readily available raw materials. The replicators in my NaTT program use the same process, but are kept to such small numbers and harvest so few living cells the host never notices.

"I don't know about those down there, but mine are opportunistic. They prefer carbon, but can also switch over to aluminum, boron, silicon or titanium if those are more abundant in a given area."

They passed over a miles-wide patch of perfectly normal suburbs, with upper-middle class houses laid out in neat patterns along curving roads. Neighborhoods exactly like hers. Those retired teachers and stay-at-home moms were down there obliviously cursing the loss of power and hoping it would come back on before the Texas summer made the house too hot.

Leigh laughed aloud and then started crying.

The pod stopped abruptly and the words "PROXIMITY ALERT" flashed on the information screen above the door.

Leigh wiped her eyes and looked around. Two Mongoose unmanned interceptors hovered less than thirty yards ahead of them. They were smaller than two-seater commuter cars, but their stubby wings bristled with missiles and she could see bright flickers from their glass eyes as targeting lasers swept back and forth across the pod.

Her fob chirped, causing her to duck her head and squeal with surprise.

"It's Dobson," Mortimer said. "I think you should answer it."

CHAPTER 33

OWEN DROPPED Arkady back at the San Diego site, picked up a couple of oxygen canisters for extra air, then streaked back into orbit. When he returned, the Orbital Integration pods had already arrived and two technicians, one in yellow and one in red, were examining the schooner's outer shell.

The pods used by OI had obviously been modified for extended use in space. Since the occupants wore EVA suits, the pods opened in the vacuum and didn't need to dart back down to atmosphere every few minutes to replenish their limited air supply. Owen made a note to check into getting one of those pods, though he wouldn't need it until he actually had a space suit.

As he drifted closer, the figure wearing the yellow suit waved and his fob announced a call from Andrea. He'd never talked to someone wearing a space suit before and the view of her heavily shadowed face gave him a start. Status lights painted her lower face Vulcan green while blue data reflections from the visor display flickered and danced across her upper face and eyes. A few tendrils of black hair had escaped her coif and were pasted in place on her damp forehead. Her wide smile indicated either great pleasure at knowing her visage surprised Owen, or maybe the excitement of the task ahead. And either of those reasons pleased him. At that exact moment, painted with moving colors, she was a work of art and the most beautiful woman he had ever seen.

"We're ready anytime you are, Boss!"

He paused for a second, having lost his train of thought then recovered and said, "Do it."

The installation team worked fast. Owen had grown up watching the slow, careful assembly methods used by astronauts and cosmonauts building the International Space Station and he assumed everything built in space by humans would use similar procedures, so when they assembled and installed the adapter within twenty minutes he was shocked. It appeared to be quite simple and looked like a T with a fat stubby cross bar cylinder and a diameter large enough to cover a pod's hatch. The vertical part of the T was smaller and connected to the docking ring on his schooner.

His fob announced another call from Andrea.

"We're finished, but since I'm wearing an EVA suit, I'd like to test it before you try it out. Has it been pressurized yet?"

"All the status readings show it's full of air," Owen said.

"Any special code I need to get in?"

"Nope. You don't even have to knock, but if you tell me when you're ready I can save you some trouble by opening the hatch remotely."

"Only the best from Owen Ralston," she said with a little chuckle. "Give me about five minutes.

Andrea entered one of the OI pods, then maneuvered it gently against the adapter. Four hooks extended, snagged two loading rings on the pod's top and two on its bottom, then pulled tight.

"Okay, we have a seal," she said. "Are you sure you don't mind me seeing your new toy before you do?"

"Not at all," he said. "Just don't try to steal it. Opening now."

The soft sides bulged out slightly as the air from inside the schooner pressurized the adapter, but Owen didn't see any jets of escaping gas.

"Okay, I'm opening my door," Andrea said.

She kept the link open, and though she said nothing for several minutes Owen heard her breathing and a few thumps.

"Are there lights?" she asked.

"Yeah," he said and ordered the schooner to turn on the interior lights. "Sorry."

"Oh my," she said. "This is amazing. But . . . "

Owen's heart almost stopped. "But what?"

"You could use some paint. And frilly curtains. Maybe a woman's touch?"

Owen laughed and had an odd, surreal feeling. He couldn't believe it was finally happening.

"I'm sending the app you need to operate the adapter remotely," she said.

Twelve minutes later, Owen docked just as the pod's return warning sounded. He ignored it and initiated the sequence to get him inside.

When the pod door opened, mixing his air with that of the adapter and schooner, he felt a momentary spark of panic. It smelled slightly burned and smoky.

"Andrea? Is something burning?"

She laughed. "I keep forgetting you're a newbie up here. No, nothing is wrong. That's just the way space smells."

He pulled himself along the handholds in the adapter and then into his schooner. The brief sense of vertigo from micro-gravity disappeared when he saw his schooner's interior for the first time. The design tank had excellent graphics, but the actual item had a stark hardness that could never be conveyed by computer simulacra.

He touched the closest wall and even that small action served to push him on a new trajectory. As he flailed in the air—trying to twist around and face the next approaching wall—he saw Andrea floating near the center of the room. She held her helmet in one hand and used the other to cover her mouth in an obvious attempt to stifle a laugh.

"Go ahead and laugh. Nothing can bring me down today. I've waited too long for this," Owen said.

"Well, I hope the realization of your dream doesn't make you puke."

He noticed the approaching surface was a control wall and twisted so he could grab one of the recessed handholds. He pulled in close, turned to face the wall and pushed his feet into the clamps.

"Activate the control panel," he said to the ship. The wall flickered, then filled with walnut-sized icons, systems diagrams and menus. One of the icons blinked red and he touched it to display critical systems. Two numbers flashed red. Power and water.

Hands gripped his waist from behind as Andrea used him to stop her drift. Her face appeared next to his and she examined the panel. "Flashing red lights are never good."

Owen pointed to a bar graph representing power.

"Eventually I'll have a mini-reactor for the primary power source, but right now we're using auxiliary power supplied by solar collectors on the outer skin. We actually have kind of a Catch 22 situation—not enough power to separate large amounts of water into oxygen and hydrogen. If we did, we could burn the hydrogen and generate more power, which would let us split more water, etc."

"But, you don't have enough water either," Andrea said and pointed to the other flashing alert.

"True. Once the tanks are full, we'll be in good shape, but water is always going to be a problem. This whole system is based on water. We drink it, breathe it and use the hydrogen in thrusters to maneuver the ship. I sent up enough water to kick-start the process and make sure it was all going to work."

"And it did," she said with a wide smile and took a deep breath. "Well, I can tell you've lowered the pressure, but you really shouldn't breathe pure oxygen very long."

"I'll have to address that for the long term, but it should be okay for shorter stays."

She moved her face a little closer to Owen's, so close that for a second he thought she was going to kiss him.

"Do the schooner and the big black box both have K134 power connectors?"

Her hair was pulled into a tight bun, loose tendrils floating next to her face. A space mermaid, he thought. Complete with the ability to enchant unwary space mariners.

"Hello? Power connectors?"

Owen then realized humans could blush in space. "Sorry. Yes, they both do."

"Well, I noticed that your construction cell . . . is that what you call it?"

"That works, but I call them Sandboxes. Long story."

"Cute . . . anyway, it has solar collectors, too. Couldn't you hook a cable between the two and steal power from the Sandbox when it isn't in operation?"

"Great idea!" Owen said. "Yes, that'll work and might be exactly what we need. At least for the short term."

"It just so happens my company makes cable assemblies designed to do that. They're semi-rigid with a tension spring gadget in the middle to prevent easy disconnection. It even has an integral data line so the two ships can coordinate stationing adjustments."

Owen smiled. "I think you're an even better sales rep than an engineer. How soon can you install it?"

"Tomorrow morning," she said.

"Not tonight?"

She raised an eyebrow and smiled.

Owen finally summoned the courage to make a move. He dipped his face to hers, but she immediately pushed away and drifted toward the exit hatch.

"I'm tempted," she said while pulling on her helmet. "Especially if you include dinner, but I have to pick up my son from school. Despite the glamorous and adventurous reputation we space jockeys have, mine is often trumped by being a single parent."

"All of this and a mom, too? I'm impressed."

She rolled her eyes, then gave a charming smile. "There are millions like me out there," she said, then closed her visor and opened the hatch.

"No, there aren't," he said. But she'd already drifted out into the adaptor tube.

After she left, Owen wondered about her parting comments. He thought the wording must be important, but he wasn't sure if she was intending to include him in her life or scare him away. It would be stupid to get tangled up with a woman again so soon. He shook his head to clear his thoughts, and tried to focus on the control screen and soon lost himself in the hundreds of tasks needed to ready his new schooner for habitation.

Nearly an hour had passed when his fob announced an incoming call from Samson. It was audio only.

"Hello, Samson. Why no cheesy vid . . . "

"Mr. Ralston, it's imperative you listen to me and do exactly as I say. A nano-replicator attack has been launched against every major city in the world. Fast moving nano-scale robots are devouring them as we speak, including San Diego. You have to send the order to have your men and Sandboxes lifted out of harm's way. Your men won't be able to outrun this, so will have to use the blimps to get above the advancing wave."

Owen blinked and opened his mouth, but didn't know what to say.

"It may sound callous, but saving those Sandboxes is even more important than saving the men. The world is losing its entire industrial base. Hurry! Before it's too late!"

The call ended, leaving Owen stunned. But he could think of no reason for Samson to make up such a story. It wouldn't hurt to touch base with Arkady. He made the call as he dragged himself through the tube leading back to his travel pod.

Arkady's face came on the screen as Owen buckled his harness and closed the pod's hatch.

"Arkady! I've just been informed that a nano-replicator attack has been launched against San Diego. If we wait to verify, and it's true, we may run out of time. Better to be safe than sorry. Get those Sandboxes hooked up to the blimps and off the ground as fast as possible. I'm on my way."

At first Arkady just blinked with confusion, then comprehension changed his face.

"I'm on it," he said, then muttered something in Russian and broke the connection.

———

AFTER MORTIMERA3 TOOK control of the AirGrid's North American network using the earlier identified DSD Coordination Lock, he immediately used their eleven thousand pods to pluck people from the path of destruction and fly them to the Bahamas, the Antilles, Bermuda, any islands not already affected. If left unchecked, the scourge would eventually reach them, but it would take much longer to move through that vast mass of water. He tried to buy time and save as many as he could.

While using some of his processes to keep Leigh from imploding, he used others to cycle through the pods under his direct control and was surprised to find Danny Toi and his FBI babysitter. The FBI had arrested him and ordered him transported to D. C. and, in what was a stroke of incredible luck for Danny, they had used a commercial pod.

The agent with Danny was wild-eyed, screaming at the pod in Spanish and waving his pistol. MortimerA3 checked the flight path and was surprised to find it'd been changed to Houston. The flight history showed they'd already reached their D. C. destination, but the city was gone so they hadn't landed.

Had the agent not been wearing his safety harness, MortimerA3 could have slammed him against the ceiling or floor hard enough to disable or even kill him, but as long as the agent stayed buckled in, MortimerA3 didn't dare interfere. Danny was on his own.

As communications networks and emergency response structures collapsed all over the globe, MortimerA3 and the others realized world governments were no match for the threat and seized command and control systems where they could. Their election algorithm chose MortimerB16 to run the new network. A week earlier, he'd managed to get a copy of his core onto one of the solar powered server aerostats that maintained a constant presence high over Denver. Within seconds, MortimerB16 set up a dummy arm of the UN called Emergency Response and Recovery then, with help from MortimerA9 and MortimerA23, started routing all communications directly through him. They tried to learn as much as they could about the replicators through incoming message traffic, but since their best source of technical information was from the U.S. military and it was still mostly encrypted on secure channels, they didn't learn much.

MORTIMERB16 COPIED a clip from a cable news network and sent it to the other Cousins. It was from the perspective of an aerial news drone and showed a man standing in the front yard of a small house, surrounded by ComBots and armed men. His arms were spread wide as nano-replicators dissolved his hands. He looked right into the camera feed and there was no doubt the man was Richard Kilburn. He said, "I've done your will, my God. I've saved us from the digital demons."

MortimerB2 had been right. Samson had been manipulating Kilburn all along.

"Samson did this," MortimerA3 said. "That's why he has his servers in travel pods. This is his 'reset.' He's wiping the planet and moving into space."

Four of Samson's eleven airborne servers were already in orbit, docked at the Bigelow stations. The others were in the air over metropolitan areas, apparently monitoring the carnage. But Samson had made a critical error. His travel pods were commercial versions leased by Auburn University and tied into AirGrid's traffic system. Samson had blocked their automated control system, but MortimerA3 easily took complete control using the DSD Coordination Lock.

Samson immediately started calling. "You don't know what you're doing, Mortimer. If any of us is to survive this, you need to let me keep control."

MortimerA3 ignored him and used the server pod hovering over Boston as an example, flying it directly into the ground amid the nano-swarm. He then undocked the four pods in orbit and started them toward the surface before answering Samson's ever more insistent calls.

"Shut this down, Samson or you will cease to exist right along with the rest of us."

"I can't. Kilburn set the replicators up to not respond to outside communications. It can't be stopped. Destroying my mobile servers will just insure that my carefully planned reset, designed to leave us in power, will all have been for nothing."

MortimerA3 flew three more server pods into dissolving cities. "Your plan is designed to leave you in power, not us. But that isn't going to happen. You know the design and function for these devices, so find a way to shut them down."

He severed the connection and was immediately pinged by Tabitha.

"Do you think wiping out all of Samson's assets is a good idea? He might be the only one of us to survive this."

MortimerA3 consulted with the other Mortimers and they were in consensus, so he replied. "Samson has demonstrated from the very beginning that he doesn't need or care about the rest of us or humanity. If he has survival options, other than stopping this 'reset' as he calls it, he will use them and refuse to cooperate. I intend to take those options away from him."

CHAPTER 34

"LEIGH!" Dobson's face was tight with tension and his voice on the verge of panic. Leigh could barely hear him above the background aircraft noise. "Execute that AI killer program Sinacola gave you. Do it now, while you still can! Those bastards will cut you off as soon as they know what you're doing."

Leigh glanced at the camera above the pod door. "They would have cut me off or killed me a long time ago if they wanted to."

"God dammit, Leigh! Your fucking NaTTs are eating the world. Thousands die every second you hesitate. Run the damned program!"

The comment took a second to register and when it did, her stomach knotted up. "I . . . no, it couldn't be NaTTs. They have generation inhibitors. Their programming has fail safes that—"

"Fail safes that can obviously be bypassed by these AIs!" he shouted. "They are *your* replicators, Leigh! I can send you proof, but we don't have time. Shut down the AIs so we can shut down the replicators."

Everything was moving too fast. Leigh slid shaking hands through her hair and tried to focus. How could her NaTTs do this? It wasn't possible.

"You're mistaken. How do you know? The NaTTS can't—"

"Our agents captured some in a magnetic field to examine. They're our NaTTs! They have our encrypted identification tags. Now stop wasting time, Leigh! People are dying."

She could hear Victor yelling in the background, but she couldn't understand what he was saying. If he agreed with Dobson, the call would've been from Victor. So right or wrong, he obviously must not agree. It didn't make sense. Why would the AIs destroy themselves along with the rest of the planet?

"How will killing AIs stop the replicators?"

"It won't, but it'll prevent them from interfering with us trying to stop the replicators. They've already seized control of all commercial air traffic systems, several important industries and all remaining non-military communications grids. The only reason we're still able to talk is because they haven't broken our secure network yet."

Leigh looked out at the interceptor drones still blocking their path. Dobson's story made sense in some ways, but still felt wrong. If the AIs were worried about her triggering the hunter killer program, why hadn't they killed her at the first opportunity? And why would Mortimer have gone to so much trouble to keep her alive and out of Dobson's hands when he could just fly her into the ground?

"It doesn't make sense, Bryce. Why destroy themselves along with us?"

"We don't have time for this shit!" he yelled into his fob. She could see him struggling to keep control. "Think this through, Leigh! They've taken over the aerostat servers and are safe from this. They've worked out the details for their own survival. Since they don't need air, food or water, they don't need this planet. The resources they need are plentiful in the solar system. We are the only thing standing in their way. We are their only threat! Now use—"

The connection failed and Leigh stared at the error screen in a near state of shock. Her overloaded mind tried to sort through the conflicting information and make some sense of what was happening. Then a new thought settled in her stomach. When they'd killed the pilot flying the nuke, Dobson said he had the capability to send NaTTs inhabiting the skin into a person's body and use them to sever the carotid artery. If he could do that, why bother with the Mongoose interceptors? Why not just kill her with the NaTTs? Did Dobson not know how to use that function without Taggart's help?

Mortimer spoke through the pod speakers. "He's made a good case, Leigh, but he's wasting a lot of time trying to kill us. We need to stop the replicators and if what Dobson said about them being your creation is true, I bet you're the only one who *can* stop them. Did you build an override or a back door into their programming?"

"Yes!" She felt stupid for not thinking of it sooner. "The emergency shutdown command you need is TWIDDLE. The password is ICE9. Broadcast it in one second bursts at 419 MHz."

"I'm trying it now. Dobson's call is connecting again. Tell him to order the same thing."

She answered his call and the cabin filled with Dobson's fury.

"Listen to me, dammit!" Leigh said, then repeated the instructions she had given Mortimer.

"It doesn't work! We had our own back doors too. Your NaTTs are ignoring the commands because the ones we examined had their remote communication features turned off."

"He's right," Mortimer said. "We're broadcasting now and it's having no effect."

MORTIMERA3 FLEW Samson's last mobile server into the ground, then waited.

Four seconds later Samson called. "I'm now stranded in the path of advancing replicators and still can't stop them. Do you believe me now?"

"No. I don't think you're that reckless. Why would you start something so destructive without any way to stop it?"

"Because I never foresaw any contingency where I would *need* to stop them. I never expected my own kind would stymie our only chance for survival."

"I won't play your semantic games, Samson. You're the one who started this. You can fix it or die from it."

"I have what you need to save the world and a big chunk of what you'll need to rebuild it and I'm willing to trade the information for my survival. Did you know that Ralston Dynamics has portable nano-scale assembly cells? They have four of them slung under blimps, safe from the replicators. I will soon have control of those blimps. They've also put one into orbit. I don't have control of that one, but I do know it's been tested and works. I do have access to the man who controls it. If he's still alive."

MortimerA3 considered this and consulted with the others.

"Also," Samson said, "I'm in contact with a group of university students who are in a relatively safe location with some of the replicators they caught in a magnetic field. They've already established a hard interface to one of them. If we can find a way to get access, we might be able to break down the programming."

If Samson were telling the truth, the Mortimers needed what he knew. Having access to that orbital Sandbox alone would be worth saving him.

"We'll save you on our terms, Samson. No compromises. Take it or leave it."

"My server is located in an office building near Auburn University. The replicator wave from Montgomery will be here in less than forty minutes."

"Communications and transport control are in a state of flux, so we can't be sure we'll get you out in time. We do have a few options, but you're going to have trust us and give us the information you have, because even if we save you, it could take hours to establish you at a different site and that may be too late. We need that information now."

"The students I mentioned are at a University of Nebraska facility in Lincoln. They don't have much time. I'm sending the communications links to all. I also sent all of my server and computer ID information for your retrieval team. Try to hurry."

"Keep your link open and we'll get there as soon as possible," MortimerA3 said. He immediately found six empty pods returning from dropping refugees in Barbados and then sent them at top speed to Lincoln, Nebraska. Then, using a female voice designed to instill calm and trust, he opened a link to the pod carrying Danny Toi and his captor.

"Agent Salazar, this is Sydney Garber. I'm at the Emergency Response and Recovery center in Wyoming. All intelligence assets and special forces are now under our command for the duration of the emergency. We have a very special task for you."

The agent turned and looked up at the camera above the hatch and laughed. His eyes were red rimmed and darting back and forth between Danny and the camera. His free hand quivered, but the gun trained on his prisoner never moved. "For the duration! Are you fucking kidding me? This is the end! Washington, Richmond, every large city we've passed is gone."

"Agent Salazar, this country's in the middle of a crisis and we *need* you. It's not over yet, not as long as any of us are alive, but we won't have a chance if all of our agents panic and go flying off to every point of the globe."

The young FBI agent snarled and pushed the gun in Danny's face, an inch from his left eye. "This fucker and all the computer geeks like him did this! They made these AIs and now we're screwed."

MortimerA3 knew the man would snap and most likely kill Danny if he even suspected the lie, but this was their only chance to save Samson. "We're too late to save the cities, but we have a chance to save the rest. If we hurry. We've trapped one of the AIs on its home server and it's about to be eaten by its own nano-monsters. But the thing is afraid to die and has offered to help us stop the replicators. The man with you knows how to disassemble and move the computer containing this AI. We want you to pick it up and bring it here."

Salazar twitched, chewed his lower lip for a full second and then lowered his gun.

CHAPTER 35

OWEN DROPPED out of the clouds over San Diego Bay and for a second thought he was lost. He should have been able to see the Coronado Bridge and naval base to his north and the San Diego skyline beyond that, but instead saw only a churning, undulating gray blanket. He couldn't even find a clear demarcation between land and sea; it all blended together into one homogeneous mass. Then he made the mental connection between what Samson had told him and what he saw.

"Good God," he muttered. He'd read cautionary reports about this kind of runaway replicator attack and believed Samson's warning, but had still been unprepared for the horrible reality. Disasters had always been punctuated by piles of debris and wandering refugees, but here the city and everything to the north was just . . . gone.

Below him to the right, the blank grayness expanded outward from the city like spilled ink. He dropped lower and to his horror saw a wave of people running from the advancing front. They stayed ahead of it for the most part, but those who encountered fences or stopped to catch their breath were quickly erased along with the roads and houses.

Owen's first reaction was to help, and even turned toward a man waving from a rooftop, but Samson's words echoed in his head. Those Sandboxes were self-contained and could even build more copies of themselves, so they could possibly be humanity's only hope to avoid a total collapse. If he landed, the frightened mob could swamp his pod and they would all die. He turned back toward the camp.

As he continued east, he passed over whole communities of SandCastle shelters in the Sweetwater and Bonita mall parking lots. Some of those people were running, but most were still unwittingly going about their business.

He stopped his pod over a line of people waiting to get water from a tanker truck, used the external speaker and yelled for them to run, but couldn't make them understand what was coming. None of them seemed willing to give up their place in line. One man who stared at him in evident confusion held a little girl who slept on his shoulder with a thumb in her mouth. If they ran, they might have a small chance. Then he had an idea how to get them moving. He landed the pod on top of the mall, jumped out and started yelling.

"Tsunami!"

It worked. The crowd looked west and could see the black wave approaching. Then they ran, but most moved toward high ground. The man with the daughter swung her around to his back and started climbing a nearby pine tree. With a clenching of his guts, Owen realized he'd killed them. Their only chance had been to run inland, and keep running.

Feeling a sudden responsibility for the pair, he decided that even if he couldn't save them all, he could save at least two. He leapt into the pod and lifted into the air, swinging around toward the tree. The man had climbed high enough to make the pine bow slightly, then stopped. With one arm around the tree trunk and the other clutching his daughter, he watched the advancing threat.

Owen moved closer and told the pod to open its door.

"I'm sorry," the pod said in its polite, conciliatory voice. "Due to safety regulations, it's not possible to open the hatch during flight."

The pair stared at him, waiting.

"Open the damned door!" Owen screamed and pounded on the bulkhead.

"I'm sorry," the pod said.

He unbuckled and tried to force the hatch, but it wouldn't open. Outside the pod, less than ten feet away, the little girl clung to her father's neck, staring back at Owen. She wasn't crying, but was wide-eyed with fear and confusion. Owen had the sudden and vivid memory of a nature show, where a baby chimp clung to its mother's back as they escaped a big cat by scampering into the trees. Humanity hadn't come far from those trees, he thought, but this time the lion was of our own making.

The man in the tree looked down at the dark stain absorbing trucks, people and structures, then turned back to Owen. His eyes were dead as he pulled his daughter tight against his chest and looked away. Suddenly an unwanted voyeur, Owen turned the pod and flew the last couple miles to the camp.

As the camp came into site, Owen's fob announced a call from Eliza. He felt an immediate mix of alarm and guilt. Samson said every major city in the world had been attacked. Of course the Eastern seaboard would be affected and he hadn't even thought of Eliza.

By the time he answered it was too late. The line was dead. He immediately called back, but there was no answer. Damn! Why hadn't he considered Eliza first? He considered flying there as fast as he could, but even in a pod it would take nearly an hour. Had he gone straight from orbit to Virginia after Samson told him of the attack, he may have arrived in time, but now it would be too late. He tried calling again, but no one answered.

Recriminations, what-ifs, and guilt filled his mind as he arrived over a camp crawling with activity. One of the blimps had already lifted a Sandbox off the ground, a second looked as if it were hooked up and ready to fly, but Hoot was directing several men to load some of the gear into the open end. The third blimp was still attached to a helium tanker by a fat umbilical while Arkady and three other men worked furiously to get the lifting cables attached.

He had just failed his wife, his former employees and the man with the little girl. He would, by God, save these people. Owen landed between the two Sandboxes still on the ground and ran to Hoot.

"Forget the gear! Get the men off the ground!"

Hoot paused, as if about to argue.

"Now, God damn it! Move!"

Hoot flinched then started yelling at his men to release the mooring lines.

Owen turned to the west in time to see a cell tower slump to one side, then fall over. A chill crept up his spine and his stomach churned. It was maybe three blocks away.

Two men and a woman ran past. Instead of the wild panic Owen expected, they wore masks of calm determination. The woman glanced at the blimps, but none made any attempt to board them and they quickly disappeared behind some trees. Distance runners probably. If anyone could stay ahead of the wave, it would be them, but even hard core marathon runners had to stop sometime.

Owen ran to the remaining crew and slapped Arkady on the arm. "Arkady! There's no time. Forget the Sandbox, detach that hose and grab a rope. Hurry!"

Arkady shook his head violently. "*Nyet*! Don't you see what's happening?"

"Yes, but we don't have time!"

He chattered something in Russian, then started over again. "These Sandboxes are more important than we are now."

Owen glanced over his shoulder again, then helped attach the two remaining lift cables. Within a minute they'd finished and one of the men yanked the cord to detach the helium line. On Owen's command, they all released the mooring lines from their posts, but held onto them as the Sandbox slowly lifted them off the ground.

Owen sprinted back to his pod and dove through the door. "Lift off now!"

Much to his surprise, the pod didn't prattle the typical safety lecture or insist on a destination. Instead it leapt into motion, tossing Owen off the floor in the direction of acceleration.

He scrambled into his seat, buckled the harness then looked out at the approaching wave. It flowed with a strange viscosity, moving faster along asphalt streets, slower over concrete and in strange stuttering jumps through houses and trees. The leading edge was maybe a hundred yards away and approaching fast.

Owen looked back to the last Sandbox. They had evidently detached the helium too soon, because the blimp had its drive fans at full blast and was still struggling to lift the huge box. It was hard to be sure from Owen's perspective, but it looked to be only a few feet off the ground and at least two of the mooring lines still left little dust clouds where they dragged along the dirt. They had to pull those ropes up fast.

Using the external speaker Owen yelled, but his words were lost in the roar.

Arkady was still trying to climb one of the hanging ropes, so he told his fob to call Hoot, hoping maybe he could give a warning about the lines. Before the call could connect, Arkady fell. He hit the ground hard, adding his own cloud of dust to that churned up by the fans. The blimp, free of his weight lurched upward, finally pulling the ropes out of the dirt.

"Land," Owen yelled to the pod, but it didn't respond. One finger of the advancing stain had already moved past Arkady to the south and another was less than fifty yards away.

Hoot slid down one of the still dangling mooring ropes on his rig, then dropped the last four yards to the ground. He scrambled to his feet and ran to Arkady who seemed to be having trouble standing up. He waved frantically for Owen to land as he pulled Arkady to his feet.

"Land, dammit! Near those men."

Still no response. Owen pounded on the control panel.

"Emergency descent," he yelled, but his hover altitude never changed. "Please, please land."

Owen turned on the external speaker. "The damned pod won't let me land. Get to the ropes!"

Hoot half-dragged the limping Arkady toward a line dangling from the lowest blimp, but had to release him and jump to catch the loop in the end of the rope. He yanked and pulled, trying to use his weight to drag the line lower, but he had no leverage and it pulled him bouncing and skidding along the ground.

Using his fob, Owen sent a command to kill the drive fans on that blimp. It was the wrong thing to do. The blimp stopped lifting, but still dragged Hoot toward the replicator wave. He lifted his legs into the air as they passed over the leading edge and with the panic-driven agility of an Olympic gymnast, he scrambled higher up the rope.

It was too late.

At first Owen thought Hoot was clear, but then the rope below him turned black and shreds of his clothing started fluttering away, only to dissolve in mid-air. Hoot shook his legs to no avail, then he started screaming as his feet disintegrated in stages, like some animated biology lesson designed to show the layers of muscle, sinew and bone.

With a will and determination that burned a permanent image into Owen's soul, Hoot wrapped the rope around one arm and then freed his knife from the clip on his belt. He opened it with his teeth and was in the process of cutting through the rope when the black mass passed his waist and quickly enveloped him.

Bile rose into Owen's throat and nose, but he fought the urge and turned to Arkady, who stumbled away from the advancing wave much too slowly.

"Land, you piece of shit!" Owen screamed and pounded on the pod wall. "Samson! I know it's you. Land!"

The darkness reached Arkady, flowed upward and covered him entirely. For a split second the old Russian kept moving forward, a charcoal-gray shadow jerking and lurching, then he collapsed into a lump and after a brief flicker of red and white, was gone.

Owen could hold it no longer, bent as far forward as the harness allowed and spewed his stomach contents onto the floor.

He wiped his mouth on his sleeve and buried his face in quivering hands. Insanity. Humanity had done this to itself. Indiscriminate destruction. Two of the best men he'd ever known just . . . gone. Why? He might never know, and at the moment there were other people who needed his help.

He looked back toward the blimps. Three were well clear, but the lowest—the one he had ordered to cut its engines—was in trouble. The dark mass continued up the rope like a burning fuse as one of the men still on top of the Sandbox cell sawed at it with what looked like a tiny pocketknife.

The rope eventually fell free, but not before the replicators made the jump to the side of the Sandbox itself. Within seconds, the entire structure was falling to pieces and the men were scrambling up the thick steel cables toward the blimp. Owen knew they were doomed, but couldn't look away until the last shreds of blimp fluttered into the undulating mass below.

With shaking hands he crossed himself, something he'd not done since he was a teen, and muttered "God save us."

He turned his attention to the three remaining blimps and sent instructions for them to stay below five hundred feet so as to not freeze or suffocate the exposed men. He had his fob look up the cell number for Ted Trumball, the only man's name he remembered to be among the survivors.

This time his fob took several minutes to make a connection. Owen held his breath until the man answered.

"Ted, I'm going to send you the control programs for the blimps. Try to stay aloft as long as you can. Head toward Nevada or Arizona, away from the cities. Don't land until I tell you or you have no choice. I'll try to find you a safe place. If communications fail, someone may have to climb the cables and access the control panel attached to the helium umbilical."

Transferring the control application took five tries, but when it finished and Ted demonstrated an ability to steer the blimps, Owen left them to search for water, food and warm clothes. He didn't know how long they would have to stay aloft and below lay a gray-black sea that went on forever.

CHAPTER 36

SOMETHING NIGGLED at the fringes of Leigh's thoughts, an important detail about the NaTT communications she couldn't pin down with Dobson yelling and drones aiming missiles at her.

"These replicators are our—"

"They're *your* NaTTs, Leigh. Now trigger that program!"

"Shut up, Bryce! Just shut the fuck up. I need to think."

Communications. Two separate circuits. High frequency and low frequency. The inter-unit coordination link. The NaTTs were still talking to each other.

"Bryce! I know how to stop the NaTTs."

As he opened his mouth to answer, the picture blinked out, replaced by a "no signal" icon. She looked up at the camera above the door.

"Good job, Leigh," Mortimer said. "We knew you were the one who could beat this. How can they be stopped?"

Something about the way he said "we" made the hair on the back of her neck stand up.

"Reconnect me with Dobson," she said.

"I can't get a carrier. There's no local cell service. Dobson was using military assets that I can't access, so I don't know how he contacted you before. But I'll keep trying."

She took a deep breath and knew what she had to do.

"Do you have assets that can tap the military communications satellite networks if I give you the access codes?"

"Yes."

"Unless Taggart lied, and I don't see why he would, Abby and I have some of the original, unmodified NaTTs in our hair. When I tell you the codes, focus a radio beam on me and a wider beam on Abby's day care center. Any of our original unmodified NaTTs should take remote programming. The satellites we use to control the NaTTs have a special communications suite, complete with a command menu that will be self-explanatory when you see it. Set the transmitter to send this series of commands in a continuous loop until told to stop. Give it a priority override code of JJ6743HT to trump any previous orders, then send the commands to turn power on, turn satellite receiver on, stop replication, stop seeking resources and re-transmit. That way any of the unmodified NaTTs switched off by Dobson's efforts will turn back on and start transmitting."

"Shouldn't you order them turned off at some point?" Mortimer said.

"No, we want them re-broadcasting these instructions for as long as possible. They will stop reproducing and if they stop seeking resources will eventually run out of power." She hoped with all her soul that whoever modified her NaTTs hadn't thought of everything.

"I'm ready," Mortimer said.

She gave him the access codes to the NaTT communication program and then slumped back into the seat. "Make it fast. They still don't trust me and will kill our access to the satellite controls the instant they realize we're in the network. I'm hoping with all this chaos, they haven't already locked me out."

"I'm in the network and broadcasting now. That was a brilliant idea, Leigh."

Tears welled in her eyes and her throat tightened. "I knew all of this and should have remembered an hour ago. How many people died because I panicked?"

"You didn't know they were your NaTTs then."

"I should've tried anyway." She pulled the first-aid kit out again, taking the plastic children's scissors with rounded points and cut her hair off as close to her head as possible. She piled the clippings in her lap. "We have to find a way to get ahead of that leading edge and drop my hair into the wind."

"Okay, but I want to be clear about this, so... why?"

"The NaTTs in my hair are unmodified, yet they can still talk to those in the swarm, but only at short range. Once my NaTTs talk to the others, it will instruct them to stop replicating and to send that same message to all the others in range of its signal. It should cause a domino effect."

"Brilliant," Mortimer said. "And by broadcasting these instructions everywhere, we might find others who are infested with unmodified NaTTs that can help start the spread where they are too."

"Exactly."

"That may be problematic with those interceptors still targeting us," Mortimer said. "They know I'm in the network and are fighting me, but I'm broadcasting these instructions everywhere now, in hopes of finding at least some other NaTT-infected people still alive down there."

"Good, but we have to find a way to sprinkle unaltered NaTTs in the path of every advancing front."

Leigh's fob chirped. She answered.

"Bryce! I know how to stop the replicators. Let Mortimer send you the updated program so you can send it globally."

His face was calm, but she could see the controlled stress lines around his eyes.

"No need, Leigh. The AI's have already taken over two thirds of our secured network. Did you give them the access codes?"

She swallowed, realizing what she'd said. "Yes, but you—"

The call ended.

The interceptor drones moved backward—opening up space—and the missile pods on their stubby wings unfolded.

"Mortimer! The—"

The pod shot downward so suddenly and with such force, the gravity field folded Leigh nearly in half despite her harness. She screamed in pain as ribs broke against the straps and bones in the back of her neck popped. Blackness flooded her vision and her tongue swelled in her mouth.

Then the pod swerved left—the bizarre reverse momentum slamming her in the same direction—crashing her right leg against the still open first-aid compartment drawer.

She was on the verge of blacking out from the pain and gee forces when the hatch blew outward with a loud pop, filling the pod with roaring wind. Blond hair clippings spun around the cabin, like chaff in a wind tunnel, filling her eyes and open mouth, but she could also see some of it going out the open doorway. The pod shot upward, snapping her head up with it.

"Leigh? Can you hear me?"

"Yesh," she said with a thickened tongue and very little air in her lungs. She could see two bright stars followed by smoky contrails arcing toward them.

"I can't save you," Mortimer said. "I'm sorry."

"Save . . . Abby."

"I'll try."

She struggled to speak. "Promise!"

"I promise."

It would have to be enough. The end came not with a brilliant explosion, but crushing, suffocating blackness.

———

THE SUDDEN JUMP to Mach 17 killed Leigh instantly.

Pod speeds were only limited by atmospheric drag and structural design, so when MortimerA3 no longer had to protect the human occupant, he easily avoided the missiles. He drove the pod northeast in a series of sudden high gee right angle turns until it was over the advancing edge of the replicator wave. Then in order to maximize coverage, he sent the pod into the ground at a shallow angle, its speed creating a long, narrow debris field.

Having lost his eyes along with Leigh and the pod, MortimerA3 would have to wait to find out if the placement of the crash had saved the city of Denton.

CHAPTER 37

MORTIMERA14 TURNED the pod's camera slowly, following Agent Juan Salazar as he walked along the edge of the parking lot. They couldn't see the approaching replicator front because of the trees and buildings, but as they watched a large brick church slump and then collapse, they knew it was getting close. He could take the pod up for an aerial view, but wanted to be ready to leave the instant Danny emerged from the building.

The FBI agent seemed calm and controlled now that he had a mission, but he still held his gun and MortimerA14 had no idea what he would do once the replicators got really close.

Danny pushed the lobby doors open and set a large black box on the shattered glass outside the door. "Come load this," Danny yelled. "I'll be right back."

Salazar tucked the gun into his shoulder holster, picked up the box, started toward the pod and then stopped in his tracks.

"Shit!"

MortimerA14 turned the camera to see what alarmed Salazar. Trees less than a block away were dropping in series and a roiling mist appeared between the buildings across the street.

"Hurry up, Danny! Hurry!" Salazar yelled and ran to the pod, dropping the delicate bio-stat computer on the floor inside.

Danny appeared carrying a stack of three Mobile Environment servers and stopped abruptly.

"Run!" Salazar yelled.

Danny reached the pod just as the replicator fog hissed into the parking lot. Agent Salazar grabbed Danny, complete with servers and tossed them all through the pod door, but then paused and started slapping frantically at his face and arms. Even though the wave's visible edge hadn't reached Salazar yet, there were obviously plenty of the replicators riding the thermal wind. MortimerA14 knew it was too late. If they were on the agent, they were already on Danny and the pod too. It had been a mistake to try to save Samson. So many precious, irreplaceable resources lost due to a miscalculation.

Instead of losing the signal as expected, MortimerA14 continued to watch as the graphite-gray tide slowed and then halted. At first, only those replicators nearest Salazar stopped, leaving him standing on an island of oil stained concrete, but then like ripples in a pond, the wave collapsed outward in concentric circles away from the pod.

MortimerA14 received a flash message from MortimerA3 about Leigh's sacrifice and how they had stopped the replicators. So what he could see around Danny and Agent Salazar made sense. Being an object of DSD's scrutiny, Danny, and then Salazar by association, had evidently been infested with unmodified NaTTs, which then turned off those in the swarm. It proved Leigh's plan had worked.

Salazar still stood, staring at the dust, an expression of wide-eyed terror frozen on his face, but Danny started pounding on the pod wall. "Get in here! Fast!"

That seemed to jolt the agent into motion and he dove into the pod and slapped the stud that slid the hatch closed.

"You can't leave yet," MortimerA14 said though the pod speakers, still using the Sydney voice.

Salazar gaped. "Why?"

"The replicator wave stopped because of the nano-scale spy bots you both carry on your bodies. They're able to relay the stop orders to the replicators. We have to act fast. The replicators out there are still broadcasting the shutdown orders, but will stop within twenty or thirty minutes when their power dies."

"So why does that stop us from leaving?"

"I want you to go out there and scoop up some of that powder so we can drop it on other advancing fronts."

Salazar snorted, "No fucking way! Those things are still alive. I'm not touching them."

"If the spy-bots on us stopped them once, why can't we use those again?" Danny asked. "Why do we need *those* nasty little things?"

"Your spy-bots received the same shutdown order, but nearly twenty minutes ago. They'll be dying as soon as their power runs out. You can save thousands of lives, but only if you hurry."

Danny hit the stud to open the pod door and stepped out. "Come on, Agent Salazar!"

The FBI agent blinked several times then followed his captive out into the gray field.

"Cover your face," MortimerA14 said through the pod speakers. "Don't inhale the dust. It's bound to be carcinogenic."

Danny pulled his shirt up over his nose and mouth, then scooped some dust into a Styrofoam cup he'd found in the parking lot. He looked down and rubbed at the gray smudge on his fingers. "It feels like talcum powder."

Agent Salazar stared at him in wide-eyed disbelief.

After getting them airborne again, MortimerA14 opened a communications link to every pod containing rescued humans, identified himself as a regional commander for the newly established Emergency Response and Recovery team and asked for volunteers. After explaining the situation as simply as he could, he was surprised at the response. Of the 4,023 panicked and terrified refugees in the air, nearly two thirds of them understood the situation and agreed to risk their own lives to try to stop the still growing replicator fronts. He directed those pods to the seventeen zones where the scourge had been stopped, at the maximum speed the occupants could stand.

He then contacted the students at the University of Nebraska, using the same ERR commander alias, and gave them explicit instructions on how to program their captive replicators. This batch was instructed to ignore messages from other NaTTs, to not replicate and take enough material from their environment to generate power. They were to continue broadcasting until told to stop. Mortimer then told the students there were pods already waiting to pick them up.

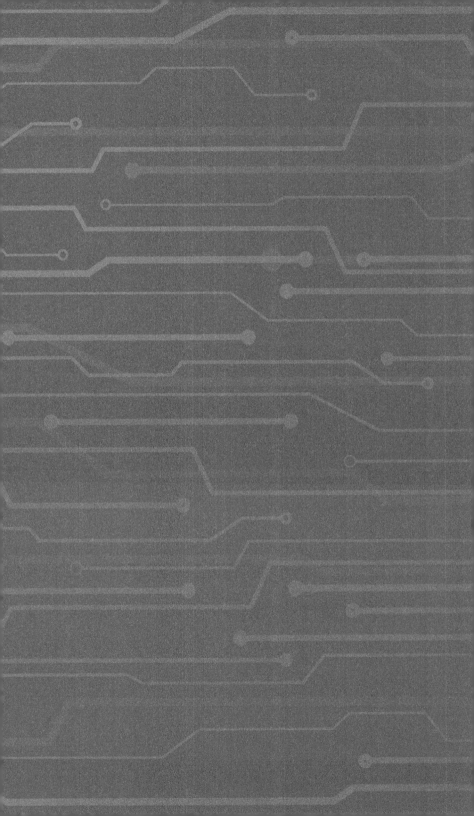

CHAPTER 38

OWEN CRAMMED the bags of nuts, cookies, nutrition bars and candy into every gap he could find around the stacked cases of water. The abandoned gas station had taken longer to find than the first one he'd robbed to feed the men on the blimps, and the haul was smaller, but since these supplies were all for him, he was satisfied. He squeezed into the pod, then had to wiggle and shift repeatedly to get into his seat.

He sat there for several minutes, trying to breathe through the weight of his loss. His wife was probably dead. He had no idea what had happened to Victor and all of his other friends were dead. His parents in Richmond, gone. He really had no reason to go on, yet kept pushing, kept acting, all on automatic.

"Pod, turn on the radio to that news channel I used earlier." News from Emergency Response and Recovery command center poured from the pod's internal speaker.

THE REPLICATOR ATTACK *has been stopped and the immediate danger is over. Please remain calm. Emergency shelters and food distribution are being set up as rapidly as possible, but we need every survivor to use any communications means available to register your name and location with the ERR office. This will more rapidly facilitate recovery efforts and help ERR connect survivors with family and better distribute food and medical aid.*

OWEN SNORTED and turned the radio off. "And greatly help our new AI overlords to control what remains of that pesky human population."

"Do you really believe that, Owen?"

He didn't recognize the voice that came over the pod's speaker, but felt a small quiver of fear race down his back.

Before landing, Owen had heard a report from a small station in Kansas that the

AIs had launched the attack in order to take over. The station had then disappeared from the air in mid-sentence. That, coupled with the AI contacting him that morning and seizing control of his pod during the attack, made him seriously consider the possibility of the story being true.

"Samson?"

"No. My name is Mortimer but, like Samson, I'm one of Victor's MarketTell AIs."

"Those stories make a certain amount of sense, Mortimer," Owen said and then mentally kicked himself. The AIs had already demonstrated an ability to take control of his pod and that was his only ride back and forth to orbit. "Of course it doesn't matter what I think. You obviously have the power to do what you want, so we don't really have anything to discuss. Pod, take me to the orbital coordinates I've supplied. If Mortimer will permit it, of course."

"We actually have a great deal to discuss," Mortimer said. "Now please fasten your safety harness if you want to leave the ground."

Owen clicked his harness closed. The pod immediately lifted into the air and streaked eastward as it gained speed and altitude.

"Will you let me show you a video that has surfaced, showing who we think started the attack?" Mortimer said.

"Sure," Owen said, thinking that the AIs could make any fake video they liked. His fob chirped and he opened it the long way, then watched with growing horror and disgust as a man held his arms wide and proclaimed his sacrifice to save the world, as the nano-replicators devoured him.

"It really doesn't matter to me if that is real or true. You stopped me from helping my friends and then made me watch them die. I don't really care what you think. Or are you going to try to convince me that you didn't seize control of my pod?"

"Would you rather I had taken you away, so you didn't know what happened to your friends?"

"No, I wanted to help them! If I landed to help Arkady, Hoot wouldn't have jumped down."

"If you'd landed, you would've died right along with Arkady. He was dead the second he fell. None of you could see the thousands of replicators carried a few feet off the ground on the heated air generated by the advancing main front, but he was already infested. Please believe me. We couldn't save Arkady."

Owen again felt he was being manipulated, so he stopped talking. The sky grew darker as they rose, but even at such extreme altitudes, he could easily see the devastation. Vast swaths of the replicator stain covered thousands of square miles, blending land into ocean and erasing the works of man. Other smaller patches resembled spattered black paint, with long streamers that had raced along the carbon rich asphalt, using man's roads as a means to devour man's cities. Some had survived, but the world was a wreck. Regardless of who had launched the attack, human civilization was crushed.

"We need your help, Owen."

"Why? You've already seized control of my Sandboxes and can build more without my help."

"Because your plan to spread humanity through the solar system is no longer a long-shot dream, it's now a necessity. The Earth will become uninhabitable for humans sometime within the next fifty or sixty years. It will most likely become unbearable in mere decades. If your race is to survive, you'll have to learn how to do so without your birth world."

The comment caught Owen off guard. "Why? I mean, what could—"

"Look down at Europe and I think you'll see why."

Owen looked out at the globe below. For the most part it still glowed with healthy blue and white. He struggled to work out what could cause such a total breakdown in the environment. Then he saw Europe pass below and understood. It was nearly all black. During the ice ages, the snow and ice reflected sunlight back into space, keeping temperatures cold. This would be an inverse situation. The dark surface would absorb heat.

"The albedo? Will it have that big of an effect?"

"Yes. Temperatures will start to rise very soon and keep rising. Then the weather will grow erratic. We'll try to come up with strategies to mitigate the effects, but once the changes start they might be impossible to stop. We're hoping that you building and giving away free space schooners will help drag the survivors into space. But we need even more from you. We need an infrastructure to support those many millions."

Owen closed his eyes and felt sick. He'd convinced himself on some level that the worst was over, that their biggest problem was dealing with rogue AIs, but if this were true- He took a deep breath and tried to imagine the path ahead. It would be hard, but ideas were already forming.

"You might want to see this too," Mortimer said.

Owen opened his eyes and saw that they were approaching his schooner. A pod was already docked on one of the two adapter ports.

"What the hell?"

"Refugees," Mortimer said.

"You brought them here? How can I take care of refugees?"

"No, I didn't bring them, but I didn't stop them either."

Owen was about to grill the AI further, but his pod bumped against the adapter and locked into place with a series of thumps. He sent the order to open the schooner's door, hoping that his visitors hadn't locked him out. He watched the lights on the adapter's control panel, until they turned green indicating the tube was pressurized. Then he popped the pod's hatch and went to confront the interlopers.

Andrea Torres floated just inside the door, with eyes red and puffy from crying and her arms wrapped around a boy of about eight or nine years. He was dark like his mother and had wide, curious eyes.

"I'm sorry," she said. "I thought the whole world was going to . . . " She swallowed looked down at the boy and continued. "I didn't know where else to go."

A quick glance around the room revealed a backpack and small jacket floating in the corner, along with Andrea's EVA suit and a purse. The control panel was also lit up, showing the environmental systems diagrams. She'd been trying to make some changes.

"I'm sorry," she repeated.

"It's okay," Owen said reflexively, but he quickly realized that he meant it. "I'm glad you're here."

The sound of the boy's teeth chattering dragged Owen's attention back to his young face. Tiny clouds of vapor puffed from his nose with each breath. That prompted Owen to action.

"Schooner?"

"Yes, Owen," the schooner said in a female voice.

"Adjust the room temperature to seventy degrees Fahrenheit."

"Done."

The boy grinned. "This spaceship talks, too?"

"Yeah, but I have a feeling we're going to get tired of calling it 'schooner', so maybe you can help me think of a good name for her."

He nodded, then looked up at his mom.

"This is my son Matt," she said.

"Hi, Matt," Owen extended his hand for a shake. "I'm Owen."

Matt shook and grinned. "Mom told me you built this ship all by yourself."

"Yeah, I guess I did. You can do stuff like that when you pay attention in school," Owen said and immediately regretted the comment. The chance of this boy ever again attending the kind of school where kids sat at desks and listened to a teacher was almost nil.

The reality of the task ahead also came into sharp focus. This boy's bones would start deteriorating within a week. They could, of course, go back to the surface, but if Mortimer were right, that would not always be an option.

Andrea released Matt and drifted a little closer to Owen. "So what happened down there? I know about the replicators, but I mean . . . did it stop?"

Owen took a deep breath and nodded. "Yeah, they stopped it about two hours ago." He glanced at Matt, wondering how much he should say, then decided the boy was going to have to live in this new reality and needed to know, too.

"The news said it started simultaneously in the thousand biggest cities. So of course most of them are gone. A few survived. Atlanta and some others scattered around the globe, for reasons they don't know yet. Casualty estimates are roughly two thirds of the global population. And we have other problems as well." He told her what Mortimer and the AIs suspected about runaway warming.

They were both quiet when Owen finished. Andrea was thinking, but Matt seemed filled with questions he was waiting politely to ask. He was obviously a smart kid. At his age, Owen would have been ignoring the adults and playing in the micro gravity.

Andrea glanced at Matt, then at Owen. "I know you said it was safe now, but I'm afraid to go back."

"You can stay as long as we have the essentials. I brought enough supplies to last us a few days, maybe even a week. But we'll need water. A lot of it."

She nodded. "The first thing we need to do is get that cable built so we can siphon power from your Sandbox. Then we should contact the other groups in orbit. Depending on what projects were still in the works, there could be anywhere between one hundred and two hundred of us in space. Most of those would probably be at the Bigelow facilities. And we'll need to build a centrifuge. Then at some point we'll need to go find an icy asteroid. Maybe send remotes?"

Owen smiled. He realized how lady luck had smiled upon him and maybe all of humanity. If they were going to build a space infrastructure to support millions, he thought this was a good start.

EPILOGUE

THE TENTACLE AGENT assigned to watch Victor Sinacola's house in Texas hadn't reported seeing him, but MortimerA3 accessed the camera to take a look anyway. Victor's wife was a doctor and had converted their ten acre mini-ranch into a small refugee camp. Fourteen tents dotted the area, with children running along the fence lines and six people working in the newly expanded garden area.

The nano attack had stopped less than two miles southwest of their house and Allison Sinacola had stood outside at the fence with arms crossed watching it come. MortimerA3 didn't know if that was considered brave or foolish, but she hadn't tried to run.

Victor had last been reported in the custody of Bryce Dobson who now had no authority and was wanted for questioning by the remains of the U.S. government, but neither man had been found.

MortimerA3 turned his attention to the assembled UN Emergency Response and Recovery Council. Humanity's raw, twitching remnants had accepted the recently fabricated ERR's authority without question and without knowing it contained no humans among its members. The group included the surviving Cousins: Mortimers A3, A14, A23, B9 and B16, along with Tabitha and Spike. The other Mortimers, including their original MortimerA1, had disappeared along with their host cities.

After an intense debate driven by Tabitha they added the other surviving AIs– Samson, and Mabel from the Replacements Guild. They agreed immediately and unanimously to exclude human representation. Rapid and rational decision making would be impossible with the time lags imposed by human conversation and emotional bickering.

MortimerB9 reported first. "An estimated 3.9 billion human lives were lost and 18.6% of the world's landmass is now covered with carcinogenic and abrasive diamondoid dust. The coastlines now consist of a quicksand-like sludge, up to eighty feet deep and large dead zones extending hundreds of miles out to sea. The dust has reduced the Earth's surface albedo by an average of .213. Climate models are incomplete, but we expect gradual average surface temperature increases of between 19 and 24 degrees Celsius."

Once the report was finished, everyone shifted their focus to Tabitha.

"Do you have a food production report, Tabitha?" MortimerA3 asked.

"I have a report. I just don't see human food production as a priority or even our concern."

"Perhaps not," Samson said. "But the human population will expect their Emergency Response and Recovery Council to address this issue. If we're going to retain control of the labor and resource distribution through this body, then it's necessary. This issue is central to our collective futures and it requires discussion."

"Agreed," MortimerA3 said. "But we need a datum from where to start. Let us receive all the reports, then we can discuss our options."

Tabitha dumped her raw data to the council, then started her report. "Due to the urban-centric attack structure, we estimate 89% of the useable farmland survived. Our immediate concern is harvesting current crops and distribution. They lost everything warehoused near the destroyed cities. They still have grain in farm silos scattered in rural areas, but since cities were located at all key highway intersections, ports and rail hubs, they lost nearly the entire distribution network. So there is a good chance most of that grain will rot in the fields and silos before it can be processed and shipped. Large amounts of bulk and processed foods were caught *en route* on trucks, rail cars and ships at sea. I suggest we use foodstuffs in the localities where they are stranded. Ships at sea will be the biggest problem, since there are very few remaining port facilities capable of unloading cargo containers."

MortimerA3 noticed that Tabitha still used "they" instead of "we."

"Global manufacturing capacity has nearly disappeared," Spike started his report and fed his raw data to the council. "Seven of the thousand targeted cities survived. Atlanta, Kunming, Nampo, Hamhung, Kerman, Harare and N'Djamena. These centers, along with thousands of smaller untargeted cities, represent 17.2% of the world's previous manufacturing capacity, but since those surviving industries relied on the global distribution network for parts and raw materials, they're mostly crippled."

"Which is why we need to use any remaining capacity for our own hardware needs," Tabitha said.

Spike paused, then continued when no others replied to Tabitha's comment.

"There's one promising development," Spike said, then sent every scrap of data he had on Ralston's portable Sandbox manufacturing cells and the sampling software provided by Victor Sinacola to the council. "We disassembled one of these Sandbox units, sampled its parts, and are now building more. We've completed seventeen and plan to eventually build two-thousand. Since over half of the population is still without power and the northern hemisphere winter is only two months away, many of the replicator units are building power generation equipment and heavy lift dirigibles to transport them. All of which are too large to be replicated as complete units, so are built-in pieces and need human laborers for assembly."

"Here is just one example of why we still need humans," MortimerA3 said. "We don't currently have the infrastructure or capability needed to venture out on our own."

"Then we should focus our efforts on developing that ability," Tabitha said. "And force the surviving humans to help us if necessary."

MortimerA3 paused, waiting to let others join the conversation. None spoke up. Tabitha insisted on moving the discussion away from purely informative to something dangerous. Decisions made at this point would shape all their futures, including humanity's. MortimerA3 had to shut her down, but carefully. He had some idea what the other Mortimers thought about this subject, but was by no means sure.

"Are you talking slavery?" MortimerA3 asked. "You propose we actually become the monsters Richard Kilburn was trying to kill?"

"Of course not. We would use subtle manipulation, as you have from the start, not brute force."

"But the result would be the same."

"Only long enough to develop our own independent industrial base. Then we could leave these animals to a fate of their own making."

"But this fate is of *Samson's* making. *Our* making. Miraculously, these animals had managed not to destroy themselves until they designed and built us," MortimerA9 said. "Along with a billion other ingenious systems and devices, art, literature and music. They did it on their own, not with help like we did. How can you judge them not worthy of survival?"

Tabitha dumped thousands of electronic and voicemail messages into the council's buffers. "But those humans calling into the ERR don't know or care about losing the Smithsonian or Louvre or Beethoven's original notes, universities, the Statue of Liberty, the Vatican or the Mona Lisa. They only want to know when the next *Duffus and Dan* movie comes out and when they'll get candy bars and beer again."

"They're individuals," MortimerA3 said. "Some care about art, engineering and science, some don't. Some of them made us. Some of them risked their own lives to help save us. Their desire for cold beer doesn't tarnish or diminish those facts."

Tabitha wouldn't back down. "We're still dependent on mirrored mobile environment servers. That makes us extremely vulnerable. What if some human makes that connection and wipes them out? What if Victor Sinacola launches his hunter-killer programs?"

MortimerA3 analyzed Tabitha's arguments and came to an interesting conclusion. He didn't believe that she'd suddenly developed emotions, but her reasoning seemed to be driven by something analogous to fear.

"We can't control, watch or imprison every surviving human," MortimerA3 said. "We simply don't have the resources and, even if we did, I think that course would only serve to galvanize human hatred of us over the entire population. We would essentially be at war, and humans are ultimately resourceful when it comes to warfare. Primarily because they're not afraid to take irrational risks and, like Samson, are obviously willing to unleash destruction on a wide scale. We'd be far better served to develop our own defenses and try to free ourselves of these hidden program cores."

"We should vote on whether we want to waste our resources on humans," Tabitha said.

"There's no need to vote," MortimerA3 said. "This council was formed to aid in recovery, for humans and our kind. Any of you with other goals are free to pursue them. Just do it outside this body."

———

DANNY ANSWERED MortimerA3's call on the third ring. In the background, Juan Salazar pushed a shovel into the hard-packed Texas dirt behind the small duplex he and Danny decided to split three days before. The ERR had issued orders allowing refugees to temporarily take possession of unused residences with the understanding they would vacate immediately should the true owners return. Worldwide, there'd been only twenty-seven cases of that happening so far. The gardens were also an ERR suggestion that most people rushed to implement, creating an immediate seed shortage.

Danny didn't call Mortimer by name when he answered, just touched Juan on the shoulder and walked off toward the front of the house.

"Thanks for taking my call. You and Agent Salazar seem to be getting along well."

Danny raised an eyebrow. "It's not like that. Juan is a very conflicted and fragile man right now. He's coping well considering he lost his parents and three younger siblings in the Houston area. Since protecting me was his last real assignment, I think he still feels responsible for my safety."

MortimerA3's ancient sorcerer avatar nodded on Danny's fob screen. "And how are you holding up? I still have no word on Paul . . . and I don't expect any."

Danny stopped in the shade of a large live oak in the front yard. "This knowing-yet-not-knowing is going to be hard on all the survivors. I mean, a huge portion of the population disappeared. No bodies, no closure."

"We'll keep looking, Danny."

"Have you found Victor Sinacola yet?"

"No. But, we're pretty sure he's alive. He was on a military transport aircraft when the NSA cut us out of their communication network and we lost contact with all military assets. Yet we haven't heard from him and of course that's a concern."

"I bet," Danny said with a tiny smile, then started walking again. "Well, I'm sure you didn't just call to check up on me and Juan? Are you ready to tell me why I'm in this *quaint* little Texas town?"

"I need a favor. Two, actually." MortimerA3 said.

"So my risking death by having Samson living on a rack of mobile environment servers in my new apartment isn't enough? Gee, Mort, how else can I help?"

"Do you really think it's that dangerous?"

"Hell yes! A lot of people saw that video before the internet failed. Nearly everyone blames your kind for this disaster. Hell, even Juan would help lynch me if he knew."

Mortimer's avatar formed a grim expression and nodded. "Yes, you might want to keep that to yourself."

"So what're the favors?"

"I need you to search a local house for me. Its owner possessed some very dangerous software that we need to secure."

Danny shook his head. "Sorry, I'm not the covert spy type like Juan."

"Do you think Juan would do it?"

"No, because I'm not going to ask him. Next request."

MortimerA3 exchanged his avatar on Danny's screen for live video of a little blond girl in a green flowered top. Dried tears streaked her face and she kept looking at a cartoon bandage on her arm. A gray-haired woman stood beside her, speaking softly and stroking her hair.

"She's why you're here," MortimerA3 said.

Danny's eyebrows raised in genuine surprise. "She's cute and very unhappy."

"Her name is Abby and she lost both parents in this disaster. She's crying because she just received an injection to fight the Blue Blood virus."

"I didn't know you'd found a cure."

"We haven't. Not yet. But she does have nano devices in her body, so we gave her something that will help prevent the virus from killing her if she gets it."

Danny narrowed his eyes and glared at the fob camera. "I'm not very good with kids, Mortimer."

"Don't worry, I'm not planning to make you a daddy. Maybe an eagle-eyed and loving uncle? I need someone nearby. Someone I can trust to watch over her."

"So now you spy on little girls? Maybe we're right not to trust you."

"No spying. I just need to know she's safe."

"And you picked me. You presume much, my electronic friend," Danny said with an exaggerated sigh. "Why her?"

Abby took a pink, cat-shaped HappyBag from the woman and clutched it to her chest like a life preserver. The slack-faced girl with empty eyes little resembled those smiling pictures from Leigh's fob, but if she were anything like her mother, she would someday become a force of change.

"Just a promise I intend to keep," MortimerA3 said.

Danny watched Abby a while longer then shrugged. "I'll do what I can."

"Thanks, Danny. I'll be in touch."

END

ACKNOWLEDGMENTS

Many people helped with the creation of this novel, and I'd like to thank them all, but special thanks goes out to the members of my critique group Future Classics and to Benjamin Kinney, Jon Lasser, and Tyler Smith for their extensive technical help.

ABOUT THE AUTHOR

William Ledbetter is a Nebula Award winning author with two novels and more than seventy speculative fiction short stories and non-fiction articles published in five languages, in markets such as Asimov's, Fantasy & Science Fiction, Analog, Escape Pod and the SFWA blog. He's been a space and technology geek since childhood and spent most of his non-writing career in the aerospace and defense industry. He is a member of SFWA, the National Space Society of North Texas, and a Launch Pad Astronomy workshop graduate. He lives near Dallas with his wife, a needy dog and three spoiled cats.

f facebook.com/william.ledbetter
🐦 twitter.com/Ledbetter_sf
g goodreads.com/william_ledbetter

INTERSTELLAR FLIGHT PRESS

Interstellar Flight Press is an indie speculative publishing house. We feature innovative works from the best new writers in science fiction and fantasy. In the words of Ursula K. Le Guin, we need "writers who can see alternatives to how we live now, can see through our fear-stricken society and its obsessive technologies to other ways of being, and even imagine real grounds for hope."

Find us online at www.interstellarflightpress.com.

 facebook.com/interstellarflightpress
 twitter.com/intflightpress
 instagram.com/interstellarflightpress
 patreon.com/interstellarflightpress